Sweet Revenge ... and Other Stories

by

Di Shelley

i

Sweet Revenge... and Other Stories

First Kindle Edition, September 2014

Copyright © Diane Shelley 2014

Acknowledgements

With grateful thanks to my 'reading/assessment group':
Theresa, Babs, Pat, Candi, Toni and Aunty Micki.
Your suggestions into what did and didn't work, your help in
filling in the gaps and in Toni's case supplying a new ending to
one of the stories (so much better!) helped me enormously in
finally getting these out of my head and into print.

A really special thanks to my dear friend Shelley, whose
continued support and insights lifted these stories from the page
onto a new level.

Thanks also to sister-in-law Ann and brother George for keeping
up the pressure and allowing me the use of their home for the
final push.

My thanks to you all, I owe you and love you.
Here's to the next one coming soon.
Watch out for '*All Shorts*'.

iii

For my daughter Theresa - the wisest woman I know
You continue to amaze me.

And for my late husband, John Merchant, who supported me in all my wild imaginings. I miss your input darling.

FOREWORD

Welcome to this melange of short stories, some of which I describe as being 'light-hearted with a bite!'

They range from revenge – which doesn't necessarily mean cutting up or cutting off – and light crime to spooky and the downright ridiculous.

Enjoy.

CONTENTS

SWEET REVENGE

'Sweet is revenge – especially to women'

Lord Byron – *Don Juan*

SWEET REVENGE

The three women sitting at the bar of the Italian restaurant exuded elegance, sophistication and supreme confidence.

I watched them through the window and was uncomfortably aware of the contrast between their smart business suits, sleek nylons and high heels and my own shapeless, long grey cardigan, flat shoes and mid-length tweed skirt. Their hairdos were shapely and obviously expensive, whereas my own was pulled back and pinned in a tight bun.

A twinge of fear twisted my gut and I almost turned away, but I knew this had to be done. Taking a deep breath, I pulled the cardigan tightly across my chest and clutching my large tote bag for protection, pushed open the restaurant door. The aroma of good Italian food wafted through the restaurant, but I was already convinced I wouldn't be able to eat.

The three looked up as I entered, then turned back to their drinks, ignoring this nonentity. The barman peered at me for a moment as if assessing my right to be there, then went back to polishing glasses.

I walked up to the women and digging in a pocket of my cardigan, drew out a slightly crumpled envelope and held it out to them.

'Excuse me.' It came out as a whisper. I hadn't realised just how difficult this was going to be. I cleared my throat. 'This is for you.'

All three turned and stared at me. I knew their names: Sadie, Carol and Lisa. Sadie took the envelope and Carol watched as she opened it. Lisa however, continued to stare at me.

'What is it?' Carol asked.

Sadie read the letter aloud. *'Slight change of plan. Bethany Jones will entertain you throughout lunch and I will join you for coffee. Regards. Jane Clark.'*

'Oh great!' Carol beckoned the waiter and ordered another drink.

'For you madam?' he asked me.

'Just a mineral water please,' I managed to stutter. I'd have wine later to steady my nerves. For now I just needed to get through this with a clear head.

3

'I know you.' Lisa leaned towards me, invading my personal space. 'Oh yes, now I remember,' she said softly. 'Just look who it is, girls. None other than Wet Betty.'

Carol and Sadie stared

'Oh my God, so it is.' Sadie glanced again at the letter. '*You're* Bethany Jones.'

I smiled nervously and nodded. 'Er, I'm to stay with you through lunch.'

'Oh this should be fun,' Carol stood up. 'Right girls, let's eat then, shall we?'

She picked up her glass and followed the waiter to a table at the back of the restaurant. Apart from us, there were no other customers.

'You're not very busy today,' Sadie said.

The waiter shrugged and having offered the wine to each of us handed us all a menu. As the women made their choices, I slowly sipped my water and watched them cautiously.

Underneath the glamour and the hairstyles I realised they hadn't really changed much at all. The cold eyes, the harsh set of their mouths – all would take their facial toll in years to come.

Not surprisingly, they chose the most expensive dishes on the menu: they intended to get their fill out of this lunch. I ordered a small salad and waited for their 'fun' to begin.

It was so calculated I could almost see their playground instincts clicking into place. As we began to eat lunch, Lisa – probably the nastiest – led the assault.

'So – *Betty* – how come you're working for Jane Clark. What do you do?'

'What could she possibly do?' Sadie joined in before I could speak.

'Not a lot,' Carol crowed. 'Bet she's just some sort of gopher. Lowest of the lowly. I'm surprised Jane let you meet us for lunch. This,' she waved a hand 'must be *sooo* upmarket for you. Perhaps we should have translated the menu for you.' They all laughed. 'But then, you can't go wrong with salad.'

'Probably too nervous to try anything more adventurous.' That was Lisa again. 'Still a coward then.' It wasn't a question.

I lowered my head and picked at my food trying not to rise to their taunts. The bantering insults went on for a few more moments and I wondered how three, seemingly intelligent women could still resort to the level of the playground. Was it

5

nerves? Was it fear and uncertainty about the upcoming meeting that created the need to belittle and humiliate another human being – one they saw as weak and helpless and one that could increase their power and enable them to feel self-important and in control? For a moment my unease was almost overcome by a pang of sympathy for these three damaged women. But then Lisa leaned towards me conspiratorially.

'Got a clean pair of knickers in that bag of yours? Don't want any nasty accidents in here, do we.'

And there it was - the reference to their ultimate triumph. Any feelings of well-being towards them were instantly shattered by the bad memories.

Why did I become the victim of their schoolgirl bullying? I'll never know, but from the first day these three had focused their unwanted attention on me. They would crowd me in the playground, push me over, tear my schoolbooks, push me over in the mud, taunt me mercilessly and encourage others to join in their vicious games.

I took to locking myself in the loos each break time – my back against one wall and my feet on the other so they could not see me under the gap in the bottom of the door. I was nearly always late back to lessons and was subsequently punished with detentions. Instead of support and understanding from the teaching staff, I was castigated as a troublemaker, lazy and weak.

The catalyst came one day after school. I'd been kept in again for *'disrupting the lesson by arriving late'* and when I left, they were waiting for me. They'd come prepared – and armed. Dragging me round to the back of the school, they fastened me to the railings with black plastic ties and began punching me in the stomach. The ultimate indignity happened. I wet myself.

After that, they cut the ties and let me go, promising worse if I told anyone. I stumbled home in tears to my mother. Of course I told her, but instead of sympathy and comfort, she gave me a tongue-lashing.

'For God's sake, when are you going to stand up for yourself? You just let them walk all over you. You'll get far worse than this in life if you don't start to toughen up. Now go and get cleaned up.'

The next day, as I walked into the school playground, I realised something was wrong. There were no footballs being slammed up against the school walls, no groups racing around and screaming at each other and none of the noise that usually

accompanied us all into the building. Instead it was silent –
except for small groups of pupils standing around whispering. As
I passed through the gates, they all turned to stare at me. I
stopped and this seemed to be the signal for them to start.

Whispering at first, their chant gradually became louder. 'Wet
Betty. Wet Betty. Wet Betty …'

I dropped my books and fled the school, their laughter echoing
along the street behind me.

My mother only took me seriously when she found me trying
to cut my wrists with a kitchen knife.

Counselling sessions and a new school saved me from any
lasting damage.

And here I was, having what should have been a civilised
lunch, my three tormentors trying to take up where they'd left off.

'So what do you all do?' It was a weak attempt to deflect their
attention away from me, but to my surprise it worked. They
couldn't wait to show off how well they'd done.

Lisa was currently a 'Director of Human Resources', Carol
was 'Head of Finance' for a large conglomerate - and Sadie?

'I did even better than these two,' she crowed. 'I married the
Chairman, so I have the big house, the *big* bank account, the

diamonds, the clothes and all the holidays and lunches I could ever want – and what's more I don't have to lift a finger for it.' She pouted 'Trouble is I'm bored. Which is why we're here, and shortly, *if* your boss ever appears, we will be heading up our own company. But oh,' she sneered 'you never told us. What *do* you do for Jane.'

'Oh this and that. I keep her diary, make sure she has everything she needs for meetings. Stuff like that.'

'So you know what this meeting is about?' Sadie asked.

'Er yes, sort of.' I couldn't meet her eye. Instead I glanced at my watch. Lisa reached across the table and tightly grasped my wrist.

'Mmm. Tasty,' she said. 'So where did *you* get a watch like this.'

Sadie leaned over and inspected it.

'If I didn't know better I'd say this is a Cartier. Some of these fakes are quite good nowadays. So where did you get this bauble?' she sneered. 'Off a market stall – or off the back of a lorry?'

I pulled my hand out of Lisa's grasp and looked down as if embarrassed.

'Actually, my husband bought it for me for our third wedding anniversary.'

'Husband!' the women looked startled, then all burst out laughing.

'So Wet Betty snagged herself a husband. Wonders and all that.' Carol mocked. 'So what does this 'husband' of yours do?' She turned to the others. 'Bet he's some sort of geek.'

'A teacher ...'

'Or an accountant ...'

'More like a computer nerd.' Carol laughed.

'What's his name?'

'Bet it's something like ...'

'Rodney,' Lisa crowed. 'Bet she's married to a Rodney.'

I smiled weakly, pushed my chair back and, grasping my bag, stood up.

'Please excuse me.' I apologised. 'I need the bathroom. I'll sort the coffee out while I'm up.'

'Need to change your knickers?' Carol said loudly. Their laughter followed me to the Ladies.

Once in the washroom, I leaned my head against the cool, pristine, tiled wall and began to breath deeply and steadily, as I had been taught to do all those years ago. Then I straightened and stared at myself in the mirror. The soft lighting calmed my soul and I felt the playground and its terrors recede. I reached up and began to pull the pins from my hair. It fell to my shoulders smoothly and sleekly as only a top quality haircut can. I fluffed it up a little, applied some lipstick and changed into the heels I was carrying in my bag. I drew out the designer jacket that complemented what had appeared to be the dowdy skirt, rolled the grey cardigan up and thrust it into the bag, then with another deep breath, opened the door and murmured *'Show time!'*

The three women didn't notice me at first; they were too engrossed in the files on the table in front of them.

I sat down.

'In answer to your question,' I said sweetly, 'my husband's name is not Rodney. It's Richard. Richard Clark, and just in case you've missed the connection, he's the Managing Director of J & R. Clark, Venture Capitalists plc. I'm J part of J and R. I'm the Chairman, but please, don't refer to me as 'the Chair'; I don't have wooden legs and I do so hate these PC terms, don't you?'

11

The three gazed at me, their stunned expressions slowly turning to horror as reality bit. Now I had their full attention.

'I'm really surprised,' I continued 'that you didn't recognise me before. But then, I suppose you weren't really looking at someone as 'lowly' as me, and the name would have distracted you – as I hoped it would.'

I beckoned the waiter and he brought me a glass of superb Chianti. I sipped it gratefully. Now I could relax. Now I was in control.

'What's the matter?' I looked at each of them in turn. 'Cat got your tongues?'

They suddenly all spoke at once.

'Oh my God.'

'Oh shit!'

'You mean you're…'

'Jane Clark, yes. I did tell you I'd be joining you for coffee, and in case you're wondering,' I continued, 'I changed my name when I left that abomination of a school. My full name is Bethany Jane, but as you can imagine, Bethany wasn't a name I wished to keep – too many bad associations. Oh by the way, Sadie,' I held out my hand to show off the watch 'this *is* a Cartier. Pretty little *bauble*, isn't it?'

I signalled the waiter again. He brought the coffee pot over to the table and began to pour for the three women. I moved my wine glass to one side, pulled a file from my bag, and began to leaf through it.

'Right, now let's get down to business.'

They looked stunned.

'You mean you still want to discuss our proposal?' Carol asked the question.

'Why not? I never let personal issues interfere with business. Now drink up. There's brandy to follow.'

I waited as they began tentatively sipping their coffee.

'Now, I've read your proposal and on paper it seems solid enough. But before we discuss the finer points, I want to know what strengths you think you'll each be bringing to this business. Lisa?'

She coughed nervously and then launched into her spiel, which included her expertise and experience as a Human Resources Director. Carol extolled her own virtues as Head of Finance and

Sadie boasted of all the contacts she already had through her husband.

'Together,' Sadie concluded, 'we're a formidable team. We know we can make this work. What we need is a bit of financial back-up, which we *can* match,' she added hastily, 'and managerial support – and of course, ' she added hastily, 'with your company name behind us, we'll soon all be in profit.'

They sipped their coffee nervously as they waited for my decision. I pretended to consider what they'd said. After a long moment I looked at them each in turn.

'I'd take a guess that you didn't really bother to research me or my company before approaching us?'

Worry began to cloud their faces. I shook my head.

'Tut, tut. You *really* should have done your homework. I did mine.' I closed the file and rested my hands on it. 'As I said, it's a sound proposal ...'

'But?' Lisa said.

'You're not going to invest in us, are you?' Carol finished, her tone flat. I leaned back in my chair.

'Of course not. Did you really think I would?' I asked.

'So why did you meet us. Why lead us on?'

14

'I was curious. I wanted to see how you'd developed. Had you become mature women, using your obvious abilities creatively? Or were you still the nasty little threesome that caused so much misery to me and, no doubt, others like me? Well I got my answer.'

I picked up the file.

'Pity really, because as a business proposition, this has great potential. You three, however, don't. Apart from the lunch we've just endured, did you think I was stupid or naïve enough to meet with the three of you without investigating *your* backgrounds? Did you think I wouldn't find out that you, Carol, are about to be taken to a tribunal for bullying a member of staff – which will be upheld by the way - I've seen the paperwork. You might have got away with it in school, and even in the 80's, but it's not tolerated nowadays. Times have changed, but you obviously haven't.

And you, Lisa, you're obviously unaware that when you get back to your office this afternoon, two senior officers from the Fraud Squad are waiting to arrest you for embezzlement. God knows how you thought you'd get away with it.'

She turned pale and visibly shrank. The other two stared at her in horror.

'Oh my God,' Sadie whispered, 'is that where our money…?'

'Where did you think it was coming from?' Lisa snapped.

'But embezzlement, Lees? That's criminal. You could go to prison.'

'Oh, she assuredly will,' I smiled.

'And what about me,' Sadie demanded. 'What have you got on me?'

'Ah Sadie. I feel quite sorry for you. Married to a rich man with all those contacts? Do these two know that he beats you up on a regular basis?' Carol and Lisa turned to stare at her.

'Oh the bruises don't show,' I assured them. 'He only hits her in the body. Where it can't be seen. He's not stupid.'

'So my husband beats me,' she snarled in embarrassment. 'Lots of men do that to their wives. At least I have the compensation of enough money to take myself off to recover.'

'Not for much longer,' I told her. 'You don't know it yet, but he's started proceedings for divorce.'

'What,' she shrieked. 'How do you know this?'

'Well, unlike you,' I drawled, '*my* contacts are my own, not just my husband's. Your husband is about to ditch you for a younger model – and you won't get a penny. Remember the pre-nup you signed?'

She looked stunned.

'He can't do this,' she whispered.

'Can and is. Well,' I picked up the file and stood up from the table, 'my work here, as they say, is done. I shall keep this,' I waved the file at them,' as a reminder that with time, revenge can be oh so sweet. Have a nice life girls, oh and by the way, there's a chemist three doors down to the left.'

They looked puzzled.

'What do we need a chemist for?' Carol asked.

'They sell emetics.' I gave them a finger wave as I walked away from the table.

'Emetics? Why do we need emetics?' Lisa called after me.

Sadie got it first.

'Poison! Oh my God, the bitch has poisoned us!' She looked round wildly. 'It must have been in the coffee. She didn't drink any coffee. Call an ambulance!' she screamed. 'Call the police!'

I could still hear their shrieks as I walked out of the restaurant and down the street back to my office. I wondered whether any of them had wet their knickers in fright.

The police came later that afternoon and were ushered into my office by my secretary.

'Ms. Clark,' the Inspector's tone was sombre. 'An allegation has been made against you – a serious allegation - by three ladies claiming that you tried to poison them in the Capri restaurant this lunch time.'

'Where are they now?'

'Er,' he was surprised by my question and glanced at his colleague. She shrugged.

'They're in hospital, still recovering from having had their stomachs pumped.'

I leaned back in my chair and closed my eyes.

'Oh bliss,' I said.

They both looked startled.

'You don't seem to be taking this very seriously,' the policeman said. 'Tests are being carried out as we speak to ascertain the type of poison you allegedly administered.'

I couldn't help it, I chortled. He stared at me as if I was mad.

'It's not funny, Miss. You could have killed those women.'

'No I couldn't – didn't. I didn't poison them,' I said scornfully. 'The only poison you'll find in their system is the poison they've carried with them all their lives. In short, officer, *they* are poison.'

I filled him in on their behaviour – past and present – and described the lunch.

He looked dubious.

'Well, if what you're saying is true - and we still have to wait for the test results,' he warned, 'but if what you're telling us *is* the truth, there may be repercussions – wasting police time for example,' but even as he said it, I could see he didn't believe it, after all it hadn't been *me* who'd called them in. He tried another tack.

'There's also the restaurant owners. I don't suppose they'll be very happy, you besmirching their reputation. They could put in a complaint against you. Luckily there were no other customers in the restaurant to witness the incident, but even so ...'

'Oh I shouldn't worry about that,' I said. 'You'll not be hearing from them and neither will I – at least not in that way.'

'How can you be so sure?'

I leaned toward him across my desk.

'Because, Inspector, *I* own the restaurant!'

19

NEMESIS

'The goddess of retributive justice …'
Reader's Digest Universal Dictionary

NEMESIS

'Maggie'.

The woman on the bed didn't stir.

PC Wendy Paine leaned over her.

'Maggie, I know you're awake. Come on, we have to talk.'

'Go away.'

'Maggie please.'

The woman opened her eyes and turned her head carefully.

'How many more times are you going to let him do this to you?' the police officer asked.

'I fell down the stairs.' She spoke slowly, deliberately and painfully through swollen lips.

Wendy nodded, her tone scornful.

'Just like you *fell* in the bath last time and broke your arm, and just like you *tripped* over the pavement the time before and broke your nose and just like...'

'Go away.'

'Maggie, he will kill you.'

'No, he loves me.' For a moment her voice was stronger and she struggled to sit up. Then with a sigh, 'I love him.'

'But Maggie...'

'No.' She was becoming increasingly distraught. 'I will not leave him. I will *not* go into a women's refuge.' She sank back into the pillows. 'I know what you think, but he's my husband, we *will* sort this out - and anyway,' a faint smile creased the puffy flesh around her mouth 'I fell down the stairs and dislocated my shoulder. It hurts like hell, so I'd like to sleep now if you don't mind.' She closed her eyes and turned her head away. Wendy stood watching her for a moment more, then sighing, turned and left.

'Maggie.' This time a man's voice. Gentle, loving, desperate.

She opened her eyes.

'Maggie love, dearest love, can you ever forgive me?' He took her hand and held it to his cheek. 'I didn't mean it. I wouldn't hurt you for the world, you know that.'

She stared at him for a moment through bruised and blackened eyes.

'I fell down stairs.' she said. He began to weep.

'It will never happen again,' he sobbed. 'I swear it will never happen again.'

She stroked his face, her eyes full of pain - and pity.

'Maggie?' Wendy was back. 'How are you?'

'Much better, thanks. They say I can probably go home later today.' She paused. 'What do you want?'

'Maggie...'

'I told you what happened. That's an end of it.'

'Maggie, I've got someone I want you to meet.'

'No.'

'Please Maggie - you *must* do something.'

'No.'

'Maggie...' the pleading voice enraged her.

'I don't *need* anyone.' Her voice rose sharply. 'I don't *want* a social worker, or a therapist or any other do-gooder you feel like producing. Just go away and leave me alone!'

The police officer opened the ward door, but she made no move to leave. A man stood behind her.

'I've brought you some help anyway,' she said, ushering him to the bedside.

'Help me to what?' Maggie demanded, anger masking the tears in her voice.

'Bring peace and harmony to your household.' His voice stayed her anger instantly. It rang like a soft bell and reminded her of - what? The memory remained elusive, but instinctively she knew it was good. And powerful, she added to herself.

Instantly she knew that she liked this tiny man standing at her bedside, knew she could trust him and also knew that despite herself, whatever help he was offering, she was going to accept it.

'Maggie, this is Veeran. Let him help you.' Wendy glanced at her watch. 'I must be getting back. I'll leave you two to get to know each other.'

Maggie gestured for the man to sit down. As he did so she studied him closely. His eyes dominated his wrinkled, brown face. Deep, hypnotic eyes held hers without apology as he watched her watching him.

He reminds me of a walnut, she thought whimsically and smiled at the thought.

'You are very strong,' he observed, 'but your soul is weary.' It was a statement.

She gazed at him in astonishment. That was it! For so many months now she had been trying to define the way she felt and after only moments, this man had named it for her.

Weary.

Weary of being on the edge day after day.

Weary of the knot of fear in her chest.

Weary of the love that she held in her heart, but was afraid to unleash. Weary of waiting.

Weary of watching for the signs that would predict yet another beating, weary of soul.

'Yes,' it came out as a sigh, 'I am weary.'

'Now this is the plan,' he said, and she instantly relaxed. She knew that from this moment she was no longer alone. She knew she would do whatever he asked, whatever it took to allow him to organise and order her life.

Two weeks later the pain in her shoulder had diminished to a slight ache, her bruises hardly showed at all. Fortunately the weather was bright, so the dark glasses that she wore were not out of place. She knew that the neighbours watched her carefully, waiting for the next episode in this long-running drama.

Being a fairly wealthy neighbourhood however, it did not 'do' to appear nosy, although she could imagine the sympathetic noises that were made over morning coffee and afternoon tea.

She had no close friends.

After the first beating she had been so stunned and ashamed that she had deliberately severed all close ties. Even then, she knew that this was not a solitary aberration and the thought of a future pandering to the lascivious needs of bored housewives filled her with a horror far greater than the physical pain she knew she would have to endure in the future.

They weren't regular, these beatings. There was no pattern to them. Sometimes a year would go by before it happened again. A year of wondering, *Is it over? Is he better? Can I let my guard down and begin to live a normal life?* The answer had always been no and although she expected it – waited for it even - each time it happened she felt renewed surprise and shock.

The phone rang.

'Darling, it's me. How are you? Look, I'd like to take you out for dinner tonight - to make up for - you know. I thought the new French Restaurant? I've heard good reports. What do you think?'

'I'd love to.' She smiled as she pictured him behind his executive desk, still wracked with guilt at what he had done. 'I thought I might get my hair done this afternoon anyway, so it will give me the chance to show it off.'

'Great.' There was pause. 'Are you really OK?' He was hesitant.

'Yes, I'm fine'

'It won't happen again - I promise.'

'No, ' she smiled again. 'No, I know it won't.'

The neighbours watched closely, nodding knowingly to each other as she closed the front door behind her.

'There she goes, poor dear. Same time every day. I wonder who he is? Still, you can't blame her,' and they clucked delightedly over their bone china.

He poured her some more wine. 'You seem different.'

'How?'

'I'm not sure.' He frowned slightly and she leaned over to smooth the wrinkles away.

He caught her hand. 'You seem -' he struggled for words '- tranquil, serene - I'm not sure. Different.'

'I'm fine.' she said. 'Don't worry.'

'Maggie...'

Another apology was coming

'Look, forget it.' She squeezed his hand reassuringly. 'It's over. I know it won't happen again. I love you.'

Summer turned to autumn and then it was Christmas and the start of a new year – and a new beginning she told herself.

New Years Day dawned bright and warm. Today was the day if she was ever going to do this. She cooked a special breakfast and served it with champagne.

'What's this,' he smiled. 'Alcohol so early?'

She waited until they had eaten and then raised a toast to their future.

'Are you OK?' he asked, obviously puzzled at this unfamiliar behaviour.

'Perfectly. Look, I feel like celebrating today - starting the year as we mean to go on. As it's such a lovely day, why don't we go out for drive into the country? Find somewhere for a light lunch, then back for dinner. I've got steak in the fridge. We'll have it with all the trimmings and a decent bottle of red.'

He agreed cautiously, wondering again at her serenity.

After dinner, as he relaxed with a brandy, she knew this was the time – she just hoped she was strong enough and prepared enough. But there was no going back. This moment would define her future – *their* future. She stood from the table and moved to his side.

'Darling, we need to talk.'

He looked up at her and for a fleeting moment she caught the flicker of an emotion that darkened his eyes: puzzlement, uncertainty, expectancy, suspicion - one of those, she couldn't be sure which, but she knew that if *this* didn't trigger the expected reaction, nothing would.

'There's something I have to tell you …'

Carefully and deliberately, he placed the now empty brandy glass down on the table and stood up, closing the space between them.

'Oh yes?' he said, his tone soft, yet menacing.

'There's this man…'

She got no further.

That night the neighbours were woken by the sound of police sirens. They watched the by now familiar sight of a stretcher being loaded into the ambulance.

'Maggie?'

She opened her eyes.

'Are you all right?' PC Wendy Paine sounded anxious.

'I'm fine.' Maggie smiled. She looked at the figure in the bed.

'Ben's not so good. I'm afraid he's broken his arm and dislocated his shoulder. He's in a lot of pain – bless him,' she added. She looked back at the police officer. 'He fell down the stairs,' she explained.

'Of course,' Wendy smiled and nodded. She leaned forward. 'Strictly off the record - what happened?'

Maggie looked at her thoughtfully.

'Well,' she said eventually, 'I suppose you deserve the truth. If it hadn't been for you – and Veeran - it would have been me again. Veeran is a good teacher. You were right to bring him into my life. He taught me how to achieve peace of mind. He taught

30

me how to harmonise my life with everything around me. He taught me gentleness, patience and assurance. He taught me strength - of mind and body - and,' she grinned wickedly, 'he taught me how to use Ben's strength against himself.'

She looked down at the bandaged figure on the bed.

'Quite simply, as he raised his arm to hit me I threw him and he fell heavily enough to break his arm. Mind you,' she continued, 'I'd worked it all out in advance. I'd already calculated the best place for him to fall so that he would break his arm, then I dislocated his shoulder to show him what it feels like and then I told him that if he *ever* tried it again, not only would I break his other arm, I would also cut off his balls and feed them to the cat! I think he believed me, because at that point he turned white and passed out. You see,' Maggie continued, gently stroking the unconscious man, 'he knows that the difference between us is that when I say something - I mean it!'

For a moment the police officer was totally at a loss for words. Uncertain, almost uneasy now in the company of this stranger that she thought she once knew, she said the only thing she could think of.

'I didn't know you had a cat.'

OBSESSION

'A compulsive, often unreasonable, idea or emotion'
Reader's Digest Universal Dictionary

OBSESSION

The accident had been easy to arrange.

We buried him in the family grave with our mother, father and paternal grandparents.

Poor Father, if he knew what had led to this, he would be turning in that grave.

Father was the cause of it all though - albeit unwittingly.

Father - who refused to acknowledge his own mortality and consequently the need to his make a last will and testament.

When he died suddenly of an aneurysm, it was the solicitor who suggested a way round the intestacy laws. As a result, all Father held dear went to our mother who, on the advice of the solicitor, immediately passed his most treasured possession – the land – to her son, my younger brother.

The land had been in the family for over four hundred years. Poor land, but ours. It was *our* heritage. It should have been his *and* mine

'But it's in his blood, dear,' mother said, as she signed the transfer deeds. 'He'll care for it. He'll nurture it. He'll farm it well.'

Like hell he did! He did nothing for the land except prostitute it. Mostly he let it out to neighbouring farmers to graze their cattle or reap the hay while he enjoyed the status of 'gentleman farmer'.

Each year I watched in anguish as the yields went down and the occasional house went up as planning permission bit into the soil.

Oh yes, he was not averse to selling the odd plot, but *that* was after he married. He said he needed the money from the developments to plough back into the land, but the land continued to deteriorate.

I wasn't concerned with the money he was making, I had enough of my own, but I *did* care about the land. It should have been mine as well as his - but now it belonged to a stranger - the wife, now his widow.

And there she stood at the graveside, regulation black and regulation tears.

But underneath the regulation grief, I saw smugness tinged with resentment.

Smugness?

Well, she now owned everything for which she'd sacrificed her frigid virginity.

Resentment?

If she'd had her way it would have been a quick trip to the local crematorium and a suitably pious stone in the anonymity of the local cemetery. Laid to rest and promptly forgotten, except maybe in the occasional silent toast to her good fortune.

But she couldn't be seen to be breaking with village tradition. To do that, she'd lose face. To do *that* would partially destroy the reputation she'd carefully built up over the past few years.

She played her part well at the wake. I watched from the sidelines of the muted blue carpet. She'd actually produced sherry, good quality too, and this in a teetotal household. Her rules. My poor brother. Denied in life, toasted in death.

Around me in the elegant hush of their designer house were the relics of my childhood - treasures that retained nothing more than a monetary value to her.

Sentiment?

For the birds!

Well *this* bird has learned her lessons well! Oh yes, I've really learned my lessons. It was a pity my pathetic brother had to be the one to be sacrificed, but it had to be done. I raised my glass in a silent tribute to his memory and I continued to watch as my plan began to play out.

I'd been watching this mistress of manipulation for some years now. I'd seen the clever erosion of our land – *my* land - all in the name of progress and village enhancement, and I'd watched her gradual ingratiation into village life.

And now I watched the next stage unfold.

The vicar was drifting from group to group, re-establishing his role as head of the village, while willing members of the WI poured and served the requisite funereal sherry, tea, thin crust-less sandwiches and slabs of fat free sponge oozing strawberry jam and whipped fresh cream. As mourners mingled and the older generation swapped reminiscences about the family, I watched Tony make his move.

'We've not met before.'

His soft tones reached me from across the room as he bent solicitously towards the widow.

'I knew him so well. He was a great friend. I meant to get in touch with him when I returned from the States, but you know how it is. You think you've got all the time in the world ...'

I smiled.

I couldn't have done it better.

I'd taught him well.

I'd met Tony at a party. It was one of many I'd attended during my search for the right man. I'd considered other likely candidates, but none had that certain light in the eye: that need, that greed. Tony had it in abundance. It was easy to convince him that he loved me and would do anything for me. The money carrot clinched his devotion.

Seven months after my brother's funeral the village was buzzing with the news.

A marriage had been arranged. Mutual consolation, of course. So touching that the man who had sadly 'lost a wife to cancer' should find happiness with the wife of his old friend.

Odd that no-one should think to question the existence of that *late* wife of his.

They planned the marriage for the following year. It wouldn't do to offend the sensibilities of the villagers at this stage. After all, she still needed the final planning permission for her latest venture and she needed all the sympathetic support she could get.

She needn't have feared. The villagers had taken her to their hearts. But then, they hadn't experienced the tantrums of the spoiled brat, the cold-heartedness shown to her invalid mother-in-law while she lived, the lack of feeling for the older members of her dead husband's family - her greed.

No. They only saw the grieving widow 'struggling' to keep her late husband's legacy alive. They were unaware of the planning applications, the detailed drawings, the clandestine meetings with local government officers and builders. All these had been put on hold while she re-grouped. She would be long gone before the reality of these impacted upon the gentle village innocents.

I'd discovered the plans quite by accident some years before. They weren't plans in the strict sense you understand, but the idea had been formed, had taken root and was in the initial stages of discussion.

Interestingly enough, it was my brother who was objecting for once. It was too much even for him, this desecration of the land. But I knew him. He was weak. All she had to do was threaten to leave and he'd crumble. He needed her too much.

But this was *our* heritage she was planning to destroy. Four hundred years of heritage, and all for a housing estate.

It was then I knew I must act.

I too must plan to destroy.

But I was patient.

Five years patient.

The marriage took place in the village church, that hub of our childhood community. It was a warm May day and the village turned out to celebrate. Tony looked a little uncomfortable when he caught my eye over the glass of champagne. Oh yes, alcohol was now socially acceptable, if not encouraged.

I later took a bottle from the reception and poured it over the family grave as a libation, and toasted the family future as I moved on to the next stage of my plan.

The accident was easy to arrange.

Her funeral eleven months later was a suitably sad occasion – for an anonymous cremation! Tony seemed to take it very badly, which surprised me somewhat. I found later she'd been pregnant and he'd begun to fall in love with her.

But a bargain is a bargain.

We married last month here in the Seychelles. A simple ceremony, completed by the drawing up of his will. He has no-one else to leave it to, and after all, the land has been in my family for over four hundred years.

I gave him his cheque as promised and suggested that maybe as we were here, we should spend a few months in the sun and live it up a little. After all, we'd waited this long, we deserved it -

and he's not a bad looking guy. I've not weathered too badly over the years either.

He's lost his sparkle though. The light has gone from his eyes. He's no fun any more. In fact, with what he knows about me, he could be dangerous.

The accident should be easy to arrange.

SAUCE FOR THE GOOSE

'What's sauce for the goose is sauce for the gander'
Late 17thC

42

SAUCE FOR THE GOOSE…

'Jen? It's me.'

'Oh hi dad. Sorry. I was going to phone you earlier, but the ferry was delayed for three hours and we didn't get back in until four this morning. Jerry's just gone off to take the kids to his mothers while I get the washing on and the house sorted properly before they get back, so …'

'Jen.' The strain in his voice stopped her in mid flow. 'It's your mother.'

'Mum? Why, what's happened? Is she hurt? Oh God she's not …'

'No, nothing like that, but I'm very worried about her. I'm sorry to do this to you as soon as you get back Jen, but can you come over? I don't know what to do, I'm at my wits end.'

As soon as she put her key in the door, she knew that things were very wrong.

43

The smell for a start.

Her mother always kept a clean, fresh house that spoke of polish and flowers, but now stale air overlaid with old food wafted through the hallway. The small table by the stairs was filmed with dust and dead stems wilted in a vase next to the telephone. A brown halo of petals and leaves stirred gently as she closed the door. There was no sign of her mother. Tom Morgan stood in the kitchen doorway watching his daughter's reaction, then started to turn away, tears threatening to fall.

'Oh dad.' Jenny reached out and put her arms round him, trying not to recoil from his grubby shirt and stained appearance. She was shocked by the change in him over such a short period of time.

'Is mum in bed?'

He shook his head miserably.

'Where then?'

He pointed mutely towards the back garden.

'And she's not hurt or injured?' Again the silent shake of the head. 'Then let's put the kettle on and you can tell me all about it.'

The kitchen was a tip. The rubbish bin had overflowed onto the floor and fat blowflies drifted over the piles of dried fast food packets littering the surfaces. Jenny looked round despairingly.

She had to empty the sink of dirty dishes before she could get to the tap. Wrinkling her nose, she washed the kettle out thoroughly before filling it. There were no clean cups or spoons and the sugar stood in a lump on the table, still in its bag. She opened the fridge door for the milk and sour fumes wafted out. She sniffed suspiciously at the half empty bottle.

'Black coffee it is then,' she declared, washing the lumps down the sink.

'Sorry,' he mumbled. 'I've not been out to get fresh this morning.'

'OK dad,' she handed him a steaming mug. 'What on earth has been going on?'

'It's been like this since just before you went away,' Tom slumped at the small dining table in the corner of the room.

'But that was three months ago.'

'I know.'

'So what happened?'

'I don't know. She just suddenly – stopped. Everything. She's even packed up her job.'

'What? But I thought she loved working in the hotel.'

'So did I. But one morning she just didn't get out of bed. She said she was all right, not ill or anything, but wouldn't say why she wasn't getting up. Just looked at me and smiled and started to read a magazine. I felt I ought to do something, let them know at least that she wasn't coming in, so I phoned the hotel and they told me she'd given in her notice. I didn't know what to think, I was that cross. I felt so stupid. Why hadn't she told me?'

'More to the point, why didn't you tell *me*?'

'Well I didn't like to bother you with it. Gerry had his job to consider and you were coping with the kids in a foreign land. Anyway, I thought it would just blow over. For the first few days,' he continued as he slowly sipped his coffee, 'she just stayed in bed until about midday, then slopped around in her dressing gown with a glass of wine. She watched a bit of television, had a bath and then went back to bed and stayed there 'til the next morning.'

'She is still washing then?'

'Oh yes. Spends hours up there sometimes.'

'Well I suppose that's something.' Jenny frowned. 'But what about meals and so on? Is she cooking?'

'No. I've had to resort to take-aways. You know me, I'm useless in the kitchen.'

'And is she eating?'

'Oh yes. Mind you we eat most of it out of the packages – as you can see. She eats whatever I put in front of her – when she's here that is.' His voice cracked. 'And then all she does is pour us both a glass of wine – and smiles at me. She just keeps smiling at me.'

He stood up and went to the window, nursing his now empty cup. 'I'm beginning to hate that smile.'

He leaned his head against the window. 'Look at her, sitting there in the sun as if she hasn't a care in the world. She's knows I'm watching, but she won't react.'

Jenny sensed his utter weariness and desolation and her heart ached for him. He took a shuddering breath.

'About a month ago she started going out mid morning and coming back halfway through the afternoon and sometimes it's evening before she returns. Almost every day. A couple of times she's been out in the evening too. Doesn't tell me where she's going, just says 'see you later' and leaves. I've tried asking her where she goes, but she just smiles at me, tells me not to worry. How can I not?'

His voice cracked with despair. 'I wondered if she'd got another man, but somehow I can't believe it. Surely there'd be other signs if she were being unfaithful. And I don't like to follow her,' he added, 'I don't want her to think I don't trust her. It's just that …' he hesitated, and then expressed the fear that had been lurking between them since she'd arrived. 'Jen, do you think it's…?' He left the sentence unfinished as if the word would create the reality.

Senility or Alzheimer's was every pensioner's dread. The thought of losing everything that defined a loved one – even oneself.

'I don't know. Have you talked to the doctor?'

'He said to bring her to surgery, but she won't go, and unless there's some physical emergency they won't come out. I'm telling you Jen, I'm at my wits end.'

'Right. I'll go and have a word with her, and if I think she needs to see a doctor, we'll take her down to the surgery and fight our way in if necessary. You stay here and try to stop worrying. We're sharing the load now.'

'Hello darling. Good time in France? How's the wine business doing?' Elizabeth Morgan put her book down on her lap and reaching over to a small shaded garden table, lifted an open bottle of white wine out of a cooler and filled two glasses.

'I knew he'd phoned you and I must say I'm pleased to see you back. I don't think I could have gone on with this much longer'

She handed a glass to her daughter.

'Chardonnay,' she announced, displaying the label. 'Probably not quite as good as those you've been tasting over the last three months, but passable as a pre-lunch tipple. I've booked us in at the Trattoria by the way. After all that French cuisine I thought you might appreciate a change. Anyway, cheers.'

Jenny automatically raised her glass. The cold, pale liquid rode over the after-taste of the black coffee and for a moment she was back in France, drifting through warm vineyards in the sunshine. But only for a moment. She glanced round at the neglected garden.

'Right, mother.' She put as much disapproval in her voice as possible. 'Are you going to tell me what's going on? You know dad's in there worrying himself sick and imagining all sorts. Doesn't know whether you're ill or losing your mind - although I must say you don't look sick.'

She put her head on one side and studied her mother closely. In fact, sitting there in the sun, Jenny thought, she looks remarkably fit, younger than I've seen her in years, and surely that's a new hairdo. And my God, she's wearing eye makeup!

'Mum, what *is* going on.'

Her mother sighed and adjusted her sun lounger to a more upright position.

'Men can be so stupid,' she announced, reaching once more for the bottle. She topped up both their glasses. 'I suppose I shall have to spell it out for him in the end. You see, it's a matter of ganders and geese.'

Jenny waited.

Her mother sipped her wine and looked over the rim of the glass at her daughter.

'Do you remember your dad's sixty fifth birthday?' she asked.

'Well of course I do. We had a whale of a party.'

'Mmm. I know. Not easy to forget really was it? All those people and of course the presents. He was really spoiled. Deserved it mind. He'd worked hard for a long time, supporting us and giving us the best he could.' She reflected silently for a moment. 'But do you know what stands out for me that day?'

Jenny shook her head.

'That morning, I took him breakfast in bed. First day of the rest of his life. And do you know what he said? "Liz," he said, "that's it. I'm retired. No more working for me, I can now spend time doing what *I* want to do, when *I* want to do it."

She took another sip of wine, her mood reflective. 'I'm sure he didn't mean it to be as selfish as it sounds, but I knew he meant every word and that from that moment on that's how it would be. Well, as you know, just after you left for France, I turned sixty and that morning, July 24th, the morning of my birthday, I woke up and repeated every one of his words to myself. I handed in my notice with immediate effect and I haven't done a stroke of work since. I've been taking myself out to lunch, having facials, having my hair and nails done, going to the cinema, catching the odd afternoon matinee at the theatre – and reading, lots and lots of reading. Absolute heaven. Mind you,' she sipped her wine contemplatively, 'I'm not sure how much longer I could have gone on living in that squalor. I started to go out more, not just to avoid the mess, but also to avoid the temptation of starting to clean it up – but it wasn't easy.' She shuddered. 'All those take-away packages strewn around the kitchen, sour milk in the fridge when he forget to buy fresh – although I must admit, when he went out I did sort of clear round a bit – not too much though, I didn't want him to notice and think things were getting back to normal – *his* normal that is. And the *smell*, not to mention the dust! It's a wonder we're not both suffering from asthma by now. Anyway darling, I'm glad you're home. Now we can put an end to this nonsense. Cheers!'

'How is she Jen? Did you find out what was wrong? Should we go to the doctor?'

'No, you don't need the doctor, dad.' She put a reassuring arm round her father's shoulders. 'What you *do* need is a cleaner, a gardener and a travel agent. Now go and have a shower, find a clean shirt and freshen yourself up. Come on, we'll explain it over lunch and then you can both decide which cruise you'd like to book.'

He looked puzzled.

'Cruise? What…?

'Quite simply,' she said, 'Mum has retired - and about time too!'

Later that evening, washing done, dinner cleared and children in bed, Jenny and Jerry relaxed with a bottle of their duty free brandy.

'Jerry?'

'Mmm?'

'Are you still hoping to take early retirement?'

'Well I'd like to think so. They reckon the package will be very good. I'd be silly not to advantage of it while I've still got some life left in me. The kids will be soon be off our hands, so financially we should be reasonably comfortable and I've known too many people who retire and then don't live to enjoy it. Why, is there a problem?'

'No. I just wondered.'

Jenny tipped her glass in silent tribute to her mother and thought of beauticians, long lunches, theatre matinees, … and geese   and   ganders.

THE HELLION

'unrestrainable person ...'
Reader's Digest Universal Dictionary

THE HELLION

'But that's *appalling*!' The Assistant Gatekeeper stared at the Guardian in horror. 'How could you let this happen? You were supposed to keep her alive until …'

'I know, I know AG. But you don't know what she's like.'

'But I *do* know. We *all* know. That's why you were given the task of keeping her there. For as long as possible! So she would mellow. Lose that bossy edge. Stop being so pushy and trying to organise everyone. Remember?' He shook his head. 'God *knows* what went wrong when that one was created. OK,' he sighed resignedly. 'You'd better tell me what happened.'

'Well AG, it's not been easy…'

The AG began to growl.

The Guardian continued hastily '…she went to the Post Office. It was as simple as that. Well, you know how slow they are. Four available tills and only one of them manned at any one time. Are you sure there isn't a central training complex somewhere…? No. Sorry.'

He began pacing.

'Anyway, I thought I'd got at least ten minutes while she waited in the queue. The sun was shining, and there was this tree just begging me to sit in its shade and chat for a while and she seemed safe enough with all those people around. I just thought a few minutes peace and quiet away from that voice and the *constancy* of the woman … I was just so exhausted by it all and I thought – why not? What could go wrong?'

The AG joined in the pacing. 'So what happened?

'Armed robbery! All hell – if you'll pardon the expression – broke loose. Turns out that this was the day the Post Office was scheduled for a raid, but nobody warned me,' he said petulantly trying to offload the blame a little. 'I thought we were supposed to be kept up to date with any possible incidents...?' His voice tailed off as the Assistant Gatekeeper glared at him. 'Anyway, there were four of them, all masked and carrying guns. They yelled at everyone to "hit the floor" – but would she do that? No, of course not. Instead, she started shouting at them, telling them what lazy layabouts they were and how they should get off their backsides and get a decent job like everyone else. She then started poking one of them in the chest and told him how inefficient and sloppy their whole operation was and that they

56

might as well give themselves up before they made any more stupid mistakes. And then he shot her - and ... here we are.'

'Yes. Indeed. Here we certainly are. We'd better let Peter know before it's...'

'WHAT THE HELL IS GOING ON HERE!' It wasn't so much a question as a demand for an answer.

'... too late.'

The Assistant Gatekeeper and the Guardian scurried to the Main Gate to find a very angry young woman confronting a very startled Gatekeeper.

'But – but you're not supposed to be here,' he stuttered as he hastily checked a long list on the desk in front of him.

'Sod that for a game of soldiers,' she yelled, 'I am! So what are you going to do about it?'

'Um ...'

'Don't you 'um' me,' she snarled.

'Er ... You do *know* where you are?' he asked nervously.

'Of course I bloody know. What am I? Stupid? I got shot.' She pointed at the gates. 'Duh. Pearly Gates, which means you're Peter,' she poked him in the chest, 'which means I'm dead. OK? Deal with it. I want to know where I'm supposed to be, what I'm supposed to be doing and *who* I'm supposed to be doing it with. And it's obvious you haven't a clue.'

'There seems to have been a mistake …' Peter winced as she leaned on the writing desk, grabbed a bundle of parchments and shook them in his face.

'And how many more 'mistakes' are there in this lot? Huh? Huh? What a shambles!' She threw the parchments back down and turned to the crowds hovering anxiously behind her. 'Right, listen up you lot! Any of you think you shouldn't be here either?'

A few hands went up.

'Right. Form an orderly queue on this side,' she pointed to her right. 'The rest of you line up here.' She pointed to her left. 'Right. Let's see if we can get this lot sorted out.'

'She says "right" a lot doesn't she?' the Assistant Gatekeeper murmured.

The Guardian shuddered. 'I used to dread hearing that word,' he whispered. 'It usually meant trouble.'

'Right, you two,' she yelled. The Assistant Gatekeeper and the Guardian looked at each other. 'Yes, you! Get over here.'

They shuffled reluctantly over to the front of the desk.

'Right,' (the Guardian groaned) 'You can start by rounding up the groups – that way it'll make it easier to process them. You,' she prodded the Assistant Gatekeeper's chest 'can start with the ones who are asking for their quota of virgins. They're quite easy to identify, they're the most vocal. You,' she turned to the Guardian 'can deal with the whingers – they're the ones in dog collars demanding their just rewards. You,' she turned to Peter 'can sort out that little clique over there. They're all claiming this is a figment of their imagination. As that's your fault …'

'Hang on a minute,' Peter squeaked 'How can it be my fault?'

'Well you obviously didn't do a very good of convincing them when you had the chance, did you? Anyway, that's by the by. Just go and sort them out and can we *PLEASE HAVE SOME HUSH AROUND HERE.*'

Heaven went silent as the shuffling, complaining hoards froze.

Somewhere in the heart of Eternity the Holy One was also startled out of His normal state of complacency as the Cherubim and Seraphim ceased their continuous songs of praise.

'What happened?' The question was asked of no-one in particular. Then the heavenly host, shocked by their own silence, threw themselves back into their music.

59

The Holy One, not having experienced silence for many eons, reflected for a moment that a bit of peace and quiet was actually quite refreshing.

Maybe I should try it again sometime, He reflected, it would relieve the boredom a bit.

Meanwhile Peter was trying to re-establish command.

'Er ...' he shuffled the papers in front of him in a vain attempt to convince her that he did know what he was doing.

'Oh for God's sake...'

'I wish you wouldn't keep saying that,' he murmured, hastily making the sign of the cross whilst looking nervously over his shoulder.

'Let me have that list.' She snatched the parchment from him and began to scroll down the list of names. 'You see? I'm not even on here.'

'I know that but ...' Peter tried unsuccessfully to grab the list back.

'So what am I supposed to do? Are you going to send me back?'

Peter looked even more nervous and unsure as he scrabbled to re-align the parchments.

'Erm ...' he began

'No, of course you're not.' She ignored him. 'Dead is dead, right? There *is* no going back! You have screwed it up big time and I want to see the Boss!'

'But that's ...'

'Not possible?' she sneered. 'You bet your sweet ass it's possible. If I want to see Her -' Peter winced ' – *no-one* is going to stop me. So get it sorted! Now!'

Peter glanced helplessly around and spied the Guardian and Assistant Gatekeeper starting to creep cautiously amongst their charges.

'Hey, you two,' Peter yelled, 'come back here.' They pretended not to hear and as they tried to hide themselves amongst the throng, Peter's voice rose above the hubbub.

'This is all your fault,' he howled.

They fled.

Some time later, (although there being no time in Paradise, the duration was therefore not quantifiable) Peter was still trying to contact the Holy One. He'd managed to retrieve the lists and was attempting to continue with his checking in, but as he would freely admit, he wasn't very good at doing two jobs at once.

In the meantime, the lines of waiting souls had grown. The woman was still organising them into groups, but each time she thought she'd sorted it a fresh batch arrived.

'Oh this is impossible.' She stamped her foot. 'Can't you get some more help for this lot? I can't do it on my own.'

'Serves you right! You started it. I was doing quite well until you started to interfere. And in case you hadn't noticed,' he sneered 'I'm still trying to sort out *your* problem.'

'It's not *my* problem,' she reminded him nastily. 'It's yours. Oh for God's sake – and don't start that again,' she smacked at his hand as he began to make the sign of the cross, 'give me that.'

She snatched the list from him and started calling names. The queue began to shuffle forward silently, except for the clerics, the virgin seekers and the atheists who all surged forward expecting to be dealt with first and were clamouring for answers. Those who believed they shouldn't be there were now the most vociferous of the lot, threatening all kinds of action and attracting the attention of a few barristers.

She ignored them all and continued her roll call. At one point she paused.

'Your writing is appalling,' she told Peter. 'What's this name here?'

'Um ...' Peter squinted. 'I'm not too sure. Jones? Or is it Johns?'

'Oh for God's sake! Stop that!' she ordered sharply as Peter's hand moved towards his forehead again. 'Why are you still using a quill and ink?'

'Will introduced them to us. That's Will Shakespeare of course.' Peter smirked 'We were so lucky to get him,' he preened. 'Mind you, it was a close shave. Anyway, the quill and parchment were a huge improvement on the wax tablets and styli that we used to use.'

She groaned. 'Has no-one introduced you to the computer?'

'Well, we know of it obviously, but we're still waiting for Bill to arrive. Bill Gates?' His tone was tentative. 'Do you know of him?'

'Know of him? Is the Pope Catholic?'

'We-e-ell ...'

'Oh never mind all that. Let's get this backlog cleared then we can start to get some sort of order in here.'

As word spread throughout eternity of this disturbing anomaly, it was eventually decided to convene an emergency meeting of the heavenly host.

The air was electric.

'We've not had this much fun since the Big Split,' one archangel murmured to a colleague.

'*Right*,' As Peter held up a hand for silence, the Assistant Gatekeeper groaned quietly to himself. Now she's got him at it, he thought.

'As you all know by now, we have a problem. One of our souls has returned before her time and is causing mayhem in each area.'

'Well, what's done is done.' The chorus of Peace Keeping angels did their best with their version of soothing oils.

'That's the trouble,' Peter was not to be consoled. 'It isn't done. She's not supposed to be here. We've nowhere to put her. There's no category. She's just wandering around, totally out of control and poking her nose into everything. We have to stop her before she finds her way to the inner sanctum of sanctums.'

'Hang on.' Michael, the archangel and mighty warrior of God held up his sword 'What do you mean 'wandering around'?' He bristled at the idea of someone, anyone, roaming unattended through the realm. 'Is no-one with her? Is she not supervised?'

'Well, we tried,' Peter dropped his head into his hands, 'but she's not easy to deal with. Take the nursery…'

Following her tirade on the antiquated methods of Gate-keeping, it was decided that the Guardian, 'who was responsible for this cock up in the first place' (Peter rarely used such descriptive language, but this time he felt he'd been pushed too far and was therefore justified in this outburst) should take her on a tour of Heaven to keep her out of harm's – and God's way.

It was to backfire – spectacularly.

She was taken to the nursery.

'Why do they all look so miserable?' was her first question as she beheld a host of new souls all waiting for the Word to set forth for their earthly destination.

'Well, wouldn't you?' The Guardian felt peeved. Surely this was a punishment too far. Hadn't he suffered an earthly lifetime of this dreadful being? Was he also to endure eternity? He shuddered.

'So?' she persisted.

'Obvious, isn't it. Who would want to leave the peace and tranquillity of heaven for God knows where? On second thoughts, actually He does – know *where* I mean…'

'She!' she snapped.

'Pardon?'

'God is female,' she stated, brooking no arguments.

The Guardian winced and opened his mouth to protest that contrary to perceived feminist belief, the Holy One actually was a 'He', which is why he'd created *man* in His own image in the first place. Simple really.

'Oh get on with it.' she snapped again – he wondered if she ever spoke quietly – or gently. No, he supposed not.

'Anyway, God draws up the rosters and they're sent on their earthly way. They don't like it though. Why do you think babies cry the minute they're born?'

'I never thought of that.' She looked puzzled. 'So are you saying I was here once?'

'Yep!'

'And I was that miserable?'

'Mmm, actually – no. You were looking forward to it. You always were a difficult soul. That's why I was put in charge of you.'

'So...' she paused 'If I was sent out from here, presumably you were expecting me back at some stage....

The Guardian nodded. 'But not yet,' he added hastily. 'You were due to mellow into something like a normal soul.'

'So why is there no record?'

'Pardon.'

'Well you've got a list of those coming back, surely you have register of those going out?' The Guardian gazed at her blankly. 'Otherwise, how do you know how many you've lost on the way?'

The Guardian looked bewildered.

'Don't you reconcile your birth registers with your gate registers?'

The Guardian gaped.

'Oh for God's sake!' (More signs of the cross and furtive peering.) 'It's simple. It's like VAT.'

A shudder ran through the very fabric of eternity.

'You list how much has gone out, how much has come in, and any shortfall or whatever is due to the HM Customs and Revenue Office – otherwise known on earth as Hell.' She pulled an Ipad from under her fledgling wing and began making notes. The Guardian gasped.

'Where did you get that?'

'Black market.' She glanced at him. 'See? There's your first failing. Not keeping proper records means that any hoi polloi can get in. You were so busy matching names to that list of yours you didn't notice that a few villains got in through the back door so to speak. Your whole system needs upgrading pal. Right. Next?'

'…so now she's got *me* on a fast track computer course. Don't ask.' Peter shook off the inevitable questions. 'She's got the lesser spirits working all the hours God sends ... all right, all right, I know,' he waved a hand petulantly as a chorus of celestial beings disputed the term 'hourly' – 'anyway she's got them inputting all our past data and the bad news is …' he paused, the

68

heavenly host held their collective breath, 'she's right! There are major discrepancies between in and out. She'll let us have the figures later.'

The resultant groan was enough to waken the interest of the Holy One Himself. But after a few moments, as no-one begged His Indulgence, He settled back with His new toy. Someone - He had yet to find out whom - had left this amazing piece of technology on one of the steps leading up to His throne. He'd nearly fallen over it after returning from a visit with one of his more sublime galaxies. He was used to finding small gifts – slaughtered lambs, fatted calves and the like, but this was different.

Despite being God of Gods and Lord of Lords, he'd led a somewhat sheltered existence and had never heard of television before now.

'By Me,' He mused, *(others would have said 'By God', but as he was...)* 'I thought *I* was creative, but this is pure genius!'

Once one of the younger members of the Cherubim had shown him how to tune it in and change channels he'd become hooked. *Coronation Street* in particular had taken His fancy and He was busily catching up with the doings of Ena Sharples and Elsie

Tanner – accompanied of course by the now muted tones of the angelic host as they strained to hear the dialogue without neglecting their duties.

'So what's she doing now?' Archangel Gabriel asked as he surreptitiously logged on to his laptop. As the Messenger of God he was beginning to show unholy signs of interest in this new fangled method of computerised communication.

'Trying to block the leaks apparently. She's also convinced one of us is responsible for the shortfall and she's instigating an investigation into the culprit.'

'What?'

The cries of protests rose and echoed throughout the known and unknown universes and creatures of all worlds shuddered at the discord. Peter frantically shushed them, but it was too late: the swelling angry chorus reached the very throne itself - but as the Holy One had just reached the exciting bit between Elsie and her son Dennis, He decided to ignore it.

'After all,' He grumbled, 'I don't get much space to myself. Let someone else sort it out for a change,' and He put on the pair of headphones which had miraculously appeared at His right hand. He smiled beatifically as he realised that not only did it shut out the ugly sounds, it also shut out that constant, irritating warbling. Realising that they were no longer being listened to, the cherubim & seraphim stopped singing and clustered around the next episode of *Corrie*.

Meanwhile, back at the meeting, another bombshell had been dropped. The senior members of the heavenly chorus, whose voices were reserved solely for high days and Holy Days, were told that there was a possibility that they could be disbanded.

'But she can't!' the chorus whispered despairingly. 'What would we do?'

'She's says it's ergonomically unsound and a waste of angel power just using you on the odd occasion. She says you could be put to better use.'

'Like entering her wretched data I suppose,' one of the chorus said bitterly, promptly bursting into tears. Archangel Raphael rushed to console the forlorn spirit as the rest huddled round disconsolately.

'Where's this going to end?' someone asked.

'Well, I heard her talking about checking on the number of cherubim and seraphim next. Feels there's too many of them around the heavenly throne. Feels He – although she insists on calling the Holy One 'she'...' they all groaned, 'deserves a bit more peace and quiet.'

The representatives of the said C's and S's began to whimper. 'What's to become of us? What do we tell our members?'

'And then there's the harpists.' Peter ploughed on remorselessly.

'What?' a sharp arpeggio rang out. 'What about us?'

'Well, she reckons you could all be replaced by a couple of decent organists playing *electronic* organs no less. She'd noticed from the *new* records,' his sarcasm did not go unnoticed, 'that a couple had recently come home.' Peter glanced around at the blank stares. He named one of them. 'Spent 60 years as a church organist, also played for concerts and produced something called a radio programme during his time away from us.'

The faces cleared.

'Oh *that* organist,' one of harpists muttered. 'Yeah. He was good. I remember him as a fledgling soul. Knew he had talent, but surely the harp is the chosen instrument.' He gasped as a thought struck 'What if he starts playing - *jazz*?'

'Or *theatre?*' another whispered.

The harpists thrummed in agitation.

'Never mind.' Peter snapped. 'We've got to decide what we're going to do about this – before she gets the Apostles, the Saints, the Martyrs and all the rest of the heavenly mob in her sights – not to mention …' He glanced upwards. The host gasped at the possibility of the unthinkable.

'She wouldn't. Would she?'

'I'd put nothing past her.' Peter said grimly. 'So – any suggestions as to how we're going to deal with this hellion?'

Silence reigned.

'I've got an idea.' The small voice of the smallest cherub could barely be heard. His mates laughed and began to josh him and started pushing him around the heavens.

'No, let's hear it.' Peter beckoned the young being to his side.

'Well, you called her a hellion. So why don't we – ' he paused, 'send her to hell.' He finished in a rush and scuttled back to the security of his brethren.

The silence was awesome.

An archangel began to chuckle. Another joined in. Soon the whole host was laughing uproariously. Peter however, was looking thoughtful and one by one, as they noticed, the laughter subsided.

'That's not a bad idea,' Peter said.

'It would get her out of our wings,' Michael said.

The transition was remarkably easy.

'Well let's face it – they will take anyone.' Michael cynically remarked, as the big four celebrated their success with a heavenly libation.

She had been intrigued by their proposal.

'Your mission is to identify and retrieve any souls who should be with us. Also cause as much chaos as possible. At the same time…'

'But surely that's what hell is?' she queried. 'Chaos?'

'Just go,' pleaded Raphael, ever the peace-maker.

And she went – but only after doing eons of research into the meaning and beings of hell.

'*WHAT IN GOD'S NAME IS GOING ON HERE?*' the voice rang through the fiery nether regions.

The screams of the tormented ceased abruptly and only the crackling of flames could be heard. Demons and damned alike stared at the newcomer.

'Is anyone in charge here? Don't you have a gatekeeper or something? Where's Lucifer? Where's Beelzebub?' No-one spoke. 'Well? No-one?'

Silence.

'Oh for God's sake …' the satanic throng drew back in a hiss of horror. A small imp, braver than the rest, poked her with his branding fork.

'You shouldn't blaspheme like that, the Dark Lord won't like it.'

'I don't give a fuck what the Dark Lord does or doesn't like,' she snarled. 'Find me someone in charge.' As he turned to flee, she kicked him hard in the backside. He ran yowling into the smoky darkness.

'Right.' She turned to the rest of the crowd gathered round the rim of a pit of boiling sulphur. 'So which of you is new here?'

A shivering skeleton of a man stepped forward hesitantly.

'I've just arrived,' he whispered fearfully. 'And I have to say I don't like it.' He leaned forward. 'Can you get me out of here? Please?'

She tilted her head to one side.

'Do you deserve to be here?' she asked.

'I don't think so. I mean, it's not as if I killed anyone – not physically that is. Financially, maybe, but in my profession that was regarded as just good business.'

'What did you do? What was your profession?'

'I was a banker.'

'Mmm. That could be tricky. But I see where you're coming from. OK. Let me have a word.'

'What is going on here?'

She turned towards the silken tones of true evil as the company of demons behind her fell onto their faces, moaning and clawing at the ground.

'About time too. What kept you? Beelzebub, I presume?'

'At your service. And this is my colleague, Balthazar.'

The tall, courtly demon at his side gave a slight bow. By now the moaning had become an unearthly din.

'Oh shut up you lot,' she snapped at the grovelling hoards. 'We can't hear ourselves speak.'

The silence was abrupt and startling.

'Well,' murmured Beelzebub to Balthazar, 'that was unexpected. Who the hell is she?'

Balthazar shrugged.

'Do you mind telling us who you are?' Beelzebub asked 'Are we expecting you? If so, why have you not been tossed into the fiery furnaces?'

'She just turned up master,' a cowering demon ventured a few paces forward, then scuttled back to hide behind the group of shivering souls.

'Never mind who I am,' she snarled. 'More to the point, do you know who this lot are?' She beckoned the lost souls forward.

Beelzebub shrugged. 'Not my job to know,' he sneered, 'we have lower demons for that chore.'

'So where are they?'

'Um...' he looked round.

'Exactly! God,' a hiss of alarm rose behind her, Balthazar frowned, 'what a shambles. No wonder the world's going to hell in a handcart …'

'Huh?'

'Just a saying we had back on Earth,' she explained dismissively. 'Right! Let's start getting some order around here.'

'Order?' Beelzebub squeaked. 'But it's supposed to be chaotic. It's Hell.'

'Nonsense! How can you have true chaos if it's not organised. Right. Let's start with your booking-in system.' She snatched an Ipod from the grasping claws of a small demon. 'Give that back,' she snarled as she powered it up, 'Don't you know that stealing is a sin?'

The demon giggled. 'Precisely,' he screeched.

'So,' she continued, 'booking-in system?'

The two Princes of Hell shrugged, their red eyes beginning to glint dangerously.

'Uh huh. You don't have one do you? God, you're as bad as the other lot.' She began typing.

'Other lot?' Beelzebub mouthed to Balthazar.

'Right! Now first I need to know how many workers you have out there.'

The silence was ominous.

'Have you got anyone out there?'

Beelzebub cleared his throat.

'Well, the point is, we don't really need to do anything 'out there' as you put it. They're doing a pretty good job all on their own.' He giggled somewhat insanely. 'Wars all over the place, corrupt governments, selfish bankers,' the banker gave a squeak and scuttled behind the nearest demon.

'Greed everywhere you look, envy, sloth, murder, child abuse …' Balthazar took up the litany. 'Honestly? We couldn't have done it better if we'd tried.'

'Fundamentalism and fanaticism running rife' added Beelzebub.

'That was one of our better schemes bro,' Balthazar gloated, and they high-fived each other. The imps and devils followed suit, slapping hands, screeching, giggling and farting.

'Enough!' she roared. 'And could we please stop using the slang. It doesn't become you.' She turned back to the Ipod. 'OK, so no-one knows how many – or *if* any of your legions are working the earth. You don't know how many souls you should have and therefore you don't how many are missing. You obviously have no recruiting policy…'

'Recruiting…?' Balthazar murmured.

79

'Thought not. As I said, this place is a shambles.'

Silence again.

'So – there's only one thing for it. Take me to your legions!'

'She says "Right!" an awful lot doesn't she?' Beelzebub complained to his Chief of Staff. 'I've come to dread the word.'

'What's she doing now?' the demon asked.

'Well, so far she's identified a clutch of souls that don't belong to us and sent them off to you know where,' he shuddered. 'She's got the imps rounding up all the souls we've had here for centuries and she's got the minor demons categorising their levels of evil. Says it will prove how effective we've been – or not.' He groaned. 'She's got the higher demons working out the *statistical probabilities of increasing our effectiveness* as she puts it, and has done a comparison of the results of the last five Earth years – which, by the way, are pretty disappointing - and is setting quotas for the next millennium. She's threatening to take all her reports to the Dark Lord for discussion and reappraisal.'

'But she can't do that.' The fiend recoiled in horror.

'And are you going to tell her? No. Thought not.' Beelzebub shivered. 'She's got a devilish mind and if we're not careful, she'll ruin us' He lowered his voice to a whisper, ' She's even talking of filling in the sulphur pits, says it's a waste of natural resources.'

The demon gasped 'But she can't do that either! It will be the end of Hell as we know it. Oh Lucifer,' he whispered 'Her earth name wasn't Margaret Th…'

'No, no, no.' Beelzebub dismissed the demon's fears. 'No, we got lucky there.'

The demon sighed with relief. 'That really would be too much,' he murmured. 'Does the Dark Lord have *any* inkling what's going on?'

'In a vague sort of way. Luckily though, she got him hooked onto that television thing of hers, so he's leaving it all to me.'

'So what are you going to do?'

'There's only one thing that can be done. Find Balthazar for me and call a meeting of all the Legions and Squadrons.'

Balthazar wasn't happy about being disturbed. He'd just discovered Facebook and was busy updating his profile page.

The meeting was noisy as the upper and lower squadrons and legions of the infernal hordes howled in anguish at news of the latest proposed changes to their diabolical world.

'Right,' Beelzebub shouted above the screams and groans and winced as he realised what he'd said. It worked though. The bedlam began to subside. 'As some of you know, I've had word from one of the souls who left us,' he held up a struggling imp holding an Ipad. 'You may remember the banker? He was new and hadn't had a chance to properly savour our delights. Anyway, apparently before she came here she was – there.' (Even now he couldn't bring himself to say the word 'heaven'.) 'They sent her here to get rid of her.'

The hoards bayed in protest at the audacity of being used in such a way. Beelzebub raised a hand and the noise subsided again.

'It means of course that we can't retaliate by sending her back. They wouldn't take her. So,' he paused dramatically 'I've come up with a plan.'

It was a small gathering. Just the four of them on an idyllic earth bound island, the loan of which had been negotiated by Gabriel and Beelzebub.

'Lucifer.' God nodded coolly at his archenemy as he sipped a cold Margarita.

'God.' Lucifer nodded back, his eyes smouldering as he sat down alongside the Author of his downfall. 'Can I get one of those?' he nodded at the glass.

'Provided you move downwind.' God waved at a waft of sulphurous smoke. 'How can you stand that *smell?* No matter,' He snapped his fingers and a glass appeared in Lucifer's hand. God chuckled.

'Not quite as easy as wine, but a lot more fun. So what do you think of this place?' He waved a hand at the crystal blue sea lapping the silver white sands. 'Not bad for one man is it? Not many humans own their own islands nowadays.'

'And whose fault is that? There's not enough to go round.' Lucifer scowled. 'You will keep churning out new souls.'

'Now, now! No need to get churlish.' God topped up his own drink.

'Have you read my boy's proposal?' Lucifer demanded impatiently.

'Yes.'

'What do you think?'

'Bit extreme, old chap.'

Lucifer gritted his teeth. 'It's been done before.'

'Once. And that was slightly different.' God smiled benignly as he thought fondly of His Son. 'This is resurrection in another body.'

'I don't care, so long as it gets her out of my realm.'

'She has caused a bit of mayhem, hasn't she?' God sipped contemplatively. 'You do realise you may get her back next time round?'

'Not if I can help it.'

'Mmm. She may have to stay in limbo next time then.'

'So will you do it?'

God sighed heavily. 'I suppose I'll not hear the end of it unless I do. Go on then. I'll talk to the guys about a suitable donor and time and let you know. In the meantime,' he shuddered 'you'd better send her back to us. Anyway, that's enough of business. May as well make the most of this while we've still got it. Now, have you seen the latest episode of...?' God topped up their drinks as talk turned to their favourite TV programmes.

Meanwhile, the agreement having been reached and ratified, Beelzebub and Gabriel toasted each other's efforts with the beverage of their choice – large gins and tonic - whilst extolling the virtues of instant communication and debating the possibilities for good and evil of the World Wide Web.

The hospital room was silent save for the bleeping of life-retaining machines and the soft sobbing of the woman sitting by the side of the still, pale form of her daughter lying in the bed. Her chest rose and fell mechanically as the breathing apparatus kept the vital supply of oxygen circulating through her body, but to no avail To all intents and purposes she was dead. All that was required was that the machines be switched off and she could continue her interrupted journey heavenwards.

A sickly child from birth, the girl had been the love of her mother's life, but a great disappointment to her father. He stood at the window, glaring grimly down at the passing day, fretting at the time that he had to spend fruitlessly watching his daughter die and wondering why and how he had sired such a pathetic creature. Not that he didn't love her, he did, but God, how he would have loved a child with guts so much more. Didn't matter if it was a girl or a boy, all he'd wanted was an offspring with the same sort of get-up-and-go that he had, with grit in the soul. Instead he'd been blessed with this insipid creature who couldn't even cross a road safely.

He'd tried of course. Tried to instil that spark of life, but to no avail. She was her mummy's girl. Soft – not just around the edges, but in the centre as well. 'A bit slow on the uptake' as his grandmother would have said. Which of course was why she was here.

Day dreaming as usual, she'd not noticed the car careening down the road towards her until it was too late. A hit and run, the police said, but the perpetrators had been caught. Earlier that same day they'd shot another young woman to death during a Post Office raid, so they were up on charges of murder and now, he assumed, manslaughter.

His daughter had lain in a coma ever since. The doctors were puzzled. There was no brain damage as such, but her body, or soul, it seemed had just given up. He wiped a tear from his eye, not because he was losing a daughter, but for the loss of what might have been.

He turned as his wife's sobbing began to reach a crescendo and he realised the doctor had entered the room. The time had come.

Nothing was said, but as the doctor looked enquiringly at him, he nodded and pulled his wife to him. She clung to her daughter's hand as she buried her head in his shoulder.

The silence was deafening as the machines stopped their life giving function. And in that silence the father swore he heard someone say 'Now!'

Suddenly, he felt his wife tense.

'Oh my God,' she whispered. 'She squeezed my hand.'

'It's natural,' the doctor reassured her, 'just a muscle spasm.'

The man looked over his wife's shoulder, not sure whether to believe what he thought he was seeing.

'I think,' he said hesitantly, 'I think she's breathing.'

All hell broke loose, and again, as he and his wife were ignominiously herded out of the ward, the man thought he heard an unearthly chuckle.

'Physically she's fine.' The doctors were reassuring.

'But?' the father asked.

'Well, she has no memory – of the accident, of who she is and who you are. Her past life appears to be wiped out. It may all come back of course, but I think you have to prepare yourself for the fact that her memory may never return. We can recommend a good psychiatrist to help her readjust to normal life ...'

'I don't understand it,' his wife sadly commented one evening six months later. She sipped her wine as she watched their daughter hunched over the computer. 'She never showed any interest before, why now? Don't you think she's changed?'

'How do you mean?' the father was also watching his daughter, the warmth of the amber whisky mingling with the growing warmth of his feelings towards her.

Yes, of course he'd noticed a change, but he waited for his wife.

'Well, she's no longer interested in clothes or make-up. We don't go shopping – unless it's for the latest computer update.' Her voice became mournful. 'She doesn't talk to me like she used to. She's – I don't know – different? Harder?' She glanced at her husband and thought, but didn't say, more like you.

He smiled.

Oh yes! She'd changed all right. If he didn't know better he'd have thought that the girl busily re-organising his business practices for the better was a changeling. Instead of the dull, feeble girl that *was* his daughter, he now had the feisty, fiery, organised and organising child he'd always longed for. Oh yes! He thought again. She'd definitely changed. He smiled at his wife.

'I hadn't noticed,' he said.

The Dark Lord returned to his appointed place as Master of Hell and the comfort of his television, while Beelzebub and Balthazar rubbed their hands with glee as they ordered the evil minions back to the sulphur pits, toasted their success with their favourite tipple and listened contentedly as the screams of the damned once again filled the darkness with their music.

The Almighty returned to the comfort of His Self Appointed place as Master of All He Surveyed and Peter and his heavenly compatriots sighed in relief. The Cherubim and Seraphim high fived each other as they settled down to start catching up with East Enders – their latest favourite soap.

Both Masters agreed that, thanks to that pushy soul, some things had changed for the better.

Order had been restored.

Except for the Guardian.

'Right!' The nursery manager bustled up to him with a bundle of computer printouts. 'As you made such a balls up of the last one…' (the heavenly language was beginning to get ripe thanks to the influence of the latest TV dramas) '… we've got another one for you. Don't bother coming back if you get this one wrong!'

EVIL IS AS EVIL DOES

Just add a 'd' and there you have it: ignore it at your peril…
Anon

EVIL IS AS EVIL DOES

'Medieval claptrap!'

'Superstitious nonsense!'

'This is the 21st. century, you can't really believe in the devil in this day and age?'

Ah, but I can and I do, I wrote. *Not the horned, hoofed, fork-tailed version of our forefathers, but the devil nonetheless - the personification of evil as an insidious, powerful force that works in the minds and lives of mankind.*

Is it goodness or evil that inspires men and women to beat, maim and sometimes kill their children?

Is it goodness or evil that kills, rapes and robs?

Is it…

Is it what? I wondered. And did I really need a third 'is it…?' Still, it was a good start.

I sat back in my chair allowing myself a slight frisson of relief. It didn't stop me feeling cross with myself though. Every week I vowed that I would not wait until the day of my deadline to start writing my piece. But I always did. And here I was, yet again on the borderline of despair - panicking.

I'd been given the weekly column by the editor of our Regional Evening paper just over a year ago. My brief had been to comment on any issue that might be of interest to the readers and also to be controversial. I'd certainly achieved *that*. Within the first few months I'd been thoroughly branded! The Tories believed I was a Communist, the Socialists thought I was Fascist; I was in turn condemned as being racially and sexually prejudiced, an anarchist, politically incorrect, and oh yes, a bigot! I dined out on that one for weeks. Some guy, who preferred to remain anonymous, sent me a letter via the paper calling me a 'boring, bigoted, old bag!' As I wrote in reply in my next column,

'Boring? Possibly. Bigoted? Probably. Old? Pistols at dawn Sir!

Most journalists would have given their exclusives for a by-line. I had no choice.

'If you can't stand by your opinions,' the Editor told me, 'don't express them!'

I needed the work and the money, so there I was each week, complete with a head and shoulders photograph and my name in big typeface below each caption, right in the firing line.

It was difficult enough producing five hundred words every seven days as it was, without the added knowledge that someone, somewhere was going to castigate me for my opinions. It taxed my mind and originality to the limits. Believe me, a five hundred-word column is far more difficult to write than a thousand-word feature. Each word has to be carefully considered and crafted, it must justify its existence and each sentence must carry powerfully into the next.

As a result, I left it later and later each week, waiting for inspiration to strike. In the end, the source of my inspiration was fear – fear of missing my deadline, fear of the editor's wrath and fear of looking a fool.

This week had been no different. I'd scoured the papers for ideas, I'd listened to news bulletins and I'd even eavesdropped on conversations. I'd walked on the beach, taken relaxing baths in the middle of the day, practised self-hypnosis and meditation - nothing.

Until yesterday.

Yesterday an elderly woman had taken her dog for a walk in the woods. The dog had returned home alone, its mistress's life-blood slowly soaking into the woodland floor. She wasn't robbed or raped, just knifed enough times to kill her. A harmless, gentle, elderly woman, murdered on a warm, autumn afternoon.

I was overwhelmed with anger at both the horror and the complete senselessness of it. The story simmered in my mind all night and I woke with a heavy head and a heavy heart, but I knew what I was going to write about.

I re-read my opening sentences and crossed out my third '*Is it...*'

'*Evil walked in the woods this week,*' I continued, '*not goodness. It was evil that stalked an innocent victim and evil that plunged the knife into her chest and killed her. Can you truly say that you don't believe in the devil?*'

Instantly, the computer shut down.

I stared in disbelief at the dead screen.

Oh my God! A power cut – at a time like this. It took a few seconds to realise that my printer light still glowed. Not a power cut then.

Frantically I hit keys, any keys, desperately trying to re-boot the system. Nothing. Then a flicker of light flashed across the screen and I watched in an agony of anxiety as the computer slowly went through its set-up programmes. I crossed my fingers until they ached.

It was taking so long.

I tried to remember if the auto-recovery tool had been doing its job. It usually saved automatically every few paragraphs. Had I written enough for it to operate? How much had I lost? What had I written? I'd never remember.

Slowly the screen came back to life, and there were my words. Every last one of them. I nearly cried with relief. Pressing *Ctrl S,* I saved my work and then to be on the safe side, I copied it onto a memory stick.

I tried adding a few more words, but I was very shaky and I'd lost my train of thought.

'A cup of coffee,' I thought, 'that'll do it. A good strong shot of caffeine.'

As I waited for the kettle to boil, I stood in the open doorway of the kitchen that led out to my small back yard.

The sun was warm on my face and I began to calm down. I loved days like this: Indian summer days. They had a special quality, a special feel to them. I knew that if I closed my eyes my other senses would sharpen. I would hear the bees hovering over the red and pink geraniums still cascading down the old brick wall from my hanging baskets. I would smell the subtle perfumes of the creamy white datura, whose large, white bell-shaped flowers filled the air each evening with their fragrance.

Evil was a long way from this perfection.

The old fashioned whistle on the kettle brought me back to reality. I closed the door on the day, and cup in hand returned to my computer screen. To my relief, the screen saver was busily doing its thing. I touched a key to return to my work in progress.

For one shocked moment I thought I'd lost it all again, because all that came up was a blank page.

'Shit,' I thought, 'I haven't got time for this.'

I checked my watch, two hours to go. It was getting tight – tighter than usual. I hadn't been that long getting the coffee surely? Frantically hitting the 'open' icon, I tried to access my saved file, but the message came up 'file open.'

'It isn't,' I howled, then realised that the computer was right. The file *was* open, the page had simply scrolled down to a new page. Breathing a huge sigh of relief I scrolled back up to my work, but something looked wrong.

I read it through from the top and found that not only were some of my words missing, but the two main paragraphs had changed places.

'*Christ*' I muttered, and moved the mouse. The words on the screen danced a crazy jig. I tried to highlight a sentence. Nothing. What *was* wrong with this bloody thing? Now I really was panicking. I tried again – still nothing. I tried to shut the damn thing down. Hopeless. Nothing was responding, and then as I watched, individual words shuddered, vanished and re-appeared in another place. My article was now gobbledygook.

Suddenly I felt cold. Was this just a faulty computer? Or were there other forces at work here? Nah. Too much imagination – or was it? Was I challenging evil by writing this piece? Was evil retaliating, mocking my efforts and causing this mayhem? Oh, come on!

However, I decided to play safe. I needed protection of the heavenly sort. Now I'm not necessarily religious, but I have a healthy respect for those who are and I knew that various icons are believed to provide that protection: for instance, St Christopher medals for travellers – and of course that most powerful icon of all – the crucifix. Who was I at this moment to question this belief? I needed all the help I could get. Opening my desk drawer, I reached for the silver crucifix that had belonged to my darling father-in-law. I knew exactly where it was, except – it wasn't. I pulled the drawer out further and shuffled through the oddments of stationery that I'd accumulated.

Still no joy.

Now I pulled it out completely and tipping it up on the floor began scrabbling through the litter.

'But it *was* here,' I sat back on my heels, confusion mingling with doubt. Perhaps I had moved it during one of my rare blitzes on the office. I stood up and stared down at the computer screen trying to ignore the tingle of fear that stroked the hairs on the back of my neck. Words still danced randomly across the screen.

In desperation I pulled the plug from the wall and held my breath. For a long moment nothing happened and then the screen slowly faded to black.

I breathed again. I was still very shaky, but at least I was back in control and I was determined to stay that way.

I went down the stairs, through the kitchen and out into the garden. There, I broke off two stems of geranium flowers. Why geraniums? I'll never know: It just felt right. Perhaps it was the purity of their scarlet colour, the woody strength of their stems - whatever, it was instinct, a gut feeling that told me I needed something of nature to make this work, rather than something man-made and possibly tainted with impurities. Carefully carrying the blossoms back to my desk, I laid them in the form of a cross on the tower of my computer monitor, then switched it back on.

For a moment the screen juddered and then went blank. I watched and waited. Slowly it came back to life. There was a message saying that it had not been shut down properly and was in emergency mode. Fine. I didn't care so long as it worked. Tentatively I opened the relevant file and there it was, clean and as I had saved it. Not a word out of place. Resisting the temptation to look at my watch, I gritted my teeth and began to type.

It took two abortive attempts to e-mail it to the paper, but as soon as it was gone, I phoned Henry, a computer whiz friend of mine. Knowing how essential it is to my work, he said he'd come straight over and run through the system for me.

'Probably a loose connection or something like that,' he said. 'Don't worry, I'll sort it.'

I went down and put the door on the latch so that he could come straight in and then pouring us both a glass of wine, I went back up to the office to sort out the mess that I'd left strewn across the floor.

I didn't hear Henry come in.

I wasn't even aware of his presence until he helped me to my feet.

'Christ,' he said, 'what have you been doing?'

Geraniums lay crushed around the room and strewn over the computer – dozens of them. Instead of being scattered across the floor as I'd left it, the detritus from my desk drawer was now stacked bizarrely on my desk and the computer screen was going crazy.

Henry led me from the room and closed the door.

'Are you hurt?' he asked, as he led me down the stairs and out into the garden and the sun. I shook my head: no, I thought, just spooked – and terrified. He sat me down at the garden table and went back into the kitchen and fetched the wine. I couldn't stop shaking. He poured the wine and then, taking my clenched fist, gently tried to prise my late father-in-law's crucifix from my grasp. He failed. There was no way I was letting go of this protection.

I had just one question. If it hadn't been in that drawer when I'd looked for it - and I'd swear on everything I held dear that it wasn't - then how come I'd just found it balanced right on the top of that grotesque structure currently sitting on my desk!

'Henry,' I said, gulping my wine 'I think I need a new computer – and a priest.'

CIRCLES OF DEATH

The fairest things have fleetest end, their scent survives their close...
Frances Thompson 1859-1907 *('Daisy' 1913)*

CIRCLES OF DEATH

My mother had always been psychic.

As a child she would frequently fall into trances. Once, she told me, she'd fallen into a trance in the middle of the street in Chelsea, just up the road from where she'd lived. Just like that: traffic screaming all around her and there she was in a silent, spirit world. She saw things then that she learned not to talk about.

People said she was simple. Daft. Something missing. Not quite right in the head. But she knew that she knew things that they would never know. She began to talk to me about them as I grew older, when she knew that I would understand. She needed to talk, and she knew that as her daughter I wouldn't dare query or question. As it was, I was fascinated by this extraordinary power she possessed.

Friends and relatives would 'pass over' – they never 'died' in our house – and they would always come back to visit. I always knew when they did. The next day she would put fresh flowers in front of a lit candle that she kept tucked away in a corner of the

104

living room above the small bookcase. My father never commented on this. Apart from warning her of the danger of fire from naked flames, he preferred to ignore it, burying his head in his history books, and his mind in all the other interests he pursued. She'd tried to tell him once, but he hurumphed it away as 'a load of nonsense.' She never mentioned it to him again.

She didn't mind the visits. They were a comfort, compensating for the sadness of the death. She didn't really mind the deaths; they were a natural part of life. At least, she didn't mind them then.

It began with a phone call early one morning in April. She asked if I could pop round for a minute and give her a hand. I'd had my day planned, but she sounded concerned and anyway, I only lived a few streets away. I found her, not in the kitchen as I'd expected at that time of day, but in the bedroom sniffing under the bed.

'Can you smell it?' she asked.

I sniffed.

'No, nothing. Why what can you smell? It can't be gas, you don't have any,' I joked.

'It smells like something's rotting. Decaying. I thought it was the cat. I thought she'd brought in something half eaten and left it somewhere; a mouse or something, but I've searched everywhere. Under the beds, behind the wardrobes, under the chairs, I can't find anything. Are you sure you can't smell it, it's really strong.'

'No, all I can smell is your furniture polish. There's nothing here, mum.'

' Oh well.' She stood up and smoothed her skirt. 'I suppose it will go.'

And it did. Life - and death - went on and three weeks later mother had another visit. A distant uncle had died the day before and he'd come to bid her farewell. The flowers were picked and placed in front of the lighted candle.

A few months later I got another call from her.

'That smell's back.'

'What smell?'

'Don't you remember? Horrible, decaying or something, I thought it was the cat at the time. You must remember.'

'Oh yes. I shouldn't worry, it's probably the drains or something.'

'Yes, you're probably right.'

Shortly afterwards, my cousin died of a heart attack during a dialysis treatment in hospital. He was too tired to cope any more. He'd lived, loved and laughed and I knew I would miss him more than any of my many cousins. He'd been like a brother to me and I adored him. When I popped in to see mother the next day, I was pleased to see the flowers in place. They were a small comfort and the knowledge of his visit to her softened the sharp edges of my loss.

It was the holiday in the caravan in the middle of a field in Wales that finally convinced her of what she'd already begun to suspect.

Apparently, she woke up one morning and the van was filled with the stench of rotting decay. My father couldn't smell a thing. They returned home a few days later with my mother in a state of trepidation. She waited - and three weeks later to the day, another relative died. Now she knew. She could smell the approach of death in the family.

She was white and shaking when she confided this horror to me. I tried to comfort her, but it was useless. Unknown to me she had noted the dates of the smell and the subsequent deaths in her diary. She showed me and sure enough, the evidence was there. It wasn't so much the deaths that frightened her; after all, she of all people knew that life went on. No, it was the uncertainty of it all, that period of waiting and wondering - which of us would it be next?

She never grew used to it and I knew she dreaded each occurrence. She never mentioned it again either, or told me when it happened, but occasionally, I would catch her looking at me under hooded eyes and know that it had. Three weeks later she would breathe a sigh of relief as her closest relatives were spared – until the next time.

And then it changed again. She phoned me one morning, unusually cheerful.

'I had that smell again the other week.'

'I know.'

'How?'

'I can always tell.'

'Oh. Well anyway the good news is that the three weeks are up. No-one's died and no-one's been to visit. Perhaps it's all gone. Perhaps it *was* all in my mind.'

Then she received the letter.

A close friend in the States had written to tell her that her husband had passed away. The date? Three weeks to the day of the smell. Now even her friends were being drawn into the circle of death. She grew depressed for a while and then seemed to develop a calm acceptance.

There was only one exception to the pattern. My father. He was attending a meeting of one of his many interests, had just handed out the Minutes to his fellow committee members, then sat down and died. Mother had had no warning smells, no three week waiting period, no sign of any sort, so it was a huge shock for her. But what she did tell me was that as he left the house that day, a wonderful, sweet aroma of flowers filled the air behind him. She never saw him alive again, although thankfully, he did come to visit and asked if she was all right.

She's gone herself now, almost a month, but she came back to see me. After she went, I built a little shrine in the corner of my lounge. Each day I light the candle and each week I place her favourite flowers – freesias - in front of it. She knows I love her and miss her.

There's only one problem.

This morning when I woke, there was this stench in the room. Dank. Rotten. Decaying. Tom, my husband could smell nothing. I checked everywhere for possible causes, but there were none. To be on the safe side, I also checked the children out for illnesses, but they seem fine: no sniffles, no temperatures, no apparent illnesses in waiting and I've told Tom to drive extra carefully for the next three weeks. I've also phoned my sister and brother, just to be sure. They all think I'm being over fussy and neurotic, laughing at my so-say 'sixth sense.'

The trouble is I have no control over what will happen and to whom.

Now – I just have to wait.

BEWARE

WHAT YOU WISH FOR

'Beware, madam, of the witty devil,
The arch intriguer who walks disguised
In a poet's cloak ...
Robert Graves (1895-1985)

111

BEWARE WHAT YOU WISH FOR

It was an ordinary sort of day with ordinary sort of weather. The sort of weather you expect in England in early summer. Not too hot, not too cold and thankfully today, hardly any breeze off the sea, or the drenching fine drizzle that seemed to soak more effectively than a deluge. The grey ceiling overhead was peppered with screaming gulls, but apart from that, nothing moved – except me and my dog, Rufus.

As we strolled along the beach – well I strolled, he ran, barking at and jumping into the waves, I thought about what I'd got waiting for me at home. Actually, not a lot, I reflected. I sighed. When did life become so dull?

I'd cleaned the house that morning more thoroughly than usual. I'd put the washing on; I'd had my lunch with my customary glass (or two, but who's counting) of wine and even prepared my evening meal before I left for our walk. Other than that? An evening of television? As I said – not a lot to go home for.

I knew I should try to get out more, but there wasn't much on offer in the small village in which I lived, especially for middle-aged women. There was the odd coffee morning for charities and the occasional invitation to a drinks do - but I suspect that was more out of pity than a need for my scintillating company. To be honest, I wasn't that keen on going to places on my own anymore, so opted for slobbing around at home.

The village had been a 'new build' thirty years ago, providing expensive 'homes for the discerning' – in other words those well off enough to be able to pay for the idyll of country life and with enough personal mobility to dispense with the need for local trades people.

As a result, there was no corner shop where residents could gather and gossip, no local pub for a swift game of darts or a relaxing glass or two of Pinot - Grigio or Noir - neither was there a church to provide a central focus to life in the village; so, no Women's Institute, no choir, no gardening clubs, no fetes or committees on which to serve.

As the original residents gradually moved away, either downsizing to residential housing or their graves, most of my neighbours were now much younger than me. They were friendly enough when they were there, either at weekends or late evenings, passing the time of day as they tended their immaculate gardens or washed their expensive cars, but mostly they were out all day, dashing to their city desks or working in one of the nearby towns.

The nearest one for me was twelve miles away and if I fancied taking myself out to lunch or an evening meal, I had to get the car out – and without a husband to share driving duties, there were all the attendant risks of drink driving.

The local bus ran to town and back three times a week – yes, really – out at 9.30 and back at 12.30 for shoppers with no cars - and even that service was under threat because those passengers it attracted from the surrounding villages were non paying, free bus pass users.

So, apart from the odd trip out I spent my days cleaning an already clean house, paying bills, ordering my shopping on line, and – to my shame – watching day-time television or playing solitaire on the computer. Oh, and walking the dog on the beach.

Thoughts of Rufus brought me back to the present, I realised he'd stopped barking and was digging at the water's edge.

Thinking he'd found a dead fish – or worse, a jelly fish – I called him back, but he ignored me and went on digging.

'What have you got then, boy?' I asked as I knelt in the sand next to him. He looked round at me and then shifting round slightly he began digging with renewed joy and vigour, showering me with wet sand.

'Oi,' I shouted, as I stood and backed off. 'Do you mind, that went all over me.'

At that moment, he pulled his treasure free and would have run off if I hadn't grabbed his collar.

'Give!' I commanded and held out my hand. He reluctantly dropped his find onto the beach and I picked it up. It was just an old bottle. Quite thick green glass though, I noticed, with dimples around the base and a thick cork in the top. Actually it was quite a nice shape. Mmm, I thought, this would look quite effective on the bathroom windowsill.

I turned it over in my hands looking for cracks or breaks, but could see none. Then I dipped it in the sea and began to wash off the sand.

That's when it happened.

Suddenly the cork shot out and smoke began to wreath and grow around me. I dropped the bottle, thinking it might be some sort of acid. Rufus let out a yelp and began tearing up the beach. I turned and yelled after him.

'Rufus! Come back here this instant.'

'What is your wish, oh mistress?'

The voice came from behind me. I turned back - and screamed. An ugly great brute floated in the smoke a few feet off the beach, complete with turban and flowing robes - the epitome of the genie from Aladdin's lamp.

I stumbled back up the beach a few paces, wildly looking round to see if anyone else was around. No-one. Totally deserted. Isolated. Just me and Rufus – and the *thing*. Now I was scared as well as disbelieving.

'Keep back,' I shouted at it. 'Keep back or I'll set my dog on you. Rufus! Rufus! Here boy. Now.' I shrieked in panic.

'But mistress, I only wish to grant your heart's desire.' The creature rubbed his hands together like some Turkish Uriah Heep. 'I am yours to command. What is your wish?'

116

Then an extraordinary thing happened. Rufus ran back down the beach towards me, but instead of coming to me, he went straight to the creature and began licking his hand.

'No,' I muttered, shaking my head. 'I don't believe it. This can't be happening. I must have dozed off. I knew I shouldn't have had that third glass of wine with lunch.'

'Good boy, Rufus. Good dog. Oh that feels good,' the phantom said, holding his hand up to his face, 'the touch of another living creature. It's been so long.'

He looked wistfully at Rufus who, tail thumping and tongue lolling, gazed lovingly at him and promptly sat down at – well I can't say his feet because he didn't have any – just this wisp of smoke wreathing back and forth over the bottle.

'Please mistress, just make your wish and I'll be on my way.' There was an edge of desperation in his voice and he begged once more. 'Please?'

Feeling encouraged by Rufus's behaviour, I took a couple of steps closer to the thing. Curiosity got the better of me, but I still wasn't sure if I was awake or not.

'So, are you really here? Are you for real?' I asked cautiously.

'I am, mistress.'

'And I'm not dreaming? I mean, you're not the product of three glasses of wine?' I asked, crossing my fingers hopefully, thinking if it was the wine, I'd have to seriously consider going tee-total.

'No mistress. You may continue to safely indulge, but I would recommend you cut down a little.' He looked me up and down quizzically. 'It's starting to go on round your waist.'

Cheeky sod! I automatically pulled my stomach in.

'You could always wish for a sylph like figure,' he suggested tentatively.

'You're beginning to push your luck, sunshine,' I snarled.

'A thousand pardons, mistress. I do not wish to offend. Although personally, I've always liked a bit of flesh on my women.'

He held up his hands to ward me off as I took a threatening pace towards him.

'Please mistress,' he begged 'just let me know your one wish and I'll be on my way.'

'Hang on a minute,' I said. '*One* wish? I thought you lot always granted three.'

He sighed. 'That was in the good old days mistress. Haven't you heard? There's a worldwide recession going on. Ever since your three-day week back in the seventies, we've been restricted to one per person.'

'Well, I think that's a bit much.' I muttered. 'What's a person to do with only one wish?'

I thought for a moment. 'I suppose I could wish for world peace.'

He went white. 'Please don't do that mistress. You'll upset the finely tuned global equilibrium and cause chaos. No,' he held up a hand to stop me talking further, 'just take my word for it. World peace is not an option. Besides, it has to be something personal – just for you. All I ask is,' he gritted his teeth, 'that you hurry up.'

'All right, all right! No need to get snippy. Now … what do I wish for? Mmmm. I'll need to give this some thought.'

An hour later, I was sitting against a rock still trying to decide. The genie continued to chivvy me and then began to get restless.

'I don't like this weather you have here,' he complained. 'Where I come from the sky is blue. Not this dreary colour - and the sun is hot as well,' he added.

'Well if you don't like it, you'd better change it.' I snapped.

'Is that your wish, mistress?' he asked eagerly, 'that I make the sky blue?'

'No, it bloody well isn't. Now bugger off and let me get on with my choice.'

He shrugged, muttered something and the clouds parted letting the sun through.

'Mmm, so you do have your uses,' I conceded and settled back to soak up the sun. He grumbled under his breath and began to float down the beach with Rufus in tow. 'And if you're thinking of going for a stroll,' I called after him, 'you'd better do something about your appearance. You'll frighten the natives.' Then I closed my eyes and leaned back.

What to wish for – that was the question. It's not as easy as it sounds.

I guess most people would wish for more money, but that didn't apply to me. Thanks to a guilt-ridden husband, I didn't really lack for anything. He paid me enough to cover all my bills each month, together with a generous personal allowance that allowed me to live in the style to which I'd always wanted to become accustomed. He'd also signed the house over to me as part of the divorce deal, so I was quite comfortable – and even better, I didn't have to share it with him.

The relief when he came home that night two years ago and told me he'd found someone else – I can't begin to tell you. I 'grudgingly' allowed a quickie divorce to go through, pretending all the time to be the heart-broken, dumped wife, while all the time rejoicing at my good fortune.

After all, if he hadn't left me, I'd have had to leave him.

So thrilled was I, that when all the paperwork had been completed and the deals done, I sent his trollop a huge bouquet of flowers with a thank you card, and just because it gave me an added frisson of vengeful satisfaction, I hired a young, handsome, male model to deliver a pair of jump leads and a note which read *'You're gonna need these!'* (An old joke I know, but effective and rewarding: borrowed from the stable of the comedian Bob Monkhouse if memory serves me right.)

So no, I didn't need money, or a house, or even a yacht or a private jet – or any of the things money can buy. Mmmm…

I woke with a start, water pooling around my feet. The tide was coming in. I sat up and looked round, wondering where Rufus had got to. The good weather had brought out other sun worshippers and bodies in various states of undress were dotted along the shore. The normality made me wonder if it had all been a dream and I peered along the water's edge hoping not to see him. But no, there he was, strolling along the beach with a bikini clad blond babe on each arm and Rufus at his heels.

'Huh, so much for liking a bit of flesh!' I muttered. 'Not much on them - except where it matters.'

He'd taken my advice though and sorted out suitable clothing. He actually looked quite handsome in his black, figure hugging trousers and a white lawn shirt. He'd lost the turban too and swept his raven coloured hair back in what looked like a ponytail.

Seeing I was awake, Rufus ran back to me and sat down beside me panting. I reached for my bag and produced the bottle of water and small bowl I always carried for him when we went out.

He drank greedily and I felt a bit guilty that I'd neglected him as I slept. I ruffled his fur and pulled him to me in a hug.

'You're such a good boy, aren't you,' I told him as he slobbered cold water over me. He barked once and sat down looking at me intently. Although he was a large mongrel with a wiry coat, he was handsome in his way and certainly loving and loyal and I loved him to bits.

'What is it, boy? What do you want?'

He barked again.

'Oh Rufus,' I stroked his sand covered fur. 'I wish I could understand what you're trying to tell me.'

Instantly there was an enormous flash of light and a billowing cloud of smoke and I heard a voice say:

'Thank Allah for that! I thought you'd never choose. Nice to have met you – and thanks, Rufus, for getting me set free.'

'No problem old chap.'

I stared at Rufus in disbelief.

'Did I just hear what I think I heard?' I stuttered. 'Did you just talk?'

He looked at me pityingly, as if I were a simpleton.

'I've *always* been able to talk,' he said, 'it's just that *you* haven't been able to understand me – until now.' He peered through the clearing smoke. 'Pity he's gone,' he said, 'I quite took to him. I shall miss him.'

He stood and shook himself.

'Now,' he looked at me, 'can we please go home. As I tried to tell you a few moments ago, I'm getting hungry.'

The next morning, the news was full of 'the weird incident on the beach' as the newsreaders were calling it.

The police arrived first, alerted by several concerned sunbathers reporting the 'explosion' and had begun shepherding those who hadn't already run away screaming, up to the road. They took our names and addresses and told us we could go home, but they might be in touch later. I was worried Rufus would say something and give the game away, until I realised that I was the only one who could understand him. (That was a relief I can tell you.)

Then the army arrived. Apparently, the official thinking was that the incident had been caused by some sort of incendiary device left over from the war, and they were busily and carefully going over the ground with bomb detectors. Of course they found nothing: except the usual detritus – and a green bottle.

Damn, I thought, I'd wanted to bring that home with me. Oh well.

It had been a weird night.

Now he'd found his voice, Rufus wanted to talk – non-stop. It was fascinating. First we discussed his name.

'Why Rufus?' he asked.

'I don't know really.' I told him. 'It's the first name that came into my head when I saw you and I thought it suited you. Besides that, *he* hated it, so I insisted.'

'Yeah, he didn't like me much. I could tell.'

'He didn't…?' I asked.

'No, never hit me. I'd have bitten him if he had. No, he just avoided me, for which I was grateful. So what happened there? One day he was here, the next he wasn't.'

Once we'd exhausted the topic of the divorce and sex and the lack thereof, (which he found very hard to understand, monogamy not being in a dog's make-up) he then wanted to discuss his diet.

Typical male, I thought, sex and food.

He didn't like dog food – at all, he told me.

'Not at all?' I asked.

'Well,' he compromised, 'I can take or leave it, but given the choice I'd rather leave it.'

So we then began to prepare a daily menu for him to approve. Meat featured strongly: fillet steaks, sirloin at a pinch, but not rump …

'Too chewy.'

…loin of pork…

'Not shoulder. Too fatty.'

…chicken of course,

'Breast preferably, although I can tolerate wings and legs. But please remove the bones. There's something about chicken bones that puts my teeth on edge.' He shuddered at the thought.

'But I thought all dogs ate bones.'

'Yes, usually because we're hungry. You lot really don't feed us enough – or properly.' He sounded quite severe.

'Vegetables?' I broached tentatively.

'What do you think I am?' he said indignantly, 'A vegetarian? I'm a carnivore in case you hadn't noticed – and none of those dog biscuits either, they're as dry as dust and just as tasteless.'

'But I thought…'

'Same answer – hunger.'

126

At some time during the evening after feeding us both, (I shared my meal with him because he flatly refused to eat another tin of dog food) I turned the television on to watch the late evening news. I expected him to lay down at this point and go to sleep as he usually did, but to my astonishment he began commenting on the various items, even shouting at the television when he didn't like or agree with the commentator or interviewee.

Eventually I turned the set off, hoping that would shut him up, but then he wanted to discuss all things politic and economic. I must say for a dog he was very well versed in these matters.

'Not surprising really,' he told me when I queried how he'd come to be so knowledgeable about world affairs. 'You have that box thing chattering on all day...'

'You mean the radio.'

'Yeah, that's the one, and the television on all evening, I can't help hearing everything that's said. By the way, do you think we could watch *East Enders* from now on? I know you prefer *Coronation Street,* but I've seen a few trailers and it looks quite interesting. Also *One Man and his Dog?* I think that's on again now, and there's some real honeys rounding up those sheep.'

In the end, fascinating though the evening had been, I could hardly stay awake.

'Bedtime!' I said firmly.

'OK. Could I – um – go outside first do you think?' he sounded somewhat embarrassed.

'Oh, of course,' I got up and went and opened the back door for him, 'And don't…'

'I know, don't piddle on the roses,' he called jauntily. 'By the way, there's a pile of doo-dah under the tree you'll need to clean up in the morning.'

Mmm, I thought, now we understand each other, perhaps I can change a few of *his* habits, as he's so intent on changing mine.

But that could wait for the morning.

It wasn't a good night.

He was so excited he was restless and kept waking me up for a quick chat.

Then he was thirsty.

Then he fancied a snack.

Then he wanted to go out again.

128

Then, when I was finally fully awake and unable to drop off again, he flopped across the middle of the bed, fell into a deep sleep and began snoring – loudly.

I crept out of the room and climbed into the single bed in the spare room, something I'd not needed to do for the last two years, since my ex had left in fact.

'*This* has got to change,' I muttered grimly to myself. 'I'm not going through this again – not for man nor beast!'

The next day I set a few ground rules. He was happy to go along with most of them, but not so happy about moving into the spare room.

'But I've always slept with you,' he protested.

'Yes. *Sleep* being the operative word. You kept me awake for most of last night talking, and to be honest at my age I can't be doing with it. I can't guarantee you'll let me be, so it's either the spare bed or your basket in the kitchen.'

He grudgingly agreed and that night, with barely a hint of bad grace, curled up on the single bed and closed his eyes.

I performed my ablutions and sank back onto my pillows, drowsily reflecting on this extraordinary event and wondering how it was going to affect my life.

He woke me just after 3am.

'It's this rich food,' he said prancing around my feet. 'Hurry up or I'll never make it.'

I groggily went down stairs and opened the backdoor. He bolted out and was gone for a good ten minutes. Suddenly it seemed that all hell broke loose.

'What the hell do you think you're doing in my garden,' he shouted. 'Get out. Get out now, or I'll have your guts for garters.' There was a loud hiss followed by a screech and a scrabbling noise. I closed my eyes and groaned.

'Bloody cat from next door,' he said, as he strolled back into the kitchen. 'Still, saw it off good and proper. By the way, what's 'garters'?'

'I'll tell you tomorrow,' I said, switching off the light and preparing to go back to bed.

'Hang on a minute. I'm feeling a bit peckish after all that. Any chance of a nibble?'

The next evening my neighbour knocked on the door. She was quite polite and asked me nicely if I could keep the noise down. My dog's incessant barking had ruined their weekend, which they'd hoped to spend quietly in the garden. And not only that they'd been woken several times during the night for the last two nights and quite frankly it just wasn't acceptable. She emphasised once again that this was a friendly request, but left me in no doubt that unless things improved she would 'take action'. I'm not sure what that would have entailed, but I promised I would keep Rufus under better control.

I had a word with him about it, but he couldn't really see what all the fuss was about, but promised to try and keep the noise down, especially at night. In return I promised him that we'd go for longer walks where he could talk and shout to his heart's content.

From then on we spent hours walking on the beach, in the neighbouring fields and nearby woodland, and on occasion I took him into town with me, something I'd never done before because of the hassle of shopping with a dog in tow. But now he could understand me I was able to explain *why* he had to stay outside and *why* he had to wait for me. I took him to the pet cemetery and waited silently as he paid his respects at the graveside of other departed canines.

I found him fascinating to talk and listen to, to discover his take on life and a world that was so dominated by mankind – a mankind that regarded all other species as inferior, particularly in the realms of intelligence. I was intrigued by this rare insight into the mind of another species and impressed by his capacity for learning. I felt enormously privileged to be witnessing such a phenomenon.

But there is only so much of a good thing that a body can take.

It was his voice that first began to grate. I hadn't noticed it initially, but it had a sharpness about it that made my ears ring when he became excitable – and he was often excitable. I was constantly aware of the neighbours and spent more and more time each evening shushing him.

His curiosity, that I had initially found so refreshing, began to pall, his incessant questions had lost their charm and his dietary demands were not only time consuming, but were proving to be expensive.

I was getting very little sleep as the consequences of his diet continued to lead to broken nights. I seemed to spend my life cooking and cleaning up after him for very little in return. He dominated our television viewing, insisting loudly that we watch his favourite programmes 'live' while I recorded my own choice for later viewing, and of course he continued to harangue all the news programmes.

One morning, as I recovered from yet another broken night, I realised the awful truth: that this was much like living with my ex husband. The snoring, the farting from over-rich food, the waiting on him, the shouting at the television, the occasional late nights when he went out on the prowl – suddenly I was back where I'd started – or rather finished. Fuming about my stupid wish, I thought *something's* got to be done!

I tell you, I became so desperate that night after night, in the early hours, I began fantasising about the ways I could solve my problem.

Send him to a dog's rescue centre? I could get away with it on the basis that as an elderly pensioner I could no longer afford to keep him, and someone else might love him as much as I did without the added complication of communicating with him. But come morning I knew I couldn't do it, the thought of someone else caring for him actually made me feel jealous. After all, he was *my* dog. And anyway, irritating as he had become, for all his faults I still loved him – which was more than could be said for the ex!

Should I take him for a long walk and – well – abandon him for a few days while I recovered? No. Again, the thought of him starving and wandering lost over some barren moors brought tears to my eyes.

And then after a particularly irritating day when I couldn't do anything right by him, I even - yes, I admit it - I even considered *murder,* getting him put down. I felt so guilty the next day for having even contemplated the idea that I over-compensated with the food – and of course was up for most of that night.

And then one evening it happened. We'd been watching Graham Norton presenting a programme about dogs and he – Rufus that is – began holding forth on the ethics and morality of humans 'owning' other beings, keeping them as pets and moulding them to their own standards and behaviours. I suddenly became aware that he'd asked me a direct question – and I hadn't answered.

'Are you OK?' he asked.

I sat bolt upright. 'Yes, I'm fine,' I answered. 'Sorry, I must have drifted off for a moment.'

'Mmm. You do look a bit peaky,' he said, his head tilted on one side, but then continued with his theme as if there'd been no interruption.

That night in bed, I could hardly contain my excitement and relief. I knew I hadn't 'drifted off': I'd *switched* off. For a few moments, I'd actually blocked out his voice. The enormity of this discovery and how I could develop it kept me awake for most of the night. It needed careful planning. I knew I couldn't do it all at once because he'd start suspecting – after all he was a clever dog.

The next night, after he'd gone to bed and was thankfully still asleep, I devised a time line. Luckily the one thing he hadn't learned was how to read, so I crept down and fixed it to the fridge door with a couple of door magnets where I could see it each day, knowing he wouldn't know what it was. If and when he asked I would tell him it was his meal plan.

I started that next morning.

'So what would you like for breakfast?' I asked him

'Toast and marmite – as usual,' he added looking slightly puzzled. After all this is what he always had.

'Sorry?'

'Toast and marmite,' he repeated.

'Come on,' I coaxed him. 'Stop messing around. I can't understand you when you bark.'

'Bark?' he squeaked. 'I'm talking normally.'

'Well, whatever.' I feigned puzzlement. 'I'm going to give you toast and marmite as usual. Let me know when you feel like speaking to me properly.'

I made the toast and marmite for him and poured myself some cereal. He ate his breakfast slowly, obviously unsettled by this turn of events.

'Would you like some more?' I asked as he finished.

'No, that was plenty, thank you,' he replied.

'Oh now he deigns to speak to me properly.' I said.

'But I was speaking properly before,' he protested.

'Well, I couldn't understand you,' I replied as I finished my breakfast. 'All I could hear was a lot of barking. Now how do you fancy a trip into town.'

I continued with my ploy of pretending I couldn't understand him, increasing the level a bit each day, until eventually after three or four weeks he'd given up trying. Life became much quieter after that.

One morning my neighbour came round to thank me for taking note of her concerns and even complimented me on how his behaviour had changed for the better. Rufus overheard this and lifted his head and began to howl mournfully.

I felt a bit sorry for him, but on the other hand thought life had changed for him for the better, so he shouldn't really have any complaints.

I still gave him his favourite foods and we still watched television together, although I balanced the programmes between those he enjoyed and those I wanted to watch. I now recorded *East Enders* for him and let him watch it when I was cleaning or cooking. I eventually let him back on my bed at night and he seemed to realise that if he disturbed me he'd be back in his own room.

For a while I still talked to him about politics as if he could understand me, but he looked so reproachful I decided it wasn't a kind thing to do, so I stopped.

Our conversation reverted to the usual human/dog subjects: 'Who's a good boy then? Who wants his dinner or walkies?'

Slowly, slowly, he began to accept the situation and began to behave once more as a dog, enjoying his trips into town and his walks in the fields, woodland and on the beach.

It was on one of these latter walks that it happened.

It was an ordinary sort of day with ordinary sort of weather, the sort of weather you expect in England in early summer; not too hot, not too cold and hardly any breeze off the sea. The grey ceiling overhead was peppered with screaming gulls, but apart from that, we were alone. Nothing moved except us.

I strolled along the beach with Rufus running ahead barking at and jumping into the waves and reflected on that strange day a few months ago. I'd almost lost the ability to understand him and life was pretty much back to normal. The balance between human and animal had been re-instated and I was grateful for that.

Suddenly I became aware that Rufus was calling me. He was digging frantically in the sand and urging me to join him.

'What have you got there, boy?' I asked him as I joined him at the water's edge. Just below the surface something glinted – green. Uh oh.

Very carefully, so as not to rub the surface, I unearthed a green dimpled bottle. Rufus watched me, quivering and panting with anticipation. For a moment, I held the bottle in my hands, and then, with a loud shout, I drew back my arm and threw it with all my might into the sea. For a moment, Rufus looked at me in utter disbelief.

'You really didn't want to play with that old thing, believe me.' I assured him. 'Come on. Let's go home. Nearly time for dinner and it's your favourite. Steak.' And I marched up the beach, totally in control, with a bedraggled, forlorn dog trailing behind me, occasionally casting a woeful glance over his shoulder at the sea and the green bottle catching the light as it bobbed away to the horizon.

STAKEOUT

We must recollect ... what it is we have at stake...
William Pitt (1759-1806)
Speech 22nd July 1803

STAKEOUT

It was a tedious business, knocking on doors. But despite the varied rejections, the smiles never faded, the bonhomie remained undaunted.

The two men moved inexorably from suburban door to suburban door, their yellow and blue rosettes declaring their political bias and intent. At each house, each one semi-detached, they would pause, consult their matching clip boards, fix their smiles and move purposefully towards the front door. Sometimes a man answered, sometimes a woman. This time it was a man.

He'd been idly watching their progress through the Close with a sense of inevitability. If he didn't talk to them now, they'd only be back.

'Better get it over with.' he muttered to himself.

God, he hated politicians, amateur or otherwise!

'Good evening, sir. I hope we're not interrupting your evening meal or your favourite television programme.'

He shook his head waiting for the inevitable spiel. It didn't come.

'Sir.'

It wasn't a question. A moment passed before he recognised the urgency in the voice.

'Sir, try not to look surprised. Just nod your head as if you're agreeing with us.'

He looked blank.

'Sir, we need your help.'

Confused, he looked more closely at the one who was speaking to him. Tallish, heavyish, his manner was authoritative beneath the urgency.

'Who are you?'

'We're police officers, sir - and we need your help,' he added hastily, as the door began to close.

A long pause.

'Why? How?'

'If we might just come in, sir, and I'll explain.'

He didn't catch the names at first, but dutifully rang the number they gave him to check with the local station.

Drugs? In the Close? This quiet backwater of genteel semi-suburbia? Still, as they said, a good cover. And they wanted his room, his bedroom.

Surveillance they said. Maybe one, two weeks, just to build up some photographic evidence.

'Don't worry,' they said, 'you'll hardly know we're here.' A discreet cough, 'Use of the kitchen would be helpful.' A hasty reassurance stilled the question. 'Don't worry, we'll bring our own supplies.'

Then they were gone, placidly moving up the street, leaving confusion in their wake.

What was a Liberal Tory anyway?

They moved in the following evening, discreetly using the back of the house for cover. He'd moved out of his bedroom into the small, spare room that was never used. For a while he'd watched the house across the road. They were right. He'd never noticed the number of callers there before.

Filthy trade!

He was glad to be of some use.

143

They settled in, and before long he realised he was glad of the company. They made no demands, as other visitors would. They required nothing of him except the use of his house. If he wanted to be alone, they respected it. If he wanted to chat, they were ready to listen.

They'd questioned him at some length about his neighbour, but he knew little. He'd seen him move in about four months previously, but apart from passing in the street, he'd had no social contact. Indeed, he had no social contact with any of his neighbours. He hadn't realised until now what a lonely existence he lived.

He began to join them during the evenings on their vigil, sipping sherry while they drank their tea, chatting about this and that. He was flattered by their attention and began to talk about his childhood, those golden days in a countryside unspoiled by vandalism; the shock of losing his father; the forced move that took him and his mother into the soul-less suburbs; her debilitating illness that bound him to her side until death had relieved him of all responsibility.

He quizzed them about their job, envied them the excitement of it. Told them of his plans for the future when he retired, of his intended travels to the great cities of the world. For the first time, they saw a light in his eyes as he spoke of Istanbul, Delhi, Moscow, the Far East. He intended to see it all.

'America?' they asked.

'Not America,' he said. That country 'with all its greed and false values' sickened him. He wanted to meet *real* people, the people who'd built their land with their blood and tears.

He wouldn't be coming back, he told them. England was following her American cousins too closely for his liking. She was getting fat on the backs of third world nations, her policies were becoming flabby, and there was no backbone any more. He needed a country where the people believed in their cause and were not afraid to fight for it.

He'd never talked so much, but they were good listeners, and they seemed sympathetic to his views. They admired his principles they said, and the conversation turned further on the war zones of the world.

For the first time, somebody seemed to be taking an interest in him, found him interesting. He began to dread the thought of his visitors leaving, as they surely would within days.

To his regret, they left early one evening, their job complete, and despite invitations to visit anytime, he knew in his heart that they wouldn't.

He soon reverted to his previous existence, his time divided between work and home, but he couldn't help noticing the emptiness of the house. Soon, he decided, he would move. Just a few more months, time to complete various projects that needed his attention.

They came at four in the morning. Heavy with sleep, his immediate reaction was one of joy.

'More drugs?'

But no, he thought, that case had been closed. He'd seen the handcuffed man driven away in a flare of blue flashing lights. In his puzzlement he realised they weren't smiling.

A chill hit his stomach and he retched.

It was over.

The police returned to the house later that day and removed all traces of the bugs and cameras they had so carefully planted during their occupation of his house.

It had been a lengthy operation stretching over several months, but it had paid off. They removed his computer together with every scrap of paper they could find.

He'd been careful in his treachery, but even the most careful traitor overlooks the obvious. It wasn't difficult to build the case against him once they'd tracked down the money, more than he could possibly earn at the Government Research Centre where he worked.

It would take a while for them to completely assess the damage he had done, and maybe they would never know the full import of the betrayal of his country.

All they could do now was sift - and pray.

REMEMBER, REMEMBER...

Middle English *banefyre*
...a fire in which bones were burned: BONE + FIRE
Reader's Digest Universal Dictionary

REMEMBER, REMEMBER...

First off, I thought I'd put him in the bonfire.

Then I thought – nah - bin there, done that, should 'ave got the T shirt so to speak, and anyway, why spoil the little kiddies fun? Mind you, knowing some of the little bleeders round 'ere, I bet there's nothing they'd like more than burning a real live guy.

It's a lovely big one though, the bonfire. Do a treat. Fair makes me mouth water. Long time since I lit a decent fire. I really miss it. That lovely crackling noise as it takes hold, and then the roar as the air gets to it...

Anyway, enough of that, Much as I'd love to, I'd better not. For one thing it'll piss 'Arry off and I don't want to do that. For another it's not classy enough. The trouble is, 'Arry does like a bit of class where his 'contracts' is concerned.

'James,' he calls me James on account of that's me name, but most people calls me Jim.

'James' 'e says in that posh voice of his, 'murder is an art form and it should be treated with respect. Anyone can *kill* another person, but to do it skilfully with originality *and* remain

149

undetected, that takes a great artist. You James, are going to be a great artist.'

'Course I've heard that speech many a time now over the years we've been together, but I can tell you, that first time, phwoar, it fair knocked me out. Me! A loser all me life, suddenly I'm gonna be a great artist? Made me feel all warm inside it did, and I knew there and then that I would do anything for 'Arry. Any man that can make you feel that good deserves all the loyalty you can give 'im.

'Arry Pemberton, the Honourable no less, come to visit me when I was doing me juvie for burglary. Told 'em that he was a sort of distant cousin who'd only just heard of me problems like and had come to help sort me out. They was pleased. Apparently he was well known in the prison service for his work with wrong doers and given 'is past success rate with offenders, they thought he'd be a good influence on me. ('Course what they didn't know – and neither did I at the time - was that all his 'successes' was now gainfully employed in his own criminal set up!) But they was convinced he'd help me get back on the straight and narrow. Fat chance, I thought! I didn't want some do-gooder messing wiv my life. I'd never heard of 'im and told 'em so, but they left us alone anyway - to chat they said. They even brought us a cup of tea. First thing 'Arry did was lace it wiv a drop of whisky from a flask. I was right impressed I can tell you. Gawd knows 'ow he got that past security!

Anyway, he introduced himself. He wasn't no cousin, well I knew that, but he said he'd read about the fire in the papers first off and had made a few 'enquiries' about me. He'd bin keeping an eye on me ever since, waiting for the right moment - 'til I was 'mature enough' he said. Said he liked my work, even though it was my first attempt, and was impressed wiv' my attitude towards - and 'ere he sort of twisted his mouth a bit, then delicate like, whispered 'murder.' 'Course I denied it right away and was all for getting back with the other lads in the rec room. What? Did he think I was stupid or something to fall for that? Bloody coppers – try anything for a cough!

Between you and me I also thought I'd done a pretty good job. They never did prove I'd set the fire, let alone killed the old bastard. Well, silly old bugger, going on at me like that. On and on and on. So what if he was me dad, I'd had enough I can tell you, so I 'dispatched' him. Me mum was a bit upset, but as I told her, she's better off without him, and I would appreciate it if *she*

151

didn't keep going on. She moved away just after that. Didn't leave a forwarding address or nothing and 'asn't bin to see me since. Good riddance I say.

Where was I – oh yeah. 'Arry. Anyway, he said no, he wasn't no cop, but if I liked, when I got out, I could go and work for 'im. He needed someone with my 'special talent' to do a bit of work like. That's what he called it – talent. No-one's ever told me I'd got talent before. That's when I got the artist speech. I knew then he was the real thing – the genuine article. He said I'd need a bit of polishing, but he was willing to put in the time and money and he'd kit me out with all the right gear. All I had to do was keep me nose clean 'til my time was up and he'd see me right.

So that's what happened.

When I came out I joined 'Arrys outfit and gradually, over the years, became his right hand man so to speak. I bin sorting out 'is little problems for – what? – ten years now? Must be. It's a nice little earner, and I've built up a nice little nest egg over the years. Very nice indeed! Between you and me, I've invested some of it in a little property Spain, but no-one else knows about that, right? Anyway, 'Arry stayed true to his word. Anything I want, I just have to ask. But I tell you, it fair taxes the old grey matter trying to come up with something different each time - and to be honest, I'm getting a bit fed up with it all. Especially as he won't let me use fire. Shame really. It works so well.

'Long memories they've got, James. They'll forge the links with the first one and that's you gone.'

'Arry was a bit disappointed with my early efforts.

'My deah James,' he said after the first couple, (a nice cement overcoat in the M46 and a pair of concrete boots in Lake Windemere), 'you really do have to apply a little imagination to your palette. Colour, that's want we want: colour and decent brush strokes.'

'Course, I knew what he meant, or least I think I did. So I puts me mind to work. First off, I read all the Agatha Christies I could lay me 'ands on. They wasn't much good. Dead boring if you ask me, no pun intended. Then I turned to Dick Francis. Always fancied a bit of a flutter meself, but he wasn't much better. No real bodies to speak of, and all these geysers playing the 'ero. I tried watching all the James Bond movies, but they was so way out, there was no way I could copy anything there, I mean – jumping on crocodile heads? I don't fink so!

I was starting to get a bit worried like, 'cos 'Arry was beginning to line up all these bodies for me – except they wasn't bodies if you see what I mean – not at that point anyway, and they wouldn't be unless I did something pretty quick.

That's when I discovered this woman writer, Patricia Cornwell – I think that's her name anyhow. Now she really did know how to kill a body. Talk about blood and guts! And her a woman too. Didn't seem right somehow. Anyway, I began to see what 'Arry meant. There was an art to all this. All I had to do was to find my style like. So I began experimenting.

Mushrooms was a good one. First off, I found that my 'assignment', (that's what 'Arry likes to call 'em) ate at a local caff every Friday morning, and he always had the same thing. A big breakfast! Easy peasy. Get a job as a part time washer upper – slip in a few – let's say *unusual* mushrooms when chef's not looking (well he wouldn't be would he, not when I'd just dropped a five gallon jar of cooking oil) and Bob's you're uncle so to speak. And who's to blame? Not me. I'm just a simple washer upper – clumsy at that. Anyway, 'Arry was pleased with that result. Said I was 'coming along'. Gave me a bonus.

Well, after that there was no stopping me. I've done a fair number since then I can tell you, and it's bin a real eye opener. Trouble is, as soon as I dispatch one, 'Arry comes up wiv another, and it's getting to be quite difficult finding new methods. I tried telling him, but all he said was 'I trust you James. You will not let me down.'

Actually, between you and me I didn't quite like the way he said that, but anyhow, he smiled nicely as he always does and offered me a drink of me usual, brandy and coke.

But I tell you, this one's a bugger. The bonfire would be so easy. You know, dress 'im in old clothes, cover 'im with paraffin, stick him on top and light the blue touch paper so to speak. He wouldn't be dead of course, not straight away. He'd be well passed it though. A couple of ruffies in his drink would have done the job – that's the rape drug in case you didn't know. Rohypnol, that's its full name. Sometimes called roofies, rophies, rope, or roaches, take your pick. Does the same job. A couple of tabs and suddenly you know nothing. I've got quite a stash of it actually - bought it off Billy the Kid. No – straight up – that's his name – his dad was into cowboys or something. Mind you, I'd never use it on a bird. No. If she won't come willing, then I don't wanna know. I can't understand these blokes that use the stuff for that. Where's the pleasure? That's what I want to know. I reckon it's for losers, but it's good for my business. Works a treat. One drink and they're anybody's so to speak.

But this don't get me no further on with this *assignment*. It's gotta be done tonight. 'Arry says there's a lot riding on it. Trouble is, this one's a cop. I ain't never done a cop before and I don't mind admitting I'm not happy. Cop's is dicey. They don't like losing one of their own. They never lets go. I mean 'Arry's been helpful with this one. E's given me an 'itinererary' as 'e calls it, so I knows where to start. It's where to finish that's bugging me.

Between you and me, I think 'Arry's getting a bit above 'imself. It's one thing rubbing out the competition when they gets a bit too close, but coppers? Nah. I think this is gonna bring a whole heap of crap round our ears, and guess which muggins will be sitting slam dunk in the middle of it. And another thing, I don't like the way he's bin looking at me lately – all thoughtful like. Not only that, he's got this new lad, Tom. He's bin spending more and more time wiv 'im. I 'eard them talking the other night and they was obviously plotting to 'dispense' with some geyser

156

or other, and then I 'eard my name and the word 'stale.' I tell you I was gob-smacked! Couldn't believe it! Me? Stale? I was that mad. Even just thinking about it now makes me mad all over again.

You know what? Sod 'Arry. Just for tonight, this one's for me! The bonfire it is. OK, so I know he won't be pleased and I know this could have 'terminal' consequences for me, if you get my drift, but I'll sort that tomorrow.

I mean, just look at it. Who could resist? All nice and dry, big enough to give a good blaze and with a good drop of petrol on the base it'll be gone before you know it. Just this once won't hurt, and let's face it, the kiddies can always build another one before tomorrow night and by then I'll be long gone – and so will 'Arry.

Well it's 'im or me!

Daily News UK: December 29th.

A body, believed to be that of the Honourable Harry Pemberton, who went missing on November 6th. last year, has been found washed up on a beach in Dorset.

Mr. Pemberton was on his way to visit his cousin in Jersey at the time and when he failed to arrive on the overnight ferry it was feared that he might have fallen overboard.

Fellow travellers reported that at dinner that evening, before the ferry left port, Mr Pemberton appeared to be "rather the worse for wear". One passenger, who wished to remain anonymous, voiced the opinion that the man wasn't drunk, but drugged.

An extensive sea search was made at the time, but no body was recovered.

Mr. Pemberton was well known for his voluntary work within the prison service, successfully helping to rehabilitate offenders, including James Beech.

'I owe everything to Harry,' said the former burglar, speaking from his villa in Spain.

'He said I had potential and that he could put me on the straight and narrow, and he did. He gave me a job and a future. Without Harry I wouldn't be where I am today, I'd be nothing – probably be back inside by now. Yes, I'll always remember Harry. Always.'

RUNNING LATE

Timing is all
Anon

RUNNING LATE

I was running late.

We'd agreed to meet at 6am and I'd set my clock for five. I'm not very good at getting up early at the best of times and this, in the words of Dickens, could definitely be classed as 'the worst of times'!

I reluctantly crawled out of bed in answer to the buzzing summons, shuffled to the kitchen to put the kettle on, then slumped at the breakfast bar midway between nightmares. My dreams had been distorted into horror by the task that now faced me – the task itself was a nightmare. I was about to prove conclusively that my long-term friend, the one person I would have trusted with my *own* life, had murdered my sister.

Until eight days ago I'd thought, along with the police and coroner, that she'd died in a road traffic accident, her car plunging into the river that ran alongside the road, just over three miles from home.

Home, although without her presence I've found it difficult thinking of it as such, is a small end of terrace ex-council house

160

on the edge of the village of Waverly on the east coast. On a clear night you can hear the surf breaking on the shore just over a mile away. It's frequently cold and bleak, but we loved it. The house had been our family home and when dad died we managed to buy it between us from the local authorities. Mum had gone five years before that and between us we'd cared for the old man until he died.

'My girls,' he'd say, 'what would I do without you?'

We knew very well what he would have done. Being of the old school and cared for by women from the moment he was born, he would have starved to death!

On his marriage to mum, he left one woman – his mother – and went straight to another, with only hotel catering filling the honeymoon gap.

He had no idea how to cook, wash, iron or clean. He had no reason to. His women did all of that for him and we, my sister Katie and I, took over where mother left off.

Katie was a year older than me and we'd been born quite late into our parents' marriage. We'd grown up in the claustrophobic security of village life. We knew everyone and they knew our business, but unlike many of our peers we had no hankering to leave.

As we grew up, our horizons were expanded somewhat by travelling to school in the nearby town ten miles away. We each had our own circle of friends, but stayed close friends with each other. Neither of us wanted to go on to further education, so Katie took a job in the local chemist, while I went to work for an estate agent as their Publicity Administrator. It sounds very grand, but what it meant in reality was that I was sent out in all weathers to take photographs and the measurements of properties as they came on the market and hype them up into dream dwellings.

And if I hadn't been out doing my job that particular day, my nightmare would have never begun.

The night the police called, Katie had been going to see Gerry Irving. They'd been 'going steady' for several months and the old biddies were predicting a spring wedding – even though they weren't engaged. Gerry was a policeman and had no intention of getting married until he'd been promoted and could guarantee his future wife the sort of security that children could be born into safely. Sensible lad.

162

It was actually my night for the ancient car that we shared, but I had no problem with Katie using it instead. Being between boyfriends I decided I'd much rather spend a cosy night in with a hot bath, a decent steak, a bottle of claret and an Eddie Murphy film, instead of gallivanting out around town.

I'd had the bath and a glass of claret when the doorbell rang.

They were uneasy in their sympathy.

'Wet roads,' they said, 'patchy fog – no other vehicles involved – death probably instantaneous – is there anyone who can stay with you?'

It was Ginny they sent for, Ginny who stayed, Ginny who gently led me out of grief.

Ginny had always been in my life. We'd shared chickenpox, measles, various flu bugs, and as we grew older, the occasional boyfriend.

'My youngest daughter,' mum would laugh, as we giggled and preened our way through childhood and puberty.

I saw little of Ginny when we left school, but we remained close friends and stayed in touch by phone, Facebook, email and text We occasionally met in town for lunch in a wine bar, spent evenings 'doing' the town in the local clubs or going fishing in her father's battered old tub of a boat - a favourite pastime.

Ginny had gone on to college to take a business course and had then got a job in one of the major chemical labs. She seemed to be doing well. Whenever we met she was expensively dressed and drove a smart car. I was really pleased for her and proud of her achievements.

I should have realised then.

'You silly bitch!' It was the venom in the voice that caught my attention.

It had been five months since Katie had died and I was slowly getting back into the routine of living.

I usually popped home for lunch, but already late from my last appointment and with not much time before my next assignment, I decided it would be quicker for me to grab a sandwich in the wine bar. With its high backed booths along each side and down through the middle, the décor provided a degree of intimacy that appealed to the business fraternity and those conducting illicit assignations. Because they couldn't see or be seen over the tops of the booths, they could convince themselves that no-one could hear them either, as they discussed their confidential affairs

Wanting a bit of privacy of my own, I waited at the bar for my food order and then, with my files tucked under my arm and balancing the plate and a glass of wine, I headed for a booth at the back. I curled into a corner facing away from the door to avoid the distraction of looking up every time it opened. As I nibbled my sandwich and sipped the cold Pinot I began catching up on my notes from the morning's visits.

I was vaguely aware that someone moved into the booth behind me, talking in hushed tones, but was too engrossed to give them much thought. However, when the man raised his voice I couldn't help overhearing. For a moment I wondered if I should make my presence known. But at the same time I reasoned that if I stood up now, they would know I had heard and that would have made it worse; so I sat mutely, hoping their argument wouldn't become too personal. Talk about a rock and a hard place. I sat there trying to close my mind to their conversation, but by now I was tuned in.

'What else could I do?' the woman hissed.

165

With a sense of shock I realised that I knew that voice, but it was different. It didn't have the warmth or softness I was familiar with. It was hard, almost coarse. It was Ginny! I'd no idea who the man was. I'd not heard him before. I knew he wasn't a boyfriend. Only last week she'd boasted that she was gloriously unattached at the moment and intended to keep it that way for while.

So who was this man? And why was he giving her grief?

'You are endangering the network,' he continued. 'We're not pleased.'

Network, I wondered? What network?

'*Me* endangering the network!' Her fury was palpable. 'If it wasn't for me you'd have the police on your backs by now.'

Police? What was this Ginny was involved in?

'And whose fault was that in the first place?' The silky voice seemed to silence her for a moment – but only a moment. 'First that girl Katie and now this junkie.'

I froze. Katie? What about Katie?

Her next words filled me with horror.

'He would have died anyway. I just helped him along a little – think of it as a mercy killing. And at least I had the guts to sort them out.' She was in a vicious temper now. 'I warned you about forcing me to deal in my backyard. I'm too well known. Anyway, no-one suspects a thing. Katie's death was 'an accident',' the quotes were clear in her tone, 'and the junkie OD'd. OK? End of problem! Now,' I heard the sounds of movement and shrank further down into my seat, 'I have to get back to work, so unless there's something else…?'

She sounded sarcastically triumphant – and then was gone.

To say I was reluctant to pick up the phone was understatement of epic proportions, but for Katie's sake I knew I had to do it – to face the truth of it, and to face Ginny.

She responded warmly to my voice.

'Hey, how are you?'

Fortunately she didn't wait for a reply, but hurried on with all the sort of irrelevancies we normally exchanged.

'Let's go fishing,' I interrupted abruptly.

'What…?' she started to say.

'It's ages since we went fishing. You know – two girls together against the elements – and the weather forecast looks good for the weekend and I could really do with the break…' I faltered. My voice sounded false even to me. There was a stillness at the other end of the phone. I held my breath.

'Yes, why not,' she said eventually. (Was it my imagination or did she sound cautious?) 'How about Sunday? Let's leave early and catch the tide – say six? You bring the food. I'll bring the wine and the rods.'

'Right.' I couldn't think of anything else to say.

'Are you OK?' she asked.

'Yes, yes.' I put the phone down without saying goodbye.

That was Friday. Now it was Sunday. And I knew I was running late – putting off the evil moment.

My head was still groggy from lack of sleep as I slowly dragged on my waterproofs. I *really* didn't want to do this. Dread slowed me down even further. I was dreading the confrontation, dreading the truth. Even now, I truly hoped that I'd heard wrong, that Ginny was still my Ginny and she would have an explanation that I could believe.

I'd gone through the motions of packing a picnic basket the night before and I could almost convince myself that it was for a genuine fishing trip, the sort we used to revel in. But as I put the basket in my new car, I abandoned all pretence. Should I just forget the whole thing? Phone Ginny and pretend a migraine? Pretend nothing was wrong? But before the thoughts were fully formed, I knew that for Katie's sake I could not turn away. This had to be faced.

The old jetty looked forlorn in the early morning light. A ramshackle affair, it had been there for as long as I could remember. Patched and repaired by the local fishermen over the years, it withstood most of the North Sea gales. In recent times, an old shed door laced with barbed wire had been fixed half way along to deter the local vandals. It was reminiscent of the barbed wire beaches of the Second World War, giving it a forbidding air, but it was effective. This morning it looked particularly desolate, but that was probably just the way I was feeling knowing what was ahead.

I stopped half way along the sea wall and I glanced at my watch. Despite my tardiness I was only ten minutes later than the time we'd agreed. I could see Ginny's boat moored just off to the right at the end of the jetty, but there was no sign of Ginny. She might already be on board, of course, but I didn't think that was likely. There was no sign of rods or fishing paraphernalia. I dropped the picnic basket onto the concrete and dug out my phone to try and reach her and realised that I'd not turned it on. A text was waiting for me. It was Ginny. She'd sent it thirty minutes earlier.

'*Rning l8. Find key. Go in. See U there.*'

This threw me because Ginny prided herself on her punctuality. I started to walk to the steps that led down to the jetty wondering what to do. Should I do as she said? Go on board? Or wait for her here? Before I could decide, however, the decision was taken out my hands.

I had seen them on television many times, but hadn't realised the impact an explosion could have on the body, even at that distance. One moment I was breathing normally, the next it was if my chest had imploded and I was thrown sideways. As I saw the jetty heave in the middle and begin to disintegrate, I was blinded by a sunburst of flame as the boat blew up. It seemed an age before my eardrums were assaulted by the roar. And then – nothing.

I don't know how long I was on the ground, but it was Ginny's voice that broke the screaming silence.

'You're late,' she spat. She was standing over me, hate in her eyes and a gun in her hand. 'Now I'll have to think of something else.'

I sat up and shook my head to clear it. Despite the heat from the burning boat, I felt icy cold.

'Just out of interest,' she said, 'how did you know?'

My throat burned, my tongue felt swollen and even my teeth hurt. My voice sounded hoarse even to me, but I told her.

'How did *you* know?' I rasped.

'I could tell from your voice. I didn't know how you knew, but I knew. You always were transparent.' The sneer cut deep. 'And now,' she continued, 'I suppose you want to know why. Why drugs? Why your sister? Well, I'll tell you. Money. Pure and simple. Like my drugs really. I don't take them,' she added hastily, 'I'm not that dumb. I deal! That's why Katie had to go. She saw me one night in town collecting from one of my 'clients'. She recognised him. He was a regular in her chemist shop. She knew he was a junkie, put two and two together and got what she thought was four. Silly bitch decided to tackle me

171

about it. She was going to tell that copper of hers. I couldn't allow that to happen.'

'So you killed her.' My voice seemed to come from somewhere else. 'How?'

'It was almost too easy,' she laughed at the memory of it. 'I gave a beautiful display of hysterics, told her I'd been conned into it and wanted to get out of it but didn't know how. She fell for it. She suggested I go with her to see Gerry, give him all the relevant names and he would look after me. Your family always was too nice,' the sneer was back. 'I begged her not to tell you and suggested we meet that night to go and see him, but not to warn him I'd be with her. I pretended that I was scared that someone would find out and that it was better if only she knew until we actually met Gerry. She was so gullible; she bought into the whole thing and agreed. She talked you into letting her have the car and picked me up as arranged. I couldn't have timed it better. It was dark and drizzling, the roads were wet and there was patchy fog. When we reached that bit of back road that follows the river, I quietly undid my seatbelt, smashed her head hard against the car door window, grabbed the steering wheel and as we went up over the bank and into the river I opened the door I

172

jumped out. I managed to shut it again just before it hit the water. It was risky, but I couldn't leave any unexplained anomalies, could I? I fell in myself and got soaked. That river is bloody cold at the best of times. But it was worth it. She drowned. Problem solved.'

'And the bomb was meant for me?'

She frowned.

'I timed it perfectly. No-one would have known. The evidence would have been blown away.' She laughed at her own joke, then frowned and put the gun to my head. 'Why were you late?'

I didn't answer. I didn't need to. It was all over.

Later, at Police Headquarters, I sat in the canteen, with a female police officer for company, drinking a huge mug of scalding tea. I had been checked over by paramedics who reassured us all that I had suffered no injuries, but should watch out for the symptoms of delayed shock. As I sipped my tea I began re-playing the events of the morning over in my mind.

Ginny had badly underestimated me. I was neither foolish enough nor brave enough to meet her alone. After that shattering revelation in the wine bar I'd gone straight to Gerry and told him what I'd heard. The police decided to set a trap. Gerry was all for being the bait, but I knew she wouldn't fall for it. It had to be me, I insisted. They agreed, albeit reluctantly. It was simple enough. I just had to tackle Ginny about Katie and the conversation I had overheard and the police would record every word she said, both through the small microphone that was hidden in my clothes and the powerful backup mic hidden with the police in the dunes.

'Don't go on board,' they said 'It'll make it difficult to control the situation. We need to keep her on *terra firma.*'

They didn't to warn me, there was no way I was going to allow myself to be left alone with Ginny.

'At least we have the element of surprise,' they said, but none of us had reckoned on the fact that she'd seen through my picnic ploy, or that she would use an explosive device to shut me up. They were still castigating themselves and each other for the danger to which they'd exposed me. They'd also nearly ruined the whole thing. When the bomb went off they were about to rush to make sure I was OK, but ironically, Ginny herself had saved the day by getting there first.

She was now in an interview room doing exactly what she had told Katie she would do – singing her heart out. The shock of betrayal had broken her spirit. She was further shocked by the news that her attempt to make murder look like an accident would have failed in this case. Forensic science was now so advanced that even water and fire could not have destroyed the evidence of explosives. Every scrap of the boat would have been collected and examined. With her scientific background, they said, they were surprised she hadn't known that. Furthermore, they said, they would now be launching an investigation into Katie's death and the charges against her would ensure that it would be a long time before she walked free again.

Suddenly I began to shake. The full horror of the morning filled my mind as I began to absorb the full implications of what had happened. I had literally been moments from death. As tea slopped from the mug, the policewoman gently took it away and holding my hands began muttering soothing words. All I could hear though was my own voice saying over and over again in wonderment:

'Oh my God, if I hadn't been running late...!'

175

THE LADY OF USHER

With apologies to Edgar Allan Poe!

THE LADY OF USHER

This is my last day on this earthly plane.

I woke this morning to the warmth of the sun through the open window and knew that today I would surely die. I am not afraid. I have met death many times in small ways through my illness, and once – that dreadful once – I faced him in my tomb. But today he will come for me and I will embrace him fully and finally. A great serenity has settled on my mind. There is a peace in my heart the like of which I have never known in life.

I remember feelings of joy and happiness as a young woman and before that as a child, but that was when my dear mama was alive, surrounding us all with her love.

But peace? It is an unexpected and welcome bonus.

My brother - he is no longer - and I, were borne to the House of Usher in the fifth year of our parents' marriage. We did not know – how could we – that it was a cursed marriage?

They were deeply in love and I well remember the sound of their love ringing through the halls of our beautiful House of

Usher. But the infection of their love infected us, their children, with the physical and mental ailments that can only come from such a cursed coupling.

They had met in Italy. Papa, as an only son, had newly become the head of the House of Usher. Mama was with elderly relatives taking the air of Lake Garda when they met.

What evil fates decreed that meeting? What malicious gods plotted gleefully to lead each to the other unknowingly – the legitimate son and the bastard daughter?

Their common parenthood was uncovered ere long, but by then it was too late. They would die apart and so they chose to sin, their secret locked in the bosom of the family, who looked on in despair and disapproval as the priest, sweetened by a generous purse, read the rites of marriage over them. They returned to England, to the House of Usher, where they were received with goodwill and celebration.

The House lived, nay thrived, under my mother's influence and my father's utter devotion to her. Flowers bedecked every room. At dusk, lights glittered from every window. The delicate perfumes of polish and cleanliness pervaded the air and seemed to infiltrate the very fabric of the building until it glowed with its own sweet life. The servants, and there were many, rejoiced in the rich atmosphere of the House, and fulfilled their tasks gladly. The vast corridors rang with the sound of music and laughter.

Papa would fill the house with weekend guests and mama would organise lavish, glittering parties. Orchestras would be hired for the evenings' entertainment, and the banqueting table could scarce bear the weight of the dishes prepared for the feasting.

On the day of our birth, a cold October morning, the whole village was invited to celebrate the event and papa himself carved meat and poured wine until all had had their fill. It was an event that was told and retold to local children and their children in the light and warmth of the autumn fires. Roderick and I never ceased to tire of hearing the wondrous, ancient tales of the House of Usher at our nurse's knee.

Life was full, and we grew and played and learned in an environment that was safe and warm and full of light and joy. We played in the grounds in summer as the servants tended and coaxed the gardens to the elaborate profusions of mama's designs. In winter we would run through the elegant, draped halls of the House, pausing awhile to gaze in awe at the sombre features of our ancestors gazing down with disapproval on our antics, and then with a whoop of joy we would be off again, teasing and tormenting our poor nurse, who tried in vain to maintain an authority over us.

As twins, we could read each other's mind and a certain telepathy added to our mischievousness.

In quieter times, I would sit on the bank with my books, watching Rodney cast his line over the waxen flower heads of the water lilies into the clear, deep, dark waters of the tarn.

And then it turned.

Mama became ill. All laughter and music ceased. The House appeared to darken under an unknown, menacing shadow. There were no more parties, no more guests, and it seemed to us as children, no more love.

Physicians began to call with ever more frequency and from our nursery window we would watch them leave, heads bent low as if weighted by some great burden. Papa began pacing the corridors. We could hear him late at night from our rooms. The servants began whispering amongst themselves in corners. Even the flowers seemed to exude a sickly perfume of their own, as they wilted and died untended in their vases.

Our lessons continued each morning, but soberly. The joy of learning had gone. In the afternoons we would wander listlessly through the hush of the house or in the grounds. We were aware of a sensation of waiting, of holding our breath, of being suspended in time.

The silence shattered in the early hours of one bleak morning. I was awakened by a sound that I thought to be an animal in distress. As the sleep cleared from my mind, the sound grew from a whimpering to the most dreadful howl of anguish, the like of which I have never heard since. It proclaimed the moment of my poor mama's death. My heart chilled to stone and I knew that the glorious days of the House of Usher were at an end.

Little did I know that the nightmare was just beginning.

Mother was laid to rest in the family vault, at some distance from the house. I watched my father as her tomb was sealed, his countenance dark and rigid, and it seemed to me that he was no longer of this world. The part of him that once lived was now sealed in the tomb with her.

We saw little of him from that day. It was as if the sight of us, with her colouring and her life, was more than he could bear, as if we were tormenting him with his loss. He sent Roderick away to school and hired a personal maid to care for me, and so my dear Susan entered my life.

I missed my brother dreadfully and for the first few months we wrote to each other daily, but his letters became full of melancholy and he wrote less and less. I tried to cheer him with vignettes of village gossip, but to no avail. Eventually his correspondence ceased entirely.

Meanwhile papa's health began to deteriorate. Susan and I despaired of him as he began to whither and decay before our eyes. And as papa withered, the house seemed also to wither. The servants crept away one by one until only my faithful Susan and Ben, Papa's man servant, remained to tender to our meagre needs. We tried, Susan and I, to maintain the standards of dear mama, but it was useless. The house was too big, too demanding.

182

My own poor strength precluded strenuous cleaning and poor Susan grew old before her time with the struggle.

By now Roderick and I were fifteen years of age. He returned home from school unexpectedly the day after our birthday and declared his intent not to return. Too old to be a boy and yet too young for manhood, he was now dark and good-looking, but the darkness seemed to emanate from his very soul. There was no laughter in his eye, no peace in his countenance. He took to locking himself away for days, only allowing Ben into his studio with simple refreshments and to dress him for the day or prepare him for the night. Occasionally I would catch him watching me from beneath his brow with those large, luminous eyes that so matched mine. When I caught his eye, he would look away furtively. We no longer conversed at length.

Susan and I continued to the best of our abilities to keep the house running with some semblance of routine and order. Papa was now so emaciated that it came as no shock to find him gone one morning. Death had overtaken him during the night, and for the first time since mama's passing, he looked calm and almost happy. We laid him with mama and took our leave of them both.

The day after the funeral Roderick summoned the lawyer and remained closeted with him in the library for several hours. Susan and I were at lunch in my room, a practice we had begun soon after she arrived, when we became aware of raised voices. Suddenly the door of the room burst open and Roderick stood there, dishevelled and wild of countenance and shaking with rage. In his fist he held a paper, which he shook savagely at me. He was shouting incoherently. I ran to him and took him in my arms and tried to calm him. Gradually as I soothed his hair and stroked his face, the fire began to leave his eyes and the rigidity of rage began to seep out of his body. He began to weep uncontrollably. When I felt him to be calmer I led him to a chair and helped him to be seated.

'What is it, my dear? What has distressed you so?'

He started up, but I gently pushed him back into the chair. I stroked his hand and turning to Susan sent her for brandy and to enquire after the lawyer who remained in the library.

'Now my dear, we are alone. You can tell me.'

He passed his hand, clutching the paper, across his eyes and moaned.

'No, I cannot. It is the destruction of the House of Usher. Better never to be told than to bear this burden with me.'

'Nonsense.' I stood up and briskly wrested the document from him. I saw at once that it was a letter and I recognized my father's writing.

The next thing, of which I became aware, was my brother and Susan bending over me in great distress. I was in my bed. My head ached and the light seemed to blur my vision. A third figure, the family physician, moved to my side and lifted my wrist.

'Well young lady, that was some fright you gave us. We'd all but given you up for dead.'

I learned later that my illness, catalepsy, was not unknown, but the causes and the cures were. It was the first of many times that I suffered my 'small deaths' as I came to know them. Roderick sent me away to Italy to recover.

Was this destination contrived? I've often wondered how far the sickness in his mind dictated this irony. He knew I'd seen the contents of the confession and had understood the full implications of the potential consequences for us as their offspring. Was he punishing me for succumbing to an illness that

185

could have been caused by our parents' relationship? Punishing me for the demons in his own head? I'll never know. By then his mind was closed to me. Even the simple telepathy we'd shared as children had gone.

Italy was dazzling. The softness, the warmth, the colours, the light - a place for love. Susan was with me, and each morning we would walk. My health improved daily and I began to feel what I can only describe as a surging of joy in my soul as I revelled in the sounds and the sights which surrounded me.

We began to receive invitations from the families who wintered on these shores. I began to dance again, and on my eighteenth birthday I fell in love.

The Rochford's, who hailed from Oxfordshire, had taken us under their wing shortly after our arrival. They had three daughters, the eldest being a few months younger than myself. We were not the best of friends, but we liked each other well enough and kept company often. It was Isabella who learned of my birthday and proposed that her parents should arrange a small celebration. I was overwhelmed. The last party I had attended had been when mama was alive.

'You must have a new gown,' Isabella declared, clapping her perfectly formed hands excitedly, and the next day introduced Susan and myself to a small couturier that she and her mother used.

The gown was exquisite.

As Susan helped me prepare for the party, my sense of excitement and anticipation grew so that I could hardly draw breath. As the guest of honour, my host, Mr. Rochford, escorted me into the ballroom. Not since a child had I seen so many flowers, so many beautiful people, so much glitter and glamour. At the end of the room a small orchestra was playing softly. I was led to the seat of honour and the guests, many of whom I recognized from my stay, began to present me with gifts. I could scarcely contain my joy, and was excitedly tearing the tissue from one small parcel, when I became aware of someone standing in front of me. I raised my head and found myself gazing into the eyes of the most gloriously, handsome young man I had ever seen. He smiled at me gently and held out his hand.

'Please dance with me.'

In a dream I placed my unopened gift on my chair, took his hand and moved into his arms. I had come home. He held me close, closer than I'm sure convention should permit, but as we moved to the music I cared nothing for convention.

'You are so beautiful.' I felt his breath on my hair. 'You are so, so beautiful.'

I danced with no-one else that evening and as midnight drew near he whispered 'I must kiss you.'

No words were spoken, but by mutual consent we dared to meet in the garden under a bright, Italian moon. I remember that moment so well. The lush, green vegetation, shielding us from prying eyes, the music of the cicadas in the undergrowth, his eyes looking deep into mine and, having no doubt of his love for me, my own voice boldly whispering 'You know I love you.' His gentle 'Yes,'

And then he kissed me.

That first meeting was so short. We were not so irresponsible as to shock our hosts, and returned to the ballroom separately.

Our courtship continued on more conventional terms. Society, in the form of the Rochfords, took responsibility for my moral welfare and they arranged and chaperoned our meetings. And then Mr. Rochford decided it was time to contact my brother to acquaint him with the facts of our relationship.

I was all in ignorance of this move until one morning, as Susan and I returned from our morning stroll, I saw Roderick striding towards us. His face was dark and angry and dismissing Susan from us, he roughly clutched my arm in a tight grip, rushed me into our villa and slammed the door behind us.

I will not repeat the words he used as he raged at me. At first I felt nothing but shock, and then a cold fear clutched at my heart as the import of his words reached my mind. I was to be separated from my love. I would never see him again, never feel his arms around me, never hear his voice, never know that love.

And as the grief began to seep through my soul, I saw another emotion in my demented brother's eyes. I shrank from him, but to no avail. The last words I remember as he raped me were, 'You belong to the House of Usher.'

We returned to England to the rain, the cold, the greyness of the sky, the landscape and the people. We shut ourselves away in the House of Usher.

189

Susan was allowed to stay with me, but she became surly with despair for me and was less than no company. Ben continued in his role of valet. My small deaths increased yearly and my brother kept a watching brief over me. I felt his eyes watching me at every turn, but he made no attempt to touch me again. Indeed, his act of violation had in some strange way given me power over him. He cowered when I came near and seemed afraid of me, and yet at once afraid to be without me. I rarely spoke to him and he knew that he would go to his grave unforgiven. I had made no attempt to contact my love. No-one would want a woman so defiled.

We began to slowly close the house down. The gardens had gone years before. Neglected, allowed to run wild, the dank sedge had taken over. The tarn no longer sparkled. Some poison had entered the water and killed all life there. The house seemed to be crumbling around us stone by stone and un-cleaned windows restricted the light so the house appeared to grow as dark as our lives. Dust, damp and dirt filled the corners and there was no life in anything.

The years passed unnoticed in this joyless domain. People shunned us, and only my physician called with any regularity. It was as if we were locked in time.

We had one visitor towards the end: a friend of Roderick's who had attended school with him. He came into the study unaware of my presence and seemed pleased, if not disturbed, to see his old friend. I remained silent in the shadows as they greeted each other, and my brother, self-absorbed as always, began the long, self-centred gloomy discourse of his maladies. When he finally began to bemoan my own illness and 'the approaching dissolution of a tenderly beloved sister,' I could bear no more of the hypocrisy and left the room.

I saw no more of the visitor, but heard evidence of him as they conversed, played weird music and sang strange songs. I took to my bed in exhaustion. Grief for my love had taken its toll over the years and I was weary to death.

But I was not prepared to die in my coffin.

That day had begun like any other.

Susan brought me some food, which I could barely swallow. Today I felt more than ever a deep listlessness. I know I slept towards noon and when I woke it was growing dark. I knew I was not alone in the room. I became aware of my brother standing at the foot of my bed, his cold eye fixed on me. I struggled to sit up, pulling the covers up to my neck. The movement seemed to disturb him and he began to laugh. A cold fear ran through me and I began to shiver uncontrollably. Suddenly he stopped.

'Why?' he demanded, 'why won't you let me be? Why will you give me no peace? Why do you torment me so?'

I gasped, stunned by the arrogance of his utterings.

'*You* can say that to *me*?'

He passed a shaking hand over his eyes – a tortured soul. For a moment I felt a stab of pity for this brother of mine. He saw it in my face. It was all he needed.

'Why couldn't you love *me*? Why couldn't you do as dear mama? Why did you need someone else? Was my love not good enough for you?'

He said more, but I had clapped my hands over my ears to stem the flow of such filth. I could see his lips move with the madness that inflamed his mind. And then he moved towards me. I made to ring for Susan, but he gripped my wrist. My whole being screamed in silent denial, 'Not again, please not again,' and then - nothing.

I woke to suffocating blackness, a dank, dark smell filling my nostrils and lungs. I tried to move, but found myself confined on all sides. Panic rose like bile in my throat and I began to scream.

I must have passed out again, for when I awoke the next time I felt calmer. Terror had sharpened my mental capacities. I began to order my thoughts, and as I reasoned my position, I knew with dawning horror that my brother had indeed interred me alive. But where? Not below earth – oh God, that would have been too much to bear. But no, with a supreme effort of will I collected myself, he would not do that, could not do that. Too many questions would have been asked. He could not have stood the whispers and the gossip.

No – it must be the family vault then.

To test this hypothesis I shouted long and loud and with blessed relief heard what I willed to be an echo. Tears of relief burned my eyes. I knew where I was. I knew that outside of this infernal box lay, amongst others, the coffins of dear mama and papa, that there was space and air.

Air! Dear God, how would I breathe? For how long? In desperation I pushed up at the lid above me and heard – a grating sound? For a moment, the full import of it did not register, but then the full realization of that sound suffused my being with such joy and such hope that for a moment I wept tears of gratitude.

I knew what had happened.

Anxious to be rid of me, Roderick had obviously performed the job in haste and therefore completed it clumsily. His dereliction to death had given me life. I had air. I would not suffocate. But could I escape my tomb? Tentatively I pushed up again. It was not easy, there was so little room to move, but by lifting my knees and hands at once and pushing upwards, I heard the joyful sound of the screws grating in their sockets. In a frenzy I began pushing with every ounce of strength I could muster until I collapsed, weeping tears of frustration and exhaustion. But I would not give in.

How many days and nights passed? I know not. How did I survive those days of thirst and hunger and pain? I know not. But I believe the intense desire to avenge myself on my brother gave me the will to live and to escape my tomb.

194

Fighting the agonizing cramps that gripped my muscles, grunting and shouting and moaning in my anguish and anger, pushing and resting, pushing and resting, ignoring the thirst and the hunger, feeding my mind and my soul with hatred, little by little I raised the lid of that terrible tomb.

And then that glorious moment, that blissful bursting forth as the lid broke from its fixings and crashed to the floor.

I was still in darkness, but now I had freedom. I struggled to haul my weakened body up, but my strength was all but gone, and my limbs due to their long confinement would not obey my commands.

I fell clumsily out of the coffin onto the floor and for long moments lay stunned. Slowly I became aware of the cold, smooth texture of the floor. Something was amiss. This was not the cold damp stone of the burial chamber. I patted at the floor around me, my hand fluttering in its weakness and confusion. And then at once I knew it. Copper! Oh such joy. I didn't understand it, but now I knew where I was. I was still in the House of Usher, and this chamber I knew well. The wine cellar.

Empty now of the fine wines it once held, it was located in the bowels of the house beneath the guest apartments. It had been a favourite hiding place of my childhood. Pulling myself slowly across that floor, I worked my way around the vaulted room until I touched the cold iron of the door. Reaching up I grasped the handle and pulled myself upright. My legs were barely able to support me. My body was wracked with pain as the blood began to course through veins unused to such life for so long, but I was exultant. I was free.

I tried to turn the handle of the door, but had no strength in my hands. I couldn't move it. For a moment I believed myself thwarted and let out a wail of despondency, I began to rattle the handle frantically, willing it to turn. And then - did I imagine it? The handle did indeed begin to turn of its own volition. I moved back in horror. What new evil was this? Was I going mad after such confinement? And then the grating of the hinges rent the silence of my tomb and the door moved slowly inwards. A lamp was raised high, the light glaring into my eyes causing intense pain and tears. And through the mists of my tears I saw Ben and Susan clutching at each other in terror.

The sight of these dear people was too much for me and I fell swooning into Susan's arms. I was aware of them lifting me between them and carrying me upwards through the house, Susan weeping and muttering and proclaiming at my state with every step.

'Oh my poor lady, my dear heart, what have they done to you?'

As we drew up into the great hall, she would take me straight to my bedchamber, cleanse my wounds and summon the physician, but I resisted her caring with such strength as I could summon. With each step towards life, my anger renewed, boiling and bursting through my weakness. With such a rage in my heart I would first confront him, my brother, my incubus.

They stood me at his door and on my signal moved anxiously to one side, ready to rush to my assistance. As I raised my hand to open the door I heard my brother's ranting voice.

'MADMAN!' he shrieked, 'I TELL YOU THAT SHE NOW STANDS WITHOUT THE DOOR!'

In that moment I pushed the door open and gazed on the pitiful creature standing before me. And then my weakness overcame me, and I fell forward onto Roderick. I was aware of a figure rushing past me, of my brother's limp, dead body beneath me, and then hands lifting me and carrying me away from that chamber of death.

197

I learned later that Susan and Ben, terrified by the events of that night and unwilling to stay with a corpse, had hurried me straight from the house to the physician.

He had listened to their garbled tale of terror and after tending my wounds and organizing my nourishment, had gathered a party of village men to accompany him to the house to collect Roderick's body. But they were too late. Terrible storms and freak whirlwinds had raged throughout the region that night and had finally taken their toll on the crumbling, decaying structure of the house. It had fallen into the tarn and was gone.

My brother's body rose to the surface a few days later, battered and bloated. He now rests in the family vault.

I have had a few good years here in Italy.

The light, the softness, the warmth, the colours, the sounds – it hasn't changed. It's still a place for love.

I shall be buried here, in the sun. I am the last of the line. With my death the family name dies. No bad thing. It will be an end of darkness and disease and inbred mental instability.

It will be the end of the House of Usher.

ABOUT THE AUTHOR

Di Shelley (nee George) was born in Buckinghamshire and brought up in a house surrounded by books. She was taught to read at an early age, for which she is eternally grateful to both her parents.

Prior to winning a scholarship to Aylesbury Grammar School, she attended Waddesdon Church of England School where she was lucky enough to have been taught by Tom Bingham.

Not only did he encourage her with her writing, but excused her from many other lessons so she could pursue her passion. This eventually led to a career in broadcasting with the BBC.

She now resides in the West Country and can usually be found at her computer with a glass of wine to hand!

Email: dianeshelley1@gmail.com

Printed in Great
Britain
by Amazon

A Symphony for Blue

by

Boyd Brent

Author contact: boyd.brent1@gmail.com

Prologue
Meet your Author

How do you do? I am Fate. Your ever-present companion. I'm the one you turn to when life seems unfair with questions such as: 'Why me?' or 'What have I done to deserve this?' and more recently, 'Are you having a laugh?'

Yes, quite possibly. Roll with it.

A Universal Truth: it's never *me* you thank when things go well.

Perhaps you believe in me? If you don't, it's because you would rather believe that nothing is fated. That you decide your own destiny. Reader, despite what you've been told, I am NOT a thief of free will. The truth about me is not so black and white. Things rarely are. And so, before we embark upon our extraordinary journey to meet Blue, I'm going to take a moment to set the record straight about myself.

Wouldn't you?

Simply put, I loom over an orchestra, holding a baton, and conduct the soundtracks to your lives. These melodies, which are unique to each of you, can be heard just beyond human perception by what's commonly called 'the sixth sense.' It is here that my melodies are able to inform and inspire you.

The Big Question (actually it's massive): why don't I conduct more harmonious melodies? Ones that make people kinder and more tolerant of each other's differences. Drum roll...

If you want proof of the existence of free will, you need look no further than people who bully, harm, or impose their will on others. Those who refuse to embrace the beautiful harmonies that the majority of you yearn for. I'm not bitter about these people. Even if they do distract from the beautiful melodies of my orchestra and give me a bad reputation. You see ...

Good actions are inspired by bad.

And beauty results from good.

And so, the cycle goes on.

What is important is that the beauty of humanity outweighs the hideous. Why do I care? That is something you're about to discover. In fact, letting you in on this age-old secret, and revealing why things happen the way they do, is my biggest motivation for sharing this story about Blue. As you are about to discover, her name had nothing to do with the colour of her eyes, they were autumn brown, and everything to do with her somewhat unenviable start in life…

Chapter 1
Blue embarks upon a voyage

The year is 1912. And our journey begins at the docks in Southampton, England. It is here that Blue was carried aboard a ship that's almost as famous as I am: HMS Titanic. Titanic was the biggest, fastest and crucially, most unsinkable ship ever built. Spoiler for the tiny percentage of you who are unaware (there's always a tiny percentage of you), she sank. Indeed, a more accurate message on the posters for her maiden voyage would not have read: 'Travel to New York in record time!' but 'Travel to the bottom of the Atlantic Ocean toot sweet!' In case you imagine me unsympathetic, here's universal fact number two: every raindrop that falls is a tear that I have shed for the loss of an innocent.

And so, with the benefit of hindsight that you and I have in common, let's join the three fatalistic dots that led to Titanic reaching the bottom of the Atlantic Ocean and not New York:

1. Poor visibility
2. Travelling too fast
3. Iceberg

The confidence of those clutching tickets and boarding the marvel of her age was understandable. And there she is! Baby Blue. You see her, don't you? Wrapped in red swaddling and being carried up the gang plank by her mother. At this time, her name wasn't Blue, but Tilly. Only her mother was aware of this and she wasn't going to survive the sinking. Reader, welcome to my world; a place where difficult decisions must be made to balance the scales in favour of the greater good. As the saying goes, you can't make an omelette without breaking some eggs. I hold up my hands: I make what *seems* like a mean omelette at times. Fate? My name might also be Mr Damage Limitation.

Talking of omelettes, Blue's mother enjoyed a jam one. Her name was Iris. As I watch her now, climbing Titanic's gang plank, a cloth holdall in one hand and Blue clasped to her chest in the other, I'm reminded of those millions of refugees who have been forced to flee their homes, usually as a result of war, and travel far in the hope of a better life. What was Iris fleeing from? Nothing as disruptive as sections of my audience declaring war on one other. Iris was escaping from the judgment of others. She was a single mother at a time when it was deemed a sin by many of her peers. Those gossiping, sneering, and judgmental members of my audience, leaning forwards in their seats with opera glasses pressed to their eyes, included Iris's family. And so…

Travel to America!

Aboard the greatest ship ever built!

A new life awaits!

Iris had been a seamstress since the age of 13. She had squirrelled away enough money for a single trip in third class – a bunk room with shiny, whitewashed walls, where a dozen other travellers had also been billeted. Iris was the last to be shown into the room by a harassed, red-faced steward. She wrinkled her nose and, casting her gaze around, saw that eleven of the twelve bunks had been taken. For Blue to survive the coming tragedy, Iris had to befriend one of the room's occupants. And so, I raised my baton, turned a page of sheet music, and led my orchestra in a little ditty entitled, 'A Watery Connection'.

"Here, you'd better take my bunk," said the gallant Irishman in question as his tune began to play. He climbed off his bunk and glanced at the one above. "It'll suit me just as well up there."

"Well, only if you're sure?" said Iris, dropping her holdall and switching Blue to the lesser of her two aching arms.

6

"Be my guest," he said, transferring his belongings to the upper bunk. "You've a baby. Your need is the greater."

"She's a good girl," nodded Iris. "Hardly ever cries."

"Probably the same could not be said for the rest of us in here," said the man, glancing around at their fellow passengers who sat, lay or stood quietly beside their bunks, chewing fingernails, checking pocket watches, or wiping sweat from their brows. "So, what's the tiddler's name?"

"Tilly. And I'm Iris."

"Max. Nice to meet you both," said Max, stepping closer and looking at Blue. "You know, she doesn't look like a crier. Not at all. She looks full of wisdom, that one. Like a little sleeping Buddha. Go on now, take the weight off your feet. Try out your bunk for size."

"Thanks. We will," said Iris, stepping past him and lowering her bottom onto the bunk.

Max studied her for a moment. "There's no need to look so glum. A grand new life awaits us all over the other side of the pond."

"Yes, quite," said Iris, finding a smile.

It's several hours later. Iris and Max are sitting side by side in the third-class mess hall. They are being served cold meat, cheese and pickles. The quiet reflection of the bunk room had been replaced by rowdy chatter. Even so, baby Blue, asleep on Iris's lap, is about as serene as a creature can be.

Blue alone can sense it.

The comforting, protective melody that surrounds her.

She has always sensed it.

Max forked some cold meat and pickle and, relishing the sight of such a tasty combination so close to his mouth, paused to savour the moment. "I reckon she must get it from you?" he said, raising his voice above the hullaballoo.

Iris glanced down at Blue. "Get what?"

"Taking things in her stride."

Iris shrugged.

"Her father's a laid-back sort then?" said Max, putting the food in his mouth and chewing slowly. Iris felt her hackles rise. She'd had enough sly questions about the identity of Blue's father to last her a lifetime but, glancing at Max, and seeing how good natured his smile was, she smiled back, stabbed a pickle with her fork, and placed it in her mouth.

"To a better life," said Max, picking up a glass of water.

Iris nodded, picked up her own glass and clinked his… "Yes. To a better life."

Oh, Reader, let us draw a veil over this! A sinking is destined to occur. We all know it. So why prolong the inevitable?

We jump forwards in time several days to when, with a solemn heart, I swung my baton and a drum roll from my percussion section accompanied an iceberg from the star lit murk. In the crow's nest, the senior lookout lifted a telephone receiver, and communicated the sighting to the Captain on the bridge.

Like all else it is now simply a case of cause and effect. Or Fate.

Poor visibility.

Travelling too fast.

Iceberg.

For those fated to survive (710 out of 2208 passengers), my orchestra is playing *the most* enchanting melody led by a flute. The louder the flute played, the safer baby Blue, wrapped in the arms of her sleeping mother, felt. Iris was dreaming about flying a kite on a beach, a red kite that danced against a blue sky. As the iceberg struck, tearing a hole down the side of the ship, the kite slipped from her grasp and leapt away on the wind. Iris opened her eyes and peered at the other passengers, many of whom mirrored her own questioning body language. There was a grating sound and the ship listed to one side. My attention was focused on Max, sitting up, wide-eyed and alert on the bunk above Iris and Blue. I swung my baton down and, like an enthralled member of my audience, he scrambled off his bunk. "Come on!" he whispered, "let's get topside."

"What… what do you think it was?" Iris whispered back even though everyone else was speaking in increasingly raised voices. Max gazed into the middle distance, listening. He'd always had the gift of perception, and now he perceived his own discordant melody.

"What's wrong? What is it?" asked Iris, breathlessly.

"Nothing now. Probably nothing. But we're going topside nonetheless."

Iris nodded, gathered Blue up in her arms, and followed him out into the corridor.

In the corridor, people were poking their heads out of doors, while others stood in shabby nightclothes, their expressions dazed as they listened. You might imagine for sounds of the ship's anguish. No, Reader, at times such as these, people instinctively listen for their own informative melodies. Those with better than average intuition, like Max, are making their way to the end of the corridor and up a stairwell to the next deck.

To a clash of cymbals from my rhythm section, he manhandled Iris through an exit, moments before a steward slammed and locked it.

They spilled through a door and stumbled onto the deck where people hurried in both directions as though eager to get back to where they started. Others leaned over the guard rail, attempting to see what damage the iceberg, now a fair distance behind them, had wrought. Shouts of reassurance rang out…

"Can't see nothing here!"

"None here neither. Must have sounded worse than it was."

"There's no hole here!"

"None here neither!"

"A passing graze?"

"Looks as such!"

What these optimistic souls failed to see was the gaping hole below the water line where thousands upon thousands of gallons of sea water were filling the ship's engine rooms. As you know, I'm not one to prolong things. So, let's jump forwards in time one hour and thirty minutes…

Titanic is listing dangerously to one side and feels close to rolling over. It had been a frantic hour to say the least. One where I was called upon to lead my orchestra in melodies that suited a wide range of emotional states. These included: hopeful, exasperated, resourceful, resentful, tearful, stoic, apologetic, fearful, regretful, angry and resigned.

As you might imagine, my musicians broke into a sweat that night.

As yet, Max had failed to find a place for Iris and Blue on board a lifeboat. Taking hold of Iris's hand, he led her through a crowd of life jacket wearing passengers towards one of the few remaining boats.

"Why are you doing this for us?" she asked.

"You're women and children! They go first."

Iris glanced around at the other women and children. "But why *us?*"

"I have to do something!" said Max, forging a path through a gathering of passengers towards the lifeboat. As with most gatherings, this one was being influenced by the same melody. And so, albeit begrudgingly, they made way for the young man who was clearly desperate not for himself but his wards.

The lifeboat, when they reached it, was only a third full. Something you might imagine would inspire confidence that room could be found for a mother and her baby. But Max had already seen other boats lowered in this way. "Excuse me!" he shouted in the face of the steward in charge of the lowering. "I've got two more here. *Please*, allow me to lift this woman and her baby onto the boat before it's too late."

"No can do," replied the steward, "no one boards a lifeboat once the lowering process is underway. It's company policy."

"*Company policy*! We're talking about a couple of lives!"

"There are more lifeboats on the aft deck. Now move along."

"No! There aren't. We just came from the aft deck."

A man rushed forwards clutching his own child by the hand. "What are we supposed to do?" As the steward wiped the man's spittle from his eyes, Iris looked over the guard rail and made eye contact with a portly woman from first class who, as I swung my baton and raised the volume of a compassionate harp in her melody, rose slowly to her feet and held out her arms.

"Goodbye my darling, *precious* girl… your mummy will love you always." Iris kissed her baby for the last time and released her into the woman's outstretched arms. Despite the increasing panic, Iris remained rooted to that spot, Max beside her, and watched until the lifeboat had dissolved into darkness and safety.

Chapter 2
An orphan needs a name

Titanic sank below the surface to the accompaniment of my orchestra's lone piper, Woebegone. Woebegone stopped playing and lowered himself back into his seat. I then led my orchestra in a swashbuckling composition entitled 'Carpathia to Blue's Rescue!' HMS Carpathia was the first ship to respond to Titanic's SOS. When they arrived to discover that Titanic had sunk without trace, and that only a smattering of partially filled lifeboats remained afloat, Woebegone climbed back to his feet.

Blue was carried aboard the Carpathia by the plump aristocrat who'd caught her. The woman's bluster of entitlement had been quelled somewhat by the cold and final cries of the drowning. She handed her shivering bundle to the seaman who helped her out of the lifeboat. "Is your baby alright, ma'am?" he asked, cradling Blue to his chest.

"I'm no relation to the poor creature. Her mother and father went down with the ship."

"I'm very sorry."

"Not as sorry as she is, I imagine."

"What's the little un's name?"

The woman shrugged. "It's well behaved. Never cried or made so much as a peep." The seaman gestured to another to take his place, and then turned towards a door, determined to get his shivering bundle inside.

Down in the Carpathia's infirmary, the ship's matron, busy preparing medicines, bandages and beds, turned and placed her hands on her hips.

"What's this?"

"A baby, matron. Her ma and pa didn't make it."

The matron crossed herself. "Bring the infant here. What's its name?"

The seamen shrugged.

"Boy or girl?"

"No idea, matron."

A little later, the matron, having examined Blue for injuries and found none, placed her down on her back. "What a *God-awful* start in life," she murmured, and then, following the most philosophical of shrugs, she reached for a name tag and pencil.

Chapter 3
Fate finds a father for Blue

The year is 1917. Five years since Titanic sank. And three years since the start of the First World War. If you thought the loss of life on Titanic was a tragedy, it was but a tiny historical footnote compared to the monumental slaughter that took place during World War One. The pounding of my drums and wailing cries of my string section have never been so energetic before or since. Seventeen million lives brutally extinguished. Twenty million more horribly wounded.

So much for free will.

Come with me, if you will, to the battlefields of Flanders. I'd like you to meet a British soldier called Harry Tibbs. Harry, like so many others, had wanted to do the right thing by stopping an aggressive nation, Germany, from conquering its peaceful neighbour, France. He therefore saw it as his duty to volunteer to stop them. But one morning, as he sat in a muddy trench, reading a letter from his wife Sheila, he wondered if he hadn't been a little quick to volunteer. After all, the war had not been won as quickly as many believed, and it was now clear that the generals, who belonged to a bygone age without machine guns and poisonous gas, were prepared to sacrifice the lot of them to capture a few metres of mud. These things considered, the letter brought Harry some much-needed good news. As Fate would have it, Harry and Sheila had been unable to conceive a child of their own and...

Harry, my love, the letter read, *the agency has found us a little girl! I've met her. Her name is Blue, and she's the most darling little five-year-old! I can't wait for you to meet her. She's quite the most adorable little creature. The nuns at the orphanage were loath to see her go. Harry, my darling, come home to us both!* Harry folded the letter and placed it back in its envelope with some difficulty. His hands had started trembling of late, the result of spending months in trenches where deafening shells had not only shaken the soil but Harry to his core.

At 12 pm on the same day, Harry was lined up in a trench with thousands of others. They were waiting for a whistle to be blown, whereupon they would scramble over the top of the trench and into the Rat! Tat! Tat! blasts of a hundred machine guns. Death would result for all but the indestructibles. '*Indestructibles*?' I hear you think. '*No one is indestructible. Not in real life. Only the superheroes of fiction are indestructible.*' That is where you're wrong. Those whose Fate it is to survive any particular day are indestructible for that day. You weren't aware of it yesterday, but yesterday you too were indestructible.

Harry was indestructible that morning. And it was Blue who ensured his survival. So how, from so far away, did she manage such a feat? Well, as Harry stumbled towards the German trenches, clasping his bolt action rifle, his friends falling dead and wounded around him, he tripped on a churned-up tree root and fell to his knees where, catching his breath, he was delayed from standing by the following thought: *I wonder why she's called Blue?* This momentary pause meant that the bullet that would have killed Harry only dented his helmet. Harry stumbled on. He didn't stumble far. An artillery shell exploded, and a wave of compressed air lifted him several metres into the air and then dropped him into a muddy crater. As Harry lay on his back, ears ringing, numb to his core, he felt a sense of acute loss. Not at the lives being extinguished around him, his grief had long ago reached overflowing for his friends, no, this stunned, dreamlike grief was for the landscape: the once lush green fields, tall trees, hedgerows and wildflowers that had been obliterated from the face of the Earth. Harry had always loved nature. As Fate would have it, he was a landscape gardener. This would become an important factor in Blue emigrating to the United States with her new family. This is how I join the dots. Why things happen the way they do. Dots. It's all about the dots. And the melodies that accompany them.

Chapter 4
A family for Blue

Harry was discharged from a hospital in France three months later and sent back to England.

And so, on a crisp November morning, Harry, several shades paler and half the weight he'd been when he left, arrived back at the little suburban house he never imagined he would see again. As Harry climbed unsteadily out of a taxi, guess who was standing in the open front door waiting for him? You see her, don't you? The little girl wearing a red dress, her curly brown locks swept from her face by a blue headband, watching the only mother she had ever known hug the breath out of the father she was about to meet. "Look!" said Sheila, looking over her shoulder at her little girl. "Blue, darling, daddy's home. What do you say?"

"Welcome home daddy!" said Blue, repeating the words that Sheila had rehearsed with her. Harry raised a trembling hand and found a smile that had been a stranger to his face for so long that it made his jaw click. "Why… hello there," he said, clutching Sheila's hand for support and making his way over.

Harry knelt to take a closer look at the little stranger and, looking into her smiling eyes, the same thought occurred that had occurred to him in France. The one that had saved his life. "Why is she called Blue? Her eyes are brown. And she looks happy…"

"Yes!" gushed Sheila, aren't they just the most beautiful hazel eyes."

Blue twirled one of her curly locks. "Don't you like my name?"

"Of *course*, he likes it," said Sheila.

Blue gazed at Harry's face. "What's the matter? Don't you feel very well?"

Sheila cleared her throat. "Your poor daddy has been working hard. But he's home now. Where things are going to be different. The colour will return to his cheeks in no time. And we'll soon feed him up. Just you see. Which reminds me, lunch is cooking on the stove," said Sheila, hoisting Blue up and holding her against her hip.

Inside the house, Sheila put Blue down amongst her playthings and, as Blue reached for a little wooden ship, Harry and Sheila went into the kitchen. Sheila pulled the door half closed. "Isn't she just the dearest little thing! Couldn't you just eat her up! She's everything we ever dreamed of. Well, isn't she?"

Harry sat down at the table that had been neatly laid for three. "Forgive me," he said, gazing at her through exhausted eyes, "it's going to take a little while before…"

"I can't imagine the things you've seen," said Sheila, lowering her voice to a whisper.

"No. You can't. And be thankful for that," replied Harry doing the same.

In the next room, Blue, accustomed to the nuns at the orphanage lowering their voices whenever they discussed her, rose to her feet, and took three tentative steps to the partially opened door…

"Your hands, they're *trembling*," said Sheila, taking one and pressing it to her cheek.

"The doctors say it will stop in time."

"What has…"

"*Please*. I can't talk about the war. Not yet," said Harry, reaching for a glass of water. "On a happier note, you and Blue have obviously bonded."

"She's been the easiest child to bond *with*."

Harry drank the glass dry and placed it down on the table. "Like I said, I wondered about her name?" As Sheila dropped her voice further, so Blue pressed her ear to the crack in the door. "What I didn't mention in my letters," Sheila began, "I only found out about it myself recently, was that Blue and her mother were passengers on *Titanic*. Her mother didn't make it, Harry."

"My God."

"No one knew her name so…"

"I see… and the rest of her family?"

"Her mother was, how can I put this, an embarrassment. Which is why she was taking flight with Blue. The family wanted nothing to do with her orphaned child. But her family's loss is our gain," said Sheila, squeezing Harry's hand.

Chapter 5
Green fingers and opportunities

During the years that followed, Harry built up a successful landscape gardening business. For Harry, gardening was as much about therapy as it was about supporting his family. He was on a mission to make up for the pulverised countryside in Flanders. And so Harry designed, planted and grew the most lovingly created lawns, trees, hedgerows and flower beds for his suburban clients. As the trees in Harry's gardens grew, so too did Blue blossom into a seemingly shy, occasionally feisty teenager, with brown, slightly curly hair, a determined bounce in her stride, and large, inquisitive eyes. They lived in the same little house in Surrey but, as Fate would have it, on Blue's fourteenth birthday, a letter arrived that would see them upping sticks and moving to the USA before the year was out.

It was nineteen hundred and twenty-six and, as a treat for her fourteenth birthday, Blue was being taken to see the latest moving picture release with a friend. We find her sitting in the back of Harry's Ford Model T, the first mass produced automobile that came in any colour you wanted just so long as it was black. Harry was driving with Sheila beside him. They were going to see The Wizard of Oz. Not the musical version you may have seen; that film wouldn't be made for another twenty years. This was the original black and white, silent version. Speaking of silent, our movie goers had barely uttered a word to one another. The letter that had arrived that morning had left them all deep in thought. It contained a job offer for Harry. Not any old job offer, but the chance of a new beginning for the whole family in the United States.

Harry had spent the morning at the local telephone exchange where, on a crackling line to America, a lawyer with a broad New York accent had confirmed that he was being offered the position of head groundsman at a palatial mansion in Long Island, a suburb of New York City. As Fate would have it, the mansion's owner, a Mr Edward De Croy, had visited a friend in Surrey that summer. As Mr De Croy drank tea in his friend's garden, I began a new melody for him and, lo and behold, he enquired as to the name of his friend's gardener. To cut a long story short, my close friends, Cause and Effect, sprang into action and three months later, when Mr De Croy's head groundsman reached retirement age, he remembered how peaceful and content he'd felt in that beautifully maintained garden in Surrey.

And so, we pick up the thread of that chain of events in a car on the way to see The Wizard of Oz. Sheila was the first to speak, breaking the silence like a ping pong ball thrown into a tower of paper cups. "It would be *such* an upheaval, Harry."

"Can I see it again, Dad?" asked Blue from the back seat.

Harry reached into the inside pocket of his blazer, pulled out the letter and handed it to her over his shoulder. Blue slid the letter from its envelope. It contained three paragraphs. The first explained how Mr De Croy was a businessman of considerable standing, indeed, he was one of the wealthiest men in America. The second paragraph, the one that Blue and Harry had enjoyed reading the most, said how much he had savoured spending time in the garden that Harry had designed and cultivated. The third and final paragraph offered Harry the job of head groundsman at his two hundred room estate with twenty acres of 'prime Long Island ground. It is no exaggeration to say,' the letter went on, 'that Chateau De Croy is the finest example of French architecture outside of France, where the great and the good are entertained regularly in its palatial rooms and formal grounds.'

Once she had finished reading this sentence, Blue, sensing her friend's sorrow at the possibility of them being separated, reached out and squeezed her hand. Inwardly, however, Blue's spirit of adventure had been ignited. Just as Dorothy is whisked away to a land far away to go on an adventure, so too did Blue sense the adventure that awaited her in the land of the mysterious Edward De Croy.

Do you imagine the family's interest in seeing the Wizard of Oz is a coincidence? Reader, coincidences have much in common with fairies. They don't exist either.

Chapter 6
Blue boards another ship

Three months have passed and, once again, we find Blue at the docks at Southampton. Now, as then, she is boarding a transatlantic cruise liner bound for New York. No longer a baby wrapped in swaddling, she's a teenager clad in a shiny red raincoat, its hood pulled up to protect her hair, which is easily frizzed by moisture from the rain. You see her making her way up the gangplank, don't you? She's that blaze of red amongst the greys and browns of the other passengers.

How prophetic that she should stand out in this way.

I'll let you in on something else that's prophetic: the ship that she boarded was going to be torpedoed by a German submarine and sink. Relax. That eventuality is not pencilled into my Book of Orchestrations until June of 1942, some sixteen years from now. This crossing is scheduled to take six days and will arrive a little ahead of time. While this liner isn't in quite the same league as Titanic, she's certainly an eye opener for a fourteen-year-old whose only experience of being on the water until now (at least that she can remember) is being rowed about on the Serpentine Lido by her father.

I should also mention that Blue was moving up in the world. No longer was she a third-class traveller. Mr De Croy had paid for a family cabin in first class. How Iris would have delighted in seeing her daughter now, running her hand along the brass rail of the first-class corridor, and gazing up at framed photographs of the famous passengers who had travelled on this ship before her.

The door to their cabin was opened by a fawning steward. "If you need anything, please ring the bell-rope beside the fireplace, and I'll be with you in a jiffy," he said. Blue stepped around him into the cabin; her eyes lapping up the wood-panelled walls and ceiling, the Rococo style three-piece suite that would not have looked out of place in a French palace, and the round dining table, its walnut surface so polished that she could see her own delighted expression reflected in it.

"Is this all *really* for us?" said Sheila.

"It seems so," said Harry, glancing disbelievingly at the ticket in his hand.

"You've worked hard enough for it, Dad."

"Look Blue, this must be your room," said Sheila, standing in the doorway of a room that led off from the lounge and dining area. Blue skirted over and entered the little room. It contained a single bed, a chest of drawers, a writing bureau and chair, and a porthole with a sea view. "It's absolutely perfect," she breathed. Blue came back out of her room and watched Harry take a little plant pot out of a holdall. A tiny green bud sprouted from its soil.

"Here, let me find a place for it," smiled Blue, reaching out a hand.

"Right you are," said Harry, handing it over.

Blue reached up and placed the little pot on the mantel above the fireplace.

Sheila glanced at it. "It's a snipping from the first rose bush he planted when he got back after the war. Always has been a sentimental fool."

Harry sat down at the table and Blue sat beside him. "I'll plant it in the garden of our new home," he said, "where it will always remind us of where we came from."

Blue nodded. "It's a lovely idea."

Harry withdrew a small flask of whisky from his pocket. He unscrewed the lid, took a sip, and placed the flask down on the table. "There'll be no more where this came from."

"If you ask me, the prohibition laws in the States are a good thing," said Sheila. "Never had time for the demon drink. I'm glad alcohol is illegal over there."

"Would you get into trouble for having this?" said Blue, pointing to Harry's flask of whisky.

"No. But I could only replace its contents by breaking the law of the land. By dealing with gangsters and bootleggers," winked Harry.

"Your father won't be doing that," said Sheila as a grandfather clock in the cabin began to strike four.

Blue had a date with Destiny.

What is Destiny? Nothing more than the title on the front of my book of orchestrations.

I tapped my baton on the podium three times to get the attention of the relevant section of my orchestra and, as they started to play, Harry reached a hand across the table and cupped Blue's. "While we get settled in, why don't you go and explore? I can tell you're champing at the bit to have a look around."

Blue looked up at her mother. "Might I?"

Sheila cocked her head a little, the tell-tale sign of someone sensing a melody that's playing for them. "... I don't see why not."

A minute later, Blue was semi-skipping down the first-class corridor towards a bank of elevators. The tune that my orchestra was playing for her, up-tempo, explorative and exciting, was slightly tempered by the drone of a bow being drawn slowly across the strings of a double bass. The double bass was the only thing that prevented her from skipping down the corridor without due care and attention. Blue's enthusiasm, while necessary and lovely to behold, needed a little restraint to prevent her from colliding with...

"Oops! I'm sorry," said Blue.

"Do take more care in the future young lady," said a portly fellow who'd just exited an elevator.

"I will," said Blue as she stepped past him. She stood beside the elevator attendant, a young man not much older than herself, who stood straight-backed and proud in a navy-blue suit.

"Which floor, Miss?" he asked.

"Um," pondered Blue, "the Recreation Deck, please." As Fate would have it, the brass button and accompanying plaque with 'Recreation Deck' engraved into it, was in Blue's direct line of sight. See how gentle my direction can be? I hope you feel that you're getting to know me a little better. The better you know me, the more philosophical, less confused, and happier you'll feel about everything.

The lift's doors opened onto the Recreation Deck, and Blue stepped out into the Bluebell Reading Room; a place where first-class passengers could choose from a selection of books, periodicals and newspapers. The reading room was styled to look like a grand gentleman's club, and it conspired with my double bass to ensure that Blue moseyed through it respectfully, hands clasped behind her back. Among the sprinkling of well-to-do ladies and gentlemen in here, she was about to encounter a woman who had broken the laws of the United Kingdom many times and been locked up in a maximum-security prison as a result. I had done the groundwork that would ensure their meeting took place and Blue recognised the ex-convict instantly. How? Well, as Fate would have it, one morning, her form teacher, Miss Schuster, had picked up a discarded newspaper on a bus. Inside, she had come across an article about the law breaker. And what she read inspired Miss Schuster to dedicate a lesson to teaching her pupils about her. Indeed, the first time that Blue had seen her was on a laminated newspaper clipping. When it came to Blue's turn to look at the clipping, I slowed the tempo of her melody and, lo and behold, she held onto it rather longer than the other students. During the lesson that followed, Blue listened intently to the story of the woman who, in the same year as her own birth, had played a pivotal role in winning the vote for women in the United Kingdom. Her name was Lady Constance Fellows. Lady Constance had been a suffragette and was partly responsible for creating their battle cry of 'Deeds Not Words!' It was a call to arms that had roused a sense of justice in the breasts of women, inspiring them to fight for equality, regardless of personal loss or sacrifice. She became a hero of Blue's and now, six months later, Blue was about to spot her sitting alone on a sofa, engrossed in a book. A rousing tune was required, something with plenty of brass as Blue needed extra courage if she was going to seize the moment and… there she goes! Veering off across the room, surprised at her own tenacity, and making a bee line for the other end of the sofa. On her way, Blue picked a magazine up off a crescent-shaped table. Without daring to steal another glance at Lady Constance, she sat down, opened the magazine, and blushed at the sight of a model dressed in the latest skimpy flapper fashion. For those of you who are unaware, this decade, the 1920s, was known as the Roaring Twenties. And for good reason, it was the western world's reaction to the gloom and misery that the First World War had brought in the previous decade. The killing fields of Flanders were followed by a decade of decadence typified by the Charleston dance, flamboyant fashions, and parties of wild abandon where champagne flowed like water. Blue had heard about these extravagances, but only in the same way as you're hearing about them now. What's more, the sight of this sultry, decadent woman in the photo couldn't have been in sharper contrast to the stern, heroic woman of the Edwardian era who was sitting on the sofa beside her. Blue blushed. She was about to turn the page when her sofa partner said something that took her blush to another level.

"Louise Brooks. *Quite* the beauty, isn't she?" said Lady Constance, as though she had eyes in the side of her head.

"I… I suppose so," replied Blue, indulging her curiosity by staring, practically open-mouthed, at her hero.

Lady Constance put on the pince-nez spectacles that hung from a chain around her neck. "Mark my words. You'll be just as pretty when you're her age."

Blue glanced at the photograph of the beauty with the bob hairstyle that she had made fashionable. "Thank you," she replied with a shake of her head.

"Holidaying across the pond?"

Blue shook her head again. "We're emigrating. My Dad has a job on Long Island."

"How exciting."

"Yes, very."

"And what line of work is your father in?"

Blue closed the magazine and hugged it to her chest. "Dad's a gardener. The very *best*."

"I'm sure he must be if someone has requested his services on Long Island. And you? What are you going to do in the brave new world?"

"I'll be starting school. In September, *after* the summer break."

"Not overly keen on school?"

"I don't mind it."

"An education is important. Particularly for our sex."

"Oh, yes," nodded Blue, "if not for school, then I would never have recognised you and…" Blue fell silent.

"I see," said Lady Constance whose stern expression broke into a smile. She extended a hand for Blue to shake. "Lady Constance Fellows. How do you do?"

"Blue Tibbs, how do you do?" said Blue, reddening again.

"I must confess, it's not often that I get recognised these days, Miss Tibbs."

"My teacher laminated you."

"*Laminated* me?" said Lady Constance, her chin vanishing into her neck.

Blue nodded wholeheartedly. "It was a photograph she cut out of a newspaper. The things you did…" said Blue, her mouth dropping open at her recollections of Lady Constance chaining herself to a statue outside the Houses of Parliament, of being violently arrested on protests, and going on hunger strikes that saw her being brutally force fed. "*Thank you*, Lady Constance," said Blue as though speaking on behalf of her entire sex.

Lady Constance gazed at Blue down her pince-nez spectacles. "You're very welcome, young lady."

"What are you reading?" asked Blue, trying to steal a peek at the cover of the book she was holding. The smile on Lady Constance's face fled as though chased away by a bad memory. "It's called *Mein Kampf*. In English it translates to *My Struggle*."

"Did you write it?"

Lady Constance shook her head. "No. I most *certainly* did not. Its author is a man called Adolf Hitler. It's only just been published. A friend in Germany sent me this rare English print edition."

"What's it about?"

"The author's diabolical hatred of Jews. He's using them as scapegoats, blaming them for Germany's post-war troubles."

"Then why are you reading it?"

"It's important to understand such dark things, so one can prepare to fight them."

"With deeds not words," nodded Blue as a grandfather clock in the room began to chime.

"Deeds not words, *precisely*. And it's going to take the good deeds of a great many to cleanse the hatred that this dreadful man is planting in people's minds," she said, tossing the book onto the coffee table beside her. "If you'll excuse me, I must take my leave. I'm meeting a friend for lunch." She stood up.

"It was an honour to meet you," blurted Blue.

"The honour was mine, young lady."

As Lady Constance walked away, Blue called out, "You forgot your book!"

"I've read it. And have no intention of adding it to my collection."

"Can I have it?"

"Of course," said Lady Constance over her shoulder. "But only if you promise you won't read until you're older. I fear for the effects of such loathsome rhetoric on a young mind."

"I promise." Blue sat in stunned silence for several minutes, and then jumped up. She returned to her cabin and, discovering her parents had gone out, left the book on the writing bureau in her room, before venturing out again.

She returned a little later to discover her father pacing up and down, holding her copy of Mein Kampf, and looking troubled. The moment that Harry clapped eyes on his daughter, he said, "This *book* was only published last week. And only in Germany. How on *earth* did it find its way into your room?"

"It was a gift."

"*A Gift*? From who?"

"Lady Constance Fellows."

"The Suffragette?"

Blue nodded. "It's *amazing* who you can meet on a ship like this."

"That's beside the point, Blue. She had no right giving you such a book."

"I promised I wouldn't read it until I was older."

"Why would you want to read it?"

Blue folded her arms defiantly. "It's important to understand such things so one can prepare to fight them," she replied, repeating what Lady Constance had told her.

Harry Tibbs then did something he'd rarely done since returning from the trenches of the First World War – he began to chuckle so hard that tears streamed down his cheeks. Laughter is infectious and it wasn't long before tears of laughter were streaming down Blue's cheeks, too. This was how Sheila found them when she exited the bathroom. "Would someone care to share the joke?" she asked.

"Our daughter has a copy of Mein Kampf! Must be one of the first outside of Germany to get her hands on one," said Harry, holding up the book.

"She does? Well, I fail to see the joke."

Reader, the joke she failed to see was Adolf Hitler.

Chapter 7
Blue arrives in the USA

Three days later, the ship arrived in New York. It was greeted by a crowd of hundreds, there to welcome friends and family to the new world with flags, wolf whistles and cheers. The Tibbs family disembarked into the excited throng, where Blue was quick to spot a man holding a large sign, 'TIBBS FAMILY.'

"Look!" shouted Blue above the din.

"That's our ride," said Harry.

Blue bobbed and weaved around several people carrying luggage and stood before the man. "We're the Tibbs family," she announced.

"Very good, Miss," said the square-jawed chauffeur, doffing his cap and reaching for her holdall.

"You really don't have to it's not heavy," said Blue.

"It's my job, Miss."

"Hello there!" called Harry above the hullabaloo. "I'm Harry Tibbs. This is my wife Sheila. And my daughter Blue."

"Welcome to the United States of America, sir, madam," replied the chauffeur, "if you'd like to follow me, the car is this way."

Harry glanced back at the ship. "We'll need to wait for our luggage to be unloaded."

"No, sir, that won't be necessary. It's all being taken care of. If you'll just follow me the car is over here."

"Alright then. If you're sure?"

"I am, sir."

The chauffeur led them through the thinning crowd to a small roped off area where a lone Rolls Royce was parked. It was silver, the size of a small bus, and had more polished chrome than any of them had seen in one place.

Blue's mouth dropped open. "Is that your car?"

"Not mine, Miss. But I'll be driving you to your new home in it today," said the chauffeur, opening a rear door. Blue climbed in and bounced along the wine-coloured leather seat to the other side. Sheila climbed in after her, followed by Harry. The chauffeur closed the door.

The limousine exited the docks and purred through a grey wasteland where scrawny street vendors peddled roasted nuts, old pots and pans and discarded furniture from outside boarded up shop fronts. Looming over these faded people were faded advertising hoardings for products long since consigned to history.

"Mr De Croy lives *here*?" swallowed Blue.

The driver caught her eye in his rear-view mirror. "Not here, Miss."

Blue gazed through her window. "What happened to these people?"

"They're poor," said Sheila.

I can see that, thought Blue.

"Times are hard for a lot of people," said Harry, his troubled gaze finding one of the few fresh advertisements, a gigantic hording that depicted a sharp-clawed dragon that announced, 'Congratulations Ku Klux Klan! Six million members! Join the KKK today.' Harry sighed, "Discontentment, it's the perfect breeding ground for hatred."

Blue looked at her father.

"The KKK preach hate against the black race. They can't abide immigrants either. Blame everyone but themselves for the hardships that many are going through. That being said, their views are not so dissimilar to that man Adolph Hitler whose book you have."

"I know who the KKK are, Dad. I thought they were around in the last century."

"They were. But now they're back again. And with a vengeance it seems."

Blue thought for a moment, and then returned her gaze to the poverty-stricken streets outside the car.

Once they had crossed onto Long Island North Shore, it was as though they'd entered another world. Tall, pampered trees stood along the road like guards concealing the mansions behind them. Even so, Blue caught glimpses of high gleaming windows, ivy festooned red bricks, and fountains that sprayed water high into the air of their private kingdoms. The car slowed and turned into a driveway. A security guard emerged from a gate house, gave the chauffeur a nod, and then heaved open a heavy iron gate with the initials CDC at its centre. As they cruised up the tree lined driveway, Blue sat forward in her seat, eager for a good look at Chateau De Croy, tantalising glimpses of which she could see beyond the trees' branches. When Blue *finally* got her first proper look at the home of her father's new employer, a sprawling mansion modelled on an 18th century French palace, it stole her breath away. Sheila squeezed her arm reassuringly. "It's just a house, Blue."

"That's no *house*. Do you know what it reminds me of?"

"A swanky hotel," said Harry, his eyes lapping up the already beautifully maintained gardens.

"No. It reminds me of one of the stories you used to read to me, Beauty and the Beast. It looks *just* as I imagined the Beast's palace to look."

"There are no beasts here," said Sheila as they turned off the main drive. Blue spun in her seat and gazed out of the rear window, way up to the tip of the chateau's highest turret.

They swept down a winding lane and through a stable yard where stable hands were hard at work mucking out stables, brushing down horses, and beating horseshoes at a smelt. "I had no idea Mr De Croy kept horses," said Harry.

Sheila sighed. "It seems to me that we know very little about him."

The driver cleared his throat. "Mr De Croy runs a polo team, sir."

"Does he play?" asked Harry.

"Mr De Croy? No, sir." No sooner had the car left the stable yard when it came to a halt outside a picture book cottage, complete with thatched roof and hanging boxes filled with flowers. The driver switched off the ignition. "This is Green Lodge. The head gardener's residence."

"Is this *really* where we're to stay?" asked Sheila, disbelievingly.

"It's where we're going to *live*," said Harry.

"This is our new home!?" said Blue, yanking on her door's handle and discovering it was locked. She tapped her foot impatiently while the driver climbed out and opened the door beside Harry. Once Harry and Sheila had got out, Blue bounced along the seat and stepped down onto the pebbled driveway.

"And which fairytale does this remind you of, I wonder?" Harry asked her.

"Hansel and Gretel…"

"It's lovely, but this is no gingerbread cottage," said Sheila.

Blue wrinkled her nose. "It certainly doesn't smell like gingerbread."

"Horse manure," sniffed Harry, "when the wind is blowing down from the stables."

Sheila raised a handkerchief to her nose. "As it clearly is today."

"Could be a valuable supply of compost," said Harry, looking on the bright side.

The driver cleared his throat. "Here are the keys to the cottage, sir."

"Thank you," said Harry taking the key chain and holding it up. "What are the other keys for?"

"The outbuildings where the gardening equipment is stored. There'll be somebody along to give you a guided tour tomorrow morning."

"And Mr De Croy? When might I meet him?"

"Mr De Croy is a busy man. He'll send for you when he's ready."

"That's all very well but in the meantime how am I to know his gardening tastes?"

"Like I said, he'll send for you when he's ready."

Inside they discovered that the cottage had recently been redecorated. A three-piece suite was still in its plastic wrapping, and there was a whiff of fresh paint from the crème coloured walls. Blue stepped into the middle of the sitting room. "It's charming…"

"It's certainly very fashionable," said Sheila, casting a gaze over the Art Nouveau décor and furniture. Blue crossed the room to a bay window with sashed curtains that looked out onto a lawn. Harry came over and stood beside her, and Blue placed a hand on his shoulder. "You're wondering about the last family to live here. The last head groundsman," she said.

"I do wonder sometimes if you're a mind reader."

"Maybe the Beast had him for breakfast," said Sheila opening a door. "Blue, I seem to have a knack for finding your room."

Blue stood in the doorway of the spacious room. It contained a single bed, a chest of drawers, and a dressing table with a large vanity mirror. Behind the dressing table, a set of bay doors looked out onto a little garden, complete with a picket fence and lily pond. Reader, it was necessary for Blue to have her own means of coming and going from the cottage. "Look, I have a little garden!"

"So you do," said Sheila. "I don't know," she went on placing her hands on her hips. "I hope this move doesn't spoil you rotten."

"Rotten? Never," said Harry, standing in the doorway.

Blue glanced over her shoulder and smiled at him.

Chapter 8
Terry and Chateau De Croy

The following morning, Blue awoke with an excitement that stole her breath away. She jumped out of bed and pulled back her curtains to reveal the lily pond twinkling in the dawn's rays. She snatched her wristwatch up off her dressing table. "7 am?" she murmured as she struggled to attach it to her wrist with eager fingers. She put on a red summer dress and black shoes and opened her bedroom door. Except for a carriage clock ticking on a mantel, the cottage was silent.

In the kitchen, she took a banana from a fruit bowl, peeled it, munched it down, and tossed the skin into an empty bin where it landed with a thud. Blue opened the front door and went out. Her intention? To get a closer look at Chateau De Croy.

She followed the lane back towards the chateau and quickly came upon the stable yard. A man was transferring straw from the back of a truck into a wheelbarrow and, inside a stable to her left, a black boy was brushing down the finest horse she had ever seen. It was white with a magnificent white mane and looked every bit as magical as a unicorn. The boy, who was of a similar age to Blue, was so engrossed in his grooming that he didn't notice her approach.

"Morning!" chirped Blue, clapping her hands together.

The boy jumped, his brush flew from his grasp, and would have struck Blue on her head had she not ducked. "Don't kill me! I come in peace. Honest," she said, straightening up.

The boy looked her up and down, trying to gauge how important she was because, if she wasn't important, he might give her a piece of his mind.

"I'm sorry for startling you. I just moved into the Green Lodge," said Blue, pointing over her shoulder in the direction of home. The boy drew a deep breath, stepped past her, and picked up his brush. "*You're* the new head groundsman?"

"Ah, no, my Dad is. Oh, you were pulling my leg."

The boy nodded and almost smiled. "You near enough gave me a heart attack, Miss," he said, making his way back to the horse.

"Oh, please, call me Blue," said Blue, extending a hand for him to shake.

The boy looked uncertain of her gesture but, having given it a moment's thought, he shook it.

"And you are?" asked Blue.

"Terrance. But everyone around here calls me Terry."

Blue stepped towards the horse and stroked its mane. "It's nice to meet you Terry. What an *incredible* creature! You look like a unicorn. Well, except for a missing horn."

"Sheba's almost as rare as a unicorn, Miss."

"Honestly, call me *Blue*."

Terry raised an eyebrow. "You mean like the colour? Is that really your name?"

"It really is."

"You don't seem so blue."

"That's because I make a special effort to be cheerful. Dad says that I'm trying to make up for a name that makes me sound miserable." Terry nodded as if this made perfect sense. "Sheba must like you. She only bows her head to me and her mistress like that."

"Her mistress? Mr De Croy's wife?"

"What? Mr De Croy's a single man. Sheba is Miss Apricot De Croy's horse. I take care of her."

"Miss Apricot De Croy?"

Terry was about to shake his head. "Oh, you were making a joke."

Blue smiled. "It sounds like a very important job."

"It is," said Terry in earnest.

"Her name is *Apricot*? Like the jam?"

"Yep. In these parts she's pretty famous. An heiress. Mar says her name really suits her on account of her being so jammy." Terry turned about as pale as it's possible for a black face to turn. "I... I hope I haven't said something out of turn..."

"Nah. We're all friends here. Aren't we, Sheba?"

Sheba nodded as though she'd understood the question.

"So, who is Miss *Apricot De Croy* then?"

"She's Mr De Croy's niece."

"She lives here?"

"No. She stays during the holidays."

"Nice lady?" said Blue, rubbing Sheba's nose.

"Miss Apricot's no lady. She's no older than you."

"*Really?*" said Blue, casting her gaze about as if to see her. "You mean our age."

"I guess."

"So, what's she like?"

"I'd say she's real serious," said Terry, lowering his voice.

"Goodness. How serious?" asked Blue, lowering hers.

"I only ever saw her smile one time. She snapped at Jim, another stable boy, told him to fetch her saddle right quick, and Jim slipped and landed in a pile of horse dung."

"And she found that funny?"

"I reckon it must have been the funniest thing she ever saw," said Terry with a shudder. "That accent you have. Is that British?"

"Yep."

"You came all the way from England?"

"Yep."

"Why?"

"So my Dad can make the grounds even nicer."

"You ever met the King of England?"

"Nope. You ever met Mr De Croy?"

Terry rolled his eyes. "Yeah, me and him, we were introduced this one time and he shook my hand and asked, 'how do you do, Terrance?'"

"You must have seen him. What does he look like?"

"No. I never have seen him."

"So, you just started working here then?"

Terry pointed over Blue's shoulder. "Been living on the estate in a cottage with my ma since I was a kid."

"And you've never *seen* him? He never comes by the stables?"

"Not during working hours, anyway."

"Well, Terry, I am *determined* to get a good look at the mysterious Mr De Croy. I'll see you later!" said Blue turning and heading off in the direction of the chateau.

Terry wiped his brow. "Miss, I mean *Blue*," he called out, "don't get any closer to the big house than the outskirts of the wood. Don't *never* cross the lawns."

"Who says so?" asked Blue over her shoulder.

"Who? Everyone. That's who."

"Appreciate the advice," she said as she walked away with a wave.

"Yeah?" murmured Terry under his breath, "something tells me you aren't all that good at taking advice."

Blue stood on the edge of the small wood that spanned the south side of the estate. She gazed out over lawns awash with dew, the watery effect reminding her of a castle moat. *I won't drown but I will leave footprints,* she thought. Her gaze rose to the chateau and lingered on its four turrets. They were mauve in colour and each had a window and balcony that any self-respecting princess would have been proud to be rescued from. The turrets had been inspired in the mind of the architect by a melody played by my harpsichordist. I deemed their inclusion necessary to ignite Blue's imagination and encourage her to cross the lawn in search of adventure. And there she goes! Holding the shoes that she had just slipped off and hoping to leave the smallest trail possible in the dew. Once across the lawn, she came upon a series of hedgerows. They were tall enough to obscure the chateau's ground floor. She rounded a corner and froze at the sight of people swarming in and out of a side entrance into the chateau. They were carrying wicker baskets from a cavalcade of vans outside. A smile spread across her face as it dawned on her that she could use the hustle and bustle to her advantage. And so, as my orchestra played a forthright, she who dares wins melody, she slipped on her shoes and strode casually towards the throng. On her way she navigated a statue of the Greek God Poseidon, holding aloft his trident, from where she could see that the wicker baskets were filled with freshly cut flowers.

"Hurry it along! Chop chop!" said a man dressed in a white coat and holding a clipboard. Blue's melody drew her attention to a group of teenagers who, as Fate would have it, had been employed by the catering firm for the summer. They lined up and formed a queue to get another basket. *I couldn't get into trouble for helping out, surely?* thought Blue as she joined the end of their ranks. Despite this charitable defence, when she reached the truck, Blue lowered her chin and held out her hands. A man on the truck plonked a basket, overflowing with roses still attached to their stems, into her arms.

Blue's heart thudded as she walked through the service entrance into Chateau De Croy. She was in a wide corridor that was lined with servants' clothes pegs. A set of double doors loomed at the end of the corridor. Blue walked through these into the din of pots and pans clattering, meat being chopped, and a matronly woman barking orders in her kitchen. Her gaze sought out another basket carrier who, having made his way down the far left-hand side of the kitchen, turned left through a door and disappeared. Blue picked up speed and followed him. On the other side of the door was a servants' staircase that corkscrewed down. "Aren't we on the ground floor?" she murmured as she held the basket to one side so she could see the steps. At the bottom, she came upon a short flight of stairs that led up into bright sunlight. At the top of these Blue lapped up the scene of a sea of tables being laid, silver cutlery being given a final polish, and the hanging of a kilometre of fairy lights around a bandstand. She heard a whistle, a shrill noise that indicated that someone had placed two fingers in their mouth and blown. "Wake up!" said a man who then clicked his fingers and pointed. Blue snapped to attention and hurried towards a group of white coated men who were busy trimming the stems of flowers and placing them in vases. She placed the basket down with the others, turned, and made her way back the way she'd come. She saw a man dressed in black tails, holding his head so high that he could only observe people by gazing down his nose at them. He balanced a silver tray on the palm of his hand, upon which lay some letters and a newspaper. *Mr De Croy's butler*? thought Blue, as the man turned on his heels and walked towards a set of veranda doors. Blue glanced around for the busy body who'd whistled at her. *If anyone's keeping an eye on me, it will be him.* She was relieved to see that he'd been distracted by a waiter whose own melody, 'Butterfingers' had been responsible for him dropping a box of champagne flutes. Blue turned her attention back to the butler. *I could always say I got lost. People do…*" she thought as she followed the butler towards the veranda doors.

Blue stepped through the doors and gasped at the extraordinary scale of a ballroom. It spanned the entire length of the chateau and went for an *obscenely* greedy distance in either direction. She glanced up at the ceiling, so far above her head that she wondered if she'd be able to toss a ball high enough to hit it. With the exception of a white table upon which sat a red telephone, the ballroom was empty. The butler's shoes clipped the polished wooden floor as he made his way towards a door on the other side.

Blue whipped off her shoes, almost losing her balance, and stepped across the floor in pursuit. She emerged from the ballroom into the mansion's main entrance hall. Before her, a staircase swept in two directions to the floors above. Except for the butler, there was no one else around. And yet the place was spotless. *Where are all the servants*? she thought as the tails of his frock coat disappeared around a bend in the staircase. Reader, as Fate would have it, an urgent staff meeting had been called that morning. I expect you're wondering where Blue found the courage to explore in such a brazen fashion. Well, you should have seen how my orchestra sweated with the sheer exertion of playing her thunderously adventurous ditty! It was the same one they played for the famous charge of the Light Brigade in 1854. Fortunately for Blue, there were no Russian cannons on the floor above waiting to blast *her* to smithereens. But there was a painting of the charge. And it was the first thing she saw when she stepped off the top stair. The painting depicted soldiers on horseback, swords raised, and charging headlong into cannon fire. Blue regarded it for a moment before turning her attention to the butler. He was making his was down a corridor towards a cage elevator. Blue stepped behind a marble pillar and listened to the elevator's cage door being slid open and closed, followed by a quiet hum as it began its ascent. She skirted down the corridor in pursuit of the un-pursuable and, grasping the elevator's outer cage door, attempted to look up the shaft as though she still might still catch a glimpse of the Beast. She murmured a word that Harry had used many times when he imagined her out of earshot, glanced left, and spotted an open window.

The window looked out over the lawns to the west of the chateau and, leaning out, she looked up and saw one of the fairytale turrets soaring high above her. "This *has* to be his turret," she murmured, sliding back inside. Satisfied with her discovery, she decided not to push her 'luck' any further and made good her escape.

Chapter 9
Miss Apricot

That night when Blue went to bed, she heard the distant sounds of a party getting underway at the chateau: whoops, cheers, laughter and music, all carried in her direction on the cusp of a breeze that swept across the lawns, through the wood, and down the lane to her cottage. At midnight, she climbed out of bed, opened the bay doors in her bedroom, and tried to imagine what all those beautiful and rich people were getting up to.

In the morning, Harry went to meet his ground staff, and Blue and Sheila set about unpacking some luggage that had just arrived.

Harry returned at midday to find them laying the table for lunch.

"Well?" asked Sheila as Harry lowered himself into his chair at the head of the table.

"How'd you know about the well?" replied Harry, distantly

Sheila looked at Blue. "Do you think he's caught heat stroke?"

"Spent too long in the sun this morning, Dad?"

Harry looked back and forth between his wife and daughter.

"So? You met them? Your groundsman?" pressed Sheila.

Harry nodded and wiped some invisible lint from the table.

"*Well*?" asked Sheila again. She balled her hands into fists, fully prepared to bop him one if he mentioned an actual well.

"Thirty!" said Harry as though calling out a number at bingo.

"Wells?" said Blue, mischievously.

"Groundsman!" said Harry.

"Congratulations," said Sheila.

"What for?"

"I wish I had thirty helpers."

"Helpers? They're highly skilled men."

Blue placed her elbows on the table and her head in her hands. "I wonder if they helped clear up after last night's party."

"Party? I told your father I could hear something. What makes you think it was a party?" Blue opened her mouth to explain what she'd seen the previous day and then closed it again. "My hearing's first-rate. It was definitely a party, Mum."

"It must have been some party if you could hear it all the way over here."

There was a loud knock at the door.

Someone spotted me yesterday, thought Blue.

"You've turned dreadfully pale all of a sudden, Blue," said Sheila, standing and heading for the door.

"No. I'll go," said Harry, "I know who it is…"

Blue breathed a sigh of relief.

Harry retuned half a minute later. He stuck his head inside the kitchen door. "I'm going to meet Mr De Croy."

"Now? What about lunch?"

"It'll have to wait."

Blue jumped to her feet. "Can I come?"

"Sorry, darling. Important business to discuss."

Blue thudded back down into her seat as though felled by an arrow.

"I'll tell you all about it when I get back," said Harry from the hall. The front door closed.

After lunch Blue went out. As she ambled up the lane that led to the stables, hands thrust into the pockets of her skirt, a flash of white came thundering around a corner, forcing her to hurl herself head first into a drainage ditch. Despite seeing stars, Blue scrambled to her feet, blew some dirt from her lips and readied herself to yell at its rider. The rider, a girl, pulled her horse to a halt

46

and spun it about. Blue clenched her fists and opened her mouth to give her a piece of her mind when the girl beat her to it. "YOU BLOODY LITTLE FOOL! Take more care where you walk in the future! Do you hear me?" The girls locked scowling eyes and, as is often the case with two people who, unbeknownst to them, have something tragic in common, their scowls softened. *Apricot De Croy?* thought Blue. The rider tutted, turned her horse around and galloped off.

Terry was stacking bales of straw in the Queen of Sheba's stable. When Blue entered, he put down his pitch fork, wiped his brow, and looked her up and down.

"*What*?" asked Blue.

"Haven't you got mirrors in that cottage?"

"Of course,…"

"You might want to look in one before you go out."

Blue looked down at herself. "Oh, right. I just had an encounter with a *lunatic* riding a horse. She would have killed me if I hadn't jumped out the way."

"You landed in that ditch, yonder?" said Terry, trying not to smile.

Blue glanced behind her and nodded.

"You've seen Miss Apricot then?"

"Talk about irresponsible," murmured Blue.

Terry gave one of the stacked bales a shove to make it fit better. "… Ma says rich folks stay rich by putting themselves first. Says it's like the law of the jungle."

"That certainly seems to be true in Apricot's case," sighed Blue.

"*Miss* Apricot," said Terry who punctuated the 't' with a tut. "Her family's had money forever. It's in her blood. Ma says that's why she doesn't know to treat folks better. 'Always keep a civil tongue in your head around Miss Apricot. She's never known the love of a mother like you have.'"

"Is that why you put up with her being rude to you? She's very clever your ma."

"Like I had a choice. Did I *say* Miss Apricot was rude to me?"

"No. But she is, isn't she?"

"Of course she is."

Blue folded her arms. "How will she ever learn how treat people if nobody corrects her?"

"Correct Miss Apricot? Now I know you're crazy."

"Do you know how she lost her mother?"

Terry took a cloth from his belt and patted his brow. "How'd you know she lost her?"

"You said she's never known the love of a mother. So, I presume…"

"Truth is she died a ways back," said Terry with a resigned nod. "I heard she was killed in an accident." Blue winced as she scraped some dirt off her bruised elbow. "I could almost feel sorry for her."

Chapter 10
Not a beast after all

Later, when Harry returned from his meeting with Mr De Croy, Blue jumped up from the kitchen table where she'd been peeling potatoes and hurried to greet him.

"So? Is he the Beast?" she asked, taking his trilby hat and hanging it on the hat stand.

"Thank you. You mean… is he eight feet tall with claws?"

"Well, is he?" asked Sheila from the living room doorway.

"I'd say more like nine and a half feet."

Blue looked over her shoulder at her mother. "Told you."

Harry navigated a route around them both and went into the living room. He sat down in an armchair and motioned towards the couch. Blue and Sheila sat down. Harry withdrew a pipe from the breast pocket of his blazer with a shaky hand. "He seems a nice enough fellow. And broadly speaking, he's given me free reign to cultivate the gardens as I see fit."

"How old is he?" asked Sheila.

"Our age I should imagine."

"And his family?"

"I got the impression that he's a single man…"

"No wedding ring then?"

Harry shook his head. "There's a portrait of a woman above the fireplace in his study."

"His mother?" ventured Sheila.

Harry withdrew a tobacco pouch from his pocket. "That would be my guess."

"Is she still alive?"

"No idea."

"I know he had a brother," said Blue.

Harry and Sheila looked at their daughter.

"It's true. He was killed during the Great War. Terry told me."

"Terry?" said Sheila.

"He works at the stables, Mum."

Sheila rolled her eyes. "I wouldn't go paying too much attention to the gossip of a stable boy."

"He's not any old stable boy," said Blue, mysteriously.

Harry stuffed some tobacco down into his pipe. "Isn't he?"

"No. Terry looks after *Miss* Apricot De Croy's horse," said Blue, looking back and forth between them. Harry struck a match and placed it to the end of his pipe. "Miss Apricot De Croy?" he puffed.

"She's Mr De Croy's niece. She comes to stay at the chateau during the holidays. She's my age. *Incredibly* irresponsible but gets away with it because she's a famous heiress."

"It sounds as though your imagination is running away with you," said Sheila.

Blue lifted her elbow and showed off her bruise. "Is this real enough for you?"

"When did you get that?"

"Earlier. When *Miss* Apricot De Croy practically ran me down on her horse."

Sheila leaned forward for a closer look at the bruise. "Why didn't you say anything?"

"Our daughter is rather fond of keeping secrets," said Harry, blowing a smoke ring up towards the ceiling. "Anyway," he went on, "Mr De Croy is having another party tomorrow night. That's why he wanted to see me. He wants me to make sure the gardens in the immediate vicinity of the house are tip top. There are going to be a lot of very important people attending."

"Did he say who?" asked Sheila.

"Did he?" said Blue her eyes widening.

"No. But he did mention something about 'the great and the good.'"

Reader, I expect you're familiar with the expression 'like a red rag to a bull'.

In this instance, as intended, the words 'the great and the good' acted as the red rag to Blue's bull. One way or another, she would be spying on that party.

Chapter 11
Blue in Wonderland

The next day, as Sheila drank her morning coffee, the idea of asking Blue to paint the picket fence around her little garden was delivered to her in a melody appropriately entitled, 'Blue Paints a Picket Fence Red.' As it played, Sheila nodded absently. "The paint's peeling on the fence outside your room. And besides, wouldn't you rather have a red one? It would match the rose bushes around the pond."

"I suppose it would keep me busy before…" nodded Blue.

"Before what?"

"Before dinner. What else, Mum?"

And so, Blue spent the day, paintbrush in hand, turning a white picket fence red. She finished at 6 pm and, having placed her brush in a bucket of water, she wandered over to the garden gate. *I'd better leave the latch off. It'll be dark when I leave.*

At 11 pm, a smile spread across Blue's face as she heard the faint sounds of a band through her open window. "The great and the good are gathering," she breathed excitedly, pulling away her bed sheet to reveal the black dress she'd chosen for her mission. Blue climbed out of bed, unlocked her veranda doors, and opened them just wide enough to slip through into the night. As Fate would have it, she needn't have worried about it being too dark. The night's sky was awash with stars, not to mention the biggest full moon she had ever seen. Yes, Reader, my influence reaches that far. And beyond.

Five minutes later, Blue emerged from the wood onto the lawns that encircled Chateau De Croy. A firework screeched into the air and EXPLODED in a shower of red that caused Blue to slip and lose her footing. It was a reminder from yours truly to keep her wits about her. I'm thoughtful that way. But, as is often the case when I help to keep people on their toes by having them topple on them, Blue murmured a sarcastic, "Thanks a *lot*." Having admonished me, she crossed the lawn, her heart racing, towards the sound of clinking glasses, music and laughter.

She navigated the maze-like hedgerows and, having smiled at her father's shapely handiwork, she turned a corner and got her first view of the festivities. Blue stood transfixed at the sight of a sea of guests – they were dressed as kings and queens, pharaohs, Greek Gods, Roman emperors, and movie stars (some were movie stars). They were dancing, utterly free of inhibition, to the Charleston, the most popular tune of the day. Flappers in stilettos kicked their legs out with the dexterity of circus performers. And actual circus performers; jugglers and fire eaters loomed high over the revellers on stilts. Blue snapped her mouth closed and moved closer, scanning the area for a good, albeit hidden, vantage point. I was about to reveal the perfect one.

A volley of fireworks exploded and, in the burst of colour overhead, up on a bank that overlooked the party, Blue spotted a true to life scale replica of Cinderella's carriage. As I swung my baton and led my orchestra in an enchanting fairytale melody, she set off, anticlockwise, around the outskirts of the party. Blue climbed a rockery of stones to where Cinderella's carriage sat nestled amid trees aglow with fairy lights. The carriage had large, oval shaped openings on each side, and a roof that ballooned like a canopy overhead. She gazed through it and out the other side to where the party was in full swing. Inside, the carriage was upholstered in purple velvet and Blue smiled at the sight of a

Cinderella manikin, seated beside Alice in Wonderland and a wooden soldier from the Nutcracker. The opposite bench, with its padded purple seat and numerous pillows, was empty and inviting. Blue pulled herself up and over the oval opening and landed in a heap in the centre of the carriage. "I'm *so* elegant," she murmured. Her clumsiness struck her as funny amid so such sophistication and, chuckling to herself, Blue slid backwards and lifted herself onto the empty bench. She leaned forwards and sighed at her splendid view of the party. "… I hope you don't mind my gate-crashing your carriage?" she murmured to her life size companions.

"Actually, we *do* mind," one amongst them replied. It was fortunate that the roof of the carriage was a metre above Blue's head or else she would have knocked herself out on it. Blue landed on the seat and slipped off onto the floor with a thud. "Ow!"

"*That* serves you right."

Blue's eyes passed over the opposite seat, and her gaze fixed on Alice in Wonderland. As far as she could remember, in no part of her story did Alice *ever* swig from a champagne bottle. "You're real!" blurted Blue.

"You're bright," replied Alice.

"But…"

"But nothing. I spy a gate crasher. I've a good mind to call my uncle's security and have you arrested."

"*Apricot*?" squinted Blue at Alice's mascara heavy eyes.

"Excuse me? *Miss* Apricot to you."

"Well, you're drunk *Miss* Apricot and that's illegal," said Blue, seeking some ammunition to fight her threat.

"Don't be ridiculous. Getting drunk isn't illegal."

Blue looked at the slightly slumped girl, dressed as Alice in Wonderland, and wondered if her extraordinary blonde hair was her own or an elaborate costume wig.

"Why are you looking at me like *that*?"

"Are you wearing a wig?"

"Does it *look* like I'm not wearing a wig?" said Apricot tugging on her hair. "Now where's that bell to call for assistance..." she went on, feeling around on the seat beside her.

"Maybe getting drunk isn't illegal," grasped Blue, "but I bet that alcohol you're drinking is."

"Oh, you do, do you? Then I suggest you tell *them* that," said Apricot, pointing outside the carriage to the revellers. "Go on. Show your gate crasher's face and shout at the top of your voice, 'This is a bust! You've been caught bang to rights like naughty children by a naughty child!'" Apricot started to giggle so hard that she knocked her head against the wooden soldier beside her. "Ow-w!"

"I think you've had enough to drink," observed Blue in her most adult voice.

"What did you say?"

"I think you heard. Does your uncle know about your drinking problem?"

"The impertinence! How *dare* you gate crash my carriage and accuse me of being an alcoholic."

"This isn't your carriage it's Cinderella's." They looked at Cinderella as though she might settle the matter for them. She didn't. "Is he here?" asked Blue, peeking outside, and keen to change the subject.

Apricot narrowed her eyes at her. "Is who here?"

"Your uncle. I wanted to get a look at him."

"He rarely attends his parties. Wanted to sneak a peek at your father's new employer, did you?"

"You know who I am?"

Apricot rolled her big blue eyes. "Whenever a careless fool almost kills me, I make inquiries as to who they are, so I might avoid them in the future, *Miss* Blue Tibbs."

"*I* was the one who was almost killed. But we both survived so..." Before Blue could stop them, the following insensitive words escaped her lips. "Wouldn't you be curious to see *your* father's boss?" *Oh, nice one*, thought Blue.

Apricot extended her already swan like neck, and her forthright reply, coaxed by her melody, came as a shock to them both. "*My* father's as dead as this dodo," she said, grasping for a pendant of the Dodo from Alice in Wonderland that hung from a chain around her neck.

"I'm sorry," nodded Blue, "I didn't mean to upset you."

Apricot shook her head drunkenly. "You haven't. He died shortly after coming back from the Great War. I don't even remember him."

"Really? My Dad was there too. He still has nightmares about it. I can only imagine the things he saw…" said Blue, a faraway look in her eyes.

"One should probably do no such thing then."

Was that a hint of compassion in her voice? thought Blue. "What about your mother?" she asked, emboldened.

"Oh. My. Goodness. You must be *the* nosiest gate crasher in the State of New York."

"I understand if you'd rather not say."

"Very generous, I'm sure. If you *must know*, my mother and father were killed in a car accident. Are you happy now?"

Blue shrugged apologetically. "I've been this way since I was knee high to a grasshopper."

"A nosey parker," nodded Apricot.

"I prefer to think of myself as curious."

"I bet you do."

"I'm adopted," said Blue, as though it explained everything. Reader, the moment had arrived to pique Apricot's interest in her visitor. And so, as my orchestra began to play the same tune it had played for Blue on that fateful day when Titanic sank, Blue gazed down at her hands and said, "My birth mother died when I was a baby. We were on Titanic. She didn't make it."

Apricot sat up as though a puppeteer had jerked on her strings. One had. "Titanic? You're joking?"

"No. I wouldn't," replied Blue, her eyes flashing up to meet Apricot's. "Not about something like that."

"*You* were on Titanic?"

Blue nodded. "I heard my adoptive parents talking about it when I was a child. It's not the kind of thing you forget. I didn't know what Titanic was at the time. But I never forgot the name."

Apricot crossed one leg over the other and tried to look as composed as her slightly muddled head allowed. "For some reason, I've had a fascination with Titanic for as long as I can remember. One can only imagine…"

"One should probably do no such thing then," said Blue, repeating what Apricot had told her.

"And your father? He was lost on the voyage also?"

Blue shook her head. "He's a mystery. My Mum was taking me to the States to start a new life on our own."

Apricot put the champagne bottle down on the seat. "How frightfully tragic."

"Yes, but I found a new family," said Blue, philosophically. "So, your uncle adopted you?"

"No. My aunt did. She palms me off on her brother every holiday. I'm a burden they both must share."

"I'm sure it isn't like that."

An awkward silence followed; a silence broken by Apricot. "Titanic? Really?"

"Really."

"Well, that makes you more important than your appearance or station in life suggests."

"Thanks. I think."

"Important enough, I dare say, to go to the ball after all. Come on, follow me," said Apricot, standing and lifting a leg over the carriage's opening.

"What are you doing," asked Blue, bracing herself to catch the girl who was clearly unsteady on her feet.

"The doors don't open so… *this* is the only way to get out," she said, tumbling over the side and disappearing from view.

"Apricot!" gasped Blue, sticking her head out and looking down.

"*Miss* Apricot," groaned Apricot from her position on her back amongst a bed of daisies.

"You alright?"

Apricot blinked up at the stars. "… Yes, I believe so. I usually am."

"I can't go with you."

"What'd you mean?" said Apricot, climbing onto her knees and pulling a daisy from her hair.

"I'm not invited."

"Well, you are now," said Apricot, waving a hand around as though she held a magic wand. "Now come on. There's someone I want you to meet. Thankfully, I know *just* where to look amongst these… these other gate crashers."

A smile spread across Blue's face and she vaulted over the opening and landed beside her. "Who is it you want me to meet?"

"You'll see. Now help me up."

"Are you sure about this?" said Blue pulling her to her feet. "I wouldn't want to get you into trouble with your uncle."

"My uncle isn't interested in anything I do. And neither is anyone else for that matter. I have always wanted an excuse to meet this person. And it just so happens they're here tonight. What were the chances?"

"I'm intrigued," said Blue.

"Me too. Which is why I can't wait to make the introduction."

Blue navigated the revellers behind Apricot, there were more rich and beautiful people than she thought she would see in a lifetime: men who were impeccably groomed but behaved like excitable, drunk little boys; and ladies in high heels, who teased them with skimpy outfits, sparkling jewels and painted faces. She felt drab and invisible amid all these impossibly glamorous people. *And to think I would have remained hidden if…* she thought as Apricot barged through a bottleneck of guests who, having glanced at the figure of Alice in Wonderland, quickly made way. Blue found herself back in the ballroom she'd crossed on her first visit. Only now it was a sea of dining tables where people ate, drank, and laughed heartily. She followed Apricot into the chateau's entrance hall and along a corridor to a reading room where books were displayed on shelves from floor to ceiling. In a corner and gathered on chairs below a cloud of cigarette smoke, sat a group of stern-looking women holding court. "Wait here…" said Apricot, holding up a palm like a traffic policeman.

Blue's eyes focused on her hand. "Are you *sure* this is a good idea? What can I possible have in common with these ladies?"

"Ah, that's where you're mistaken…" said Apricot, tapping her nose.

"I am?"

Apricot nodded and moved away towards the group. She approached a woman who was sitting with her back to them both. Blue felt butterflies in her stomach as she wondered if her new 'friend' was about to land her in a world of trouble. Apricot leaned down and spoke to the women in hushed tones. Then she beckoned to Blue with a wave.

I suppose I should be grateful she didn't stick two fingers in her mouth and whistle, thought Blue, raising her chin as best she could and putting her best foot forward. The moment that Blue entered the gathering and clapped eyes on the woman's face, a lump that had lodged itself in her throat dissolved away. "Lady Constance!"

"Miss Tibbs?" smiled Lady Constance, standing and reaching out to give Blue what turned out to be a hug. Reader, it would be no exaggeration to say that the look on Apricot's face was a study in astonishment.

"It's a small world. What are you doing here?" asked Lady Constance.

"Dad works here."

"Your father is Mr De Croy's groundsman?"

"Yes."

"You two know each other?" blurted Apricot.

Lady Constance winked at Blue. "We became friends on the ship over from Southampton. Everyone, I would like you to meet my friend Blue Tibbs who, I have just been informed, was a fellow survivor of Titanic."

"*You* were on the Titanic, Lady Constance?" spluttered Blue.

"I was. What were the chances that we'd *both* be on the same ship twice?"

Reader, the chances were actually rather good. You might even say guaranteed.

"Excuse me… you don't look old enough," drawled a woman smoking a cigarette in the longest cigarette holder that Blue had ever seen.

"I was a baby when it sank."

"And your parents survived also?" said Lady Constance.

Blue shook her head. "I'm adopted. So, in a way, Apricot and I have something in common."

"I'm sorry. Apricot? Why does that name sound familiar?" said Lady Constance.

A smile spread across Blue's face. "Lady Constance may I introduce Miss Apricot De Croy."

Apricot stepped forwards and offered her hand. "It's an honour to be formally introduced to you. My aunt gave me your autobiography last year. I read it from cover to cover."

"And what did you think of it?"

"I *loved* it," said Apricot who, realising she sounded rather mature for her years, blushed. "… It's an honour to meet a genuine suffragette."

"Thank you. I hope that we shall become friends."

"I hope so too," smiled Apricot.

Lady Constance lowered herself back into her armchair. "Now, why don't you two pull up a couple of chairs and join our little gathering?"

A servant who'd been hovering in the shadows, picked up a chair and placed it next to Lady Constance for Apricot. Then he did the same for Blue. "Thank you," said Blue as he backed away.

Apricot perched demurely on the edge of her seat. "I think it's simply marvellous how you broke that brutish policeman's nose."

The other ladies had begun a conversation, but one amongst them looked over. "Oh, please don't encourage her violent side."

"Thank you, Mary," said Lady Constance, "but joking aside, violence should only ever be used as a last resort."

"That frightful brute was trying to place you in a headlock," said Apricot.

"Deeds not words," chorused Blue and Apricot who looked at each other, astonished.

"You two must have been friends for a long time," observed Lady Constance.

"We met half an hour ago," said Blue.

"When she fell into my carriage."

"I'd never have guessed. Stick together. You're clearly destined to become friends."

The girls glanced at one another before Apricot turned her attention to Lady Constance. "The female struggle against male oppression has been going on since time immemorial," she said as though out of the blue.

"I can see you've been giving the subject some thought," said Lady Constance. "I won't deny that men have a great deal to answer for, but let's not be too harsh on their sex."

"Surely you of all people must despise them for what they put you through?"

"Despise men? Goodness, no. There are as many good men as there are many questionable women. But you know what they say about giving people an inch and them taking a mile. Women have been giving men that inch for so long that they made off with rather more than a mile. So, what are your dreams and ambitions?" she asked, looking back and forth between them.

Apricot sat back in her seat. "When I'm 21, I shall inherit my father's fortune."

"So why the long face?" asked Blue.

"It's not the sort of knowledge that motivates one."

"It would motivate me. Just think of all the good you could do with so much money."

Apricot crossed one leg over the other, placed her hands in her lap, and was clearly considering this option for the first time. "Perhaps."

"Perhaps nothing," scoffed Blue.

"And what about you, Blue?"

"Who knows? Dad thinks I'd make a good spy."

"You're certainly brazen and inquisitive enough," observed Apricot.

Lady Constance leaned forwards and squeezed Blue's knee. "Maybe rethink being a spy. Dangerous business. You might consider advising your new friend on how to spend her fortune on charitable causes."

Apricot steepled her fingers and gazed at Blue over them. "She'll doubtless end up being one."

Chapter 12
New friends

Blue returned to her bedroom at 4 am. Her excitement at a night she knew she would never forget deprived her of even a wink of sleep. At sun up, and not relishing the prospect of lying to her parents over breakfast, Blue grabbed a banana from the bowl on the kitchen table and went out.

It was Sunday and there didn't appear to be a soul around. Even the normally busy stable yard was eerily quiet as she strolled into it looking for somewhere to toss her banana skin. The silence was broken by the clank of a hammer being smacked against steel. Blue stepped from the sunlight into a darkened barn where her eyes adjusted to reveal Terry. He was holding a hammer and kneeling over a stump with a horseshoe on it. As soon as Terry saw her, he began gesticulating wildly. *Is he shooing me away?* Sure enough, the further Blue ventured into the barn, the greater the urgency of Terry's shooing fingers.

"You've stopped banging. I presume that means the shoe's ready?" came an authoritative voice.

"Almost done, Miss Apricot," said Terry whacking the shoe.

"*Apricot?*" called Blue.

"*Blue?*" said Apricot.

"Arrrgh!" cried Terry, banging his thumb.

"My goodness, you're up early considering," said Apricot, walking into view, holding Sheba by her bridle.

"That makes two of us. I'm still on cloud nine after last night. I didn't get a wink of sleep. You alright, Terry?"

Terry sucked on his thumb and nodded.

Apricot rubbed Sheba's nose. "He's never done *that* before. I expect he'll be more careful in the future. Won't you, stable boy?"

"Yes, Miss Apricot…"

"Stable boy? Don't you know his name?"

Apricot feigned looking aghast. "You mean it *isn't* Stable Boy?"

"No, it isn't. Apparently, an introduction is long overdue. Terry, meet my friend Apricot, Apricot, this is my friend Terry." Apricot looked back and forth between them and, mindful of Blue introducing her to Lady Constance the night before, heard herself murmuring, "I suppose that any friend of yours is a friend of mine."

The hammer slid from Terry's sweaty palm and landed on the ground.

"You'll catch flies in that mouth if you're not careful, won't he Sheba?" said Apricot.

Sheba nodded.

Blue walked over and stood beside Terry. "Apricot and I met last night when I gatecrashed her uncle's party."

Apricot read Terry's expression. "*No*, I didn't have her clapped in irons," she said.

She's okay with me dropping the Miss, thought Blue. "No, Apricot didn't have me clapped in irons," said Blue, holding up her unshackled wrists. "And we discovered we have a lot in common."

"Yes, and all of it rather *tragic,*" sighed Apricot.

In the far corner of the stable, atop a wooden stool, Blue noticed a book. As my orchestra played a little ditty entitled 'The Unending Majesty of the Cosmos', Blue walked over, picked it up, and read its title aloud, "The Unending Majesty of the Cosmos. Is this your book, Terry?"

"It might be Sheba's…" said Apricot, retrieving a sugar lump from her pocket. "You're a *very* bright girl, aren't you?" she said, feeding it to her.

"Yes, it is Sheba's book, Miss Apricot, but she lets me read it sometimes," said Terry, who looked suddenly sheepish.

Apricot chuckled. "My goodness, the boy has got a sense of humour after all."

"You're interested in the universe, Terry?" said Blue, opening the book.

"It's my hobby," nodded Terry. "I've got a whole shelf full of books at home about it."

"Do you have a telescope?" asked Blue.

"No, but I've got a pair of binoculars."

"Maybe you could give me a guided tour of the cosmos one starry night?" said Blue.

"Sure, if you like," said Terry, kneeling and lifting Sheba's front left leg.

"So, where are you going this morning?" Blue asked Apricot as Terry attached the shoe.

"I thought I'd take a gallop along the Sound. The fresh sea air is *just* the thing to clear a girl's head. Why don't you join me, Blue?"

"I'd love to, but I can't ride."

"Then ride pillion with me."

"Really?"

"Really. Terry would you mind fetching my pillion saddle?"

Would I mind? thought Terry, standing and wiping a hand across his brow.

"It's Sunday," said Blue, placing Terry's book back on the stool, "why not ask Terry to join us?"

Apricot placed her hands on her hips. "You're serious, aren't you?"

"Yep. You do ride don't you Terry?" said Blue as Terry made his way back with a pillion saddle.

"Of course he does," said Apricot.

"I exercise the horses most days…"

"Then join us for a ride this morning," smiled Blue.

"Would that be right and proper?" asked Terry as though pondering a mystery of the universe. Apricot regarded him for a moment, and it occurred to Blue that this was the first time she'd really looked at him. "Why don't you fetch a saddle for Thelma. She'll need a good run today anyhow," said Apricot, leading Sheba out of the stable and into the early morning sunshine.

"You mean for me to ride with you, Miss Apricot?"

"Yes, why not? The more the merrier seems to be the order of the day."

And so, as Fate would have it, these three unlikely souls rode out together that morning. Blue felt secure riding pillion behind Apricot on the magnificent white horse that seemed to sense the will of its mistress. And, whenever she glanced over her shoulder to see Terry, bouncing up and down in his saddle, riding as though his life depended on keeping up with Miss Apricot, it filled her heart with joy. They leapt over a boundary gate into the district of Long Island Sound. A minute later, the Atlantic Ocean, in its vast and glistening glory, came into view. On the other side of that great expanse of water was Blue's homeland and, midway across, three kilometres down, the final resting place of her mother.

They galloped along the shore line, to their right was the ocean, and to the left some scrubland that led up to a rocky cliff face. Blue spotted a tall, beanpole-like structure in the distance. "What's that?" she yelled above the sound of the rushing wind, the galloping hooves, and the water lapping against the shore.

"That's the lighthouse," said Apricot over her shoulder, "it's where we're headed. There's a water trough there for the horses."

As they drew nearer to the lighthouse, Apricot slowed Sheba to a trot, and Terry drew up alongside them. "Where are you going, Miss Apricot?"

"The lighthouse. There's a trough for the horses."

"Terry? You look like you've seen a ghost," said Blue.

Terry sat up straight in his saddle. "Word is smugglers use the lighthouse as a meeting place. Mean as rabid dogs, they say."

"Smugglers? Of what?" asked Blue.

"Liquor mostly," smiled Apricot.

Terry stood in his stirrups, scrutinising the lighthouse. "Mar says they're no better than cutthroat pirates. She says they've been using the shore line for hundreds of years. Attracted by those caves yonder." I swung my baton and commenced my orchestra in a little ditty for Blue entitled, 'Exploring the Caves Yonder, An Awfully Big Adventure.'

"Caves?" murmured Blue as the ditty began to play. She raised a hand to her eyes and looked towards the cliff face. "Do you think we'll see some smugglers today?"

"Not during the day," said Apricot, "they come here after dark. That's when the place is a no-go area."

"Honestly?" said Blue.

Apricot nodded. "On what was, perhaps, the only occasion when my uncle offered any parental guidance, it was to tell me '*never* visit the shoreline after dark'. He even waved a finger in my face. I distinctly remember wanting to bite it off."

"Mr De Croy's a very wise man," said Terry.

"I find this talk of caves and smugglers very intriguing," said Blue.

Apricot rolled her eyes. "Stop the press."

"Well, isn't it? It could be that the liquor at your uncle's party passed through this *very* place in the hands of smugglers," said Blue as they reached the lighthouse.

Terry dismounted. "Mar says that Al Capone himself has a hand in bootlegging…"

"She's right about that," said Apricot climbing down from Sheba. "I met him at a party last year. He's a jolly fellow. Nothing like they say he is. Although, his dancing leaves a *lot* to be desired."

"Al Capone was up at the big house!" said Terry, helping Blue down from Sheba.

Apricot nodded.

"Thanks, Terry. It's probably for the best if you don't tell your mar about Al Capone."

"I don't know that I'll be able to stop myself," said Terry as they led the horses over to the trough.

"Then tell her," said Apricot, "I wish I could be there to see her face when you do."

Terry whistled through his teeth. "The shock of you paying a visit to our place would be bigger than hearing about Al Capone."

A mischievous smile curled Apricot's mouth. "You live with your mother in the tied cottage with the red front door, don't you?"

"Yes, how'd you know, Miss Apricot?" said Terry, as Sheba and Thelma began to drink from the trough.

"I know a good deal more than people think. What do you say we pop in on the way back and give Mrs Curtis a surprise?"

"Mar's at church," spluttered Terry.

"I know. But she'll be home after the service."

"Are you serious, Miss Apricot?"

"Deadly."

"I'd like to meet your mother, too," said Blue. "But let's go and take a look inside those caves first."

"That's a bad idea. Tell her Miss Apricot, tell her again what Mr De Croy told you."

"In all fairness, he did say to avoid the area *after* dark."

Blue placed her hands on her hips. "And need I remind you of Lady Constance's mantra?"

Apricot shook her head. "Deeds not words. But, I'm not *entirely* sure how this would fit into the deeds category?"

"The daring deed category?" shrugged Blue.

"That I can't argue with."

"Who is Lady Constance?" asked Terry, sounding a little put upon.

"Lady Constance was suffragette and campaigner for women's rights," said Blue as she began to walk towards the rock face. "You two don't have to come if you don't want to. I can walk home," said Blue, lifting a hand in a parting gesture.

Apricot and Terry glanced at one another. The melodies that I now introduced provided them with a serving of Blue's spirit of adventure. However, Terry's had an intermittently jumpy string section, one that served to keep him on his toes, making him the cautious boy that he was.

"Oh, come now. What kind of friends would we be if we let her go up there alone?" said Apricot.

Terry looked at Blue walking away towards the rock face. "Alright, Miss Apricot."

Chapter 13
Dogsbody

Outside the cave's entrance was a tree root that rose and fell across the ground like a serpent. Apricot and Terry tied their horses to it and joined Blue who was examining the entrance. "You really mean to go in there?" said Terry, peering through a clump of dead branches that had been strewn across it.

"It would be a real adventure," murmured Blue as her melody played. "If you'd rather wait here and keep an eye on the horses, then…"

Terry looked at the horses, and then past the branches into the cave. He lifted a handful to make an opening. "I'm going with you…"

"Good. And thanks," said Blue, ducking below the branches. On the other side, in the thin shafts of light that had made it through the makeshift blockade, Blue spotted a brass lantern on the ground. She crouched and picked it up as Apricot, the cave's second visitor, cupped a hand over her nose. "… It *literally* stinks in here."

"You're not wrong. Bat poo?"

"Is that a serious question? How should I know what kind of *poo* it is? What have you got there?"

Blue struck a match that she'd taken from a box beside the lantern. She lit the lantern's wick and the cavernous entrance was filled by a warm orange glow. Terry climbed off his hands and knees and brushed the dirt from his trousers. "You found a lamp?"

"Your eyes do not deceive you," said Apricot, "she's nothing if not resourceful."

Reader, the insightful nature of Blue's next comment gave me goosebumps.

"Fate must have left it for us," she said, pointing to the spot where, a few hours earlier, a smuggler who, finding himself running late, had decided to unburden himself of the lantern and sprint to the boat that would soon be departing without him. I won't go into the specifics of the cause and effect that led to the hapless smuggler running late, but rest assured, the melody my orchestra was playing for him that day, 'When Nothing Goes to Plan,' had something to do with it.

Terry walked over and squinted at the glowing lantern. "You always this lucky?"

"I imagine that anyone who survived Titanic will have luck on their side," said Apricot.

"Who survived Titanic?"

Blue raised a tentative hand.

"Are you kidding?"

"No. She isn't."

Blue switched the lantern from her left to her right hand. "I was a baby. And I don't think that being on Titanic was lucky in the first place."

Terry swallowed hard. "A fair point."

"Come on," said Apricot, "if we must nose around in the affairs of common criminals, then shall we get on with it?"

"Yes, we shall," said Blue, turning, and holding the lantern aloft. Apricot and Terry followed her down a narrow path that wended its way down. The cave's acoustics magnified every sound and they felt reassured by the silence beyond their footsteps. "Just *imagine* if the police raided the caves now and took us for smugglers?" said Blue.

"Mar would never let me forget it. Not for the rest of my days," said Terry as they rounded a bend to discover water dripping through the wall into a bucket. Apricot and Terry grimaced at the mouldy, rancid looking receptacle and followed Blue around another bend into a large cavern. Dozens of wooden shelves had been erected against damp walls that rose to a stalagmite encrusted ceiling. All empty.

"No champers? How disappointing. Stocks must be low after uncle's party."

"Not really surprising considering the amount you were guzzling…" said Blue, casting her gaze around.

"You're such a charmer," murmured Apricot as Blue spotted a desk.

"They're certainly well organised," said Blue, leaning over the desk and trying to discern the spider-like scrawl on some documents.

"Hardly surprising. Bootlegging's big business these days…" said Apricot, who was interrupted by a raspy, anxious voice from the shadows. "*Get away from there*! That's Master Blake's desk! You've no business there!"

Blue spun about, lantern held high, and squinted into the furthest reaches of the light where a shadowy figure crouched. Apricot peered over Blue's shoulder. "What *are* you?" she demanded as Terry stepped in front of them both.

"*What* am I?"

Blue glanced at Apricot. "You're obviously a *person*…" The owner of the voice emerged fully into the light of her lamp whereupon all three visitors took a step back. The man was a pitiful sight; dressed in filthy rags that hung from his emaciated frame like sails torn from a mast. He had long, black, straggly hair and a greying beard to match. His back was horribly bent, forcing him to crouch low to the ground. He peered at them though strands of hair as though they were visitors from another planet. "Come away from there," he said, his tone softened, "don't touch anything, *please*, Master Blake won't stand for anything touched. He likes things organised. You want to get me flogged?"

"No, of course we don't," said Blue, taking a step forward and beckoning her friends away from the desk.

Terry cleared his throat nervously. "Is... is Master Blake here?"

The man shook his head. "And *you*, more than these, should be grateful that he isn't."

"Why him?" asked Blue.

The man placed a hand on his chin, pondering. "Colour blind?"

"No. Why should I be colour blind?"

"It's because I'm black, isn't it?" said Terry.

"The master's a grand wizard," nodded the man.

"A *wizard*?"

"In the Klan," said Terry, answering Blue's bewildered gaze.

"The *Ku Klux Klan*," added Apricot.

"Oh," swallowed Blue, and, seeing the look of trepidation on Terry's face, she mustered a reassuring smile. "When is your master due back?"

"They'll all be back after sunset," replied the man, looking at Terry.

"Are you a prisoner?" asked Blue.

The man gazed into the middle distance as though trying to process the question. "*Prisoner*?"

Blue swallowed the lump in her throat. "Only, you don't look like you go outside very much."

"No, I don't," said the man grasping at a memory, "Master Blake, he rescued me from the sea. That's where I must have left it."

"Left what?" asked Apricot.

"My memory. But no matter. I'm worth my weight in gold! Master Blake says so." To prove how useful he was, the man scuttled inside an opening in the wall and emerged moments later clutching a broom that was clearly his pride and joy.

"Oh, he's a servant," said Apricot, sounding oddly at home as he began sweeping the floor. Ignoring her insensitivity, Blue held her lamp up to illuminate a passage that went deeper into the caves, "What's through there?"

The man scratched irritably at his beard. "The Station."

"Station?"

"For the mine carts."

"How intriguing," said Blue, glancing over her shoulder at her friends.

Apricot stepped up beside her. "I've heard rumours they use the old mines to deliver contraband to the mansions."

"Including yours?"

Apricot nodded. "It's not as though they can deliver the liquor to the tradesman's entrance with the smoked salmon."

"I want to see it," said Blue.

"What a surprise. Well, we've come this," said Apricot and, casting her gaze down at the wretched man, added, "Lead on McDuff, and take us to the mine carts."

"McDuff?" repeated the man, "from *Macbeth!*"

"*You've* read Shakespeare?" said Apricot.

The man smiled. "Master Blake says I must have been a scholar before I lost my mind. I remember quotes. And poetry!" he said, straightening his back as best he could before quoting, "I wandered lonely as a cloud that floats on high o'er vales and hills, when all at once I saw a crowd, a host, of golden daffodils; beside the lake beneath the trees, fluttering and dancing in the breeze…" He fell silent and looked about as though for the words to the next verse that had escaped him.

"I, I bet you were a fine scholar," said Blue, quietly.

The man raised his hands, palms up, as if to say, 'who could say?'

"What's your name?" asked Blue.

"I forgot my name, so Master Blake gave me a new one."

"Which is?" asked Terry regarding the man with a mix of pity and mistrust.

"Dogsbody. He even christened me with a bucket of water. The others found that funny."

"I bet they did," said Terry.

"So, will you show us where the mine carts come and go?" said Blue.

Dogsbody ran his fingers through his long beard in a scholarly fashion. "I can't recall Master Blake saying *not* to show visitors. Of course, he always says nobody would dare come here."

"It will be our secret," said Blue.

"Secret?"

"Yeah, and while you're about it, best keep me a secret, too," said Terry.

Dogsbody tapped the end of his nose conspiratorially. "Dogsbody knows how to keep secrets."

"Pleased to hear it," said Apricot regarding him as someone regards a lunatic. "Now, would you *please* lead on. We haven't got all day."

Dogsbody turned and hobbled on all fours towards the entrance, on the other side of which they found themselves in a cavern where a circle, the circumference of a coach and horses, had been laid out using bricks. On the wall of the cavern was a banner with the word 'Kyklos' emblazoned across it in red. And below this word, the number '6,000,000' had been written. Reader, two decades from now, the number six million would become terrible again for a second time.

But in 1926…

"Six million?" murmured Blue.

"Members," smiled Dogsbody.

"Of what?"

"The Ku Klux Klan, what else?" said Apricot.

The penny dropped and Blue drew a deep breath. "I saw a poster on the way from the dockyard. It seems incredible that there can be so many hateful people in the world."

"Not the whole world," said Terry, "but right here, in the USA."

"The Klan have grown dreadfully popular," added Apricot.

Dogsbody moved closer to Terry.

"Why are you looking at me like *that*?" asked Terry.

"The Master was drunk, but he said that if you look closely, the coloureds have *little* horns…"

"Look… no horns here," said Terry crouching down and showing Dogsbody the top of his head.

"The master has never liked your sort."

"I don't like his sort."

"That makes two of us. What's this circle of bricks for?" asked Blue, stepping into it.

"… The blood rituals," said Dogsbody.

Blue stepped back out of the circle.

Apricot glanced at Terry. "The least that's said about those, the best, I should imagine."

"You're not wrong, Miss Apricot."

Blue looked at Dogsbody. "So, where's this mine cart station?"

"Through here…" he replied, clearly beginning to relish his new found status as a guide.

In a large open space with a vaulted ceiling, a length of raised iron track disappeared into a tunnel barely wide enough for a cart to fit through. On the track there was a train of six empty carts, while several more sat in various states of disrepair around the cavern. Terry stepped onto the track and looked down the dark tunnel. "It reminds me of the ghost train ride on Coney Island."

Blue stepped up alongside him. "But the ghouls are *on* this ride."

"Master says the track lead to paradise," sighed Dogsbody.

Apricot folded her arms. "That's nonsense. And I should know, I stay there."

Terry glanced back the way they'd come. "Now you've seen it, can we get out this place?"

Blue squeezed his shoulder and nodded.

Chapter 14
Mrs Curtis

Blue, Apricot and Terry exited the cave in silence, squinting into the sunlight. They mounted their horses and rode slowly in the direction of the shoreline. The contrast of such a beautiful morning with the darkness they'd discovered could not have been greater. Blue, who was riding pillion behind Apricot, looked over her shoulder at Terry's deflated figure, rocking from side to side, as he navigated his horse between the rocks. "Does your uncle know the alcohol for his parties is supplied by such vile people? If not, you should tell him."

Apricot shrugged. "I'm sure he doesn't imagine it's supplied by angels. And how was I supposed to discover the Klan's involvement? The *one* rule he gave me was stay away from this place."

"Which is why I'm surprised you haven't been down there before. Just thinking of that poor man, *Dogsbody*, makes me shudder," said Blue, shuddering.

"I've met unhappier people," replied Apricot, philosophically.

"*Honestly*? He's treated no better than a slave."

"Well, that's the KKK for you. They've always been partial to it."

"They're disgusting."

"Yes, of course, they are, but they're also a legitimate political party."

"You should let your uncle know he's supporting them."

"And how's he doing that?"

"By buying their alcohol."

"Uncle didn't make the ridiculous prohibition laws. How else is he to get champagne for his parties? Although I'm not sure why I'm defending him, he might even be one of the six million."

"Do you think he is?" breathed Blue.

Apricot shook her head. "No. I don't why I say these things. If he was, he would hardly employ and treat black workers so well."

"Then *tell him* how the KKK are supplying the liquor for his parties."

"Oh, dear love, he already knows *everything* that goes on around here."

Blue glanced over her shoulder at Terry. "If that boy was any more miserable, he'd fall off his horse. We are still going to meet his mother, aren't we?"

"You still want to? After that?"

"More than ever. We need to take Terry's mind off what just happened."

Twenty minutes later, Terry rode up alongside them. "Where are you going? This way leads to my place…"

"We're going to meet your mother, remember?" smiled Blue.

"You were being serious?"

"We wouldn't have said it otherwise," said Apricot.

"Ma's going to have a heart attack," said Terry, finding a smile.

They spotted Mrs Curtis a short walk from her front door. She was dressed in a red floral dress and nattering to her younger sister, Petal, who visited her every Sunday from the Bronx. The women were so animated, so engaged in conversation after their church visit, that they didn't hear the forlornly stepping horses until they were upon them. Mrs Curtis took her sister's arm and guided her to the side of the road. Apricot and Blue were riding ahead of Terry on the narrow lane and when Mrs Curtis clapped eyes on Apricot, she squeezed her sister's arm. "Ouch," said Petal. Mrs Curtis motioned with her eyes to the white horse that she'd seen ridden by Mr De Croy's niece but, as Fate would have it, only from a distance.

"It's Miss *De Croy*," whispered Mrs Curtis.

"It is?" replied Petal, pushing her thick-rimmed spectacles closer to her face.

Apricot raised a hand, waved, smiled and said, "Hello, Mrs Curtis! Oh, I'm sorry. I didn't mean to startle you. I'm Apricot De Croy and this is Blue Tibbs. We've accompanied Terry home. He's feeling a bit peaky and we wanted to see him safely into your care."

"*Very* gracious of you, Miss De Croy," said Mrs Curtis with a slight, awkward bow of her head. She looked up at her son, the expression on her face bringing a smile to his. "Terrance looks quite alright now," she murmured.

"So he does," said Apricot, glancing over her shoulder at him. "Your son speaks very highly of you, Mrs Curtis."

"He *does*?"

"Yes," said Blue from behind Apricot, "It's nice to meet you, I'm Harry Tibbs's daughter, the new head gardener?"

Mrs Curtis smiled. "Terry has said how friendly you are. It's nice to meet you both. This is my sister, Petal."

"Hello," said Petal, enjoying the spectacle.

"I bet Terry has never said how friendly I am," sighed Apricot.

"I, well…" spluttered Mrs Curtis.

"Let's face it, it's not like he had any cause to."

"You're alright as it goes, Miss Apricot," said Terry.

"*Terrance Curtis*," said Mrs Curtis, "have you forgotten who you're talking to?"

"That's quite all right isn't it," said Blue giving Apricot a discreet nudge.

Apricot cleared her throat. "Terry is welcome to speak his mind."

Terry sat straight backed in his saddle, beaming.

"You better hold onto those reins tight," said Mrs Curtis. "We just got back from Church, Miss De Croy, where the Pastor reminded us that pride comes before a fall." Terry went boss-eyed, slid sideways out of his saddle, and landed in a heap on the ground. "The Pastor was right," he pronounced.

"Foolish boy! Get up this instant." Mrs Curtis drew a deep breath. "If you're not busy, Miss De Croy, Miss Tibbs, you're very welcome to come in and join us for a pot of tea. And a slice of homemade apple pie?"

Apricot stroked the top of Sheba's head. "If it wouldn't be an imposition, then tea sounds delightful," she said, raising an eyebrow at Terry as he climbed back onto his feet.

"An imposition? Goodness no, it wouldn't be an imposition. It would be a honour to welcome you into our home, wouldn't it, Petal?"

"Oh, yes. An honour," smiled Petal.

Mrs Curtis had laid out her best china and poured five cups of steaming tea from a pot. She cut thick slices of her apple pie, still warm from the oven, and placed a slice for each of them on a plate. Apricot, who found herself seated at the head of the table, was the first to speak. "Thank you for this delightful tea. I was parched and famished," she said, plunging her fork into her pie.

"My pleasure, Miss De Croy. A humble offering surely, compared to what you must have up at the chateau?"

"The chateau may be grand but there's not much in the way of the personal touch there," she said, placing the pie in her mouth. "Delicious…"

"It's an old family recipe," beamed Mrs Curtis.

"I'm quite certain that we De Croys have *no such* recipes."

Petal picked her cup up from its saucer. "How is Mr De Croy?" she asked before taking a sip.

"Petal!" admonished Mrs Curtis, "you shouldn't enquire so after Mr De Croy as though he's a common acquaintance."

Apricot chewed her pie thoughtfully and swallowed it. "I don't see much of my uncle. *No one* does. It's no secret he's a bit of a recluse. Spends his days talking on the numerous telephones on his desk."

"He's can't be a complete recluse," said Blue. "He came to London last year and discovered Dad's landscaping talents."

"Oh, that," said Apricot. "The wife of a *very* important business acquaintance, a Mrs Eustace-Brown, passed away suddenly. Uncle said he that felt compelled to attend her funeral."

Mrs Curtis crossed herself.

"I still haven't seen your uncle," said Blue.

"My, you've only been here five minutes, Miss Tibbs," chuckled Mrs Curtis.

"Please, call me Blue."

Mrs Curtis nodded. "Alright, *Blue*."

Apricot forked another piece of pie. "Your father met my uncle. What did he have to say about him?" she said, placing it in her mouth.

"He liked him," shrugged Blue.

"And?" said Terry.

"And Dad prefers an economy of words. At least, that's how Mum puts it."

"Well now, there's no harm in choosing your words wisely," said Mrs Curtis, having chosen hers.

"You could hardly say if he *didn't* like him," said Terry.

"She absolutely could," said Apricot, exchanging a glance with Blue.

Petal raised her teacup to her lips. "How delightful to make a friend so unexpectedly."

"And how are your family settling in? Quite the responsibility being in charge of Mr De Croy's gardens," said Mrs Curtis.

"Maybe, but it's one that Dad relishes…"

"Is that for me?" said Terry, noticing an unopened brown paper package on the counter.

"Yes, Terrance."

Terry jumped up and retrieved the package. He sat back down, ripped it open, and pulled out a magazine.

"Astronomers Quarterly," said Blue, reading the title on the cover.

"What Terrance doesn't know about the planets in the heavens isn't worth knowing," said Mrs Curtis, smiling at her son.

"Who's that on the cover?" asked Blue.

"Edwin Hubble," said Terry gazing at the picture of the silver haired man smoking a pipe. "He's a genius. He just proved the existence of other galaxies outside our own milky way. Imagine that?"

"And that's an important discovery because?" said Apricot.

"Because it means the universe could be infinite," said Terry.

"And that's important because?" repeated Apricot.

Terry gazed from Apricot to the picture of Edwin Hubble and back again. "If the universe is infinite, *anything* could be out there."

"Not sure I like the idea of *anything* being out there," said Apricot. "If I'm honest, I'm not particularly comfortable with the notion of *something* being out there."

"Rest assured, Miss De Croy, there is nothing but empty space. If not, God would have told us about his other creations in the Bible."

"Is that so, Terrance?" Petal asked him, mischievously.

Terry pulled a face at his aunt. "Maybe He would and maybe He kept some things a secret."

Good answer thought Blue.

"What are you grinning about?" Apricot asked her.

"Nothing," said Blue, taking a sip of tea.

"Maybe you aren't feeling well after all. Why haven't you touched your apple pie?" Mrs Curtis asked her son.

"Must have lost my appetite," said Terry, opening his magazine and sighing at the sight of something on a page.

"What is it?" asked Blue.

"It's a Rocket 3000…" said Terry turning the page around to show it.

"That's an impressive telescope," said Blue.

"I'll say. None better."

"Would you like another slice of pie, Miss De Croy?"

"I'd love one, thank you," said Apricot, lifting her plate towards her beaming host.

Chapter 15
Something on Blue's mind

At the dinner table that evening, Sheila watched her daughter pushing her food around her plate. There was clearly something unpalatable on her mind. Harry was miles away too, trying to think about *anything* other than his memories of Flanders that would bully their way onto his mind if he didn't make an effort to think about something else. Sheila was used to Harry's long silences and understood why, but she was at a complete loss as to why Blue was so distant. She placed her knife and fork together on her empty plate and dabbed at the sides of her mouth with a napkin. "How was your day, Blue?"

Blue glanced up at her mother and then, as though she'd imagined the question, returned her gaze to her plate. Sheila placed her napkin down deliberately upon the table. "*Blue,*" she said, raising her voice a little more than she'd intended.

"Yes?"

"Don't you want your pork chops? I thought they were your favourite?"

"They're delicious…"

"How do you know? You've haven't touched them."

Blue dropped her fork onto the plate and sat back in her chair. "I'm not hungry."

"Whatever is the matter? Don't you like it here?"

Blue shook her head. "I like it very much."

"It's natural if you miss your old friends, but you'll make new friends just as soon as you start school in September."

"I've made a couple of friends already."

"Have you? That's good," said Harry as though he'd just woken up.

"Who?" asked Sheila.

"Terry, for one."

"Terry?"

"Yes, he's a stable boy. He looks after Apricot's horse."

"And who's *Apricot*?"

"She's Mr De Croy's niece."

Harry nodded. "Miss Apricot De Croy is Mr De Croy's closest relative. I gather she's heir to one of the largest fortunes in the country. Not the most likeable of young ladies, I'm told. What's more, she's allowed to ride her horse carte blanche around the grounds. I gather she has a habit of making a mess of things."

"Who told you all this?" said Sheila.

"Bob Martin, my number two."

"And how old is Miss De Croy? She sounds awfully irresponsible."

"She's fourteen, Mum."

"And how do you know that?"

"Because she's the *other* friend I've made. I'll have a word with her about where she rides in future, Dad."

Harry and Sheila glanced at one another and then looked at their daughter.

"Apricot's really nice once you get to know her. Honest."

"And when did you manage to do that?" asked Sheila.

"We spent the morning together with Terry."

"Her stable boy?"

"Uh, huh."

"Is he the black boy I've seen riding?" said Harry.

"Yes, most likely."

"Bob gave me the impression that Miss De Croy treats the staff like servants from a bygone era. Certainly not like friends."

"Dad, honestly, her reputation as an ogre is exaggerated. She's just a bit…"

"A bit what?" asked Sheila.

"Lonely, I think."

"Loneliness is no excuse for rudeness," said Sheila, pouring herself a glass of orange juice.

Harry dabbed at the sides of his mouth with his napkin. "What did you do with your new friends today?"

"We went for a ride along the beach."

"*You* went for a ride?" said Sheila.

"I was riding pillion behind Apricot on Sheba."

Harry smiled knowingly at his wife. "Sheba is Miss De Croy's horse. A thoroughbred. Purchased from the Sultan of Oman, no less."

"Is it any wonder she has problems relating to everyday people if she's so spoiled?"

"I'm an everyday person, and she relates to me just fine."

"Ah, but you are an *exceptional* everyday person," said Harry.

"I don't think so, but thank you."

"Our daughter is not so exceptional that she wouldn't break her neck if she fell of the back of a powerful horse."

"Word is, that despite her tendency for trampling hedges and bushes, Miss De Croy is a very competent equestrian," said Harry.

"Well then, in the light of making such a well-connected *friend*, why do you look so miserable?" asked Sheila.

Blue folded her arms. "I was reminded of something this morning."

"And it ruined your appetite?"

"A fact," nodded Blue.

"About what?"

"The Ku Klux Klan."

"For goodness sake," said Sheila, throwing up her hands, "the Ku Klux Klan put you off your pork chops?"

Blue switched her gaze to her father. "They have *six million* members!"

Harry wiped some crumbs from the table. "I wish I could tell you something different, Blue."

"Has this Terry been putting ideas in your head?" said Sheila.

"And what if he has?" said Harry.

"Can't you see? He's upset her."

"We shouldn't shield our daughter from the darker side of human nature. If we do, she'll grow up being ill prepared for life."

"And being exposed to the darker side of human nature has obviously done you a world of good." At this allusion to the war, Harry shrank back in his chair and looked visibly smaller. Sheila exchanged a glance with Blue. "I'm sorry, Harry, I…"

Harry waved a hand before his eyes and drew a slow breath. "I'm not saying we should send our daughter off to war. Just that she should be aware of any serious threats to society. And the Ku Klux Klan *is* such a threat."

"And what is it they want?" asked Blue.

"They're white supremacists," shrugged Harry, "they believe in the superiority of the white race. Their ideal America is one with as few black people as possible. And only then in positions of servitude. As I told you in the car, they have very little time for Jews, Catholics or immigrants either." Blue was leaning forwards, her elbows on the table, hungry for information. Harry exchanged a glance with his wife. "The Ku Klux Klan were founded in the 1800s. They flourished for a decade before going into remission."

"Remission? You make them sound like a cancer, Harry."

"That's what they were on society. *Are.* And much like a cancerous growth, they came out of remission and began to grow again a decade ago. Since then they've gone from strength to strength. A phoenix risen from the ashes. Or, should I say a dragon. It's their symbol."

"Then something must be done to stop them," said Blue.

Sheila stood up and began gathering up the plates. "That's for politicians to worry about. Not you, young lady."

Chapter 16
Blue calls on a friend

The next morning after breakfast, Blue asked her father what he had planned for the day. "I'm meeting Bob at the lake," he said, folding his newspaper and standing up. "Apparently, it smells something rotten, particularly on the southern bank."

"Can I come with you?" said Blue, standing and darting off into her room to put on her shoes.

"Yes, why not…"

On their way there, Blue and Harry passed by the stable yard.

"Dad?"

"Yes, Blue?"

"Would you like to meet Terry?"

Harry glanced at his wristwatch.

"Hey!" called Blue as Terry emerged from a barn carrying a saddle. Terry opened his mouth to meet one good 'hey!' with another, but at the sight of the new head groundsman, he opted for "Morning!" instead.

Blue took her father's hand and led him over to where Terry was now standing and gripping the heavy saddle.

"Terry, meet Dad, Dad meet Terry."

"Hello there," said Harry.

"Hello sir."

Frank smiled and extended a hand for him to shake. "How do you do?"

Terry put down the saddle, wiped his hand on his overalls, and shook hands. "How do you do, sir."

Blue glanced in the direction they were headed. "We're going to check on the boating lake. Apparently, it stinks."

Terry looked surprised. "The boating lake's a real swanky place for Mr De Croy's guests."

"Yes, and they've been complaining about the smell," said Harry.

"What can you do about that, sir?"

"That's what I'm headed down there to find out. We may need to drain and refill it with fresh water."

Terry whistled through his teeth. "It's a big old boating lake. Must hold a lot of water."

"Yes, although technically, it's just a pond."

"Yes, sir. A true lake is fed by a larger body of water."

Harry took off his trilby hat and began fanning himself. "Quite so. You must attend a fine school."

"It's okay, I guess."

"Terry's an expert on the universe," enthused Blue.

"I wouldn't say I was an *expert*."

"Then it's only a matter of time," smiled Blue.

"Speaking of time, it was good to meet you, Terry."

"Yes, sir. And you."

"See you later," said Blue.

"You all have a good day."

Harry and Blue began to walk away. "Oh," said Blue, darting back. "Have you seen Apricot this morning?" she asked.

Terry shook his head. "Nope. And there are no instructions to get Sheba ready."

"She's probably having a lie in."

"That'd be right, it's all right for some," said Terry, hauling the saddle up off the ground.

The boating lake was surrounded by tall trees, beyond which a far greater expanse of water, Long Island Sound, glistened in the sun's early rays. As they crossed a lawn towards the lake, Blue placed a hand over her nose, and Harry rolled his eyes and glanced up at the heavens.

"Reports of its stinkiness have not been exaggerated," said Blue.

"The last fella must have put this off for some time."

Blue cast her gaze over the picturesque lake with its smattering of tiny islands and pastel boathouses, arranged at perfect intervals around its edges. "Makes you wonder how he got away with it," she commented.

Harry ruffled her hair.

"What was that for?"

"For reading my mind."

"You're going to drain it then?"

Harry nodded. "It's long overdue." Across the lake a figure emerged from a boat house. "Looks like Bob?" said Harry, squinting.

"I'll leave you to it, Dad."

"Don't you want to meet him?"

"Yes. But not now. There's something I need to do."

"Oh, yes?"

"A girl is entitled to her secrets."

"Indeed, she is. But you stay out of trouble."

"I'll do my best," said Blue as she wandered in the direction of the chateau, its tallest turrets just visible above the trees.

Blue wended her way through the beautiful grounds, mindful that somewhere below Chateau De Croy was a place where bootlegging Ku Klux Klan members unloaded liquor from mine carts. She made her way past a row of sculptured hedgerows and grasped for the confidence of someone who was simply calling on a friend. A fly had taken a liking to her, and it buzzed about her head, forcing her to repeatedly swipe it away from her face. To make matters worse, she had an itch in a delicate place that she didn't think appropriate to scratch in public and it made her walk awkwardly. Despite these irritations, she held her head up as best she could. Blue remembered something about attack being the best form of defence and decided to knock at the mansion's main entrance. The one reserved for the most important visitors. She walked up the steps to the front door and stood between two fluted columns that would not have looked out of place at the entrance to the Roman Colosseum. She examined the towering black door for a knocker or a bell or *anything* to draw attention to herself. Seeing nothing, she balled a hand into a fist and rapped on the door with her knuckles. It didn't make the slightest sound, but it did hurt. Blue shook her hand, turned, and gazed down the tree-lined driveway to the barely visible gate house. "There's always someone in there," she murmured.

It was a warm morning and a welcome breeze rustled the leaves of the trees that lined the driveway as she walked below their branches.

The gate house was a dark bricked cottage where ivy climbed the walls and a sleepy-looking German Shepherd lay chained to a pole before a kennel. The dog raised its head, sniffed in Blue's direction, considered the possibility of barking, but due to the melody my orchestra was playing for it, thought the better of it. "Hello," said Blue. The dog stretched but made no reply. The sound of coughing came from the gate house and Blue looked over at its two open doors: one on her side of the gate, the other on the public side. "Is that your master?" said Blue, heading for the closest door. She poked her head inside. "Hello?" Blue heard the sound of a newspaper being hastily folded. A man in a dark uniform appeared at the end of a corridor, his mono brow crinkling at the sight of the youngster who'd disturbed him. "Can I help you?"

"I hope so. I just came from the chateau," said Blue, motioning over her shoulder."

"And?"

"And, I knocked on the door, but no one answered."

"That'd be right," he said, lifting his peaked cap and running a hand through his hair. "Any callers to the house have to come through here. Do you live on the estate?" he asked, almost adding 'kid'.

"Yes. My father looks after the grounds."

"And you have *business* at the chateau?"

"Not business. I was calling on my friend, Miss Apricot De Croy?"

At the mention of Apricot, the man stood up straighter and his tone softened considerably. "Of course, Miss. Whom shall I say is calling?"

"Blue. Blue Tibbs."

"Right you are, Miss Tibbs. I'll telephone ahead for you. Let the butler know you're on your way."

"Thank you," smiled Blue.

A minute later, Blue was making her way back along the drive towards the chateau. As she approached, the towering black door opened. The butler, whom she'd followed into the mansion on her first expedition to the chateau, stood rigid with a hand held behind his back as though it concealed a stick to chase her away with. "Miss Tibbs?"

"Guilty," chirped Blue.

"You're calling on Miss De Croy?"

"Yes. Is she in?" asked Blue, leaning to her right and looking past him into the cavernous entrance hall.

"Is Miss De Croy expecting you?"

"No. I thought I'd surprise her."

"I see. Miss De Croy has not yet risen," replied the butler as though talking about a vampire.

"I suppose I am rather early."

From the butler's poker-faced expression, it was impossible to tell whether he agreed or not.

"She did say I could call on her anytime."

"*Indeed*, Miss?" said the butler, as though he couldn't quite believe it.

"Indeed," said Blue, quietly.

"That being the case, would you like me to send Miss De Croy's maid to her room to wake her?"

"If you wouldn't mind," swallowed Blue.

"Mind? I exist to serve," said the butler, his cheek twitching irritably.

The butler led Blue to a waiting room where reading material had been provided for visitors. She lowered herself into a brown leather armchair that practically swallowed her up and reached for a copy of Time Magazine. On its front cover was a picture John Calvin Coolidge, the then president of the United States.

Twenty minutes passed by slowly due to a grandfather clock that Blue's gaze kept returning to until finally, the door opened, and a red-faced maid entered. "Would you care to follow me; I'll show you to Miss De Croy's room, Miss."

"Thank you," said Blue, pushing herself up out of the armchair.

She followed the maid to an elevator on the ground floor that was so well concealed behind an oak panel that Blue practically jumped when it split asunder to reveal the red carpeted elevator and its operator.

Blue stood between the elevator's operator, a young man with thinning blonde hair and the maid and sensed some friction. "I would *never* have imagined there was a lift, or should I say an *elevator*, behind that panel," she said, breaking the awkward silence.

"No Miss?" said the maid, scowling past her at the elevator attendant.

"No."

"Well, you never can tell what might be *lurking* in a house such as this, Miss."

Blue breathed a sigh of relief as the lift lurched to a stop and the doors opened onto a stately corridor lined with cabinets filled with porcelain.

"Wow. It's like a museum," said Blue as she followed the maid out of the lift.

"It's Mr De Croy's collection of Sevres porcelain. Only the King of England has a larger one."

"Really?"

"That's what they say."

"It's lovely…" said Blue, casting her gaze left and right.

"Priceless."

"Blimey. Must be stressful to dust?"

"I wouldn't know. They bring in a team of experts for that," said the maid as they reached a set of double doors at the end of the corridor. She tapped on the door twice, counted to a pre-arranged number in her head and, hearing no reply, opened it. Blue gazed into the room that, just as she had imagined, would pass muster for any aspiring fairytale princess, and half expected to see Beauty herself asleep on the canopied four poster bed. Sensing Blue's hesitation, the maid stepped past her into the room. "Come in and make yourself comfortable, Miss De Croy will be with you shortly." The moment that Blue stepped into the room, the maid stepped back out again and closed the door as though she'd lured her into a trap. Blue walked into the centre of the room, her eyes taking in a pony-sized rocking horse, upon which the latest fashions had been flung, presumably for the maid to put away later. There was a gothic chest of drawers that wouldn't even *fit* into Blue's bedroom, a fireplace in which she could stand with no danger of bumping her head against its shelf and, in an alcove, directly opposite, a two-metre-tall doll's house with at least a hundred rooms. Blue stood before the doll's house and peered into a ballroom where painted porcelain couples, seemingly frozen in time, danced to a waltz. "You won't find it in there," said Apricot from behind her.

"You almost gave me a heart attack. I won't find what in here?" said Blue, glancing at Apricot in her red velvet dressing gown.

"The worm you're undoubtedly looking for at this time of the morning," said Apricot as a grandfather clock in the room began to chime.

"I must say the worm is wearing a *very* fine dressing gown."

"*I'm* the worm?"

"You are."

Apricot sighed stoically. "I do resemble a worm in the mornings."

"I should look like such a worm," said Blue with a roll of her eyes. "Nice doll's house."

"Thanks. It was a birthday present when I was eight."

"*Eight*? How did you reach the upper floors?"

"With this… stand back," said Apricot crouching down and sticking a finger through a gold ring in the polished dark wood floor. She lifted out a secret panel that concertinaed silently up to become three steps. "You're sorry you asked. I can tell," said Apricot.

"No. It's just so…"

"Over the top?"

"So perfect…" said Blue, turning and facing into the room.

"I remember being impressed too when I first saw it," said Apricot as her bed covers began to move and *something* began to crawl out of them. "Relax, it's just Anastasia," said Apricot as a white cat with a ruby studded collar crawled into view.

"She's beautiful," said Blue stepping towards her.

Apricot gazed lovingly at her cat. "She's an exotic short hair."

"I've never seen a cat with such big eyes. Is it okay if I…?" she asked, holding out a hand.

Apricot nodded. "She simply adores having her ears rubbed."

"Not her eyes?"

"Funny woman. So? Are you going to tell me to what I owe the pleasure of your company so early?"

Blue sat on the end of the bed where Anastasia pressed against her, her fluffy white tail up. "Must there be a reason?" said Blue, stroking her head.

"I think somehow there *must*. Anastasia likes you. That's no mean feat. She's taken many a swipe at Mary."

"Mary?"

"The maid who brought you up here. So, what is it? Are you going to keep me in suspense all morning?"

"The mine cart," said Blue, pointedly.

"Surely you don't want to go back there?"

"No, but…"

Apricot drew a deep breath and nodded. "Oh, of course, silly me. You're curious about where the contraband is dropped off at *this* end."

"Aren't you?"

"Not particularly. I've always known that the alcohol is delivered *somehow*. Deliveries take place all the time. They're just part and parcel of a house like this."

"Maybe, but these deliveries are different."

"You mean illegal and dangerous. Have you always had this craving to seek out places that are best stayed well away from?"

"Probably. You must be a little curious? Somewhere under this house is a *mine cart* station."

"Oh, dear love. It could be you're letting your imagination run away with itself."

"So, let's go and find out," said Blue, standing up.

Apricot threw up her hands. "Give me five minutes to get dressed in something appropriate for such a mission," she said, walking towards a door that led into her dressing room.

Blue glanced at the bell-rope that hung by the side of the bed. "Aren't you going to pull this and summon someone? You can't seriously be contemplating dressing yourself?"

Apricot made a detour to a couch strewn with pillows, picked one up, and smiled as she hurled it across the room.

Blue ducked as it flew over her head. "Good throw," she said as Apricot disappeared through a door.

Apricot returned dressed in tight fitting black trousers and black shirt, her long blonde hair pushed back from her face by a diamante head band. "You look like cat burglar advert straight out of Vogue," said Blue, admiringly.

"We are going on a covert mission, are we not?"

"Yes. But you do live here so…"

"Just because I live here it doesn't mean that certain areas are *supposed* to be off limits. Particularly those areas where dangerous smugglers must surely lurk in shadows," said Apricot, making claws of her hands and stalking her way across the room. She stopped just before Blue. "They'll make mincemeat out of you in such a girly dress," she said, looking her up and down.

"I've never had a pair of trousers."

"You are joking? These are the *1*920s not the 1820s."

"Very fashionable, I'm sure."

Chapter 17
Below Chateau De Croy

"Where's this wild goose chase to lead us?" contemplated Apricot as they made their way back up the corridor.

"Down," said Blue.

"Yes, that much I had gathered."

They began their descent of the mansion's main staircase, at the bottom of which stood two burly guards in dark suits.

"Ex-army," said Apricot.

"They look it. Are they really necessary?"

"Probably not. Uncle stepped up security after the robbery."

"You were robbed?"

"Yes, I'm surprised you didn't hear about it. Caused quite a stir in the papers. The thieves got away with a valuable painting. A Turner."

"I remember seeing Turner's paintings on a school trip. Lots of golden sunsets?"

"Sounds about right. J.M.W. *loved* a sunlit landscape. It's awfully rare that one of his works comes up for auction. But one did. In London. Come to think of it, it coincided with Mrs Eustace-Brown's funeral. It sealed the deal as regards my uncle visiting your country."

"And it's been stolen already?"

"Hence the muscle," said Apricot as they reached the bottom of the stairs where the two men stood like granite statues.

Apricot led Blue to a hidden door beside a fireplace in the main hallway. It opened onto a narrow staircase. "It's a servant's stairwell," said Apricot, holding the door ajar so Blue could pass her. "Leads down to the kitchens."

"Good thinking, the kitchens would have been my first port of call," murmured Blue, edging past her.

"You mean you were contemplating this madness on your own?"

"By hook or by crook I think I would have, yes."

"You'd have *been* a crook if you'd come alone."

"I prefer to call it healthy curiosity."

"I know you do, darling. I just hope you never have to test your 'healthy curiosity' defence before a judge."

The kitchens contained half a dozen staff members having a meeting around a table. At the table's head, the chateau's cook, Mrs Bridge-Stock, sat straight of back and stern of face, while her assistants sat in order of their inferiority around her. At the sight of Apricot, the underlings facing the door sprang to their feet. Mrs Bridge-Stock glared at them before turning in her seat and seeing Apricot. "Miss De Croy? To what do we owe this pleasure?" she asked, unable to hide her irritation at being interrupted.

"Frightfully sorry to disturb you. I'm giving a friend a guided tour."

Mrs Bridge-Stock eyeballed Blue as though she thought she recognised her but couldn't quite place her. "Of the *kitchens*?"

"Oh, are *these* the kitchens?" replied Apricot casting her gaze about.

Mrs Bridge-Stock stood up and unconsciously balled her hands into fists. "If you're lost then the door behind you will take you back to the main house, *madam*."

"I was aware of that, Mrs Bridge-Stock. You look a little vexed. Does Mrs Bridge-Stock look vexed to you, Blue?"

"A tad, yes."

"Well, if she thinks she can intimidate me she's got another thing coming," growled Apricot.

"Intimidate you? I, I ..." spluttered Mrs Bridge-Stock.

"No need to trouble yourself. *Sit* and carry on with your meeting." Mrs Bridge-Stock sat begrudgingly. When Apricot didn't turn around, but walked past the table with Blue in tow, heading towards the pantry, Mrs Bridge-Stock didn't know where to look. She settled on the heavens beyond the ceiling. "Little madam," she murmured under her breath.

"I heard that!" called the little madam.

Apricot led Blue into the pantry which was comprised of a series of small rooms where the chateau's food supplies were stored. "Before you say anything, Mrs Bridge-Stock is a bully who makes her staff miserable."

"I actually thought you were polite, considering."

"Considering?"

"Considering how she…" said Blue, holding up her hands and making fists of them. "You don't think she hits those poor girls, do you?"

"No."

"How can you be so sure?"

Apricot tapped the end of her nose. "Because I have a spy amongst the servants."

"You are the dark horse," said Blue, admiringly.

"I would simply die of boredom around here without some gossip. And it only costs me two dollars a month."

"You *pay* someone? An informant?"

"Yes, why not?"

"Who are they?" asked Blue, following Apricot into a whitewashed room where canned goods were stacked on shelves. Apricot moved to the side of the door and rested her back against the wall. "Unless I'm very much mistaken, you're about to find out," she said, noticing a broken nail. As Apricot contemplated the nail with a grimace, they heard footsteps and, a moment later, a mousey haired girl with very little neck stepped into the room.

"And here she is now," said Apricot.

Blue peered at Apricot's informant as though inspecting her for cracks.

Apricot furrowed her brow. "*Must* you study her like that? You'll make her uncomfortable."

"Sorry, it's nice to meet you. I'm Blue," said Blue, offering a hand for the informant to shake.

"Annie, Miss," replied the girl, shaking Blue's hand and adding a curtsy.

"No need to curtsy. I'm not royalty."

"Are you not, Miss?"

"Does she *look* like royalty?"

"You can never be too sure, Miss De Croy. Not since you had that Hungarian princess over last year."

"You're friends with a Hungarian princess?"

"Not anymore. But that's a story for another time."

Annie glanced behind her into the corridor. "I told Mrs Bridge-Stock someone ought to keep an eye on you while you were running amok down here."

"Running amok. Nice touch."

"Yes, Miss. I think it struck a chord with her."

"We need your help finding something, Annie."

"Oh, yes?"

"Take us to where the liquor is delivered," said Apricot, motioning to the ground with her eyes.

Annie's mouth dropped open and she crossed herself. "I don't know anything about it."

"Do please calm yourself. Take us there and there'll be an extra five dollars in it for you this month."

"*Five* dollars? Really?" said Annie, glancing back and forth between Apricot and Blue.

"That's right," said Apricot, rummaging around in the front pocket of her trousers and drawing out a crumpled five-dollar bill. "All yours," she continued, holding it up.

"And no one will ever know it was me who showed you?" said Annie, gazing at it.

"Cross my heart," said Apricot, not bothering to do so.

Annie snatched the five-dollar bill from Apricot's grasp and stuffed it down her top. "Well then, follow me," she said, making her way past them.

Blue's mouth fell open and Apricot winked at her.

And so, accompanied by a melody that would have suited three inquisitive mice equally well, Blue and Apricot followed Annie through a number of interconnected storage rooms until they came upon a staircase that led down into the wine cellar. It was a chilly and musty place where bottles of wine had been left to ferment long before prohibition. "Nice stash," said Blue, touching a bottle that left her fingers covered in dust.

"Some of these bottles are over a hundred years old," said Apricot.

Annie stopped walking. "You'll find it behind there, Miss," she said, pointing to stack of barrels at the rear of the cellar.

"Find what?" asked Apricot.

"The trap door. Where they bring the liquor up from."

"Show us," said Apricot, walking towards the three-metre-high stack of barrels.

Annie remained rooted to the spot. "*Please* don't ask me to get any closer. I showed you what you asked for," she said glancing over her shoulder at the exit.

"You're frightened?" said Blue.

"Oh, Miss! I wouldn't go near that trap door for all the money in the world! And I hope you don't neither."

"Why? Because of the bootleggers?"

"No," said Annie, "because what lies beneath is haunted!"

"Haunted? Don't be ridiculous. There are no such things as ghosts," said Apricot, flashing a glance at Blue.

"Someone's been pulling your leg," chuckled Blue.

"Oh, no, Miss," replied Annie assuredly. "Everyone knows about the two ghosts."

"*Two*? Sounds awfully specific," said Apricot.

"Yes, Miss. They sit together playing chess. Doomed for all eternity." Annie gazed down towards the ground and whatever lay below. "Billy Riley *swore* he saw them."

"Billy Riley?" said Blue.

"Billy's a general dogsbody around here," scoffed Apricot. Blue's admonishing expression was a reminder of the poor man at the other end of the mine cart line. Apricot shrugged, semi-apologetically, and turned her attention to Annie. "What did Billy see?"

"The same as all the others – one of the ghosts is a British soldier from the time of the War of…"

"Independence?" said Apricot, her mouth going suddenly dry.

"Yes, Miss. That's it. He wears a red uniform. And he's got a musket by his side," she added by way of a warning.

"And the other one," asked Blue.

"The other's a black man in chains, Miss."

"It sounds like an unlikely pair to me," said Blue.

Annie shook her head. "No, it isn't. Don't you know? Back in the olden days a British garrison was right here, where the chateau is. They had a prison where they kept slaves. Those two are the ghosts of a slave and his guard. Or so they say."

"If that were true it would be quite something. I've always wanted to see a ghost," said Blue.

Apricot and Annie gazed at her. "Are you *mental*?" asked Apricot.

Blue nodded. "But I'm certain that we're not going to see any ghosts. It's obviously a story that's been made up to stop people going down there. And it's worked," said Blue, motioning towards Annie as though she were exhibit one.

"I suppose that could be true," said Apricot.

"But Teddy Riley swore blind he saw them!" bleated Ann.

"If he did, then his imagination must have been running away with itself," declared Blue.

Apricot nodded stoically. "Either that or he's a liar," she said, attempting to put her faith in her expensive education rather than the hearsay of a servant. "I imagine you still want to go down there?"

"More. Than. Ever. Come on," said Blue, edging between two stacks of barrels.

Apricot remained rooted to the spot. She glanced down at the shaking hand that now grasped her elbow, then up into the eyes of the girl who was holding her. "It will be OK, Annie. Unhand me, this instant."

"Yes, Miss, sorry I hadn't realised…"

"Relax. I will still be around to supplement your wages. Have no fear of that," said Apricot, forcing her chin up as she followed Blue around to the other side of the barrels.

"You going to give me hand with this thing or what?" said Blue, kneeling over the trap door.

Chapter 18
Back in time

They lifted up the trap door until it came to rest against the cellar's brick wall. Below them was a flight of stairs just wide enough for smugglers to carry crates up into the cellar. Oil lamps were hung from the walls and lit the way down. "Goodness… it goes on for awfully long way," said Apricot, squinting and failing in her attempt to see the bottom.

"Yes, but it's well-lit."

"Isn't it just. I have mixed feelings about that."

"Would you have preferred it to be pitch black?" said Blue, reaching into a pocket and taking out a thin, battery powered flashlight. "I brought this just in case. Although, it doesn't look like we're going to need it."

"If the lamps have been lit, it makes you wonder who for?"

"Not for a couple of ghosts that's for sure."

"How can you be so casual? I'm all for *deeds*, but smugglers are dangerous criminals, darling."

"Need I remind you who you are, *Miss* De Croy?"

Apricot considered her position for a moment. "I suppose they are business people. And employees of my uncle when it comes to it."

"*Exactly*. So, think of it as an inspection. On your uncle's behalf."

"Alright. I will," said Apricot raising her chin.

Blue counted eighty-eight steps before they reached the bottom where they found themselves in a wide, red brick corridor that smelled of…

"Gunpowder?" sniffed Blue.

"And how do you know what gunpowder smells like? Smells more like moth balls to me."

"And how do you know what moth balls smell like?"

"Funny woman. Most of my clothes are silk and moths adore it. *Ghastly* things," shuddered Apricot.

"It's very quiet… sounds as deserted as the beach end. Come on," said Blue, stepping towards an archway at the end of the corridor. They passed under the arch and entered a round space where eight fluted columns rose up to a cavernous ceiling. "… it's more like a miniature Colosseum in Rome rather than something the British Empire built."

"Us Brits were influenced by the architecture of ancient Rome," said Blue, gazing about rapt.

"Weren't most empires that came after the Roman one?"

"Well, aren't we a couple of empire building scholars? I doubt you'd have found these in the Colosseum," said Blue, pointing down at the mine cart tracks that came to a halt in the centre of the circular space.

"You found what you were looking for it seems. The end of the line below Chateau De Croy."

"I would love to be a fly on the wall during a delivery. Come on, let's have a nosey around," said Blue, taking the torch from her pocket and switching it on. "For the nooks and crannies."

"I'm not sure it's the done thing for young ladies to go looking in *nooks and crannies*. Goodness only knows what they might find."

"Precisely," said Blue, turning on the torch and aiming its beam up into the darkest recesses of the ceiling where a spider's web the size of a duvet was home to a plump arachnid. Apricot shuddered. "That's disgusting. Still wish you were a fly on the wall in here?"

Blue drew a deep, nerve steadying breath, lowered the beam and followed the tracks towards an opening in the wall. On the other side, they found themselves in a dark corridor where a flickering bulb some twenty metres away acted as their guide. Halfway along this corridor, in which they nimbly avoided treading on the raised tracks, and where, much to Apricot's chagrin, the beam of Blue's flashlight had swung wildly about in search of nooks and crannies, it suddenly landed on a face. A filthy, grinning face at waist height that exclaimed, "You came! I hoped you would come!"

"*Dogsbody*?" breathed Blue.

"Oh, it's just you…" said Apricot, clutching at her heart.

Dogsbody's smile contorted his face into something that resembled a scowl. "The Master says you should always finish what you start."

"Indeed. And what is it you hope to finish?" said Apricot, grasping to reclaim her haughty demeanor.

"Your guided tour!" said Dogsbody, clapping quickly.

"That's very thoughtful of you," smiled Blue, switching off her flashlight.

"Indeed. Well then, why don't you start by telling us about the ghosts?" said Apricot.

"Ghosts?" said Dogsbody, none the wiser.

"I told you," said Blue.

"I've never seen a ghost but look! This was all built by your people!" said Dogsbody, tapping on the red brick wall.

"You mean the British?"

"They built a fortress up above. It's no more, but the remains of its dungeon and undercroft survive. Come. Follow me," he said, scampering off down the track. "There is much to show and not much time. The Master spoke of another delivery tonight."

"Tonight?" said Blue.

"That sounds about right. The Masked Ball's upon us again. Happens every year on the first Saturday of July. Your invite's in the post by the way."

"Thanks, Apricot."

"I was speaking metaphorically," murmured Apricot as they followed Dogsbody along the tracks.

"Did you put these lights on for us?" asked Blue.

"I did," enthused Dogsbody.

"But how could you be so sure we'd come?"

"I saw how curious you were. Hoped!"

"They do say hope springs eternal," said Apricot.

"Master Blake says so."

"I have a feeling I'm going to regret asking, but about what?" said Apricot.

"The black man being sent home to the jungles of Africa."

"And your feeling was so right," said Blue as they exited the tunnel into a small cavernous space where rusted, iron bars that had once formed prison cells had melded with the earthen walls.

"It's official… I have the heebie-jeebies," said Apricot.

"It's *extraordinary*," breathed Blue, approaching a wall where rusting iron bars ran through it like ruddy veins. "It's as though nature is trying to gobble up the past."

"The glorious past!" said Dogsbody.

Apricot narrowed her eyes at him. "Says who?"

"Need you ask? Obviously 'Master' Blake," murmured Blue, looking at the red rust on her fingers. She turned and stepped towards an arched entrance. "And what's through here?"

"Come," beckoned Dogsbody scampering towards it.

They walked under the arch into a larger cavern where many more prison cells were being reclaimed by the walls. In a recess at the back of the cavern was an altar upon which stood a number of candles and a book. Dogsbody grasped the lapels of his filthy jacket and looked about reverently. "This is the Ceremonial Room. It's a very important place."

Blue stepped to the altar, moved behind it, and read the title on the book's cover: *"Kloran: The Knights of the Ku Klux Klan,"*

"Don't touch that!" said Dogsbody as Blue's hand hovered over the cover.

"Why not?"

"It's the Grand Wizard's book!"

Apricot approached the altar. "And no prizes for guessing who the Grand Wizard is…"

"You should see the master in his orange robes. He looks just as powerful as any wizard. Merlin the magician? Pa!" said Dogsbody, dismissive of the legendary wizard.

"You do know *Mr* Blake isn't a real wizard?" said Apricot.

Dogsbody's queer grin and hunched shoulders suggested that this was open to debate.

"He's not. He's just a hateful little man," said Blue.

"He's six feet six!" replied Dogsbody, reaching up as high as his bent back would allow.

"So, the Klan hold their ceremonies *here*?" said Blue.

Dogsbody spun about and held out a pointed finger. "Master Blake says it's a very sacred place. That these cells are from the golden age when the black man was enslaved to the white."

"It's beyond horrible…" shuddered Blue, stepping from behind the altar.

"You wouldn't think so poorly of the master if you met him. He's a fine scholar."

"If you say so. Did you see him yesterday after we left?" said Blue.

"The Master came to retrieve a document."

Blue shot a glance at Apricot. "And did you tell him about our visit?"

"I thought about it, but he seemed in SUCH a hurry and…" replied Dogsbody, his demeanour that of a mischievous child. "Had he known about the black boy he would have beaten me. You were right not to let him come here."

Blue approached three vertical bars that appeared to forge a path through the wall. She reached out a hand "… It's strange to touch such *vile history*." As I began a new melody for her entitled, 'The Lair of the Dragon uncovered,' she murmured, "I've seen enough…"

"I couldn't agree more," said Apricot.

Blue turned to Dogsbody. "Thank you. For our tour. Our *secret* tour."

"But must you go? So soon?"

"Things to do. People to see. You know how it is?" said Apricot, her voice trailing off to an embarrassed whisper.

Chapter 19
Blue is summoned

The following morning, Blue, dressed in a haphazardly tied dressing gown, wandered out of her room and plopped herself down at the breakfast table. Harry lowered the newspaper he was reading just enough to observe her over its top. "Penny for them?" he asked as Sheila appeared with a rack of buttered toast. Blue barely registered her father's question but, oddly for her in times of flux, the smell of fresh toast had the effect of smelling salts. Sheila placed the rack of toast down in front of Harry. "It appears our daughter has something important on her mind."

Sheila raised an eyebrow at Blue. "What's the matter? Are you unwell?"

Blue eyeballed the toast rack and shook her head.

Harry stood, picked up the rack, leaned over the table and placed it down in front of her. Blue took a piece of toast, crunched down, chewed thoughtfully, and murmured, "It's nothing…"

"Really? At least this 'nothing' hasn't ruined your appetite. So, who are you hoping to save the world from today?" said Sheila, sitting down and lifting a glass of orange juice to her lips.

"How fickle you must imagine me," replied Blue, sounding more like Apricot.

"How *is* Apricot?" said Sheila, taking a sip of juice.

"I saw her yesterday," crunched Blue.

"What a surprise."

"You don't mind, do you?"

Sheila put down her glass and exchanged a glance with Harry. "It's not that we mind. But just be *mindful* of who she is. The things you tell her may find their way back to your father's employer."

Blue reached for another slice of toast. "Apricot's not like that."

"You've known her all of five minutes, Blue."

Harry rose to his feet. "Perhaps we should trust our daughter's judgment. What have you got planned for today?"

"Nothing much. I do need to talk to Terry about something."

Sheila drummed her fingers on the table. "If you spend too much time distracting that young man, you'll get him into trouble. He's at the stables to *work*."

Blue shrugged. "He's Apricot's friend now so…"

"Just be mindful of his station, Blue."

On her way to the stables, Blue mulled over the possibility of getting Terry into trouble. She kicked a pebble off the path and considered avoiding the stables. But, as my orchestra began to play a melody for her entitled, 'The Shared Experience', it seemed to her that discovering the colonial prison below the mansion was an important part of the adventure they had begun together. *Hateful rituals are taking place so close to his home. Maybe ignorance is bliss?* Blue shook her head. *Ignorance is how things get out of control in the first place. Terry has a right to know about it.*

It was in this spirited yet philosophical mood that Blue entered the stable yard and made a bee-line for the Queen of Sheba's stable. Inside, as her eyes adjusted to the light, she saw a man dressed in a dark suit, sitting nonchalantly on a chair. "Miss Blue Tibbs?" he said, sounding like a policeman about to make an arrest.

"Yes," said Blue, casting her gaze about the empty stable for Terry. She made eye contact Sheba.

"Miss Tibbs?"

"*Yes?*"

"You're to come with me."

"With you? Where?"

"To Chateau De Croy."

"Oh, has Apricot sent you?"

The man shook his head and Blue's heart began to thud in her chest. "Where's Terry?"

"Mr Curtis is elsewhere," shrugged the man as though that ought to have been obvious.

"Is he alright? He's not in any trouble, is he?"

The man appeared to answer her question by straightening his tie. "Now if you'll just follow me, I have a small buggy parked just up the way," he said, making his way past her.

Blue turned around. "But who are you?"

"I work for Mr De Croy. I'm his right *and* left-hand man," he said, holding up both hands. "Come along, Miss Tibbs. Mr De Croy is expecting you."

"*Mr De Croy*? Are you certain you have the right person?"

"Quite certain."

"Why didn't you call for me at home?"

Mr De Croy's right-and left-hand man beckoned her to follow and made no reply.

The ride up the lane and across the lawn might have been fun in the motorised buggy except, the closer they got to Chateau De Croy, the more trepidation at the trouble she may have caused rose in Blue's breast. Reader, it would have been remiss of me to abandon our budding Hunter of Dragons in her time of trepidation. And so, I raised my baton, glanced at my horn section, and coaxed a triumphant call to arms, one that turned Blue's fear to exhilaration. *I'm finally going to meet the owner of this incredible home. Maybe Apricot has told him good things about me? She's probably with her uncle right now.*

The buggy sped past the chateau's front door and continued until it arrived below a turret where it came to crunching halt. No sooner had they climbed out of the buggy than a door into the turret opened. Inside, a stern-faced man stood with arms folded across his barrel chest. "My colleague will take care of you from here, Miss Tibbs," said Mr De Croy's right-and left-hand man.

"...Thank you," murmured Blue.

Blue stepped over the threshold and smiled at the man who reminded her of a gangster. *All that's missing is a cigar and a tommy gun.* It seemed only fitting when he didn't smile back but turned abruptly to slide open the cage door of an elevator. The man stepped inside, jabbed a stubby finger at a button, stepped back out again, and then motioned for Blue to enter it with his eyes. Without saying a word, he slid the door closed and the elevator began its ascent.

It came to a halt at its only stop whereupon another man, who looked like the first's taller brother, slid the cage door open. Blue stepped into a waiting room where a dapper looking man with a handlebar moustache sat fanning his sweaty face with a trilby hat. This seemed unnecessary due to a large ceiling fan that made the room decidedly drafty. Blue was about to take a seat when a door opened, and a harassed looking gentleman was shown out of a room. The gentleman glanced at the sweating man who grimaced as he climbed to his feet.

"Miss Tibbs?" said a woman standing in the open door.

"Yes."

"Come in, please."

"But this man was here first."

"Come in, please," she repeated, robotically.

Blue looked at the sweating man, shrugged apologetically, and edged past him into the room.

"Please take a seat. Mr De Croy will be with you momentarily," she said, indicating a chair before an expansive desk.

"Thank you," replied Blue glancing around at what looked to be every inch the inner sanctum of the fairytale character: gothic furniture that was sturdy enough for a clumsy beast to use without fear of breaking; a set of huge doors that led out onto the turret's balcony where a table laid for breakfast could be seen through net curtains. Hung around the room were original portraits of Elizabethan nobles, however, Blue's gaze found and settled on a framed photograph of a young woman on the desk – a beautiful woman with luscious dark hair who smiled lovingly at the photographer. Blue held the young woman's gaze as she lowered herself into the seat. She heard a deep, throaty cough from behind a closed door to her left, and her imagination conjured an image of a hulking beast that was completely at odds with the man who opened and stepped through the door – a man more akin to the Beast's alter ego of the prince. Of average height with fair hair, handsome eyes, perfect teeth and a smile to match. Blue sat up straight as though to attention.

"Miss Tibbs, I presume?" he said, his accent more clipped English than American. "Thank you for coming. I hope I haven't put you to any inconvenience?"

"I'm Blue Tibbs and no…" said Blue, lifting a hand and lowering it again awkwardly.

"I'm Richard De Croy. Apricot's uncle. I apologise for the cloak and dagger shenanigans. But I thought it best that we talk without giving your mother and father any undue concerns," he said, lowering himself into his seat beyond the expansive desk.

Blue swallowed hard, her mouth suddenly dry. "Thank you."

Mr De Croy regarded her questioningly.

"… For not unduly concerning my parents," said Blue, quietly.

Mr De Croy waved a hand as though it was quite all right. "Blue's an unusual name. I like it."

"Thank you. Makes me sound miserable but…"

Mr De Croy made steeples of his hands and gazed at Blue thoughtfully over his fingertips.

Blue cleared her throat nervously. "… Something's the matter?"

"The matter?" said Mr De Croy who seemed to be weighing up a yes or a no answer.

"Is Terry in trouble, only…"

"*Terry*?"

"Only I walked through stables earlier and he wasn't there…"

"Oh," replied Mr De Croy as the penny dropped, "You mean, Mrs *Curtis's* boy?"

Blue nodded.

"Is Mrs Curtis well?"

"Yes. I had tea with her the other day. She'll be thrilled to hear you asked after her," said Blue, finding a smile.

"Please do, please do," replied Mr De Croy, leaning back in his chair.

There was an awkward silence.

"You must be wondering why I asked you here today?" said Mr De Croy breaking it.

Blue nodded slowly.

"I gather you and Apricot have become good friends?"

Blue felt a smile return to her lips. "Is that what she said?"

Mr De Croy nodded, stood up, turned around, and took two steps to a window beside the balcony doors.

Blue shuffled in her seat and grasped at its arm rests.

"You see," began Mr De Croy, "Apricot has told me all about your visit."

"Visit?" said Blue, quietly.

Mr De Croy began examining the leaves of a plant on the window ledge. "How to put this. It's a delicate matter," he said, picking up a little bottle and spraying a fine mist onto the plant's leaves. "My parties are… well, they're important to my business affairs. As such they require alcohol to make them run smoothly." He turned and looked at Blue. "The fact of the matter is that homemade wine for religious purposes, as the law allows, would not suffice."

"You don't think I might tell someone and get you into trouble?"

Mr De Croy smiled, whereupon his dimples and perfect teeth looked like a well-polished double act. "No. I'm not worried about any trouble. You see, the Commissioner of Police is a close friend and a regular guest at my parties." He looked at his nails and, seeing some dirt under a thumb, used his forefinger to scratch it away.

Blue watched him.

"… The truth is… well, the truth is that the men who supply liquor for my parties are not, how to put this, particularly savoury." His eyes flashed up to meet Blue's, his expression so serious that Blue swallowed audibly.

"Look here, Blue," he went on, "it's in your best interests that I'm completely honest with you."

Blue nodded, realised that her mouth had fallen open, and snapped it shut.

"These people are criminals. Rest assured; they must abide by the *strictest* rules if our business arrangement is to continue. Even so, young ladies such as Apricot and yourself should not venture into their work space."

"She told you?"

"Not exactly. She said she'd heard rumours about how people with, how did she put it, with *frightfully hateful opinions* were involved in supplying our alcohol. I put two and two together and she confessed that you'd been doing some detective work below the house."

"I said she should tell you… about the Ku Klux Klan."

At the mention of the KKK, Mr De Croy folded his arms across his chest and hugged himself as though fending off a chill.

"They hold rituals right under your house and…"

Mr De Croy held up a palm to silence her. "As extreme as that organisation's views are, they're an accepted part of our society.

And what's more, the area below Chateau De Croy is of historical interest."

Blue felt her hackles rise. "But they're not historians. They glory in all the suffering that went on in that dreadful place."

"Don't you think I know that? I keep extensive files on their activities," he said, glancing at something over Blue's left shoulder.

"All the more reason to despise them," replied Blue, glancing over her left shoulder at a filing cabinet.

"Unfortunately, in these times of prohibition, such people are a necessary evil. And that's all there is to it. Subject closed."

Blue sighed, her gaze once again settling on the photograph of the young woman on the desk. "She's very pretty. Who is she?" she asked, leaning in for a closer look. Mr De Croy drew a deep breath and seconds passed in silence.

"Sorry. I'm a very nosey person…"

Mr De Croy exhaled slowly through his nose. "Not at all. Her name was Rachel. We were to be married but she passed away," he replied, the melancholy in his voice reminding her of the Beast lamenting happier times. "Back to the topic at hand," he said, shooting a glance at his wrist watch. "I'm sure you understand, it's for the best that you… *make an effort* not to concern yourself with those who supply alcohol for my parties. As odious as they are, they are not a threat to you or anybody else connected with the running of this estate."

"Not even Terry and his mother?"

"Why of *course* not," said Mr De Croy, standing and indicating that Blue do the same with an upward facing palm.

Blue stood up.

"Your family is settling in nicely? The cottage is to your mother's liking?"

"Yes, very much so," nodded Blue.

"Good. Good. Thank you for coming. It was nice to meet you," he said, reaching across his desk and shaking her hand.

Chapter 20
You are cordially invited

As she descended in the elevator, Blue's head felt as though a ravenous cat had been loosed amongst an aviary of delicious pigeons. Mr De Croy was nothing like she'd imagined. *A lot more handsome, awkward and...sad,* thought Blue as the barrel-chested man slid the cage door open for her.

Blue was not surprised when the little buggy was nowhere to be seen. She clasped her hands behind her back and walked with a carefree attitude away from the chateau. All things considered she thought the meeting had gone rather well. As Blue walked, she weighed up Mr De Croy's suggestion. *How had he put it? That I should make an effort not to concern myself with those who are responsible for delivering the alcohol to his parties?* Now she came to think about it, hadn't there been a lack of conviction in his request? Reader, Blue was right. And this lack of conviction had been due to the melody that my orchestra had been playing for him. A questioning ocarina solo that had conjured within this decent man the notion that it was wrong to clip the wings of a girl whose strength of conviction against the Ku Klux Klan was absolutely in the right place. Do you see how subtly I meddle on behalf of humanity? This is how the good always manages to outweigh the hideous.

Blue arrived at the stables in a buoyant mood and, seeing Terry chuckling to himself as he led a black mare across the yard in the direction of a water trough, only added to her good spirits. "You're back!" she called out.

"I am? Where have I been?"

"I was about to ask you that," she said, pitching up beside him as the horse began to drink from the trough. "What's so funny?" she asked.

"You tell me. You're the one who's grinning from ear to ear."

"You'll never guess who I just talked to?"

"You came from the direction of the chateau so, Miss Apricot?"

"No. Someone *even* more important."

"There isn't anyone."

"Mr De Croy. And we had *quite* the tete-tete."

"*What*? Did Mr De Croy catch you snooping at the big house?"

"Nobody ever catches me snooping. He sent for me."

"You serious?"

"Deadly. His right-and left-hand man was waiting for me here earlier. I expect you'd like to know what Mr De Croy wanted?"

"Only if you think it proper to tell me."

"Well," began Blue, "Apricot and I found the other end of the mine cart line under the chateau. Where they deliver the alcohol for the parties?"

"Oh, I bet that's a cheery place," murmured Terry.

"It's horrid. Apricot told her uncle how we'd done some detective work under the chateau and, well, Mr De Croy told me I should *make an effort* not to concern myself with the people who deliver the alcohol."

Terry shook his head. "He summoned you and told you to 'make an effort,' huh?"

"Yes, why are you looking at me like that?"

"Just making sure your ears are still attached to the sides of your head."

"My ears are attached just fine," said Blue, as they were interrupted by the sound of someone clearing his throat. Terry turned and the sight of Chateau De Croy's butler balancing a silver tray on the palm of a hand was akin to seeing the bogey man.

"Don't give yourself a coronary on my behalf," said the butler, looking down his nose at Terry's hand, the one clasped to his heart. He lifted two envelopes off the tray. "Mr Terrance Curtis? Miss Blue Tibbs?"

Terry shook his head.

"You are Terrance Curtis," tutted Blue.

"Well then, this is for you, *sir,* and madam, with the compliments of Miss Apricot De Croy." As Blue took the envelopes, she noticed a couple of masks, one white, the other black, on the tray. "Are these for us?"

"Indeed, they are, madam."

Blue took the masks and smiled at Terry over her shoulder.

"If there's nothing else, I'll bid you a good day," said the butler whose wriggling nose suggested that he was not enjoying the natural smells of the stable yard.

"Thanks," said Blue, holding Terry's envelope out towards him.

Terry's hands remained firmly at his sides.

"It's not a *bomb,*" said Blue observing the expression on his face.

"Isn't it?"

Blue held the envelope to her head and conjured her best fortune teller's voice. "I see not a bomb in here but, but…yes! An invitation! An invitation to the masked ball!"

Terry took half a step back. "Stable boys, *black stable boys,* don't receive invitations to the masked ball."

"Well, that's where you're wrong," said Blue, glancing at his name on the envelope. "Besides, this is nineteen hundred and twenty-five, not *eighteen* hundred and twenty-five."

"I've seen a calendar. I know what the year is. Have you forgotten about the Klan? They're right *here,*" said Terry, jabbing a finger at the ground.

"No, *of course* I haven't. I even brought up the subject with Mr De Croy."

"And he said he'd be running them off presently?"

"No, he said they're an accepted part of society. But I could tell he despises them."

"Well, there you go. If a fine, upstanding gentleman like Mr De Croy, who gave my family a home and employment can see things that way, then it might as well be eighteen hundred and twenty-five."

"If that's true then deeds not words are what's needed."

"What deeds?"

"Your accepting Apricot's invitation for a start. Look, *our* friend, has gone to the trouble of sending the butler over with these invites, so I think the least you can do is open it."

Terry looked down at himself, shook his head, and took the envelope reluctantly. "You think I got clothes to wear to a fancy party?" he said, opening the invite with such care that it brought a lump to Blue's throat. "And to the masked ball at that…" The envelope's lip fell open and he drew out the card inside as though it were a precious old document.

Blue cleared her throat. "So, what does it say?"

"*Master Terrance Curtis, you are cordially invited to the Summer Masked Ball to take place this Saturday at The Chateau De Croy.*" Terry slid the invite carefully back into the envelope. "There's no way Ma will let me be around all that liquor and dancing."

"So, don't tell her. Why'd you think Apricot had her butler deliver the invitations here and not where we live?" said Blue, glancing in the direction of home.

Terry looked at her as though inspecting an oddity. "You sure aren't one for respecting boundaries, are you?"

"Boundaries?" murmured Blue as though it was the first time she'd ever heard the word. "You can hear the parties taking place from where you live. You must have wondered what's going on?"

"Sure I have," sighed Terry.

"Well, now's your chance to find out," said Blue, holding out the masks. "Take your pick."

"Now's my chance to find out," murmured Terry, dreamlike, as he reached for the white one.

Part 2

Chapter 21

Into the dragon's lair went a hunter named Blue

Blue lay in bed, wearing a red summer dress and clutching her black mask. It was a full-face mask made from the finest porcelain, with small round holes for eyes, impossibly high cheekbones and pursed lips.

The moment the light under her bedroom door went out, a sign that her parents had gone to bed, Blue's heart began to race. The doors that led out to the garden were slightly ajar, and she could hear the faint murmurings of the masked ball getting underway. Reader, this was the night when Blue must garner a greater understanding of the Ku Klux Klan, the hate-breathing dragon in her midst. Only then would her beloved saying, 'deeds not words' take on extra significance to the task at hand. The melody that my orchestra played for her that evening was resolute and determined. She had planned to wait at least ten minutes before leaving, but her melody caused her to throw off her sheet and reach for her shoes.

Outside, Blue felt a strange chill in the summer air, one that reminded her of England. She shuddered and decided that the best way to counter it was to walk briskly. This she did, her footfalls landing in perfect time to the beat of her melody. Reader, time was of the essence. The dragon would soon be rearing its head and Fate required that Blue be there when it did. She skirted through her garden gate, clutching her mask, and made for Terry's house.

She arrived in the little cobbled lane to discover that, with the exception of a single gas lamp that hung above the front door, the cottage where Terry lived was in darkness. As she trod up the pebbled walkway that led to the front door, an owl twit-twooed. The owl sounded genuine in every respect except one: there was an unnatural urgency about it.

Twit-twoo twit-twoo!

Blue looked to her right where she made out the faint outline of a person standing beside a tree. "Terry?"

"Yes, who else?" came his whispered response. "You want to step off that gravel? Ma's a light sleeper."

"Okay," replied Blue, stepping onto the grass.

Terry was wearing his best suit, the one he wore whenever his mother insisted that he accompany her to church. "You look very smart," whispered Blue, giving his black wool suit with wide lapels the once over.

"It's my church suit."

"It looks brand new."

"Don't let Ma hear you say that. I prefer my books to going to church," he said, looking up at the heavens. He whistled quietly through his teeth. "Some night for stargazers…"

"Yes. It's incredible."

Terry nodded enthusiastically. "I'll show you some things through my binoculars sometime," he said, drawing the mask that was resting on the top of his head down over his face. The porcelain mask was white with high cheekbones and puckered lips. Terry had glued some white fabric to its top which fell down over the back of his head and concealed his short afro.

"I'd really like that," said Blue, quietly.

"So? What'd you think?"

"I think if you wanted to rob a bank you'd do just fine."

Terry nodded and pushed the mask back up onto his head. "It's just as well that folks won't know it's me. Can't see how I could have gone on this crazy adventure any other way. I even got a pair of gloves to hide my hands…" he said, patting a pocket. Blue reached out and squeezed his shoulder tenderly.

Terry looked at her hand. "What are you doing?"

"Come on friend of mine. We don't want to keep Apricot waiting."

They made their way through the little wood towards the lawns, into which the glare of the brightly lit chateau penetrated. It was accompanied by the voice of a distant female singer. Terry paused in his tracks. "… Sounds like one of those songs that's kept me awake before now."

"And now you're going to see the singer for yourself," said Blue, beckoning him forward.

"Guess I am at that."

They stepped onto the lawn where the splendour of Chateau De Croy could be seen in all its turreted, fairytale glory. "Do you think it right that one person has so much?" pondered Terry.

"I don't see why not. If I didn't, that would make me a communist, wouldn't it?" Terry didn't answer but instead slid his mask down over his face. Blue did the same.

They rounded a series of tall hedgerows where they were treated to their first view of the party in full swing. "I never thought to *see* so many happy folks," gasped Terry.

"They might be happy now, but I bet they'll have sore heads in the morning."

Terry sighed. "Drink sure has a way of making folks forget their troubles."

"Have you ever had a glass of champagne?"

"Have you ever had your head examined?"

"Come on then, let's get you your first glass of bubbly," smiled Blue.

The band was playing a song entitled, 'Ain't we got fun", and the female vocalist, dressed in a figure-hugging white dress, belted out the words with gusto into a microphone:

Every morning, every evening
Ain't we got fun?
Not much money, oh, but honey
Ain't we got fun?
The rent's unpaid dear
We haven't a bus
But smiles were made dear
For people like us

Terry, wide eyed and cautious, trod slowly towards the gyrating throng. Blue, glancing over her shoulder and seeing that he'd fallen several steps behind, beckoned to him. "Come on!" she said, over the music, the laughter and the clinking of glasses. All of which, a moment later, seemed to rush forward and engulf them like a tsunami of people without inhibition, sobriety, or self-respect. At the sight of two beautiful ladies kissing, Terry did an about turn, only to do another at the sight of a dancer who treated him to an eyeful of her cleavage. Terry clasped his eyes shut and then opened them tentatively to see Blue smiling at him. "Let's go and meet Apricot," she said, stepping through the revellers with a nimble footedness that left Terry scrambling to keep up with her.

Blue pointed up a steep bank to where the fairytale carriage sat under the branches of a weeping willow tree festooned with fairy lights. "We'll find Apricot in there."

"Really? Is that where she lives?" gasped Terry.

"Ah, no," said Blue, swallowing her laughter.

They scrambled up the bank, doing their best to avoid the little stone creatures that now peppered it, and made their way around to the other side of the carriage. Blue lifted herself up and through the carriage's oval-shaped side opening and fell as gracefully as gravity would allow onto its floor. From her crouched position, she cast her gaze over the collection of masked fairytale characters crammed along the bench to her left and braced herself.

"BOO!" cried Apricot bursting from the group of dolls and sending several flying across the carriage.

"You're *determined* to give me a heart attack?" said Blue, staring into the mascara heavy eyes now beaming at her from a golden mask that resembled an Egyptian cat.

"I simply couldn't *bear* it if I did, dear love. Hello Terrance!" said Apricot, turning her attention to the masked figure outside. Terry raised a tentative hand.

"Come in and join us."

Terry cast his gaze over the carriage's splendid interior, upholstered in red and gold velvet. "Well, okay Miss Apricot…" he said, hauling himself over the side.

Blue and Terry sat on the bench opposite Apricot who crossed one leg over the other. "Poor thing. I hear you were summoned to meet uncle?"

"Yes. He was really nice."

"He said he liked you too. I was given a similar talking to about *you know what*," said Apricot rolling her eyes. "You look very smart Terry."

"It's my church suit," said Terry pulling at the collar of his white shirt.

"Not much of a church goer then?" said Apricot.

Terry glanced at Blue.

"He prefers his books."

"How frightfully progressive," nodded Apricot, lifting her mask from her face. "Champagne?" she went on, reaching for something that had become wedged in the back of her seat. She yanked it free and it tinkled.

"Is that a bell?" said Terry.

Apricot nodded. "Yes, but not just any bell. This is a magic bell, one that befits a fairytale carriage."

"You going to magic up some champagne?" chuckled Terry.

"Yes, that's precisely what I am going to do," she replied, sliding along the seat to her right where she thrust her arm outside and tinkled assertively. She sat back and tossed the bell onto the seat where it landed in the crack, waiting to be swallowed up again. Seconds passed. "I don't think it worked..." said Terry.

"Ye of little faith... voila!" said Apricot as a servant appeared outside the carriage, balancing a tray on the fingers of his left hand. Upon the tray sat a bottle of champagne and three fluted glasses. Using his right hand, the servant lifted the bottle of champagne and filled the glasses.

"What kept you, Thomas? Rhetorical question..." said Apricot, reaching up and taking the first glass. She handed it to Terry. The second she passed to Blue and the third she wasted no time in taking several thirsty gulps from. Terry stared down into the lightly golden bubbling liquid and wrinkled his nose as the bubbles popped under it.

"Go on, it won't bite," urged Apricot.

Terry placed the glass against his lower lip and tilted it so that the nectar washed over his tongue. He winced as though in pain and licked furiously at his lips.

Apricot sat back in her seat. "Whatever is the matter? Don't you like it?"

"Never tasted anything like it..." said Terry, continuing to lick like a thirsty lizard.

"It is an acquired taste, I suppose," sighed Apricot like a disappointed mother.

Blue took a sip of hers. "Thomas must have more important things to do than stand over us? He's making me a little uneasy," said Blue lowering her voice. All three looked up at the man, standing so still and inanimate that he might have been part of the scenery. "Thomas," said Apricot, "your rowdy behavior is bothering my guests."

"Yes, Miss De Croy. Will that be all?"

"Yes," replied Apricot looking at the bottle of champagne on his tray.

"Let him take it," said Blue, "I feel as though we should all keep a clear head tonight."

"I'm already feeling... a little fuzzy," said Terry.

"After only a couple of *sips*?" said Apricot, again sounding like a disappointed mother.

"He's not used to it," observed Blue, sounding like a concerned mother.

Terry shuffled in the seat and sat up straight. "I never had it before so I guess you *could* say I'm not used to it," replied Terry, who sounded like their sarcastic offspring.

Apricot drew a long and thoughtful breath through her nose. And then, having reflected and made what seemed to her an odd decision said, "You may go, Thomas, and take the bottle with you." Reader, there was nothing odd about her decision. The cautious melody that my orchestra was playing for her *and* Blue had instilled in them both the distinct impression that they should keep their wits about them. The girls glanced at one another and shuddered as though they'd caught a chill. Terry glanced back and forth between them and, being a highly perceptive young man asked, "What's going on?"

"Is there something going on?" murmured Blue, goosebumps appearing on her arms.

"Is it just me or did it just get decidedly chilly in here?" said Apricot with a shudder.

Blue gazed out at the party. "Maybe it's time to mingle?"

Apricot nodded, they pulled their masks down over their faces, and followed her as she scrambled over the side of the carriage.

At the bottom of the bank they merged with the revellers. "This way!" said Apricot, leading them towards the grand ballroom where the most famous dancer of the day, Josephine Baker, had been hired to entertain the guests from a specially erected stage. Reader, if I'm honest, at times such as these I feel a bit like the Pied Piper of Hamelin. As Apricot led her friends towards the ballroom and my bait of Josephine Baker, Blue heard the name that she had been Fated to overhear on that spot since the day she was born.

"Mr Blake, sir. That call you were expecting has come through. If you'll kindly follow me, I'll show you to the phone in the annex."

Blue spun around and found herself behind a footman. She peered around him, drinking in the sight of the man to whom his words had been directed; he was impossibly tall and wearing a mask that reminded her of a ravenous wolf. The dark eyes beyond the holes cut into the mask sought out and found Blue's gaze in much the same way as negative and positive magnets attract. Make no mistake, these two human beings *were* at opposite ends of the spectrum. One had embraced discontentment and hatred in order to advance his own position, while the other was possessed of a burning desire to lessen suffering and make the world a better place. Blue felt someone grasp her arm. She glanced down at Apricot's hand, and then returned her gaze to Blake who was now following the footman inside. "What's wrong?" asked Apricot.

"It's *him*."

"Who?" asked Apricot, following Blue's gaze to the giant.

"*Blake*."

"Blake?" The penny dropped and, before it had a chance to reach the ground, Blue was nudging her way through the revellers in pursuit of her prey. Reader, you may consider 'prey' too strong a word. But trust me when I say that Blue's natural instinct for fighting the *good* fight, coupled with the brass heavy orchestration I was now conducting for her entitled, 'Deeds Not Words,' *had* produced within her a resolve to hunt him down. Had it simply been a case of cutting Blake's life short, I would have influenced events so that a muscle-bound assassin was in pursuit of him.

No.

A dragon needed to be slain.

A colossus for whom Blake represented just *one* of its six million hate promoting scales. To slay a monster of this size, a subtler yet infinitely more powerful approach was required: a young girl with an innate passion for making things right.

As Blue followed him, her sense of curiosity and purpose was such that she forgot about the friends who were following her. And she only became aware of them when, having rounded a corner and seeing the butler hand a telephone to Blake, she stopped abruptly and felt someone bump into her. "What the!?" she said, backing up out of sight.

"Ow! What the *yourself*," said Apricot, doing the same.

"Ouch!" cried Terry as Apricot trod on his foot.

Blue peeked around the corner to where Blake was holding the receiver to his ear. He looked at his wristwatch, shuffled a little on his feet as though it had dawned on him that he needed to be somewhere else, said something into the receiver, and then placed it down.

"What's going on?" asked Apricot, "and why am I trying to hide in my own home?"

"He mustn't see us…" said Blue.

"Why not?"

"Because we're going to follow him."

"We are?"

"Well, I am. But I'll understand if…" said Blue, moving out from cover as Blake turned a corner and began down a hallway.

"Oh, dear love, I think it *imperative* that I stick to you like glue," said Apricot, following her.

"I hoped you might. I'm going to need you if I'm caught."

"Indeed, you shall. Caught doing *what* exactly?"

"Snooping."

"I've a mind to start calling you Snoopy Tibbs," murmured Apricot.

When they reached the end of a corridor that Blake had turned down, Blue stopped and watched him walk down another corridor. She turned to Terry. "Maybe you should go back to the carriage and wait for us there."

"That's Blake? The Grand Wizard that Dogsbody told us about?"

Blue and Apricot nodded.

The cogs began to turn behind Terry's eyes, and these same cogs seemed to raise his gloved hands to his face. "I'll be okay, won't I? So long as they can't see me."

"You'll be alright. No one is going to harm a hair on *my* stable boy's head."

"Then I'm going with you."

Blue smiled behind her mask, nodded, and headed off down the corridor. She reached its end just in time to see Blake take a sharp right and go through a door.

"He's headed to the kitchens," said Apricot beside her.

"I somehow thought he might… he's going underground," said Blue excitedly.

The kitchen staff were so busy preparing food that they didn't notice the three masked teenagers hurrying through their midst. They bolted down the steps into the wine cellar and arrived at the trap door behind the barrels. The trap door was open, and they could hear Blake's footsteps as he made his way down.

Having waited a few minutes, Apricot and Terry followed Blue down the stairs. At the bottom, they stood amid some empty crates that looked as though they'd been looted. And, whereas on the girls' first visit, the corridor had smelled of gunpowder, it now smelled of something sweeter.

"Incense?" said Terry, sneezing. The girls spun about and looked at him, his masked face now buried in his gloved hands.

"Gesundheit. Couldn't you have sneezed a bit louder?" said Apricot, looking over at the arched exit that led into the rest of the old colonial prison.

Terry removed his hands from his face. "Do you think someone heard?"

They all listened. Voices *could* be heard, but they sounded so distant that Terry wondered if they were a product of his imagination. "Does… does anyone else hear voices?" he asked, as sweat edged down his brow.

"…Yes, but far enough away not have heard you sneeze," said Blue, crossing her fingers.

"Sorry," said Terry. "It pounced. Incense does that to me at church sometimes."

"Let's hope it's the only thing that pounces down here," shuddered Apricot, glancing up into the dark recesses of the ceiling.

They made their way under a red brick arch and found themselves in the cavern where eight colonial pillars rose up to the roof. Terry gazed at them. "Did those stairs just take us back in time?"

"It's the remains of a fort that was built by the British," whispered Blue.

"Looks haunted. If you believed in that sort of thing," said Terry.

"Which, of course, you don't, being a budding scientist," said Apricot, seeking reassurance.

"I guess not." Terry looked down at where the tracks came to an end. "Is this the other end of the mine cart line?"

"Yep," nodded Blue.

"So, we could ride back to the beach from here?" murmured Terry as though relishing the thought. As he finished speaking, the sound of applause found its way to them like the wispy ends of an explosion of smoke. All three drew breath and stood in a stunned silence. Blue spoke first. "… Sounds like they are having themselves quite the gathering."

"Yes… standing room only in that *frightful* room where the prison cells are being gobbled up by the walls," said Apricot.

Terry scratched nervously at the side of his head. "Prison cells?"

"There's no way to sugar coat it," said Blue, "there used to be a prison down here where, well, where…"

"They kept African slaves under lock and key."

"If you're both trying to spook me, then consider me well and truly spooked," said Terry.

"I'm afraid it's the horrible truth. I'm going to see what they're up to," said Blue, walking towards the gathering. "You can stay here if you like."

"Don't be daft," said Apricot, following her.

"Kinda late for that," murmured Terry, raising his hands and feeling the mask on his face.

They made their way down a narrow tunnel towards a single, stuttering bulb at its end. Halfway along, they heard a faint male voice that grew more distinct with every step. Blue imagined Blake, standing at the altar in *that* room. By the time they exited the tunnel, the voice was in full preacher mode, albeit a preacher of hate. Blue peered around a corner and beheld a gathering of several dozen men dressed in white robes. They wore pointed hoods that concealed their faces and stood facing the altar. Blake was standing behind the altar, dressed in orange robes that shimmered in the light of a flaming torch attached to the wall above him. An image of a fierce dragon was stitched into the front of his robes, its claws reaching up around the back of his hood and interlocking across his forehead. Looking at this man Blake, seven feet tall from the tips of his black boots to the point of his orange hood, Blue felt small and vulnerable. To compensate, I conducted my orchestra in an arrangement of frisky drums and jaunty trombones entitled 'The Brave Deeds of the Little Innocents.' It had the effect of lifting her if not in stature then in spirit. Reader, for the sake of humanity, Blue *had* to join this gathering. She drew a nerve steadying breath. "There's a table in there now. A *long* one. The end of it is close enough to the entrance for us to get under without being seen. It's for their refreshments."

"Won't they see us under the table?" breathed Terry.

"No, I don't think so. There's a table cloth… and it falls practically to the ground," said Blue, the excitement in her voice growing.

Apricot stepped around her. "That's a bit of luck."

Reader, by now you must know that there is no such thing as luck. Only me.

Bending low, Blue hastened towards the table. Apricot and Terry glanced at one another and, mirroring Blue's body language, followed her. Imagine if you will, these three youngsters, creeping with bent backs towards that place where, centuries before, unimaginable suffering had been inflicted upon innocent men because of the colour of their skin. And where this suffering was being celebrated by the masked adults now gathered there. So it was that they swept silently under the hanging table cloth and into the belly of the dragon.

Apricot and Terry followed Blue to the table's furthest end closest to the altar. They had arrived at the point in Blake's sermon that Blue had been Fated to hear ever since her mother released her over the side of Titanic into the hands of a stranger.

Blake puffed out his chest. "Gentlemen," he began, "it's the year of our Lord nineteen hundred and twenty-six, and we find ourselves delivered to a glorious new precipice. We are the masters of all we survey. As the Lord Almighty intended. Why else would He have blessed us with power? Position? Rank?" Blake placed his fisted hands on the altar and leaned his huge bulk on it as if trying to crush it. "Look around you, gentlemen, at this fine edifice. A place which dates from a time when the negro was looked upon as nothing more than a savage. An object to be bought and sold by his superiors. No better than a stray dog. These iron bars are testament to that glorious age!" Blake's black eyes twinkled in the firelight as he gazed around the cavern. "It was an enviable time gentleman, and one that will come again. In just a few short years, membership of our esteemed organisation has risen from the thousands to the millions. Our influence grows daily. Our members include Senators, Governors, Judges, leaders of industry, owners of national newspapers, respected writers, philosophers, scientists, and droves of fine upstanding people from all walks of life. Progressive, right thinking men and women who judge that now is the time for us to assert our natural authority over the coloured races, *and* over the meddling Jews and Catholics who have had it their own way for far too long."

Below the table, Apricot felt the hairs on the back of her neck stand on end, while Blue balled her hands into fists as her hackles rose, and Terry, thinking of his mother, felt sick to the pit of his stomach. They'd known the views of the Ku Klux Klan, but to hear them spoken aloud made them *real*. Blue in particular felt as though she *was* hiding in the belly of a monstrous dragon, its head behind the altar where Blake stood, its body the other men, curled and bristling around her. At that moment, had she a lance and clear sight of the dragon's heart, she would have driven it through it with all her strength. She reached out and squeezed Terry's hand. It trembled in her own. A loud BANG rang out as Blake brought his fists down upon the table. It was Apricot who clasped a hand to her mouth to stifle a cry.

"The time is at hand gentlemen! Praise the Lord Almighty for his deliverance!"

"HIS DELIVERANCE!" thundered the assembled body of the dragon, clasping their hands before them in prayer.

The room fell so silent that Blue was aware of the sound of her own quickened breath, and Terry of how tightly his eyes were clasped shut as though to make him invisible. As for Apricot, all she was aware of in that silence was the sudden and growing tickling in her nostrils that meant that the coming sneeze was inevitable. She clasped her hands to her mask, her eyes widening as she made eye contact with Blue. The sneeze, arriving as it did during a soupy silence, sounded like a muffled blow dart being fired into the dragon's thick hide. As you might imagine, the dragon's many legs began to stomp around the table, the cloth was raised, and dozens of eyes glared at them through slits in hoods. Hands were thrust towards them, dragging them from their cover, and shoving them to the ground before the altar. A thickset Klansman stepped forward and reached for Terry's mask, whereupon Apricot moved between them and whipped off her own mask. She clambered to her feet. "How *dare* you?" she cried with a level of authority in her voice that surprised even her. She can thank me for her sudden and necessary bluster. The melody I was playing for her entitled, 'Don't You Know Who I Am?' ensured that it was at hand. Then again, she can also thank me for that sneeze. That's Fate for you. If you're well meaning, trust in me.

"Don't you know who I am? I'm Apricot De Croy. And this is *my* home," she said, glancing up at the ceiling. "My Uncle will not *tolerate* your treating my friends and I in such a brutish manner."

Blue scrambled to her feet and stood shoulder to shoulder with her, creating a barrier between the body of the dragon and Terry. Behind them, Blake cleared his throat. "Gentlemen, calm yourselves." They turned and Blake's dark eyes gazed at Apricot from beyond the holes in his mask. "I recognise her. She's who she says she is. She's Mr De Croy's niece."

"What's she doing hiding under the table?" said an angry voice.

Blake held out his hands and moved them up and down in a calming manner. "That is what I am about to ascertain, gentlemen."

"We weren't *doing* anything. We were just curious," said Apricot, haughtily.

"Yes, just curious," said Blue.

"And who might you be?" Blake asked her.

"It doesn't matter who she is," interrupted Apricot. "My friends and I were bored of the party and went exploring."

"So, you were exploring, huh?" said the same angry voice from behind them. "Maybe you need to learn to mind your own business."

"I *beg* your pardon?" said Apricot, sounding so much like the lady of the manor that Blue could not help but smile behind her mask.

"Gentlemen please," said Blake. "No damage has been done here. These young people were fortunate enough to attend a meeting of our esteemed organisation. They are the future are they not? And what they have heard here tonight must have given them food for thought? I dare say, inspired them?"

The silence and body language of all three betrayed that they had not. What's more, the expression on Apricot's face, coupled with the hands now firmly on her hips, served as a very fat cherry on top of the uninspired cake. Blake gave a small, unconscious shrug and asked, "And how is Mr De Croy?"

"My uncle is in good health, thank you. And now we'll be getting back to the party." They turned and faced into the body of the dragon. It stood firm, doing an excellent impression of an immovable wall. "Make way, gentlemen. Make way," urged Blake. The dragon shifted its bulk slowly and begrudgingly, and made way for them to squeeze, single file, through its mass.

Chapter 22
A weight lifted

That night in bed, Blue stared at the ceiling, her eyes sometimes filled with tears, her hands occasionally balled into fists. When they had returned to the party, the sights and sounds of the revellers, drunk on liquor supplied by the dragon that lurked underground, had been too much to bear. Terry hadn't uttered a word since they'd arrived back at the carriage. He had the countenance of a masked puppet with several strings severed. "You had best get him home," Apricot had observed.

"You must be a mind reader."

Despite her efforts to raise his spirits on their walk back, Blue had only managed to elicit two grunts and a 'maybe' from Terry. "I'm sorry," she said as he was about to climb through his bedroom window. "I should never have led you into that basement."

"But you have nothing to be sorry for," Terry had whispered over his shoulder.

"I think I do..." she'd told his disappearing back.

The hour of sleep that Blue had managed to get had been after dawn. She awoke to discover that, despite the events of the night before, the sun had risen on a new day. She wandered out of her room in her pajamas find her mother dressed to go out, applying lipstick in the hallway mirror.

"Morning sleepy head," said Sheila, dropping her lipstick into her handbag.

"Morning," replied Blue, yawning.

"I've got a dental appointment in Manhattan. So, you'll have the place to yourself."

"Where's Dad?"

"At the boating lake. They drained it yesterday."

"Where's your appointment?"

"I just told you, Manhattan." A car horn honked outside. "That'll be my taxi. I'll see you later."

Blue poured herself a glass of orange juice and sat down at the kitchen table. Her gaze fell to the floor where her imagination superimposed a scaly dragon, lurking below ground. She shuddered and climbed out of her chair so suddenly that it tumbled over.

Five minutes later, Blue was dressed and closing the door of the cottage behind her. She walked briskly and breathed in the fresh morning air that felt as though it was cleansing her of the dragon's dank lair. Her every step landing in time to the beat of the melody that my orchestra now played for her. She had always sought Harry's company in times of confusion or strife. He had been to hell and back during the Great War and had only survived with his marbles intact due to his thoughtful, philosophical nature. Harry had never been a chatterbox; it was as though the bombs had blown the words out of him. But he'd always been a listener, and, in the absence of words, listening had become Harry's superpower. For as long as she could remember, Blue had longed for him to open up about and share the burden of that terrible time. Perhaps if he did, he would release some of the pressure that made his hands tremble, as Sheila had always said he would. Blue had always felt inadequate to the task, and if the wife that he adored hadn't been able to get him to talk, then what chance did she have? But, on this sunny morning in June of 1926, Fate had a surprise in store for her…

The lake looked very different to when Blue had visited it with Harry the first time. No longer was it a picturesque expanse of water nestled amid tall trees. Now it resembled a vast crater that contained a foot of muddy water. Harry was sitting with his foreman on an upturned rowing boat, drinking coffee from a flask. The foreman spotted Blue approaching and smiled at her. Harry looked over his shoulder and beckoned to her.

The foreman stood up, "Hello, young miss," he said, "it's always a pleasure to see your smiling face."

"Thank you. Do I smile *that* much?"

"Whenever I see you around, you're smiling."

"That was definitely my first smile of the day," replied Blue, looking at Harry.

"Well then, you'd better sit and tell me all about it," said Harry patting the spot the foreman had just vacated. Blue wasted no time in accepting his offer. "I'm not keeping you from anything?"

"Don't worry about that."

The foreman drew a cloth from the back pocket of his trousers and wiped it across his sweaty brow. "I'll make a start on pump five, Mr Tibbs."

"Alright. I'll join you presently."

"Nice seeing you again, Miss," he said as he walked away.

"And you," Blue called after him.

Blue and Harry sat in silence for half a minute, staring at the muddy crater that had been a beautiful boating lake. Harry waited patiently while Blue searched for the words that would convey how she felt without having to spill the beans about what she'd been up to. As Fate would have it, a robin flew overhead and landed in the branches of the tree that shaded them. Harry craned his neck and Blue, seeing the desperation on his face to see the little bird, swallowed the lump that had risen into her throat. She looked at the crater. "You never saw any in France. Did you, Dad?"

"See any what?" murmured Harry.

"Birds."

Harry's lips trembled, and his face lit up with hope as the robin took flight over the crater. "… No, not a single one."

Blue reached for and squeezed his hand. It trembled in her own. "It's hard to believe this crater is the same boating lake, isn't it?"

Harry nodded slowly.

"Dad… does it remind you of France?"

"Yes," blurted Harry as though he'd never expected, not in a million years, to confide such a thing to anyone who wasn't there, let alone his little girl.

"I thought so," said Blue, trying to sound matter-of-fact.

Following a pause, and to Blue's utter delight, Harry said, "Only the crater in France… well, it went on as far as the eye could see. In every direction." Blue looked around and tried to imagine *nothing* but a muddy crater for miles. "It must have felt like the end of the world."

"For many of my pals it was the end."

Blue held her father's hand firmly.

"Some of those pals of mine," began Harry as though he scarcely believed such a thing was possible, "are a part of that crater to this very day."

Blue wiped away the single tear that was creeping down her cheek. "I'm so sorry, Dad."

"Sorry? There's nothing for you to be sorry about. Those friends of mine, well, they gave their lives for the freedom we enjoy. We *honour* their sacrifice." Blue lifted her head, so she could see her father's face. Harry searched her eyes for the slightest hint of distress. Had he seen any, he would have shut up like a clam. But he saw only strength in Blue's eyes, a need to understand and be a better person as a result. "Do you know…" he said.

"What?"

"I owe my life to you."

"How?"

"Well, I hadn't long received the letter from your mother that mentioned you for the first time. During the heat of battle, I was knocked to my knees and delayed from standing for a moment."

"Delayed by what?"

"By you, darling. Despite everything, your name, it popped into my head. And I wondered about it for a moment. Why on earth is she called Blue? It was a moment that saved my life."

"Really?"

"Yes, a bullet, it passed over my head, so close that it left a *tiny* indentation in my helmet. That's why I'm convinced that you saved my life that day."

"Sounds like my name did. And anyway, you were always going to come home. How else could you have been the best dad an orphan with an unusual name could have hoped for?"

Harry drew her close. "Thank you."

"No, thank you for talking to me about the war. When I was little, I thought that if I could get you to talk about France then your hands would stop trembling."

"Whatever gave you that idea?"

"I heard Mum telling you that you needed to talk about what happened."

Harry smiled and rolled his shoulder. "I do feel lighter for our talk, but…" He held out a hand palm down. "… It's still there."

"Give it time."

Harry lowered his hand. "You wanted to talk to me about something?"

"Oh, it was nothing. Nothing as important as…" said Blue, indicating the crater with a sweep of a hand. Reader, the time had arrived for Fate to provide his hunter of dragons with her lance. I drew myself up to my full height, my shadow stretching as far as the eye could see and led my string section in a melody that whipped up a breeze, lifting Harry's newspaper up off the end of the boat. The string section fell silent and, to the strike of a single triangle, Blue jumped up, took three skirting steps, and scooped up the newspaper: her gaze drawn to the headline on the page where it had blown open. She read it aloud. "'The Ku Klux Klan's support for prohibition stronger than ever.' But… I don't understand?"

"What is it?"

"This headline," said Blue, holding up the page.

"There's nothing to understand. The Klan have always been fervent supporters of prohibition."

"But they can't be."

"I can assure you they are. It's the *key* policy on which their popularity has risen."

"But I… I heard a rumour about how they're supplying the liquor for Mr De Croy's parties."

"The Ku Klux Klan?"

"Yes."

"From who? Apricot?"

Blue breathed a sigh of relief at Harry's simple explanation and nodded.

"Then Apricot must be mistaken."

"Why must she?"

Harry glanced at the newspaper in her hands. "You're holding the reason. They simply wouldn't risk it."

"Do you mind if I take this page?" said Blue, sliding it free.

"… Ah, be my guest."

"I'll see you later, Dad! Enjoy your day! Love you!" said Blue as she hightailed it in the direction of the chateau. Harry smiled and shook his head.

Minutes later, Blue was halfway across the lawn, the chateau looming above the trees to her right, the gatehouse a blot at the end of the drive to her left. Blue cast her gaze right and left before sighing impatiently and heading for the gate house. No sooner had she started walking down the drive when she heard a car approaching from behind. She stepped to the side of the road and watched as an enormous black limousine cruised majestically towards her. As it passed, Blue tried to get a look at the passengers but couldn't see through the limousine's blacked out windows. No sooner had it sped past, then it came to a crunching halt. A chauffeur climbed out and opened the rear door. A smiling Apricot poked her head out.

"That's a bit of luck!" said Blue, hurrying over, "I was just coming to see you."

"You were? The house is *that* way," said Apricot, glancing back up the drive.

"Yes, but the gate keeper needs to call ahead. There's no *door bell,*" said Blue, exasperated.

"I'm not being funny, but you can always follow the signs to the servants' entrance. It would save you bags of time," said Apricot, sliding back inside the limousine. She patted the seat. "Get in, dear love."

"*Okay,*" said Blue climbing inside, "where are we going?" she asked as the chauffeur closed the door behind her.

"Manhattan. That whole thing with the Klan has rather upset me."

"And?"

"And some retail therapy's in order." She observed the look on Blue's face. "Not for me. If you must know, I was going to buy you and Terry a present."

"No need to get me anything. But getting a gift for Terry sounds like a great idea."

"Consider it done."

Blue pulled the newspaper's page from her pocket and unfolded it. "You aren't going to believe this."

"Aren't I? What is it?"

"See for yourself…" said Blue, showing her the headline: 'Ku Klux Klan's support for prohibition stronger than ever.'

"They're a bunch of lousy hypocrites. It's hardly surprising given how vile they are."

"It's not about them being hypocrites. Dad said their support for prohibition is what helped to make them so popular."

"And?"

"And if we could let people know what they're really up to."

Apricot began to giggle. "You think we can get involved in… in *politics*? Oh, darling. We're basically still *children*."

Blue drew the newspaper clipping gently from Apricot's hand and gazed down at it. She sat so still and looked so deflated that Apricot wondered if she was still breathing. She was about to ask her as much when Blue drew breath and murmured, "Then we should seek the advice of an adult."

"Who? My uncle? I can assure you he already knows about all this."

Blue gazed out the window and, as I led my orchestra in the same tune it had played on the occasions when she had encountered Lady Constance, a smile spread across her face. "Before we go shopping, we're going to pay someone a visit."

Apricot scratched at an itch on her nose. "Are we? Who?"

"Lady Constance. She's spending the summer with friends in Manhattan. I know her address. She gave it to me so I could write to her."

"Oh, she did?" said Apricot, folding her arms. "Well, writing is one thing, but turning up at her residence is another entirely. We can't just stop by unannounced."

"Miss Apricot De Croy lacking confidence? Who'd have thought?"

"Don't tease me. You know Lady Constance is a hero of mine."

"Mine too. So, who better to ask about all this?" said Blue, glancing down at the newspaper clipping. Apricot raised her nose as though she needed to get back into forthright character. "Alright," she said, "you had better tell Johnson the address." This Blue did and then sat back in her seat, placed her arms on the rests, interlinked her fingers, and gazed down into them.

Apricot observed her. "What now?" she asked.

"I just spoke to my Dad."

"Is that unusual?"

"It *happened*," said Blue, looking up from her hands at her. "He talked to me about the war."

The look of wonder on Blue's face brought a lump to Apricot's throat. "I get the impression you've been hoping he'd do that for a while?"

"Only for as long as I can remember."

"I'm ecstatic for you. Was it too harrowing?"

Blue shook her head. "It was moving. He told me about the friends he'd lost."

Apricot looked out her window. "I can't remember my father. But I used to dream about talking to him. And mother of course. Those were my favourite dreams."

"How old were you when they passed away?"

"Four. I was supposed to be with them in the car that day, but I came down with a fever and my doctor said I needed bed rest."

"Don't you find it strange," said Blue, "the way things happen the way they do? My birth mother and your parents. All taken so suddenly. And now, here we are, a one-time English orphan, and a famous American heiress, friends."

Apricot nodded slowly. "And on our merry way to call on a famous suffragette."

The limousine pulled up at the apartment block on Fifth Avenue where Lady Constance was staying. Apricot looked at the building's revolving door and red awning that reached to the side of the curb. "I recognise this place. A friend of my aunt lives here." The revolving door began to turn and a doorman in a red braided uniform stepped out. He exchanged a nod with Johnson who climbed out of the car and opened the back door of the limousine. "We're here to call on Lady Constance Manners," said Apricot as she and Blue climbed out. "Is she at home?"

"Yes, Miss. Is Lady Constance expecting you?"

"No. Not exactly. It's a surprise visit."

"If you'll kindly follow me. Whom shall I say is calling?"

"Miss Apricot De Croy and Miss Blue Tibbs."

Inside the lobby, they were directed to a sofa above which hung the biggest chandelier that Blue had ever seen. "It looks like a giant crystal spider died and rolled onto its back," observed Blue, taking a seat under it.

"Honestly, that imagination of yours," said Apricot, sitting beside her. An elevator door opened onto the lobby and a smartly dressed woman sauntered out holding a Yorkshire terrier. As she crossed the foyer towards the revolving door she smiled at Apricot, while her dog stared at Blue.

"I think that lady recognised you," whispered Blue.

"Not beyond the bounds of possibility. I think her mutt recognised you."

"Not beyond the bounds of possibility," said Blue as they began to chuckle.

The porter, who had been talking in hushed tones into a telephone receiver, glanced over at them, nodded, shook his head, murmured something into the receiver and replaced it. He walked over and stood over them. "Lady Constance has asked that you give her a few minutes," he said, taking his pocket watch from his waistcoat and observing the dial.

"Okay," said Apricot, "let us know *when*, would you, my good man?"

The doorman nodded, turned on his heels and headed back to his desk where he fluffed out his coat tails and sat down.

Blue raised an eyebrow. "My good man?"

Apricot crossed one leg over the other and shrugged. "Have you seen Terry this morning?"

"No. I made a bee-line for Dad. I always do when something's upset me."

"So I gathered. And Terrance has his mother to talk to if he's upset about what happened."

"Yes, but it's not as though he can broach the *actual* subject. If he could he wouldn't have had to climb through a window to get in last night."

"The indignity of it. I forget that you two have elders to answer to. People who care about what you get up to."

"Your uncle and aunt care."

"Not enough to worry about what I'm doing."

"They trust you."

"Oh, yes, because I'm *so* mature."

"You are you know."

"Regardless, I'll follow your lead with Lady Constance," said Apricot sounding her age suddenly.

"Okey doke."

They were suddenly aware that the concierge was standing over them.

"Yes?" asked Apricot, mildly agitated.

"Lady Constance's assistant is on her way down. She'll show you up."

"Thank you," said Blue as the elevator arrived at the ground floor. The doors opened and a middle-aged woman with a shock of red hair and pince-nez spectacles on a chain stepped out. "Miss Blue Tibbs and Miss Apricot De Croy?" she asked, holding her spectacles up to her eyes.

"Your eyes do not deceive you," replied Apricot, standing.

"Then would you care to follow me?" said the woman, returning to the lift.

There was an awkward silence as the elevator carried them up. A silence broken by Apricot. "I hope Lady Constance hasn't been too put out by our visit?"

"I wouldn't have thought so, she's been up since the early hours," murmured her assistant, attempting to tidy her unruly red hair with a jittery hand. Blue watched her and wondered if she'd been through a traumatic experience like her father. She had an image of the woman's hair escaping from a helmet as she clutched a rifle and charged, hell for leather, across No Man's Land. Apricot looked at Blue. "Why the weird expression? What's the matter?"

"Nothing."

They came upon Lady Constance reclined on a chaise longue. "Come in ladies, there's no need to look quite so sheepish."

"We're sorry to call on you out of the blue," said Blue, looking around at the Art Deco furniture typical of the period: sleek teak furniture, vast mirrors in silver frames, and black and white prints of the famous artists, actors and thinkers of the day.

"Nonsense," replied Lady Constance with a wave of a hand. "Sit down and make yourselves comfortable." She pointed to a high-backed couch upholstered in black velvet. "Tea? Coffee? Perhaps you'd like some breakfast?"

"Nothing for me, thanks. Maybe just a glass of water?" said Blue, taking a seat.

Apricot nodded. "Water is fine for me too, thank you," she said, sitting beside her.

"A jug of iced water and two glasses for my visitors please, Betty," Lady Constance said to her assistant. "My, what serious faces you have. Has there been a death?"

"No, nothing as natural as *death*," said Blue.

"How frightfully profound," nodded Apricot.

"Something worse than death has brought you here on this sunny morning," said Lady Constance, looking towards the room's large windows where golden sunshine streamed onto the carpet. "What could two young ladies have encountered that's worse than death?"

"A *disgusting* dragon," shuddered Blue.

"A dragon?" said Lady Constance, her chin disappearing into her neck.

"Blue's being a little melodramatic," said Apricot. "But, only a little," she added quietly.

"The plot thickens," said Lady Constance. "Does this dragon have a name?" Betty returned with a jug of iced water and two glasses on a silver tray. She placed the tray down on an occasional table before Blue and Apricot. "It does have a name," said Blue, "it's called the *Ku Klux Klan.*"

"The Klan? And where did you come across them?"

"They were having a meeting beneath Chateau De Croy," said Apricot.

"Beneath it? I don't understand?"

Blue sat forward. "There's a network of caverns and rooms under the chateau. They used to be part of an old colonial prison. It's where they locked up African slaves. The cells are there to this *day.*"

"It's true. And every bit as ghastly as it sounds," said Apricot in answer to Lady Constance's disbelieving expression.

"The Klan hold meetings there," added Blue.

"They revel in its ghastly history."

"Delightful," said Lady Constance. "And your uncle is aware that these meetings are taking place under his property?"

Apricot shrugged. "He knows the Klan are using the underground network. It runs all the way to beach, and they use it to deliver alcohol in secret to the chateau."

"The *Klan*? Are you sure?"

"Yes, that's what we wanted to talk to you about," said Blue, reaching into her pocket and drawing out the newspaper clipping. She unfolded and handed it into Lady Constance's outstretched hand. Lady Constance read the headline about the Klan's support for prohibition. She rolled her eyes. "It would appear they're hypocrites. Which is hardly surprising."

"That's exactly what I said," said Apricot, beaming from ear to ear.

Blue glanced at the clipping. "Dad said their support of prohibition is the main reason they're so popular."

"He's not wrong," agreed Lady Constance.

"Then people need to know about this," said Blue.

"Perhaps so. But *proof* would be needed."

"Proof?" said Blue, a faraway look in her eyes as she pondered the possibility of finding some.

"Yes. Proof. But this business is far too dangerous for children to be involved with," said Lady Constance, looking back and forth between them as though to gauge the impact of this news.

Blue shook her head. "Deeds not words," she said, so stoically that she reminded Lady Constance of her younger self.

"Yes, of course," said Lady Constance quietly, "but, I repeat, you are too young to involve yourselves in the affairs of such people."

"We have to do something, surely," said Blue, undeterred. "You should have seen Terry when..." said Blue, emotion evaporating her words.

"Terry?" asked Lady Constance.

"Terrance is my stable boy," said Apricot, shooting a concerned glance at Blue.

"Apricot's *black* stable boy. He was with us under the chateau, inside the dragon's lair," added Blue.

"You took a *black boy* to a Ku Klux Klan meeting? Have you quite taken leave of your senses?"

"We didn't *take* him. He wanted to come," said Blue.

"Is he all there?"

Blue and Apricot glanced at one another.

"Yes," said Blue, "he was wearing a mask and gloves, so they had no idea who he was."

"We'd been at the masked ball," added Apricot, answering Lady Constance's questioning expression.

"Regardless, do you have any idea of the danger you placed that young man in?"

"I would *never* have allowed them to hurt him," said Apricot.

"That is exactly the kind of remark that proves why young people should not involve themselves with such matters. Do you really think that if such a gathering got it into their heads to have...

to have…" Lady Constance turned pale and her hand went to her throat.

"But it's nineteen twenty-six. They wouldn't go that far, *surely*," said Blue.

"You never know what a group of men with such views might do when their blood lust is up. I'm sorry if I'm frightening you but you must be aware of how serious this is."

"You and the other suffragettes wouldn't have shied away from taking them on," said Blue.

"Not for a second," added Apricot.

"We were all grown women. You came here for my advice?"

The girls nodded.

"Then listen carefully and take heed. If you want to fight this dragon then for the time being, do so from a safe distance. Write letters to people of influence. Express your concerns. You are the future are you not? Should this organisation continue to grow it will make the world you have to bring up your children in a hateful one."

"But if we *could* get proof of the dragon's involvement in supplying bootlegged alcohol, then it would hurt it. Wouldn't it?" said Blue. It was as though she hadn't listened to a word that Lady Constance had said. Apricot braced herself on Blue's behalf but, although Lady Constance's expression was grave, it softened.

"You remind me of myself when I was your age. And I've little doubt that you'll grow into a young lady who will make a positive difference in the world. But please, I implore you, for the time being Blue, be patient."

Chapter 23
A gift for Terry

"Patience isn't really your thing, is it?" said Apricot, as the limousine sped away from Lady Constance's building.

"I can't see how we have the luxury of patience. The cause that Lady Constance fought for wasn't this urgent."

"No?"

"No. Not when you think about it. Men had kept the vote for themselves since *forever,* whereas our hate-breathing dragon has come out of nowhere and is growing fatter by the day. This is the most powerful country in the world. Isn't it supposed to be an example of tolerance? If you hadn't helped Europe beat the Germans, then who knows what might have happened in The Great War?"

"I'll take that as a compliment on behalf of a grateful nation, dear love."

"It is a compliment. And what if Europe needs your help again? And… and the dragon had a say in things?"

"Like Germany is *ever* going to start another war after what happened to them in the last one."

Reader, out of the mouths of babes.

The limousine pulled up outside of Macy's department store and Johnson got out and opened the back door. The girls climbed out and stood on the curb where envious passersby stared at them. *It's not my car it's hers*, Blue wanted to shout.

They traversed the revolving door and stood in the Art Deco entrance where the sweet smell of perfumes conspired to make Blue sneeze.

"Bless you," said Apricot.

"Thank you. Any thoughts on what to get Terry?"

"Yes, I know just the thing, but a spot of refreshment first, I'm parched."

"So, what is it?"

"You'll just have to wait as see. Come on! The tea room is on the fourth floor and the elevator's over here," said Apricot, making a beeline through the shoppers.

The attitude of the tall and stuffy maître d', standing before a podium at the entrance to the Grand Tea Room, altered significantly when he noticed Apricot approaching. "Miss De Croy!" he exclaimed in a French accent. "Always such a pleasure to see you in our store."

"I don't doubt it. This is my friend, Miss Blue Tibbs. We'd like your very best table."

"Of course! Of course! Ah, why so blue?" the maître d' asked Blue, his smile that of a concerned clown.

Apricot gave her a conspiratorial nudge. "My friend finds the current state of politics rather depressing."

"Ah Mademoiselle! You are much too young to worry about such things! But in any event, I have just the desserts to return a smile to that pretty face," he said, snatching up a couple of menus and, turning on his heels, he led them to a table in the room's only bay window. "This table is reserved for our *most* cherished customers," he said, pulling out a seat for Apricot and then for Blue.

"He's very friendly," observed Blue as the maître d' fluffed up his black coat tails and returned to his podium with a swagger.

"Whenever I come here, I tip him twenty dollars," murmured Apricot as she opened the menu.

"What? No wonder. Why so much?"

"I come to devour sweet stuff when I'm lonely and depressed and, while it may be true that money can't buy you friends, it can buy you a hearty welcome."

"Clearly," said Blue as she watched the maître d' shake his head and explain to a down at heel couple that all the tables were reserved or taken. Blue sighed at their plight and then, following a philosophical shrug, picked up her menu. "Lonely? You'd think you'd have more friends than you could shake a stick at…"

"Their raspberry cheesecake is *delicious*," said Apricot licking her lips.

"Raspberry cheesecake it is then. Thanks."

"My lonely plight surprises you?" said Apricot, dropping her menu on the table.

"I suppose not," sighed Blue. "Not after having spent time with you."

The girls looked gravely at one another, and then broke into smiles. "Before I met you, I imagined that beautiful and rich people had a lot of friends."

"A popular misconception, particularly when it comes to me," said Apricot. "Others in my social circle look down their noses at anyone who isn't as privileged as they are. They're a bad influence on me. I know they are. And *common* girls of my own age are usually awkward in my company, no offence. How about you?"

"Never been one for having a lot of friends. Just a few, Mum likes to say, *peculiar* ones, no offence."

"Touché!" smiled Apricot.

A waiter was standing over them.

"Full afternoon tea for two. And two side orders of cheesecake," said Apricot, handing her menu up to the waiter.

"Very good, Miss De Croy."

"Full afternoon tea?" said Blue, as she watched the waiter mince away.

"Yes, we might as well eat till we drop. It won't make the world a better place, but it will feel like a better one. At least for a little while."

"Which is why we're going to ignore Lady Constance's advice."

"Ignore it? What was the point of going to see her?"

"Inspiration."

"Really? She told us to write some letters and then to grow up. How was that inspirational?"

"She just doesn't want to see us come a cropper," shrugged Blue.

Apricot raised an eyebrow. "Presumably, that makes the three of us?"

"Deeds not words."

"She also said that *proof* would be needed that the Klan supplies alcohol for my uncle's parties."

"Then we'll just have to find some," answered Blue.

There was a little vase on the table that contained a pink rose. Apricot lifted and glanced under it. "None here…"

"It seems to me," said Blue thoughtfully, "that we'll need to follow the paper trail."

"Follow the *what*? If you ask me, it sounds like you've read too many detective novels."

"You heard what Dogsbody said? Blake likes to keep everything in order. He must keep accounts. Records. We just need to find them."

Apricot's mouth fell open, but the appropriate words eluded her.

"Which is why we have to find out where Blake's base of operations is," said Blue.

"Where his *what* is?"

"His base of operations."

"Stone the crows, darling. Who talks like that?"

"Army people?"

"For goodness sake. We aren't soldiers."

"We aren't forty either."

Apricot looked horrified. "Do I really sound that old?"

"Only intermittently." Blue leaned across the table conspiratorially, and Apricot found herself mirroring her body language. "What is it?" asked Apricot, lowering her voice.

"I have a pretty good idea how you can find out where it is."

"You're talking about Blake's base of operations, aren't you?"

Blue nodded and leaned in closer. "Your uncle told me he keeps a file on his activities. It's in a cabinet in his study."

"And how do you know *that*?"

"Keep your voice down," said Blue, glancing around at the other customers. "When I went to see him, your uncle told me. And he glanced at a filing cabinet when he did."

"So?"

"It's in there. I could tell," said Blue. The waiter returned and placed two four-tiered silver salvers on the table. Each held an array of sandwiches, cakes and pastries. "There's enough food on this table for a wedding reception," observed Blue, sitting back in her seat.

"Not the kind of wedding receptions I'm used to. Tuck in," said Apricot, reaching for a smoked salmon sandwich.

Blue picked up a chocolate éclair. "You'll do it then? You'll take a look in that file ..." she said, biting into it.

"You mean for the location of Blake's base of operations," chewed Apricot, thoughtfully.

"Umm, yes," replied Blue in near rapture at the taste of chocolate and cream in her mouth.

"Sure. I'll take a look. But that doesn't mean I'll find anything."

"I have the utmost faith in you."

"Who sounds forty now?" said Apricot as the waiter returned with two slices of cheesecake.

A little later, feeling bloated and more than a little sick, Apricot led Blue through the store to get Terry's gift. "You're going to buy him some shoes?" said Blue as they entered the men's shoe department.

"How would shoes cheer him up?" said Apricot.

"You really don't have a lot in common with your peer group, do you?"

Apricot stopped in her tracks. "Would you like some shoes?"

"Ah, no," said Blue, who didn't stop and found herself ahead of Apricot. "Come on, lead on Mc Duff," she said with a wave.

"No need. I believe it's through here," said Apricot, motioning into a dimly lit room to her right. Inside, they found themselves in a high-ceilinged space where thousands of tiny lights twinkled in a pitch-black ceiling. A smiled spread across Blue's face as she gazed around at the selection of telescopes on display beneath this makeshift cosmos. "You're going to buy him a telescope!"

"That's right. And not just any old telescope," said Apricot, her smile as wide as Blue's. "A Rocket 3000."

Blue threw her arms around her. "He'll love it!"

"You think it'll take his mind off his encounter with the dragon?"

"Yes!"

They heard a man clear his throat respectfully and Apricot and Blue turned to see Johnson standing beside a box wrapped in gold wrapping paper. "Oh, Johnson, I asked you to meet me here, I forgot." The smile returned to the faces of both girls as they took in the size of the box – taller than they were and wide enough to contain them both. Johnson was a powerfully built man but even he grimaced as he lifted it off the ground. "And it's a good thing you did, Miss De Croy," he said, going red in the face.

An hour later, when the limousine pulled into the stable yard, the enormous gift sticking out of its boot, Blue and Apricot gazed out of their windows for Terry. There was plenty of activity, but Terry was nowhere to be seen. The car came to a halt and the girls opened their doors and jumped out before Johnson had had a chance to let them out. "Is Terry about?" Apricot asked a beanpole of a stable boy who turned the colour of a beetroot.

"No, Miss De Croy."

Apricot gestured with her hands for him to produce more information.

"Terry didn't come in this morning, Sick, I think?"

Apricot and Blue glanced at one another. "The Curtis's cottage, please Johnson," said Apricot, climbing back inside the limousine with Blue.

The girls were relieved by the sight of Mrs Curtis's smiling face when she opened the front door. "Miss Apricot? Miss Blue? Is everything alright?" she asked, looking over their heads as Johnson hefted the package out of the limousine's boot.

"We heard Terry wasn't feeling well?" said Blue.

"That's what he tells me," said Mrs Curtis. "What's this?" she asked as Johnson, with all but his shoes obscured, struggled up the garden path with the package.

"A little gift for Terry," said Apricot.

"A little gift?"

"In a large box," added Blue.

"But why have you brought Terrance a gift?"

Apricot scratched at a temple. "As a thank you for being the best stable boy I could have hoped for. He takes such good care of the Queen of Sheba."

Brilliant, thought Blue.

"My, that is very generous, Miss Apricot."

Blue patted Apricot's shoulder. "Do you mind if we come in and give it to him, Mrs Curtis?"

"Of course not. You're always welcome. I wasn't expecting any visitors so please excuse the mess," said Mrs Curtis, patting her tidy afro.

The living room contained stacks of clothes waiting to be washed and ironed, and neater stacks that had already been tended to.

163

Blue glanced about. "Do you do the laundry for everyone on the estate?"

"Goodness no. Just for the chateau," said Mrs Curtis with pride.

"Mrs Curtis is my uncle's personal laundry service," said Apricot as Johnson cleared his throat. "Oh, right. Sorry, Johnson. Where should he put it?"

"Anywhere!" exclaimed Mrs Curtis.

"Put it down anywhere, Johnson."

"Very good, Miss."

"Where's Terry?" asked Blue, rolling her eyes.

"He's taken to his sick bed," said Mrs Curtis as she watched Johnson deposit the package beside her sofa.

"What's wrong with him?" said Blue.

Mrs Curtis looked at Apricot. "He was feeling poorly this morning," she shrugged.

"Do you mind if we look in on the patient?"

"Not at all but please excuse me while I see if he's in a fit state for visitors," said Mrs Curtis, smoothing down her overalls with the palms of her hands. She crossed the room to a door which she opened and closed behind her. Blue and Apricot could hear a muffled conversation taking place within. From the rise and fall of their tones, Blue gathered that Terry was asking his mother if she was *sure* the parcel was for him.

"What are you smiling about now? Presumably you do need a reason?" Apricot asked her.

"Terry can't understand how the package is for him."

"You can hear what they're saying? What are you? A bat?"

The door opened, and Mrs Curtis stepped out. "The patient will see you now," she said. Apricot glanced at Johnson and Johnson, having read her expression, hefted the package up.

The room was bright and airy with a large open window. There was a bed where Terry lay in green pajamas, and a writing desk above which was a shelf that displayed Terry's prized collection of books all about the moon, the stars, and everything in between. "Here's the patient," said Mrs Curtis, as Terry's mouth fell open at the sight of Johnson struggling through his bedroom door with the package.

"Anywhere will do, won't it Apricot?" said Blue.

Apricot nodded and Johnson put the gift down at the end of Terry's bed where it loomed over him like a golden monolith.

"And what do you say to your visitors?" Mrs Curtis asked her son.

"Is this for me?"

"Terrance Curtis!"

"Thank you. Is this for me?"

Apricot checked her nail varnish. "Either it's for you, *Terrance*, or I make Johnson follow me around with it out of sheer spite."

Terry gazed at her; his thoughts difficult to hide and his expression easy to read.

Apricot placed her hands on her hips. "Of *course* it's for you."

"Don't you want to know why Miss Apricot has brought you a gift?" asked Mrs Curtis, her face beaming with pride.

She wants to make up for almost getting me lynched, thought Terry, leaning forward and peering at the parcel. "Son, it's to say thank you for taking such good care of the Queen of Sheba. What a lovely thing for Miss Apricot to do."

"… It's my pleasure," murmured Terry.

"Terrance has always had had a way with animals," beamed Mrs Curtis.

"Well," said Blue, "aren't you going to open your gift? The suspense is killing me."

Terry jumped out of bed with a swiftness that betrayed a young man in perfect health. He stood beside the parcel that was a head taller than him and looked none the wiser as to where and how to start. "May I make a suggestion?" said Johnson.

Everyone nodded.

"The box has been well sealed and will require a sharp implement to open it. It might be better if I do it."

"Yes, very good idea, Johnson. We'll all go and wait in the kitchen while you open the box and set it all up," said Apricot.

"It needs setting up?" said Terry, placing an ear against the package.

"Yes," enthused Blue, "set it up. I can't wait to see the look on your face when you see it."

Apricot regarded the enormous package. "My thinking precisely."

"I'll fetch you a knife," said Terry bolting from the room. He returned with a knife that gleamed as much as his smile.

They closed the door and left Johnson to unpack and set up Terry's gift. Mrs Curtis brewed up a fresh pot of coffee, and they sat at the kitchen table and listened impatiently to the sound of a box being forcefully opened. "Have you really no clue as to what it is?" Apricot asked Terry.

"A gigantic stuffed toy maybe? Like one of yours?"

"Don't be ridiculous," chuckled Blue.

"*Excuse me*?" said Apricot. "What's so ridiculous about my collection of stuffed toys?"

"Nothing. It's ah, quirky."

"So, it isn't a stuffed toy?" said Terry, hopefully.

"No," said Blue, rubbing her hands in glee. They heard something crash to the floor followed by a groan. Everyone looked at Terry's bedroom door. "You don't think he's hurt himself? Someone should check he's alright," said Mrs Curtis, making her way over.

"No, that won't be necessary, Mrs Curtis. Johnson will let us know if he requires medical assistance. Besides, he's got a certificate in first aid."

"Well, if you're sure, Miss Apricot," said Mrs Curtis as she returned to the table and poured coffee into their cups.

Thirty minutes later, Mrs Curtis, having ironed and folded a great many items of clothing, and the impatient taps of shoes under the table having outnumbered the words spoken, the door to Terry's room opened and Johnson stepped out.

Apricot jumped up. "It's all ready?"

"Yes, Miss De Croy," nodded Johnson, unfurling the sleeves of his white shirt. Terry stood and crossed the room in one deft movement. They piled into the room to see him gawping at the shiny black telescope, secured on a silver tripod, its farthest end two metres from the ground. Terry's arm was outstretched, his fingertips suspended in the air as though, if he touched the telescope, he might wake from his dream.

Mrs Curtis clasped her hands to her cheeks. "Oh, my!"

"It's a telescope," Apricot informed her helpfully.

Mrs Curtis's mouth opened to say she could *see that* but then, remembering who she was speaking to, she closed it again.

"You can touch it, Terry. It won't bite," said Blue, standing next to him. "It's all yours. A Rocket 3000."

Terry shook his head fervently and whistled through his teeth.

"I'll have you know it is a Rocket 3000," said Apricot, "I was very clear about the model."

Terry gazed at her over his shoulder. "*This* is a Rocket 3000 Deluxe Edition."

"Oh, is it?"

"Yes! It has a magnification of *eight hundred times,*" said Terry, touching it and breathing a sigh of relief.

"So, what do you say to Miss Apricot?" said Mrs Curtis.

Terry turned to Apricot and, when the appropriate words eluded him, he stepped forward, picked her up and twirled her around.

"Terrance!" cried Mrs Curtis, "put Miss Apricot down this instant!"

Terry did this only, it seemed, so he could pick up Blue.

"Terrance! Put Blue down this instant!"

This he did and then turned and stepped towards his mother. "You had better not, you'll give yourself a hernia, son."

Terry shrugged and turned back to his telescope, beaming. "Only nine hours to go."

"Until what?" asked Apricot.

"The sun sets…"

"The moon's very bright and full today," said Blue. Terry dragged his gaze from the telescope and looked at her. "I saw it out of the car window on the way back from New York."

Terry stepped over to a lunar calendar that hung on his bedroom wall beside an old pair of binoculars. "You did at that," he breathed, bolting to and through his bedroom door.

"Terry! Where are you going in your pajamas?" cried Mrs Curtis.

"Out front to check on the moon!"

They heard a yelp and, seconds later, he was back in the room, sizing up the telescope for the purpose of moving it outside. "Shall I call Johnson in?" said Apricot.

"No, thank you. I need to learn how to move it myself," said Terry. He knelt and began turning the first of a series of wheels that unscrewed the telescope from its tripod.

Not long after, the tripod was standing on the lawn in the front garden. Blue and Apricot were sitting on the waist high stone fence that surrounded the cottage, watching as Terry cradled the telescope sideways through the front door. Much to Terry's surprise, the girls waited patiently as he fastened the telescope back on the tripod, and then wiped away any finger smudges with a cloth. As Fate would have it, the atmospheric conditions on that day were *perfect* for viewing a full moon in all its glory – the clouds arranged in such a way to block out the sun's rays.

When he was finished, Terry took a step back and looked from his telescope to the moon, a moon that shone as brightly as any he'd ever seen in the daytime. He rubbed his hands together, stepped forward and leaned over the telescope's upturned eyepiece. As he turned a dial and the moon's surface came into focus, a look of awe spread across his face, a look that Blue would never forget. Apricot missed it because, as Fate would have it, a melody was conspiring to gather thoughts in her mind – thoughts that brought her loathing for the dragon, and their blind hatred of people like Terry and his mother, into sharp focus. "Blue, you're to come for a sleepover tonight," she said.

"What?" said Blue distantly, still savouring the look of joy on Terry's face.

"After my uncle has gone to bed, we'll go to his study. Find whatever it is you need."

Blue's attention was suddenly wholeheartedly on Apricot. "Sounds like a plan," she smiled.

Later that day, Blue arrived home to discover Sheila sitting with her feet up on the couch, a hand clasped to the side of her mouth, a grimace on her face. "How did it go at the dentist, Mum?"

"How do these things usually go? He removed a tooth," groaned Sheila, pointing to the back of her mouth, "it hurts more now than before I went to see him."

"What was it you told me when I had my wisdom teeth out?"

"It'll be better in the long run."

"Exactly."

"You find my pain amusing?"

Blue shook her head. "Apricot just gave Terry a present. A telescope. You should have seen the look on his face, Mum."

"Sounds like a picture," said Sheila, grimacing.

"It was a picture. Oh, Apricot's invited me for a sleepover tonight."

"That's nice."

Blue stifled a yawn. "It's been a long day. Think I'll go and lie down for a bit. Can I get you anything?"

Sheila shook her head and closed her eyes.

Part 3

Chapter 24

The sleepover

Blue was sitting cross-legged on the floor of Apricot's room. Apricot had just drawn the curtains. "We've got some time before my uncle goes to bed so…" said Apricot, flicking a switch and blanketing her room in darkness. She felt her way over to her doll's house. "Ready?"

"The suspense could actually kill me."

Apricot reached up and flipped a switch on the side of the doll's house, and the lights inside its one hundred rooms lit up to such an extent that Blue raised a hand to shield her eyes.

"It's a sight to behold, isn't it?" said Apricot.

"It's… enchanting."

"Yes, and guess what?"

"What?"

"The family who reside here are blissfully happy."

"Where are they?" said Blue, sitting up straight and craning her beck.

"It's dinner time… so, they're gathered in here," said Apricot, pointing into a dining room on the third floor. Blue stood and looked into the oak-panelled room where a Dickensian family of three were eating dinner in the glow of a roaring fire. "How do you know they're so happy?"

Apricot reached inside and moved the mother slightly closer to the table on her chair. "… I told the toymaker that's what I wanted."

"I see," smiled Blue.

"Oh, dear love. I like to imagine what it must be like."

Blue observed her for a moment and then looked at the thumb-sized diners. "Is there really such a thing as a blissfully happy family?"

Apricot nodded heartily. "I'm sure there must be. Don't you think so?"

"Well, if you can afford to live in a mansion like this, with… five servants waiting on you at supper, then why not?"

"Six. There's a footman standing in the corner. As unobtrusive as he should be. And their wealth has *nothing whatsoever* to do with the love this family has for one another. They might just as well be living in a Victorian hovel."

"Then why aren't they?"

"How would you like to wake up beside a gigantic Victorian hovel every morning?"

"Point taken," nodded Blue, trying not to smile.

"This family is happy despite their wealth, not because of it."

"Sounds to me like the best of both worlds."

"Yes, precisely. Money and love."

"Let's not forget health," said Blue, thinking of her father.

Apricot nodded. "They are healthy. They have a live-in doctor. His name is Doctor Finer, and his room is on the top floor," said Apricot, standing on tiptoes to see him in his study. "He's *the* most well-informed doctor. And so kind."

"You really have thought of everything."

"I have plenty of time on my hands when I'm staying here."

"Still, you must miss all this when you go back to school."

"Not as a rule. Although, I suspect I will this year. That's supposing I survive the summer now I have a friend who's a lunatic."

An hour later, during which time Apricot had given Blue a guided tour of her perfect (miniature) family home, they left her room and made their way along numerous dimly lit corridors, down a short flight of stairs, up a much longer one, and arrived at a section of oak panelled wall in a corridor. Apricot observed the wall in silence, hand on chin, as though evaluating an invisible work of art.

Blue glanced left and right. "Nice wall. Are we lost?"

"I've only seen my uncle use this entrance once…"

"What? It's a secret entrance?" said Blue, stepping towards the panelling, her interest piqued.

Apricot nodded into her hand. "He used it on the night of the break in when the Turner was stolen."

Reader, I hold up my hands again. The theft of the painting, the timing of Mr De Croy's hearing about it that prompted him to use his secret entrance to telephone the police, and Apricot's decision to follow him in silence, were all my arrangements – vital pieces of the jigsaw that would enable Blue to return to Mr De Croy's study.

Apricot ran her hand along the oak panelling. "Uncle was so upset that he had no idea I'd followed him but…" Apricot smiled as she found a raised indentation in the oak panel the size of a dime. She pushed it. They heard a faint click and Blue's mouth dropped open as light slipped through a hairline crack. It widened onto a winding staircase. "Hey presto," said Apricot.

"I love it!"

"I had a feeling you would. Wait here while I go up and make sure he's gone to bed," said Apricot, treading her way up the carpeted staircase.

Blue watched her disappear around the first of several corkscrewing bends that led to the top of Mr De Croy's office tower. No sooner had Apricot reached the top when she glanced over her shoulder and tutted.

"Sorry," whispered Blue, "my curiosity got the better of me."

"Wait *here*," said Apricot, pointing at the ground.

"Woof," smiled Blue as Apricot opened a door and slipped inside.

She returned a minute later. "The coast's clear." Blue followed her through a door that led into her uncle's study where she wasted no time in making a bee-line for the cabinet that Mr De Croy had looked at when he'd mentioned the file on Blake's activities. It had four drawers. Blue clasped the silver handle of the first and slid it open and there, atop a velvet lining, lay a folder marked with the letters 'KKK'.

"You were right it seems," said Apricot, standing beside her.

"Told you so," said Blue, opening the cover and gazing at a newspaper clipping of a group of masked men standing before a burning cross.

"Your hands… they're *trembling*…" observed Apricot. "Why? If we're caught, I shall say this was all my doing."

"No, it's not that…"

"Then what?"

Reader, between you and I, Blue sensed the gravity of this moment. Indeed, at times such as these, when so much hangs in the balance, the melody that my orchestra plays, in this instance entitled, 'The Dragon's True Lair Revealed,' is as perceivable to the person that it's playing for as it will ever be.

Blue turned, as though on autopilot, and carried the file to the chair in front of Mr De Croy's desk where she sat down. Apricot headed to her uncle's chair on the other side of the desk. "What do you hope to find in there?" she asked, sitting down.

"I'll know when I see it," murmured Blue as she turned a page of the file. Blue's heart rate increased as she read the name printed in large letters at its top: *Robert Blake*.

"What is it? Have you found something?"

Blue, rapt, turned another page.

Apricot nudged the chair's headrest. "Do share."

"It's a photograph of Blake," said Blue, turning the folder around so that Apricot could see it. Apricot gazed at a black and white photo of Blake about to climb into a car. Blue spun the file back around and turned a page to discover the heading, 'The Activities of Robert Blake.' As she read the words below it, she sat forward in her seat. A minute passed in silence before Blue's eyes flashed up to meet Apricot's. Two words left her lips, and they caused the hairs on Apricot's arms to stand on end. "Rat Island."

"What island?" shuddered Apricot.

"Rat," repeated Blue, standing and making her way around the desk. "It makes sense when you think about it." Blue placed the open file on the desk. "Rat Island is where Blake lives. It says it's also where his headquarters are."

"Okay. And how does that make sense?"

"The Klan aren't so dissimilar to rats, are they?"

"I think you're doing rats a disservice," said Apricot in all sincerity.

"Sorry rats."

Reader, there has been much speculation as to how Rat Island in Long Island Sound got its name. The simple truth of the matter is this: I ensured that a number of rats scampered across the path of the man whose fate it was to name it. I did this in preparation for the human rat that would one day live there.

Blue sat on edge of the desk and gazed down at the page. "Rat Island is where we'll find the proof that Lady Constance said we needed."

"How do you know that?"

Blue turned another page. "I feel it. In my gut."

"Alright. Then what are you looking for now?"

"A map that shows where the island is."

"My uncle is hardly going to include a map."

"Why not?"

"Because he must know where it is. And being *mostly* sane, I can't imagine he has any intention of ever going there."

"You're absolutely right," said Blue, snapping the file closed and making her way back to the filing cabinet. Blue placed the file inside the drawer and slid it closed. She placed her hands on her hips and looked at Apricot.

"What?" asked Apricot, mirroring her body language, only more so.

"We're going to need a map of the local area. Of the islands in the Sound."

"Need I ask for what purpose?"

"How else am I going to work out how to get to Rat Island? You're welcome to come too," Blue added, hopefully.

Apricot extended an arm and a finger and pointed at her. "Unequivocally and *categorically* mental."

Despite her concern for her friend's mental stability, Apricot led Blue to a reading room on the ground floor. On the way there, and in no uncertain terms, Apricot shared her views on anyone considering going to a place called Rat Island that was most likely infested with Klansmen *and* rats. In response, after listening to these objections in silence for a couple of minutes, Blue responded by posing the following question, "Who's *considering*?"

"Unequivocally and *categorically* mental."

They arrived at the reading room, the same one where they'd met Lady Constance on the night of the party. It was no longer a haze of cigarette smoke in which elegant ladies languished with champagne flutes, but a sombre room that contained shelves of books that rose from floor to ceiling. The higher up books were only accessible using a step ladder on casters. Apricot pushed the step ladder to a section of wall beside the only window. She moved it a little to the left and looked up. "There are some local geography books up there."

"How do you know?"

"It just so happens…" said Apricot, climbing onto the ladder, "that I was set a class assignment during the Easter break and…" Apricot reached for a book with a red sleeve, "I spent a morning in here… I remember seeing a map of the local islands."

"Well, that was a bit of luck," murmured Blue.

Apricot climbed down the ladder. She handed the red leather-bound book to Blue who avidly read the title on its sleeve. *A Brief History of Long Island Sound.* "Not so brief," said Blue, placing the weighty tome down on a round table close to the window. She sat in one of the six chairs arranged around the table and opened the book at what seemed to her a random page. "Oh my goodness," she gasped.

"What?" asked Apricot, sitting in the chair beside her.

Blue pointed to the heading on page 147, the one she'd 'randomly' opened the book at, "Pelham Island No. 3: Rat Island."

"Well, that's a spooky coincidence."

Reader, you must know by now that coincidences, spooky or otherwise, have nothing whatsoever to do with spooks or luck and *everything* to do with the demanding schedule of Yours Truly.

Blue read the following aloud from the page: "Rat Island is one of the Pelham Islands in Long Island Sound. It is two and a half acres across and has a dual humped appearance. The island is surrounded by a bluish-looking beach made of mussel shells and bird bones." Blue fell silent as her eyes passed over the next sentence.

"What is it?" asked Apricot.

"Not sure I should tell you."

"Tell me what?"

Blue drew a deep breath. "During the typhoid fever outbreak of the 1800s, it was used as a place of quarantine for sufferers, hence the construction of The Pelham Pesthouse."

"You mean like a *leper* colony?"

Blue nodded. "Only they marooned typhoid sufferers on the island to prevent them spreading the disease."

"Charming."

Blue turned the page and came upon a map showing the location of the island in the Sound. Apricot leaned over it. "I recognise those humps... I've seen Rat Island from uncle's yacht.

You're still considering going there? The Pelham Pesthouse just sounds so creepy."

Blue nodded absently as she continued to read.

Apricot slumped back in her seat. "Deeds not words," she breathed.

"I'll understand if you don't want to come."

Apricot drew breath and, as my orchestra played a steely melody for her with a hint of adventure entitled 'The Responsibility of the Little Innocents', she exhaled slowly and said, "You'll never get there without me, dear love. Not without my motor boat."

"You have a motor boat?"

"Yes, a little forty-footer. I've been looking for an excuse to use it," said Apricot. "How were you planning on getting there anyhow? By swimming?"

"No... I thought I might stow away aboard one of Blake's delivery boats."

"Oh, for goodness sake. Do behave. We can make good use of my boat, but you'll have to hold your horses for a few days. I'm going to stay with a relative in Jersey tomorrow. It's a thing. She expects me every year. But I'll be back on Monday."

Chapter 25
Suspicion

When Blue returned home the next morning, she discovered Harry and Sheila sitting at the dining table having just finished their breakfast. They smiled at her in a conspiratorial way that made her uneasy.

"We weren't expecting you back so early," said Sheila.

"Apricot left first thing. She's gone to stay with a relative in Jersey. Won't be back until Monday," said Blue, taking a seat at the table. "You two look rather suspicious, is there something the matter? How's your toothache?"

"Much better, thank you," said Sheila.

Harry cleared his throat. "How was your night up at the chateau?"

"Good thanks. Apricot gave me a guided tour of her doll's house. It was magical."

"That couldn't have taken long," said Sheila, taking her napkin from her lap and placing it on the table.

"About an hour."

"Just how big *is* her doll's house?"

"Big," said Blue, standing and stretching her hand above her head as far as she could reach. She sat back down. "It has a hundred or so rooms."

"Does it have a garden?" asked Harry, hopefully.

"No. Just a little boating lake out front with some trees."

"A boating lake?" said Sheila, her suspicious smile returning.

Blue shuffled uneasily in her seat.

"Well then," beamed Sheila, "talking of boating lakes, your father told me about the talk you had at Mr De Croy's yesterday."

"Oh?" said Blue.

Sheila reached a hand across the table and wrapped it around Harry's. "Tell our child what you told me about your shoulders."

Blue raised an eyebrow and studied her parents.

"Your mother is quite right. Since our talk yesterday, my shoulders do feel lighter," answered Harry.

'Unburdened is what you told me," said Sheila, looking at Blue. "How on earth did you get this stubborn man to open up about such things?"

"It wasn't something I planned...' said Blue, swallowing the lump in her throat. "All it was... well, it occurred to me that the lake looked more like a bomb crater with the water drained and..."

"And in that moment, it just felt so natural to talk about the real thing," said Harry, throwing up his hands as though flummoxed by the unfathomable.

"The little bird in the tree did just as much as I did," said Blue.

"Ah, that little bird..." said Harry, a faraway look in his eyes.

"Last night your father and I stayed up talking until the early hours. He told me how he'd longed to see any living creature in Flanders."

"Other than a rat," said Harry.

"Yes, other than a rat. And about the many friends who are still in those fields."

"Men friends not rat friends," said Harry, winking at Blue.

"He's going to write to the families of some of them, aren't you?" said Sheila.

"It seems only right. Many had young children. They'll be teenagers now. They should hear how brave their fathers were from someone who knows."

Blue stood and walked around the table. She wrapped her arms around Harry. "I think it's a wonderful idea."

"I agree," said Sheila.

"I've wanted you to talk about France for as long as I can remember," said Blue, releasing him. "Who'd have thought the solution would be a smelly boating lake and a little bird in a tree?"

"But why?" Sheila asked her.

Blue glanced at Harry's hands. "Because I overheard you once… telling Dad how he needed to talk about things if he was ever going to feel better."

"When?" asked Sheila.

Harry smiled at Blue. "I do believe it was the day we met."

"I think it might have been, Dad."

"What are you two talking about?"

"The day I returned from France; we went into the kitchen to talk in private. I had a strong suspicion that Blue was listening at the door."

"Why didn't you say anything?" said Sheila.

Harry shrugged. "Why is it people do or don't do anything?"

"Well, it seems it's mission complete," said Sheila, looking at Blue. "Just don't attempt to solve anything that might get you into hot water."

"There will always be problems to be solved, Mum."

"Mark my words, our daughter is going to be a politician one day," said Harry.

Blue shook her head. "They take forever to do anything. But look what Lady Constance and her friends managed to achieve."

"It was a different world then," said Sheila.

"Blue is quite right. If it wasn't for life's right-thinking doers, we'd still be stuck in the Dark Ages."

"Is that how you see our daughter? A right-thinking doer?"

"I think that's *precisely* what she is."

"Thank you, Dad."

Sheila sat back in her chair. "Just try not to do anything stupid or reckless, Blue."

"Goodness. No, I wouldn't. Perish the thought."

Chapter 26
A sign in the heavens

It was 9.15pm. Blue was sitting at her dressing table. Outside the veranda doors in her bedroom, the sun had just begun to set. The melody I was conducting for her that evening, a combination of panpipes and didgeridoos entitled 'Rumination', had lulled Blue into a feeling of melancholy at the irrational hatred directed at folk like Terry and his mother. And why? Because they had darker skin? Been brought up in a different culture? One that embraced the same Christian God, although, as far as she could tell, even more fervently. *Hardship and injustice must have a way of making decent people yearn to believe in a loving God,* she thought. As my string section swelled and hovered on the edge of a crescendo, Blue looked through her glass doors and gazed up at the stars that now speckled the crimson sky. "What a beautiful night," she breathed. *I wonder if Terry's looking up through his telescope?* She rose to her feet. *He needs to know what Apricot and I have discovered about Rat Island.*

A minute later she entered the living room where Harry was reading his newspaper and Sheila was engrossed in a novel. "I'm going out for a bit," said Blue.

"Where?" murmured Sheila, her eyes still glued to the page of her book.

"To look at the stars through Terry's telescope."

"Terry has a telescope?" said Harry, glancing up from his newspaper.

"He does now. Apricot bought him one," said Sheila. "As a thank you for taking care of her horse."

Harry puffed on his pipe. "Why a telescope?"

"Remember, Terry's hobby is astronomy, Dad."

"Well then. Seems like a good reason."

When Blue was halfway up the garden path, Mrs Curtis opened her front door to clean away a handprint of Terry's she'd noticed earlier. As Fate would have it, Terry had stumbled over a slumbering cat and broken his fall on the door with an outstretched palm. Terry's little trip and the cat's rude awakening had been for expediency's sake: I was keen for Blue to see a message I'd left for her, a sign in the heavens that she was on the right path.

"Blue?" said Mrs Curtis, as she opened her door.

"Hello, Mrs Curtis. Sorry for startling you. Hope you're well?"

"Very well, thank you. And you?"

"Good." Blue glanced up at the night's sky. "I wondered if Terry was using his telescope to look at the stars?"

"Of course. That boy has barely left it alone. Come in, you'll find him in his observatory," she said, her voice overflowing with pride.

"Observatory?" said Blue as she crossed the threshold.

"It's what he's taken to calling it. Up in the attic," said Mrs Curtis, wiping away the smudge print and closing the door. "That boy, who has never taken to cleaning without being told, has spent the entire day tidying up there to make space for his observatory. As you might have noticed, the attic windows slant with the shape of the roof. Our resident expert insists they're ideal for stargazing."

"How wonderful."

"Come through and see for yourself," nodded Mrs Curtis. Blue followed her into a laundry room where a stepladder had been placed below a trapdoor in the ceiling. The trapdoor opened onto darkness. Mrs Curtis called to her son and moments later a light was switched on. Terry's inquisitive face appeared in the opening.

"You have a visitor, son."

"Blue?"

"Yes, it's me and I'm coming up," replied Blue, stepping onto the ladder and making her way to the top where Terry helped her to climb into the loft.

"Oh, wow, they do at that," said Blue, brushing down her dress with the palms of her hands.

"What do?"

"The slanting windows. They make for a great observatory."

"Don't they just," beamed Terry, looking at his telescope that was afforded a tremendous view of the night sky through them.

Blue glanced around at the boxes that had been neatly stacked against the walls. "Your mum said you'd been tidying up here?"

"I'll say. These boxes were all over." Terry glanced up. "I even scrubbed the windows. Got every bit of dirt off. Inside and out."

"Out?"

"Bird dung," tutted Terry. "I climbed up onto the roof when Ma went out. You won't say anything will you?"

"Course not."

A smile spread across Terry's face. "You've come to look at the stars?"

Blue nodded. "And to tell you what happened when I stayed with Apricot last night."

"You stayed up at the chateau? That must've been quite something."

"It was," said Blue, glancing over her shoulder at the trap door. "We planned the sleepover, so we could find the file Mr De Croy keeps on Blake."

"You snooped in Mr De Croy's study?"

"No. We didn't have to. I knew where to look."

Terry shook his head. "What do you want with a file like that anyhow?"

"To help find the proof that Blake is a bootlegging hypocrite. Lady Constance knows people who could use it as a weapon against the Klan."

"That grand lady put you up to it? The suffragette? Doesn't she know the Klan are dangerous?"

"Of course she does. You should have seen her face when she heard you were in the dragon's lair with us."

"You told her about that?"

"No reason not to."

"What did she say?"

"That we should stay well away from such people until we're older."

"Like I told you already at the beach. She sounds like a wise lady."

"Yes, but I think she's being overly cautious. You can't always set an age limit on something as important as deeds not words. And *especially* not when an opportunity like this comes along." Blue sighed. "We're all like little children when you think about it. You of all people should know that," she said, spotting a light switch. She stepped over to it, flicked it up, and plunged the room into darkness. The gloom was suffused by the silvery light of the moon and a trillion stars. Blue and Terry gazed up through the windows at the cosmic light show that I had arranged for them. "I don't think I've ever seen so many stars," said Blue.

"And never this bright," swallowed Terry. "I guess you're right about us all being little. This old universe spans *one hundred and fifty billion* light years. You know how far just one single light year is?"

Blue shook her head.

"Too far for anyone to travel. Ever. Right now, you're looking back in time. The light from those stars was created billions of years ago. And it's still making its way here."

Gently prompted by her melody, Blue enquired, "So, were you looking at anything in particular?"

"Take a look for yourself," nodded Terry, motioning to the telescope's eyepiece that was upturned and at chest height. Blue bent her head and looked through it. "Oh, that's beautiful! It looks like a giant bird with white and blue feathers."

"That 'bird' is a cosmic cloud in the constellation of Sagittarius." Terry cocked his head a little as though listening to something far away. "You'll never guess what it's made from," he murmured.

"No, I don't suppose I will."

"From ten billion billion billion litres of alcohol."

"Alcohol. Are you joking?"

"No. Why so surprised?"

"Because it's like… like a sign."

Oh reader! Imagine my delight.

"You mean like from God?" said Terry, reminded of his mother and glancing towards the trap door.

Blue placed her eye to the telescope's eyepiece. "It looks more like the universe to me…"

"A sign huh? Of what?"

"That alcohol is the secret to hurting the dragon. And maybe Rat Island *is* where we'll find a weapon…"

"You talking about Rat Island in the Sound?"

"Yes. We found out in Mr De Croy's file that it's where Blake lives. Apricot and I are planning on going there."

"Then you're both crazy. How would you even get there?"

"In Apricot's motor boat."

Terry chuckled. "Have you *seen* Miss Apricot's boat?"

"No."

"Well I have. And there's *no way* she can drive that machine. You'll get yourselves killed."

"Apricot seemed very confident about the boat."

"Miss Apricot is confident about anything you care to mention. But between you and me, confidence and smarts aren't the same thing."

"Maybe not, but where there's a will there's a way."

"Sure is, a way to hit a mud bank and launch that boat into outer space. If you ask me, it's a good thing then that she's gone away."

"Only until Monday. How'd you know?"

"Mr Grimshaw told me. He said she won't be riding Sheba this weekend."

"She's visiting a relative. But as soon as she gets back, we can go," smiled Blue.

All Terry could think to do was to shake his head.

Chapter 27
One good turn deserves another

When Blue awoke the next morning, she imagined she was at a loose end for the day. She needn't have worried. On my watch, what goes around comes around. And so, the melody I conducted for Harry that morning had infused him with a sense of fairness. After all, Blue had helped to lift some of his burden by getting him to share his experiences of war. And now he intended to return the favour. In plain English, Harry had resolved to answer any questions that Blue might have about her birth parents. This explained the firm knock on Blue's bedroom door that startled her. "Get up sleepyhead! Breakfast's ready. I'm working in White Rose Garden this morning. I'd like you to join me."

Blue sat up in bed, her ears prickling at the revealing tone of her father's voice. "Okay."

"This is lovely, Dad…" said Blue, as she stepped through a wooden door into a secluded garden enclosed by a red brick wall. Harry wiped the sweat from his brow with the back of his hand. "It's called the White…"

"Rose Garden, yes, you told me this morning," said Blue, gazing around at the white rose bushes that engarlanded the wooden benches, wrought iron chairs, lamps and statues of dark stone that occupied the serene space.

"It used to be part of an apple orchard. The trees are long gone… all except this one," said Harry, walking over to a tree where red apples hung from its low branches. "It was rescued by the last groundsman…" said Harry, reaching up and taking an apple. "Here…" he went on, rubbing it on his sleeve and handing it to her. Blue took a bite.

"How does it taste?"

"Great," munched Blue.

Harry turned to look at his handiwork. "It's amazing what you can accomplish with a team of green fingered men."

"It's about time you had some help, Dad."

"I have no idea how all this fell into our laps. But I'm grateful."

"We have rather landed on our feet, haven't we?" smiled Blue.

"Yes. And if we've been lucky it can only be because of you."

"Not sure how I managed that," said Blue, taking another bite out of the apple.

"You've always been lucky. Which is why I wanted to talk to you today. There are some things that I'd like to share with you. If you think you're ready?"

Blue's expression was a study in, 'Oh, I was born ready.'

Harry sighed in a resigned way.

"Am I *that* much of a nosey parker?"

"Yes, and you always have been."

"I won't deny it," said Blue, taking another bite.

"Come and sit down," said Harry, ushering her towards a wooden bench between two Victorian lampposts. They sat down and Harry crossed one leg over the other. A sign, Blue had long ago learned, that her father was composing his thoughts. He drew a deep breath. "It's about your birth parents. Do you ever wonder about them? Silly question really," said Harry brushing some lint from his trousers. "Who wouldn't be curious about such a fundamental thing?"

Blue gazed into the distance. "I've wondered."

Harry looked at her with an intensity that gave her cause to rub at her cheek. He looked away and into the middle distance as though joining his daughter there. "You already know about Titanic, don't you?"

"When *didn't* I know about it? I heard Mum telling you about it on that very first day. The day you came home from the war. The name really stuck."

"You were five years old but already so…"

"Nosey."

"Inquisitive. So just how much do you know about your birth mother?"

Blue placed the half-eaten apple on the bench beside her. She leaned forward and clasped her hands together. "Just that I was on Titanic with her. I survived and she didn't."

"And you came to terms with it?"

"I didn't know what Titanic was. I remember asking a teacher and she explained how it was a ship that sank the same year I was born. I told her I was on it. 'Stop fibbing and get on with your sums,' she said. Or words to that effect." Blue leaned back against the bench and drew her knees up to her chest. "I have to confess something… I've used the tragic tale to my advantage."

"How?"

"When I met Apricot, it was the only thing I'd experienced that she hadn't. She finds Titanic fascinating. It was quite the ice breaker."

"Titanic? Indeed, she was. Sorry, I shouldn't joke about such things."

"I think it's important to joke about all painful things. It helps to take some of the sting out."

Harry placed an arm around her and hugged her close. "I've done some research and discovered some more details about your birth mother. Not a great deal admittedly, but I'll share them with you if you'd like?"

Blue looked at him. "I would like that very much."

"Her name was Iris Flannigan. She was taking you to start a new life in America."

Blue gazed around at her serene surroundings. "I made it here eventually, Iris," she said, quietly.

Harry squeezed her shoulder and swallowed the lump that had wedged itself in his throat.

"I don't suppose you have a photo of her?"

Harry shook his head.

"Pity. I would have liked to have seen what she looked like."

"Like you, perhaps?"

"Hope not. Poor woman. Any idea why she called me Blue?"

"She didn't. You were named by the ship's nurse on the Carpathia. After you were taken from the lifeboat."

"Honestly? I must have been one sad looking baby."

"Not necessarily."

"Iris didn't name me?"

"Presumably she did. But the ship's manifest had you billed as 'Female Infant.'"

"I'm grateful that name didn't stick. Do you know why she was taking me to America?"

"Her, *your* family were strict Catholics. I get the impression you may have been conceived out of wedlock. Maybe they shunned her."

"And my father?"

"I couldn't find any information about him. Could be their relationship was a brief one. So, now you know everything I do about your birth parents," said Harry, taking Blue's hand in his own.

"Thank you."

"I've no doubt that you could find out more about your relatives. Something to consider when you're older."

"It doesn't sound like they treated Iris very well so…"

"It's up to you. Whatever you decide, your mother and I will always support you."

Chapter 28
The recce

On Monday morning, Sheila answered a knock on the front door. She was handed a letter by a man in a chauffeur's uniform who was clearly pushed for time. She closed the door, held the envelope at arm's length, squinted at the name on the front, and rolled her eyes. "I wonder who this is from?" she said, making her way to her daughter's bedroom. The knock woke Blue.

"Yes? What?"

"Don't 'yes what' me young lady."

"Sorry."

"A letter has just been delivered for you by a chauffeur. I wonder who it could be from?"

Blue opened her bedroom door and slid the letter from Sheila's hand. "I'll take that. Thanks, Mummy."

"You only call me 'Mummy' when you're up to something."

"Which is why I never would if I was," said Blue, rolling her eyes and tearing open the letter's seal.

Sheila watched her daughter read its contents. "Well?"

"It's from Apricot…"

"I would never have guessed."

"She wants me to meet her at her uncle's marina after breakfast." *For a recce of Rat Island.*

"Why are you grinning from ear to ear?"

"She wants to show me her boat."

"I wasn't aware you were into boats?"

"I'm not, but Terry said that Apricot's is pretty spectacular."

"She'd hardly have a dinghy. Don't you go boating without adult supervision."

"Alright."

The boat house overlooked Long Island Sound. The imposing structure was made entirely of oak and looked like a gigantic lavish barn. It had no front, which meant that curious day trippers on the Sound could see Mr De Croy's impressive collection of boats, stacked on shelves, as they sailed past. To say that Blue arrived with a spring in her step would be an understatement. Terry's report of Apricot's 'machine' had ignited her imagination and she was keen to see it bobbing about against the dock. Blue rounded the boat house and, squinting at the dock, could see no boat bobbing. "Oh," she said, as the spring abandoned her step. She heard the sound of heavy machinery, like a tractor being started up and, turning a corner, came upon Apricot standing with her arms folded, and scowling at the driver of a forklift truck. The truck's prongs were under an impressively long, impossibly sleek craft made from dark wood that had been polished to gleaming. The craft's name, 'Apricot's Little Runabout', was written on its side in silver letters. "Talk about an ironic name," murmured Blue.

"Good morning!" shouted Apricot over the sound of the forklift truck, "I know the feeling, trust me."

"What feeling?"

"My Little Runaround was supposed to be in the water an hour ago."

"She's quite something."

"Isn't she?" smiled Apricot.

"Do you know how to drive it?" said Blue as the twenty-metre-long craft was carried past them towards the dock.

"Of course I don't. That is why he's here," said Apricot, pointing to a man who was wearing dark overalls and reading a manual.

192

"Who's he?" said Blue looking at the man who had the initials H.B.C. stitched into the front of his overalls.

"He's the fellow that Hacker sent down."

"Hacker?"

"The Hacker Boat Company. They made my boat. He's going to show us how to, you know, make it go," said Apricot, shooing the air with her fingers.

"That's a brilliant idea."

"I know. It came to me last night."

Twenty minutes later, Blue, Apricot and the man from the Hacker Boat Company, Mr Sons, were gathered at the front of Apricot's Little Runaround. Mr Sons was sitting before a crescent-shaped wheel in the driver's seat. Apricot and Blue were strapped into the seats on either side of him. Blue tugged at the strap that secured her. "It's a bit tight."

Mr Sons tapped one of the dials on the dashboard. "We wouldn't want you falling overboard, Miss Tibbs. The waters in the Sound can get a bit choppy."

"No, we certainly wouldn't want Miss Tibbs falling overboard," scoffed Apricot, pulling at her own strap. "Why aren't you secured to your seat, Mr Sons? Are you considered expendable?"

Mr Sons flicked a switch on the dash. "I have the steering wheel to ground me. And I'm sitting in the centre of the boat. Now, if you're both ready, I'll fire her up?" Mr Sons glanced left and right and, seeing nods on both sides, turned the key on the dashboard. The engine at the rear of the boat fired up into a meaty growl. Mr Sons nodded approvingly. "That's the sound of state-of-the-art engineering."

"I should think so, too. Now take us out into the Sound and head in the direction of Rat Island. You know it?" said Apricot.

"I do. It's a couple of miles due east of here," said Mr Sons, taking hold of the steering wheel.

"Excellent," smiled Blue as she and Apricot exchanged knowing glances.

"I'll provide some instruction from the driver's seat first," said Mr Sons, grasping the wheel. "Then you'll obviously want to spend some time at the wheel yourself, Miss De Croy."

"Unless Miss Tibbs would rather do the honours?" said Apricot, looking past him at Blue.

"I'd love to learn how to drive it!"

"Good," nodded Apricot, "in all honesty, I trust your acumen when it comes to matters of speed and coordination more than my own. I was born to be *driven*."

"No arguments there," said Blue. She watched Mr Sons push the gleaming silver throttle forward and clasped her arm rests as the boat motored away from the dock.

A few minutes later, Blue, chomping at the bit to take over, suggested to Mr Sons that he swap seats and, before long, she was guiding the boat along the Sound, paying close attention to what her instructor was telling her about the tides and the channel that ran down its centre. "Stay in the channel, between the markers on either side, otherwise you'll run the risk of running aground in shallow waters," he explained, pointing out the large orange buoys that snaked away into the distance. Blue was quick to learn how to manipulate the throttle for the purposes of speeding up and slowing down, and how to turn the boat around one hundred and eighty degrees. She felt giddy with delight at having such a modern and powerful craft under her control. All the while, Apricot did a splendid impersonation of royalty as she returned the waves of the many admiring faces in the boats they encountered. "You've taken to this boat driving malarkey like a duck to water," said Apricot, waving. Blue eased the throttle further forward than she'd previously dared, and the front of the boat reared up as they sped through the water. "There's not much to it really," said Blue, raising her voice above the throaty grumble of the engine.

Mr Sons rolled his eyes surreptitiously. "There's actually a *lot* more to it than meets the eye. You can thank the engineers that built her for making her such a delight to handle."

"I'm sure we're all very grateful to the engineers," said Apricot.

Blue held firmly to the wheel. "Which way is Rat Island?"

Mr Sons extended an arm and pointed at what looked like a dark mound sitting on the water half a kilometre to their right. "If I'm not mistaken, that's the island you're after." Blue felt the excitement rise in her breast as she turned the wheel in that direction. "Look!" she said as they drew nearer, "the double hump that we read about in the book."

"That's the island alright," said Apricot, leaning forward and straining at the belt that secured her. Mr Sons tapped the throttle urgently. "If you intend to take a closer look then you'll need to slow down."

"Alright," said Blue, taking hold of the throttle and easing it back.

"Pay close attention to your surroundings. There may be areas of shallow rocks or sand banks. Be *sure* to keep your speed low and your eyes peeled whenever you leave the channel."

"It's not easy to see when you're this restrained," huffed Apricot, unbuckling her strap and standing. Blue eased back on the throttle some more and the craft slowed to a crawl.

"I have just the things you need, Miss De Croy..." said Mr Sons, turning a knob on the dashboard. The polished wooden door to a compartment dropped open to reveal a pair of silver binoculars.

"Oh! I have boat spyglasses," said Apricot, reaching for them. She raised them to her eyes and scanned Rat Island.

"Do you see any?" asked Blue.

Klan members? thought Apricot.

"I'm talking about bats, Mr Sons," said Blue. "It's the reason we're interested in the island. School project."

Apricot scanned the beach that spanned the island's east side. "I can't see any 'bats'…"

"You won't see any bats. They're nocturnal creatures. And I would strongly advise against coming here after dark."

"Hypothetically though, if we did," said Blue, "where do you think the best place to land on the island would be?"

"Hypothetically?"

The girls nodded.

"Well, you wouldn't want to land her on a beach," said Mr Sons, pointing it out. "It's a sure-fire way to get grounded. Maybe take her around the other side?"

"Alright," said Blue.

As Fate would have it, things looked a lot more promising on the island's west side where an inlet led to a small wooden dock. "There you go. That's where any visitors to the island would land. But only if they had permission. These islands are privately owned."

"We'll bear that in mind," said Apricot, handing the binoculars to Blue.

Reader, I turned the page of my sheet music and led my orchestra in a melody for Blue entitled, 'Preparation is Half the Battle.'

"I'm going to see if I can land there now," said Blue. She handed the binoculars back to Apricot and turned the wheel towards the inlet.

"Maybe you didn't hear what I just said? This island is privately owned so you'll need permission to dock," exclaimed Mr Sons.

"I'm not going to dock. Well, I am. But only for a minute to see if I can do it," said Blue, standing up for a view over the windshield.

"Yes, let's see," smiled Apricot, doing a silent hand clap.

Mr Sons shook his head. "You certainly are determined young ladies. Alright then, let's see how you do. I'll keep an eye out for shallows on this side, you do the same on the other, Miss De Croy."

"Right you are," said Apricot, looking over the side of the boat. Blue guided the sleek craft through an area where reeds were visible growing just below the surface. The closer they got to Rat Island, the more bits of flotsam and jetsam bobbed about in the form of sticks, leaves and planks. The island's beach, strewn with grey pebbles and hopping gulls, lay to their left. Blue guided the boat into the inlet where trees grew on both sides of its narrow entrance, their branches intertwined overhead to provide shade from the sun as they motored into the watery cul-de-sac. An old wooden jetty was on their left-hand side. Several warning signs loomed from the undergrowth. 'NO TRESPASSING!' 'PRIVATE PROPERTY KEEP OUT!' 'BEWARE! GUARD DOGS!' Unfazed by these, Blue eased the throttle back into neutral, and the boat drifted slowly with its momentum, coming to a halt a few yards from the jetty.

"You're a natural," said Mr Sons. "Just give her a tiny bit more gas…" Blue pushed the throttle forward for a moment, eased it back, and the boat sidled up alongside the jetty.

"You *are* a natural at this, dear love," marvelled Apricot.

"Thanks," said Blue, backing away from the wheel and scurrying over the side of the boat onto the island.

"Hey!" said Mr Sons, "that's trespassing."

"Throw me the rope to tie her up with, Apricot."

"Aye aye, Captain!" said Apricot, dashing to the rope that was resting on hooks along the inside of the boat.

"As soon as I've tied her up, we'll be on our way, Mr Sons. So, the quicker you show me *how*, the quicker we can leave."

"Miss De Croy, if you hand me the rope, I'll…" Apricot thrust the end of the rope at him. He took it and climbed onto the wooden jetty. Blue was leaning over a wooden post that had an old brass ring attached.

"Watch carefully, Miss Tibbs, this is how you tie an anchor bend knot…"

A few minutes later, Mr Sons said Blue had passed her knot tying class with flying colours. He glanced at their surroundings. "Time to go. Let's not tempt fate any more than need be." Mr Sons, you needn't have worried.

Chapter 29
Plans afoot

The next day, the foreman of the stable yard, Mr Grimshaw, walked into the Queen of Sheba's stable where Terry was sitting crossed legged on the ground. Mr Grimshaw's pale face flared red. "Curtis!" he barked, "you're not being paid to…" Mr Grimshaw's train of thought deserted him as he rounded a hay stack to see Apricot and Blue sitting cross-legged opposite him. The three friends were seated on a tartan blanket upon which lay an open book. They looked up at the furious foreman. One amongst them resembled a startled rabbit, one looked mildly perplexed, while the third sported an arched eyebrow and looked positively irritated. Mr Grimshaw's gaze settled on the irritated one with the arched eyebrow. "Miss De Croy?"

"Mr Grimshaw?"

Mr Grimshaw nodded.

"I will tell you what Terry is being paid to do, it's to take care of Sheba, something he does very well."

"I'm glad…" blurted Mr Grimshaw.

"What's more, he's become a trusted friend."

"Terry *Curtis*?"

"Yes. And I would appreciate you not using that tone with him in the future."

Terry's mouth audibly snapped shut.

"Yes, of course, Miss De Croy, if…"

Mr Grimshaw had been silenced by Apricot's raised palm.

"Your cooperation in this matter is most appreciated, Mr Grimshaw. Don't let us keep you from your duties."

"Yes, Miss De Croy," murmured Mr Grimshaw, turning and leaving the barn.

"'Your cooperation in this matter is most appreciated?'" whispered Blue.

"Well, he got the message, didn't he? You were saying before you were interrupted?" Blue leaned over the open book on the blanket. "Your uncle's file said that Blake's base of operations is close to the site of the old Pelham Pesthouse," she said, pointing to a diagram of a building in the centre of the island.

Apricot looked at Terry. "The Pelham Pesthouse is where they used to lock people with incurable diseases up to die."

"Blue already told me about that."

"I'm sure they didn't lock them up to die. It was probably like a hospital," said Blue.

"The clue being in the word 'like', said Apricot, drawing a finger across her throat.

Terry shuddered and leaned over the book. "Does it say how the island came by its name?"

"Yes, I saw it here somewhere…" said Blue, running her finger down the text on the page adjacent to the map of the island. "'One theory,'" she began reading the text aloud, "'is that the island attracted rats because of the typhoid sufferers who were taken there. Another is that men who escaped from a prison on nearby Hart Island swam there first on their way to the mainland. They called these escaped prisoners 'rats.''"

"You're really selling the place," said Apricot.

"You still mean to go there?" added Terry.

"Go? We've already been, Terrance."

"When?"

"Yesterday," said Blue.

Terry drew a deep breath. "You see anyone there?"

"No. I docked the boat so I knew I could and then we left."

"Apricot's boat?"

The girls stared at him like they'd just realised he was there.

"What? What did I say?"

"That's the first time you've ever dropped the 'Miss' and called me Apricot."

"I wasn't thinking, I…"

"Relax. We're friends, aren't we?" said Apricot, smiling and leaning back on her hands.

"I guess we are at that, *Apricot*," said Terry, trying out the name again for size. "Why'd they name you after a preserve anyhow?"

Apricot's smile fled her face. "I wouldn't push it."

"No, I won't…"

"She's pulling your leg," said Blue.

The return of Apricot's smile confirmed this.

"You got me," said Terry, holding up his hands. "So, you actually drove Apricot's Little Runaround?"

"Yep. Nothing to it really," said Blue.

"Not once she'd had a lesson from an expert."

"You gave Blue a lesson?"

"Ah, no. I'm not an expert at anything. Hacker sent someone down."

"Wow. That's really something."

"And she's going to be perfect for returning to look for evidence of the Klan's bootlegging," said Blue.

"Even if you did find some, you really think it'll make a difference? They're so popular that even Ma is worried about where this is all headed. She doesn't say as much, but I know she is."

"I'm sure she must be. Which is why we have to do something. And to think we know someone who can hurt them with any evidence we find," smiled Blue.

Terry drew his knees up to his chin. "Mr De Croy?"

"Lady Constance Manners," said Apricot.

Terry gazed down at the map in the open book. "But what about the rats?"

"I presume you're alluding to the two-legged variety who are partial to wearing robes with pointy hoods?" murmured Apricot.

"Yeah, them."

Blue shrugged. "If a rat named Blake didn't live there, there wouldn't be any reason to go."

Terry began to chew on a broken nail. "You don't know what such hateful folk might do, not when there are no decent folk around. I should go with you…"

"Ah, no you shouldn't," said Blue, pointedly.

Apricot straightened her back and looked like a prima ballerina. "You know that would be lunacy. If we're caught, Blue's pasty face will offer her some protection. And as for my own elevated position in society, well, need I say more?"

"Apricot's right. We're just a couple of kids exploring for a prank," said Blue, tapping her chin thoughtfully. "And thanks for my description by the way."

"It's nothing a spot of sunbathing wouldn't fix, dear love."

"Won't you be trespassing?" said Terry.

Blue sat back on her hands. "We're children in the eyes of the law, so…"

"And besides, my uncle is friends with the commissioner of police."

Terry sighed. "It sure sounds nice. Being privileged and pasty."

"Not exactly Holmes and Watson," murmured Blue.

Chapter 30
Seeking reassurance

When Blue opened her eyes the following morning and sensed the melody that I was conducting for her, *Making Plans to Enter the Dragon's Lair*, she hugged her pillow and felt comforted by the idea of spending some time with her father. Harry was delighted by Blue's request. They spent the morning wandering the estate; Harry jotting down notes and making sketches, and Blue revelling in his creativity and enthusiasm for gardening. She took particular delight in observing how his hands showed only the faintest signs of trembling. Blue watched her father sketch an area of thorn bushes beside a fountain, and it occurred to her that, just as a boiling pan stops shaking when its lid is removed to release the steam, so too had her father's hands been released of pressure by talking. She was sitting cross legged on the grass, a smile of contentment on her face. And what a smile it was! A smile that only departed when I conducted my orchestra in another rendition of *Entering the Dragon's Lair*. Its melody brought back Terry's words of warning from the previous day. 'You don't know what the likes of such hateful folk might do when there are no decent folk around.' As though Harry had eyes in the side of his head, he asked, "A penny for them?"

Blue leaned forward and picked something from the grass. "I've found a four-leaf clover…"

"So you have," said Harry stepping over and sitting on the grass beside her.

"Dad?"

"Yes?"

"You must have been very brave to volunteer the way you did," said Blue, twirling the clover by its stalk. Harry spotted an error in his sketch and, as he used the eraser on the end of his pencil to erase it, he murmured, "Volunteer?"

"To go to war."

Harry lowered his sketch. "Your work here is done. You do know that, don't you? Even your mother's noticed a change in me."

"I know. Just saying, you must have been brave to put up your hand and volunteer."

"I wouldn't have. Not if I'd have known what was waiting for me."

"How can anyone know what's waiting for them in the future? It's probably best that we don't know."

"And why's that?"

"It might stop us from doing what's right."

Harry ruffled Blue's hair. "Maybe it would at that."

Chapter 31
When Fate has a tight schedule

The next day, Blue had just finished her supper and placed her knife and fork together on her plate when the telephone rang. "Who can that be at this time?" said Sheila, standing and pushing her chair back. She went to the phone and lifted the receiver. "Hello? Tibbs residence." Sheila listened to the caller for a moment and then looked over at Blue. "Hello Apricot… yes, oh really…"

Blue jumped out of her seat and made her way over.

"That does sound like an opportunity… she would never let me hear the end of it if I didn't… yes, you have a lovely evening, Blue's right here, I'll pass you onto her."

Blue took the receiver. "Hello?"

"Listen," breathed Apricot, "Blake has just arrived at the chateau…"

"Why?" said Blue, her heart thumping in her chest.

"Don't worry. It has nothing to do with us. He's attending a black-tie fund raiser."

"Oh," said Blue, smiling at her mother.

"Blake and half of New York society. Bat poo crazy I know, but it occurred to me that while the cat's away the mice might play?"

Blue's trepidation was chased away by excitement. "Yes, it sounds like the perfect opportunity."

"That's because you're crazier than I am. I told your mother I want you to attend the fund raiser. Said I wanted to introduce you to some important people. So, dress for the occasion but bring an appropriate change of clothes."

"Appropriate," murmured Blue.

"Yes, for breaking and entering. I'll meet you at the marina in one hour."

"Okay, thanks for thinking of me, see you later," said Blue, returning Harry's smile. She put down the receiver. "Apricot's expecting me," said Blue, heading for her bedroom.

"What's going on?" asked Harry.

"Apricot's invited her to a fund raiser at the chateau. Although a bit more time to get ready would have been nice. Don't you think, Harry?"

"Ah, nonsense," replied Harry with a dismissive wave of his hand. "Our daughter's a natural beauty."

"She's also a natural *mess*," retorted Sheila.

"Which suits her somehow."

"Thanks Dad. I think." Blue disappeared through her bedroom door and closed it behind her. She changed into her best dress, a red evening number with silver straps, brushed some of the more stubborn tangles out of her hair, and stuffed a dark cotton frock into an overnight bag. Blue emerged from her room looking for all the world like butter wouldn't melt in her mouth.

"You look very beautiful darling," said Harry.

"Come here and let me sort your hair out," said Sheila, reaching for a brush and some hair pins she'd placed on the table. "We can't have you mixing with the crème of New York society looking like you've been dragged backwards through a hedge."

And so, while the creme of New York society gathered at Chateau De Croy, our hunter of dragons hightailed it to the marina to meet Apricot. She arrived to discover her pacing up and down on the deck of her Little Runaround. "Ahoy there. You look the part," said Blue, admiring Apricot's black all in one cat suit.

"Ahoy! Come aboard. Don't I just? I saw it in Vogue and it occurred to me," said Apricot as Blue climbed onto the boat, "just how perfect it would be if I ever decided to become a cat burglar. An odd thing to occur to me, don't you think? It's not as though I need the spoils. But I felt compelled to buy it anyway." Apricot looked at Blue, placed her hands on her hips and observed, "Such a charming dress. I hope you have a change of clothes in that bag?"

"I do." Blue unzipped her bag and, as she got changed, Apricot recommenced her pacing and began talking ten to the dozen. "You should have *seen* him, Blue."

"Blake?"

"Yes. I'm actually glad you didn't see him. It would have made you feel quite ill."

"Why? What was he doing?"

Apricot froze in her tracks. "It wasn't just what he was doing but who he was doing it with."

"I think you'd better explain."

"The guests were gathered in the hallway, having pre-dinner drinks. V.I.P.s one and all!" said Apricot, throwing up her hands.

"Where were you?"

"I was sitting at the top of the staircase, dressed in this cat suit which, as you can see, renders me invisible."

Blue nodded. "You were spying on them?"

"Through the banisters."

"And?"

"Blake... he was so... *charming,*" said Apricot with a shudder. "Nothing like the monster we saw conducting that ceremony under the house."

"The others were buying it?"

"Utterly. What's wrong with people? It's not as though they don't know he's a Grand Wizard in the KKK. Oh, dear love, it seems to me that we *have* to find a way to expose his 'political party' for the bootlegging hypocrites they really are."

"Yes," said Blue, throwing her arms around her. Blue released her friend and held her at arm's length. "Apricot? You're upset? Why?"

Apricot drew a hand across her eyes. "Oh, I don't know. Something to do with purpose. Having one for the first time in my pointless existence."

"Oh, Miss De Croy, there's nothing pointless about you. This just feels right, doesn't it?"

"Deeds not words, dear love," nodded Apricot and, had it been a thing at that time, they would have high fived one another. It wasn't, so they shook hands instead.

Blue sat in the driver's seat while Apricot climbed out of the boat and untied the rope. She climbed back on board and sat in the seat to Blue's right. Blue pressed the starter button on the dash and the engine rumbled into life. She pushed the throttle forward and the boat motored away from the dockside, its spotlight casting a reassuringly wide beam over the calm water. Apricot's melody drew her attention to the starry night. "Quite the night for stargazing," she said, looking up at the heavens.

"Isn't it…"

"My stable boy must be in his absolute element."

"Thanks to you."

"It's not as though I made the stars."

"No, but your gift brought them a lot closer."

"True and if he were here, he would tell us exactly how much closer." They sat in silence for a time before Apricot said, "You know where you're going? Things look frightfully different at night."

"There are only two ways to go along the Sound: up or down. Rat Island is about a kilometre away… look," said Blue, pointing to the mainland to their left. In the light from the heavens, Apricot could discern a narrow silhouette, sticking up like a rocket from the shoreline. "The lighthouse?" she said, opening the compartment that contained her binoculars. "I wonder if they're making a delivery tonight." She took them out, stood up, raised them to her eyes, and scanned the area.

"Anything?"

"Nothing. It's like we're the only boat out tonight ..."

"Music to my ears. We'll be there in a few minutes," said Blue, reaching for a switch on the dash. She flicked it up and the boat's search light went out. Apricot raised the binoculars to her eyes again. "... I see it, Rat Island. All that remains is to find that little dock and park."

"I think you mean moor?"

"Just do your thing, darling."

Not long after, Blue was standing and squinting over the windshield as she guided the boat into the watery cul-de-sac. Blue switched off the engine and Apricot's Little Runabout glided up against the jetty in silence. As she leapt out, Apricot bent down and picked up the rope, launching it double handed onto the landing. While Blue secured the boat to the pole, Apricot scrutinised their surroundings for signs of life. In the silvery light provided by the heavens, she read the messages that had been daubed in red paint on wooden boards. 'NO TRESPASSING!' 'PRIVATE PROPERTY KEEP OUT!' 'BEWARE! GUARD DOGS!' "Imagine *living* in a place like this..."

"It's very quiet, considering how close we are to New York," said Blue, pulling the knot tight.

"Eerily so," replied Apricot as something scampered through the undergrowth close by. "How far are we going to have to traipse before we reach Blake's house?"

"The island's smaller than your uncle's estate, so not that far."

"This path will take us there, presumably?" said Apricot, peering down a narrow walkway that wended its way beneath a canopy of trees.

"Let's find out," said Blue, as they walked towards it.

"I know Blake's at the chateau, but he must have servants. Perhaps even guards?" A twig snapped behind them. The girls spun about and scrutinized the area for signs of life. "Do you think it was a rat?" breathed Apricot.

"Could have been. I heard something just now when we arrived…"

"I did too," nodded Apricot as they turned and continued down the path that had been forged by the feet of Native Americans, European settlers, and latterly, by members of the Ku Klux Klan. They heard a dog bark in the distance. "That sounds like an awfully big…" said Apricot, as Blue grabbed her arm and yanked her off the path. They stumbled into some bushes where they lost their balance and tumbled to the ground. 'Sorry!' mouthed Blue, pointing to the left and then motioning with her eyes to the right. Apricot followed Blue as she crawled through the undergrowth to a hollowed-out tree stump with room enough inside for two teenage girls. Reader, the work that I put into ensuring the stump was not only there but had a kennel-like opening which they could crawl through was not inconsiderable. Once inside, the girls crouched amid waist height grass and gazed anxiously through gaps in the bark. To their left, a beam of light swung back and forth like a scythe cutting down wheat. They held their breath as the flashlight's owner came into view. He was a tall, thickset man with cropped red hair who scanned the woods with dead looking eyes. Another flashlight appeared twenty metres to the left. The light moved slowly at first, and then more swiftly, with greater urgency. Apricot tapped Blue's shoulder as a third light appeared, thirty metres away, between the other two. "Do you think they suspect something?" she whispered.

"Why would they?"

"Maybe someone saw the boat…"

"I switched out the lights before we pulled in."

"Then maybe they found a disappearing light suspicious? If you don't mind my saying," whispered Apricot, "you are *remarkably* calm for someone who's about to be discovered by a bunch of racist thugs on their island."

"Never have been one to get over excited."

"This could be a good time to start," said Apricot, as the three flashlights swept the forest, moving ever closer. A loud CRACK rang out from the other side of the island, like a gunshot or someone lashing out at something metal with considerable force. The three flashlights spun about and the men moved at pace in that direction.

"What do you think that was?" said Apricot.

"Our starting pistol? Come on, let's get moving!" said Blue, scampering back through the little entrance on her hands and knees.

"Has anyone ever told you how annoying it is…" said Apricot, following her.

"How annoying what is?"

"How you turn absolutely every negative into a positive?"

"How was that a negative?" said Blue, hurrying down the path.

"There you go again," said Apricot, as they rounded a clump of bushes and froze in their tracks. A large dilapidated one-storey building stood grimly before them; its red brick walls crumbling and infested with poison ivy, its dark slate roof riddled with gaps. Apricot glanced nervously over her shoulder. "Perfect. A scary old place in the woods."

"Welcome to the Pelham Pest House," said Blue, stepping towards a door hanging from its hinges.

"Where are you *going*?"

"Inside. It's the perfect place to hide."

"There's *nothing* perfect about it. What if it's still infected?"

"Don't be silly. It's been a hundred years since anyone was…"

"Locked up inside to die?"

"This is no time for being melodramatic," said Blue, squeezing through the hanging door.

"Dear love, I would say this is the perfect time for melodrama." Apricot shook her head and followed Blue inside where she placed a hand over her nose. They were standing in the remnants of a foyer where only the black and white floor tiles remained intact. A kidney shaped reception desk looked adrift in the middle of the room, surrounded by walls and a ceiling that were so waterlogged and rotten it seemed a miracle they were standing at all. Blue looked up at the four wooden beams that crisscrossed overhead, the remains of the ceiling, and thanked her lucky stars for the full moon that afforded them some light. Reader, people are very fond of attributing my work to their lucky stars.

"What's that smell?" grimaced Apricot.

"Mildew?"

"No. That other smell."

"Something must have died in here, so watch your step…"

"Thanks, I will," said Apricot, as they crossed the foyer and walked side by side through a gap that once contained a set of double doors. They found themselves in a large rectangular space, a chapel where sufferers of the once incurable disease, typhoid, had prayed for a merciful outcome. At the far side of the room was an altar, upon which stood a large wooden cross, blackened and charred from being set alight. They trod slowly over the debris of pews and stood before the altar. A rusted knife lay on it beside an image of a dragon that had been carved into the wood. Blue traced her fingers over its snarling face. "It's as though we've found the dragon's *soul*."

"Very poetic, I'm sure," murmured Apricot, feeling the hairs on the back of her neck stand to attention.

They heard someone cough outside, close to where they entered the building. "Come on!" whispered Blue, treading over debris into the next room.

Inside they discovered the remnants of fifty steel beds. The beds, that had once upon a time lined the walls on either side, were scattered about as though a tornado had blown through the room. And piled up on and around them were stacks of discarded Ku Klux Klan leaflets and posters. They were of varying heights and had the appearance of chimneys in a grimy, soulless forgotten city. A single poster lay across the rusty wrought iron slats of a bed, the red and yellow image faded to a ghostly pale, depicted a proud barrel-chested white man standing over a muscular black man with grotesquely exaggerated facial features. 'More Ape Than Human?' was the question posed below the image.

"It's *disgusting*," said Apricot.

"It's why we're here," said Blue, bending to pick up one of the thousands of leaflets that had been abandoned to rot. '*Negroes. Jews. Catholics. The scourge of any civilised society. How we would prosper without their influence.*' Blue released the leaflet with a shudder. "I bet they thought these posters revealed too much of their hateful nature. Imagined they wouldn't appeal to everyday people?"

"I see what you mean now, about this place, this *island,* it's like visiting the dragon's hateful soul…" Apricot had been silenced by the sound of a sneeze; one that had been summoned by the tinkling ivories of my lead pianist. Heeding my warning, Blue and Apricot skirted across the room towards the taller stacks of abandoned literature. They crouched behind them and listened to footsteps entering the chapel. The footsteps drew nearer until the light of the heavens, permeating through the room's tall windows, was obliterated by the harsh beam of a flashlight. The holder of the flashlight's stomach grumbled in the silence, the light swept away, and the footsteps crunched back over the debris into the chapel. "Come on," whispered Blue, as she led Apricot through a door behind them and into a corridor at the end of which was a tiled, box shaped room where broken pipes lay amid the ruins of a row of sinks. "A shower room," whispered Blue, crossing it to a large broken window. Blue climbed out of it first, taking great care not to cut herself on jagged edges of glass, and then gave Apricot a helping hand to do the same.

Outside, a fog now hung over the ground to ankle height. "I can't see my feet," whispered Apricot.

"I know, tread carefully." They made their way through the wood and spotted the orange glow of electric lights coming from the windows of a tall house. On closer inspection, peering around the side of a tree, they could see that the single storey house only looked tall because it was raised up on stilts: eight, three-metre-long legs that lent the structure the appearance of an enormous arachnid standing in the mist blanketed forest. It had a single entrance that was accessed via a narrow flight of red brick stairs that looked like an insect's tongue lapping at the mist.

"Blake's residence?" said Apricot.

"It has to be. Apart from the old hospital, it's the only other structure on the island."

At the top of the stairs was a landing that went around the house. Blue was about to make a dash for the stairs when a guard, holding a rifle in one hand and a cigarette in the other, stepped into view. He leaned against the front door and puffed thoughtfully on his cigarette.

"What now?" said Apricot.

"Looking on the bright side," said Blue, as Apricot rolled her eyes, "the only reason Blake would have so much security is because he has things to hide."

"I agree but we'll never reach that door, let alone get through it, not if that man stands there all night."

"We'll have to wait for our opportunity…"

"It might never come, dear love," said Apricot, glancing back towards the dock. My orchestra began a melody for Blue entitled, 'The Opportunity You Seek is Closer Than You Think,' and, as it played, Blue narrowed her eyes and drew a steadying breath as another guard stepped from the darkness at ground level. "Dan!" he called to the man outside the front door. Dan flicked away his cigarette, wandered over, and rested his elbows on the guardrail. "What was that racket about?"

"Tell me about it. An oil drum from the stack over on the north side of the island was dislodged and dropped onto some rocks. Probably nothing. Could be rats ate through a rope."

"Come on!" whispered Blue, darting from behind the tree and veering to her right.

Apricot drew a deep breath. "Oh, dear love ..." she said, stumbling after her.

While the guards talked, Blue skirted in a wide arc to her right, and thanked her lucky stars (those twinkling imposters!) that she was out of sight of the guard at ground level as she took the red brick steps two at a time. At the top she glanced behind her and, seeing Apricot step onto the first one, beckoned furiously for her to hurry. As soon as Apricot reached the landing, Blue moved to her right and skirted around the side of the house. She pressed her back to the wall beside the first of five windows that spanned that side and, moments later, found herself nose to nose with Apricot's flushed face. Blue smiled at her reassuringly, then spun about and tried in vain to open the window. "It's bolted..." she said, moving on to the next window and then the next, until...

"Here!" whispered Blue as she reached the fourth. "My eyes aren't deceiving me, are they? The latch *is* up?" she breathed, standing on tiptoes and squinting inside.

"It does appear to be."

Blue took hold of the window frame and attempted to heave it up. Apricot sprang forward. "On three," she whispered.

Blue nodded.

"One, two, THREE..." The girls pushed at the window and it slid up. As Fate would have it, that afternoon, when Blake's housekeeper cleaned the window, she had come across the carcass of a fly that Blake had struck with a slipper that morning. To clean the mess away, she'd had no choice but to raise the latch and, just as she finished cleaning, her assistant tripped over Blake's cat in the hallway and crashed to the floor. Quite the distraction. Yes, Reader, as well as humans, my orchestra plays melodies for flies, cats, and every other creature that draws breath or lives under the sea.

Later that day, Blue climbed through the window and dropped quietly down into the room on the other side. Apricot, releasing her hold on the window and discovering that it remained in place, vaulted rather clumsily, and out of character, it seemed to Blue, over the ledge, landing on the floor on all fours like a startled cat. "A bedroom," said squinted.

Blue negotiated her way around a double bed and placed an ear against the door.

"Do you hear anything?"

Blue shook her head, reached for the door's handle, turned and pulled it slowly towards her. The glow of an electric light in the hall crept through the crack. Blue poked out her head out and looked along the landing. "Come on, the coast's clear, let's find Blake's study." Several doors led off this corridor, all of them ajar. Blue crept along it and peered into each in turn. "This looks promising," she whispered, stepping into a room where a tall window framed the full moon that cast a mercurial light over a desk. As well as the desk, the room contained several metal filing cabinets, a drinks cabinet in the shape of a globe, and a child's rocking horse.

Apricot stepped over and placed a hand on its ribbons and yarn mane. "It's frightful to think of that man corrupting a child's mind."

"Yes," nodded Blue, as she began rifling through the documents on the desk.

"What are we looking for exactly?" said Apricot, casting her gaze around.

"*Anything* that proves Blake's a bootlegger."

Reader, I resolved to compensate Apricot for making her an orphan, and for a life utterly spoilt and without purpose until then.

That's why it fell to her to discover the all-important evidence. And so, as I conducted my cellist in a solo for her entitled, The Melody of Discovery for Apricot De Croy, she glanced uncomprehendingly up at the moon as though it had spoken to her, turned and approached a filing cabinet. Apricot's fingers brushed over the top two drawers of the metal cabinet before coming to rest on the handle of the third drawer down. She slid it open, reached in, and pulled out the only purple folder amongst a cabinet stuffed with black ones. There's a story as to how it came to be the only purple folder, an amusing yarn involving Blake's secretary, a thirsty house spider, and a spilt beverage. But by now Reader, you will be aware that there is a story behind everything that occurs, no matter how tiny or monumental.

Apricot yanked off an elastic band and opened the purple folder.

Blue was scanning the page of a document on the desk.

Apricot looked over at her. "Dear love, is this what you're looking for?"

Blue walked over and looked at the open page of the file in Apricot's hand. In it, Blake's full name Reginald Augustus Blake had been typed, and below that his signature had been flamboyantly signed. Above his signature there was a list of bottled alcoholic beverages amounting to many thousands in number, along with their production costs per bottle and retail prices. Blue turned the page avidly and scanned the names of the wealthy clients who had purchased the listed contraband. "You're a Godsend!" she whispered, sliding the file from Apricot's hands. "It's perfect! How did you know where to look?"

"It was the only purple file in the drawer. Purple's my favourite colour," she smiled, glancing at the door. "… Did you hear that?"

"Floorboard?" mouthed Blue.

Apricot nodded, slid the drawer closed, and followed Blue around the other side of the desk. They crammed themselves into the leg space below it. The footsteps stopped just inside the door, a switch was flicked, and light flooded the room. Blue and Apricot held their breath, willing the footsteps not to come any closer. They didn't. The light was turned off. The door pulled closed. Blue crawled out from under the desk, grasping the evidence they'd come for. She made her way to the door, pressed an ear to it and listened before twisting the door handle.

"What's wrong?" whispered Apricot.

"It won't open…"

"*What*? Let me try…"

Blue moved aside and Apricot took hold of the knob. "It's locked!"

"Come on. Let's get the window open…" said Blue, heading back around the desk. She climbed up on the window sill. "…There's *nothing* here," she said, feeling for a latch or a bolt or anything that would release the window. Apricot tugged on her frock and, looking down, Blue realised she was staring at the door. "What is it?"

"I heard someone…"

Blue climbed down from the sill and followed Apricot back under the desk. The door opened, and footsteps entered the room, creaking over the wooden floorboards. Apricot and Blue clung to one another, hearts thumping like pistons, until they heard a whispered voice that sounded like manna from heaven. "Blue? Apricot? You in here?" They scrambled out from under the desk and stood frozen in disbelief at the sight of Terry. "What's the matter?" he whispered, glancing down at himself.

Apricot took three quick steps and threw her arms around him. "Nothing's the matter you darling, foolish boy!" She released him and perhaps she shouldn't have been surprised to see him looking more surprised than before the hug.

"You're a sight for sore eyes," said Blue, squeezing his shoulder. "And you must be *crazy* coming here."

"Then I guess I must be crazy."

"It's a requirement," nodded Apricot. "However did you get here?"

"Stowed away on your boat. I found a hiding place in the little cabin right below you."

"*When?*"

"Got there just before you did. I called by Blue's house and her Ma said she'd just left to go meet you. I guess I put two and two together, *somehow*, and ran as fast as my legs would carry me to the marina. I knew you'd never let me come, so I skirted around you, Blue."

Blue nodded and held up the folder. "We have it, Terry. It's the evidence that Lady Constance said we needed."

"Do you really think there's something inside there that can hurt the Klan?"

"Yes! It's proof that they're up to their eyeballs in supplying illegal liquor. And thanks to you we stand a chance of leaving here with it."

"Speaking of which, the coast is clear," said Apricot from the door.

Terry stepped towards her. "The housekeeper's room is down the hall,' he said, pointing to the right. "She shut you in here and went back to bed. She must have forgot to turn the key earlier."

"The window we came through is in a bedroom to the left," said Blue, stepping in that direction.

"I know. I followed you through it." They returned to the open window, whereupon Terry climbed out first and lent a hand to Apricot and then Blue. They stood on the landing, eyes and ears alert for patrolling guards. Terry moved first, walking down the side of the house and peering around the corner for any sight of the guard outside the front door.

"Well?" whispered Blue.

"Can't see him…"

"I hear footsteps…" said Apricot, looking back past the window they'd climbed through.

"He's doing his rounds. Come on!" whispered Blue, moving past Terry and making for the red brick stairs.

So it was that the three unlikely friends took flight into the surrounding woods, doves of peace flying low to the ground, darting hither and thither, running as fast as their legs would carry them back to the boat that would whisk them away from the dragon's soul. In their possession was a weapon that, if aimed correctly from the right hands, could bring the steadily advancing dragon to its knees.

They leapt aboard Apricot's Little Runaround and while Blue started the engines and backed away from the dock, her companions gazed into the woods for signs of the dragon stirring. They saw a flash of light beyond the trees and, although distant, Apricot and Terry crouched and peered over the side of the boat. Once they'd backed out of the little inlet, Blue spun the wheel and turned Apricot's Little Runabout to face the Sound. Apricot and Terry joined Blue, sitting in the seats on either side of her. Blue placed a hand on the throttle in readiness to launch the powerful craft forward. "Want to drive, Terry?"

Terry looked at Apricot.

"You earned it and a lot more besides."

"Alright," said Terry, switching places with Blue.

"Just ease the throttle forward," said Blue. Terry placed his left hand on the wheel, took hold of the throttle with his right and moments later, the boat and its three triumphant teenagers were speeding away from Rat Island.

Chapter 32
Evidence

That night, after her parents had gone to bed, Blue went into the living room and telephoned Lady Constance. Lady Constance snatched up the receiver on her bedside table, cleared her throat. "Lady Constance Fellows."

"Sorry to disturb you, but we have it!" whispered Blue.

"Is that Blue?"

"Yes, it's me."

"Don't worry. For some reason, I couldn't get to sleep for love nor money. Have what, dear?"

"The proof you said we needed. That a Grand Wizard in the Ku Klux Klan is a bootlegger. I couldn't wait. Sorry."

"What is this proof?"

"It's a list of alcohol. Supplied and paid for. A *lot* of alcohol. And it has Blake's signature on it."

"Where did you get such a document?"

"Does it matter?" whispered Blue, glancing towards her parents' bedroom door. "You said you know someone who can use it against them."

"Yes. But you're absolutely certain of what you have? The senator's a good man and these days good men are very busy fighting the good fight."

"The senator," smiled Blue, "Yes. I'm certain. Please, *please* will you arrange a meeting with him? Apricot and Terry must be there too."

"Leave it with me. If you have what you say you have, then he'll want to see it."

221

"I *have it*. Deeds not words."

Lady Constance swallowed the lump that had come to her throat. "Deeds not words."

"So, it's okay if I call tomorrow at the same time?"

"Yes."

"Goodnight, Lady Constance."

"Goodnight, Blue."

It wasn't necessary for Blue to make that call. Lady Constance telephoned the senator the following morning and, upon hearing the intriguing news, he was eager to meet with the young people in question and see the document in their possession.

Not long after sun up, a telegram was delivered to Chateau De Croy for Apricot. And soon after, Blue was woken by her dressing gown clad mother. "Blue? Are you awake? There's a telephone call for you. Apricot. It's very early. Shall I tell her to call back?"

"What? No! I'll be right out, Mum," said Blue, jumping out of bed.

"What are you two up to?"

"That's what I'm going to find out," said Blue, snatching up the receiver. "Hello?"

"Get dressed," said Apricot. "I just received a telegram from Lady Constance. The meeting is all arranged. She wants me to make sure you get there safely. I'll pick you up in an hour."

"Yes!" said Blue, punching the air. She put down the receiver and turned to see her mother, arms folded across her chest.

"Apricot's going to pick me up in her car in an hour." Blue observed her mother's uncomprehending expression. "She won't be driving it herself."

"Obviously not. Where are you going at this hour?"

"Lady Constance has invited us over."

"Now? What for?"

Blue shrugged. "Breakfast?"

Chapter 33
Conclusion

Blue was sitting on the garden wall outside her cottage when a black limousine pulled up. As she jumped down, the chauffeur climbed out and opened the back door. Inside, Blue was very happy to see a smiling Apricot sitting beside Terry.

"I picked this one up at the stables on the way," said Apricot, sliding a little to her right to allow Blue in.

"Well done," said Blue, climbing in beside her.

"You should have seen Mr Grimshaw's face," murmured Terry as he ran a finger along the door's wood panelling.

"Would you like me to have a word with him about it?" said Apricot.

"There's not much he can do about his face."

Apricot crossed one leg over the other and turned her attention to Blue. "True enough. Do you have it?"

Blue patted the cloth bag she was hugging to her chest.

"So, we're going to see some important people?" said Terry, as the limousine pulled away.

"That's right. A senator and a suffragette," said Blue.

Terry gazed out of the window. "Sounds like the beginning of a naughty joke."

"Terrance Curtis you are a one!" said Apricot, slapping her knee.

When they arrived at Lady Constance's building, the concierge was waiting outside on the curb. "Good morning, Miss De Croy and friends," he said, as he opened the back door of the limousine. The friends lifted a hand in greeting. "I have been instructed to show you up to Lady Constance Fellows' apartment with some expediency," he said, as they climbed out.

"Right you are," nodded Apricot.

A minute later, they were in the elevator and on their way up.

The concierge knocked on the door of Lady Constance's apartment, gave a curt bow, and made his way back to the elevator.

A maid opened the door and showed them into the drawing room where Lady Constance was sitting in an armchair, talking to a tall, smartly dressed gentleman with a handlebar moustache. He was leaning against the fireplace, sipping coffee from a bone china cup, and doing his best to appear composed.

"And here they are now," said Lady Constance, rising from her armchair. "Senator, may I introduce Miss Blue Tibbs, Miss Apricot De Croy and... I don't believe we've been acquainted young man?"

Apricot glanced at Terry, who looked lost for words. "This is our friend, Terrance Curtis."

"It's a pleasure to meet you all," said the senator, stepping forward and shaking each of their hands in turn. The pleasantries out of the way, the senator stood before them, his impatient body language clear. "I have it here," said Blue, so excited that her hands were trembling as she unbuttoned her bag. She reached in and drew out the purple folder. "I've moved the evidence to the front," she said, handing it to him.

The senator nodded and took the folder, not quite a snatch, but almost. He opened it, stepped over to the fireplace and began to read. "A.G. Blake?" he murmured, reaching the signature at the bottom of the page.

"Yes, that's right. Augustus. Gray. Blake," said Blue, looking at Lady Constance.

The senator's eyes opened wide. "*The Grand Wizard* of the New York chapter of the Klan?"

"Yes, sir," said Terry, finding his voice.

The senator turned the page. "Where did you come across this?"

Blue and Apricot glanced at one another.

"On Rat Island," said Blue.

"It was in his study."

Lady Constance stepped over to the senator. "Will it be of use?"

"I'll need to check this signature against others of Augustus Blake but if it matches, well, my God… yes!"

"It's *going* to match," said Blue, with an authority that even Apricot admired.

And do you know what, Reader? It was a *perfect* match. Three days later, Augustus Blake was summoned by the senator to his office on Capitol Hill. His initial reaction, as you might imagine, was one of confusion at how the purple folder had managed to find its way from a heavily guarded island into the hands of a United States senator: one vehemently opposed to the Klan's ideology. But, confronted with the evidence of his bootlegging crimes, a felony that would have seen him jailed for many years, it took Augustus Blake precisely one hour to turn state's evidence in return for anonymity and immunity from prosecution. Simply put, this small rat, Blake, sacrificed the Klan's two most prominent rats. the serving Governor of Indiana and the Mayor of Indianapolis. On the evidence that Blake provided, these two men were arrested and charged with bribery and corruption. As a direct result of the scandal that followed their convictions, the membership of the Ku Klux Klan crashed from its high of six million in 1926, to just a few thousand disenfranchised thugs by the end of the decade. And the person who lit the fuse that brought the rampaging dragon to its knees? A girl called Blue. Of course, I played my part too. I always do. But I could never have guided Blue on her mission had she not been a right-thinking human being, one who was determined to make the world a better place.

Indeed, Blue's actions prevented a tsunami of hatred that would have led to humanity's destruction. A little over the top? Not at all. If not for the downfall of that hate-breathing dragon the KKK, then in the years that followed, when Herr Hitler and his Nazi hoards threatened civilisation, the United States, under the thrall of the Klan's ideology, would not have declared war on Germany. In this horrific alternate reality, Germany would have won the war, enslaved Europe, and eventually engulfed the globe with their monstrous ideology.

Reader, let's not dwell on such horrors.

Speaking of World War Two, as you might imagine, Blue played her part there too. And quite the secret agent in France she turned out to be! As Fate would have it, she was to meet her true love during those war years; a kind Englishmen named Francis whom she married after the war. But all that, Reader, is a story for another time. As for Apricot, she grew up into a fine specimen of humanity, a philanthropist no less, who, over the course of her 91 years, gave away the lion's share of her fortune to deserving causes. None were more deserving than a certain Terrance Curtis, whose degree in Astronomy from Oxford University she funded. Indeed, the foundation she set up funded thousands of degrees for people from non-privileged backgrounds. Terry went on to be a respected lecturer in astronomy, his passion for his subject inspiring many to follow in his footsteps.

As for Blue, let's catch up with her one last time…

The year is 2012. She has just turned one hundred years old. Her husband passed away a decade ago, and the time is fast approaching when she too must cast off her mortal coil. Where do we find her? Reader, in many ways, we have come full circle. For her birthday treat, a carer from her nursing home in London has taken her to an exhibition of Titanic memorabilia at the Science Museum. You see her, don't you? She's that wizened old lady in a wheelchair, enveloped in a red coat and wearing a silver broach with the letters D, N, W, interlinked. She's waiting for her carer to return from the restroom. All around her, as well as boisterous children on a school outing, Blue is surrounded by display cases that contain items recovered from the Titanic: pocket watches, leather jackets, life preservers, items of luggage and many more antique curiosities besides. To her right there is a black and white photograph, enlarged to cover a section of wall between two display cases. It's a still of passengers boarding the ill-fated liner. Reader, I know you'll understand when I tell you that it was with a heavy heart that I raised my baton for Blue one last time. And as my piper, Woebegone, began to play a song for her, entitled 'Blood ties' – her tired, failing eyes opened wide and, just as tenacious as ever, she raised her frail body out of her wheelchair. Seemingly invisible to the children who skirted around her, Blue made her way over to the wall-sized photo. She placed a wrinkled hand against it to steady herself, whereupon her gaze was drawn to a dark-haired woman, halfway up the gang plank. The pretty woman cradled a baby to her chest in one hand and carried a cloth holdall in the other. As Woebegone fell silent, his job done, Blue's lips parted "… *Mother*?"

A uniformed guard came over and stood beside her. "Are you alright, madam?" Blue's expression of curiosity as she gazed at Iris Flannigan transformed into one of compassion and love.

Her carer, a black woman, returned from the rest room. "My goodness! What are you doing up out of your wheelchair, Blue?"

"… Seeing my dear mother for the *very* first time."

Blue's carer and the security guard exchanged a glance. "She's one hundred years old today…" said the carer by way of an explanation.

"Many happy returns. That's some age. Any advice for the rest of us?" he asked.

Blue looked down past the line of passengers and nodded at the sight of Lady Constance Fellows climbing out of a grand car. She raised a shaky hand to her brooch. "Deeds not words, young man. And remember…"

"Remember?" asked the man.

Blue smiled as her train of thought returned. "To trust in Fate and to always, *always* fight the good fight."

The End

* * *

A final thought from your author, Fate

Listen for your own symphony, embrace it, walk, dance, play and live your life to it. Treat others well and have no regrets. Regrets apply to me and me alone.

Thank you for reading! If you enjoyed *A Symphony for Blue*, you might also enjoy the following books by the same author:

Catch 33
The Scratchling Trinity
Jack Tracy and the Priory of Chaos
The Lost Diary of Snow White Complete Collection

A book description and the opening pages of ***The Scratchling Trinity*** follow here…

Book description:
No one knew the importance of the Scratchling-born, until now.

When a Victorian orphan called Eric Kettle scratches a desperate cry for help into a wall in 1840, little does he know that it's about to be answered by luckless Max Hastings in 2016. Both Max and Eric are soon to discover that they're Scratchling-born, and that along with Ellie Swanson, a Scratchling veteran, they are destined to form the Scratchling Trinity. With an evil headmaster, a flying boat, two vengeful giants and a clutch of ghostly helpers along the way, they are off on an incredible adventure!

One
Max Hastings

London, England, 2016
Max Hastings was leaning low over the handlebars of his bike, and pedalling like he'd flipped out. The distance from his school to his home was two and a half kilometres, and Max *had* to smash his personal best time. The reason was written on a scroll of parchment, held closed by a black ribbon and jutting from his blazer pocket like a piston powering him towards a new school-to-home record. He sped up his drive, leapt off his bicycle and sprinted, arms flailing, towards the front door. Once through it, he darted into the living room, unclipped the strap on his bicycle helmet, and cast the helmet onto the couch. Max was twelve years old, of average build if a little on the chunky side, with a shock of white blond hair that grew every which way except the way Max would have liked. On his left cheekbone, just below his eye, was a birthmark that looked as though someone had signed their initials in black ink. Max drew the scroll from his pocket, gunslinger style, straightened his back, and announced his extraordinary news to his parents: 'I've finally *won* something!'

Mr Hastings looked at Max over the top of his newspaper. 'There must be some mistake,' he said.

'That's what I thought when Miss Hale announced the name of the re-cip-ient.'

Mrs Hastings, who was holding Max's one-year-old sister Maxine, put the baby down in her walker. 'Congratulations, Max! So what have you won?'

Max gazed at the rolled-up parchment in his hand. 'It's a grand prize, Mum. They picked *my name* out of a hat during the last assembly of term.'

'You've broken your duck, then?' said his astonished father. 'If memory serves me correctly, you've never won anything in your life. Not even when you went through that annoying competitions phase.'

'I know, Dad. I was there.'

'So *what* have you won, exactly?' asked Mrs Hastings.

'No idea.'

'Well, then, I suggest you untie that ribbon and find out.'

Max glanced from the parchment to his mother and back again. Mrs Hastings placed her hands on her hips. 'Whatever is matter with you?'

'It's just so…'

'So what?' said his father.

'Official-looking.'

'Which must bode well for the prize,' said Mr Hastings, putting down his newspaper. 'Give it here, son. I'll open it.'

Max shook his head. 'I'll do it.' He untied the ribbon and unfurled the parchment. His lips moved slowly as he read from it, and his brow furrowed.

'Well?' pressed his mother.

His father leaned forwards in his armchair. 'What are you the recipient *of*?'

'Of a life-time membership…' murmured Max.

'A life-time membership of *what*?' said his mother testily.

Max read the words slowly. 'The Worshippal Company of Wall Scratchings.'

'Of *what*?' said Mr Hastings.

'Of *wall* scratchings,' repeated his mother helpfully.

'But what does that even mean?' mumbled Max, his eyes glued to the parchment for some clue.

'Oh, for pity's sake, give it to me,' said his mother, sliding it from his hand.

Mrs Hastings scanned the parchment. 'Oh, my goodness. Max has been invited to a private viewing of their wall scratchings tomorrow, at Mansion House!'

Mr Hastings cleared his throat. 'What? The place where the Lord Mayor of London lives?'

'Yes!'

'There must be some mistake,' asserted Mr Hastings.

Mrs Hastings shook her head. 'No mistake. The Worshippal Company of Wall Scratchings, Mansion House, City of London, London.'

Max sighed. 'Trust me to win a grand *booby* prize. Tomorrow's *Saturday,* not to mention the first day of the Christmas holidays. I'm not going.'

'Not going?' echoed Mrs Hastings.

'Why would I? Since when was I interested in *wall scratchings*? I don't even know what they are!'

'They're scratchings on walls, presumably,' said Mr Hastings, happy to apply his keen insight to the problem at hand.

'Well, whatever they are,' said Mrs Hastings, glancing at the parchment in her hand, 'it says here that they have the world's largest collection of them.'

'Not helping, Mum,' said Max. He went to the dining table and opened his laptop, muttering absently to himself as he typed *the worshippal company of wall scratchings* into the search engine. He sat back in his seat and breathed a sigh of relief. 'Just as I thought. There's no such place. It doesn't even exist! ... What are you doing?' Max asked his mother.

'There's a phone number on here. I'm calling them.'

'But…' said Max.

'But nothing. I intend to get to the bottom of these ... these *scratchings*.' She tapped her foot impatiently as the phone rang at the other end of the line.

A woman with a cut-glass English accent answered. 'Thank you for calling the Worshippal Company of Wall Scratchings. How may I help you?'

'My name is Mrs Hastings, and my son Max has just won a free membership to your organisation.'

'Hearty congratulations!' said the woman.

'Be that as it may, there's no mention of you on the internet. No mention whatsoever.'

The woman drew a deep breath. 'Ours is an ancient organisation, Mrs Hastings. As such we frown upon all modern conventions.'

'Alright. But your address appears to be the very same as the Lord Mayor of London's.'

'That's right.'

'And the Lord Mayor?'

'What about him?'

'He's happy to share his residence with your organisation?'

'The Worshippal Company of Wall Scratchings has been located at this spot for over a thousand years, Mrs Hastings. Since the year 1065, to be exact. The first Lord Mayor didn't move in until some seven hundred years later, in 1752.'

'*And*?'

'And since then we've had no complaints from any Lord Mayor in office.'

A man's voice came on the line. 'Max is going to benefit greatly from his membership, Mrs Hastings,' he asserted.

'*Max is going to benefit greatly from his membership,*' repeated Mrs Hastings, as though in a trance.

'And he'll meet a great many important people.'

'*And he'll meet a great many important people*,' echoed Mrs Hastings.

'People,' the voice went on, 'who will be able to help him in his chosen career.'

'He wants to test video games for a living,' murmured Mrs Hastings.

'*Help him in his chosen career,*' said the man, raising his voice.

'*Help him in his chosen career,*' repeated Mrs Hastings obediently.

'Tell Max he's welcome to bring a friend tomorrow. Goodbye.'

'Goodbye!' said Mrs Hastings, putting down the phone. She turned to Max. 'You're welcome to take a friend tomorrow,' she said.

'O-kay. Are you alright, Mum?'

'Never better,' said Mrs Hastings, grinning uncharacteristically from ear to ear.

Two
Eric Kettle

Yorkshire, England, December 1st, 1840

Inside a carriage drawn by two horses, a boy sat shivering beside a large brute of a man. So at odds were they in size and attitude that an extra-terrestrial might have mistaken them for two separate species. The man sat expressionless and granite-faced, and indeed any onlooker might have thought him cut from granite. The only clue to his being flesh-and-blood was the smile that curled his lips whenever the carriage hit a pothole and the boy yelped. The man took up most of a bench designed for three adults, squashing his young companion against the carriage door like an item of worthless baggage. The boy's name was Eric Kettle, and Eric looked so fragile that he might break in two every time the carriage lurched over a bump in the road. Of which there were a great many, and many more potholes besides. Despite these hardships, Eric's big brown eyes gazed with extraordinary hope from a face gaunt with hunger.

It was gone midnight when the carriage came to a halt at its destination: the St Bart's School for Boys. The school was a crumbling mansion that rose from the Yorkshire countryside like a vampire's abandoned lair. The carriage door was opened by the driver, who was hidden by an entire closet's worth of coats, scarves and gloves. The brute heaved himself out of his seat. 'Fall in behind, sir,' he grumbled at his young ward. Eric followed as quickly as his shivering legs would allow. He hugged himself for warmth and stumbled towards the promise of heat beyond the door that now opened for them. Once through the door, Eric wondered if it hadn't actually been warmer outside.

They'd been admitted by a pale and hungry-looking boy swaddled in a threadbare coat several sizes too large. He was carrying a paraffin lamp, and, without uttering a single word, he illuminated their path across a cavernous entrance hall and up a sweeping staircase. Two flights up, he lit the way down a long corridor before finally stopping outside a door, on which a gold plaque read: *Headmaster. Augustus Mann.* Augustus took a key from his pocket and unlocked the door. He turned to the boy carrying the lamp, now hastily lighting a candle by its flame, and snatched the lamp from his grasp. The boy scurried off on bow legs, and Eric watched the candle light until it disappeared from sight at the end of a corridor. 'Fall in, sir!' came the gruff voice of Augustus Mann, from inside the study.

The headmaster placed the lamp on a desk piled high with books, and pointed to a spot on the wooden floor before the desk marked with an X in chalk. 'Stand there, arms at your sides, chin held high. That's it. And stop your shivering.'

'I'll try, sir, but it's just so…'

'Say the word *cold,* and as God is my witness, I'll thrash you where you stand. Perhaps you think that I should light a fire for you? Waste good wood? Is that what you think?'

'No, sir.'

'Speak up when I address you!'

'No, sir!'

'No what?'

'No, I don't think you should waste good wood on me, sir.'

'Spoilt! That's what you've been. Spoilt to the core.'

Eric shook his head. 'They work us very hard at the orphanage, sir.'

The headmaster sat down and opened a folder on his desk. 'It says here that your father went off to seek his fortune the day after you were born. Wherever he went, he must have liked it there.'

Eric smiled. 'Do you think so? Why do you say so, sir?'

'Liked it more than he liked *you,* anyway.' Eric's smile vanished as the headmaster grunted and went on, 'I see your mother went looking for him soon after, and whether or not she found him, nobody knows. Never seen nor heard from again. But whatever she *did* find, she must have preferred it to you.' The headmaster observed Eric through narrowed eyes. 'What is it about you that so vexes others, *boy*?'

Eric's gaze dropped to the ground. 'I'm sure I don't know, sir.'

'After so many years in an orphanage, I dare say you thought your ship had come in, with your name chosen from a hat to receive a scholarship to attend a fine Yorkshire school of good repute. Thought you'd get yourself a proper education, eh? Those abominable do-gooders, passing their laws that say the likes of *me* must look with charitable eyes upon the likes of *you*. The paltry compensation I will receive for your keep will barely cover my costs.'

'I'm very sorry, sir.'

'You will be. The fact is, you are worth more to me *dead* than you are alive – a fact that doesn't bode at all well for you,' said the headmaster, rising from his chair and turning to face a collection of canes hanging on the wall. He stroked his grey moustache thoughtfully, smiled, and then reached for one.

'Please,' implored Eric. 'I don't know why my parents left me. I did nothing wrong. I was just a baby. And that's the God's truth, sir.'

The headmaster turned and swiped the cane back and forth to gauge its suitability. 'I would strongly advise you not to take the Lord's name in vain. Not in this establishment, *sir*, or God help me...'

As Augustus Mann made his way around his desk towards him, Eric closed his eyes and willed himself back at the orphanage. It didn't work, although the heavy blow that struck his face might almost have launched him back there. Eric's legs gave way beneath him, and he collapsed to the ground, groaning and clutching a cheek that felt savaged by a thousand bee stings. Augustus Mann loomed over him, cane in hand. 'Down at the first lash? Pathetic. That is what you are, pathetic. Is it any wonder your parents left you?' The headmaster yawned, ambled back around his desk, placed the cane back on its hook and walked towards the door. 'You can spend the night there on the floor, like the dog you undoubtedly are. Although I can assure you that your life expectancy is considerably shorter than a dog's. A truth I intend to take *considerable* comfort from,' he yawned. Augustus Mann stepped through the door, closing it and locking it behind him.

Eric dragged himself into a corner, where he huddled miserably for warmth, trying to remember a legend he'd heard some years before at the orphanage: *If a child of kind heart and noble mind is ever in mortal danger, all he needs do is scratch a message of help into a stone wall, and help will find him.* Eric fumbled down his side for one of the safety pins that kept his clothes from falling apart, and with it he scratched the following words in tiny letters into the wall: *If ever a boy was in mortal danger, it's me. Please, if anyone's there, help me!*

Thank you for reading. If you enjoyed this sample, ***The Scratchling Trinity*** is available from Amazon.

Printed in Great Britain
by Amazon